A WIZARD'S FORGE

BOOK ONE OF THE WOERN SAGA

BY

A. M. JUSTICE

WISE
CREATIVE · PUBLISHING
Ink

ISBN 13: 978-1-945769-07-8
eISBN 13: 978-1-63489-923-9

Library of Congress Catalog Number: 2016950148
Printed in the United States of America
First Printing: 2016
21 20 19 18 17   5 4 3 2 1

Cover and interior design by Steven Meyer-Rassow

Wise Ink Creative Publishing
837 Glenwood Ave.
Minneapolis, MN 55405
www.wiseinkpub.com

To order, visit www.seattlebookcompany.com or call (734) 426-6248.
Reseller discounts available.

For the Refugees

CONTENTS

PART 1. ORE

CHAPTER 1

THE LOGS

Vic had never been much of a sailor. When she was a child, the other children had laughed when she bent over the gunwale, paled-faced and shaking—their people were fisherfolk, after all. Now, stomach heaving, she gulped air through her mouth, trying not to smell the stench wafting from her dress. She squeezed her eyes shut and popped them open, as if the bursting stars behind her eyelids could bring real light into the ship's hold. But eyes open or closed, the darkness remained, filled with sobbing and moans and terrified cries. She couldn't close her ears to those. Nor could she ignore her wrenched gut, sapped dry by the tossing of the ship but still straining to empty itself of misery. "Don't think about it," she whispered over and over, hearing instead the laughter of schoolmates about her white face and shaking hands.

Hands clenching her skirts, she clung to memories of jeering. They hadn't laughed the day she'd passed her exams. That morning, the youth of Ourtown had looked at her with—respect, jealousy, admiration? She wasn't sure. But being the youngest Logkeeper in history had to count for something. As Martha led her down the jaundstone path, her life had opened up. "Teach and preserve," Martha said, when she handed Vic her own Logbook.

"Until they come," Vic had recited, so pleased with herself she nearly burst. Yet the rolling misery of the ship's hold was so real she wondered if her past was a dream. Not caring whether it was, she pulled the memories over her head and let the darkness carry her home.

† † †

As she chanted the Logtitles, Vic's mind wandered. Henry had asked her to go with him to Festival tomorrow, but her spine squirmed at the thought of his sweaty palms. Her voice droned onto the next series of Logs, and she wondered why they bothered to keep them. *Ninny*, she scolded, or was it Martha's voice that scolded her? *"We do not seek to understand,"* the Master Logkeeper always reminded her, *"only to preserve."*

"Log 105.672, Ensign Chu set up the communication disk; 105.673, Civie Samantha Farrak killed by mountain sheep; lost Logs 105.674–111.13; 111.14, party sent north to find iron ore or other usable metal."

Martha nodded. "Good. Now, recite all of Log 43.17."

Vic's lungs filled with relief. Her gut had told her she would be tested on this one. Her orals done, tomorrow they would name her Logkeeper and send her out among the villages. "43.17, Captain's personal log. There's a phase-out each time we enter hyperspace. Every day I become more and more concerned that perhaps we were never meant to reach Gamorrah Two . . ." She recited the whole log in two breaths.

Martha sat with her eyes closed, slowly rocking as if listening to music. "Some say you've progressed too fast. We've never made anyone so young a Logkeeper before. What is the significance of 43.17?"

Caught off guard, Vic stammered her answer. Martha never asked for an analysis of the Logs. "Captain Wong knew the *Elesendar* would crash here—well, not here, necessarily, and they didn't really crash of course, but he knew they would never make it to Gamorrah. He realized the *Elesendar* had been sabotaged."

Martha pursed her lips and squinted one eye at Vic. "Has anyone given you these answers—your father, perhaps?"

Vic shook her head. "My knowledge is my own."

Martha nodded once. "Go rest." She paused, glancing out toward Winter's Isle, where the rest of the town's youth cavorted around bonfires. "Festival is tomorrow. And pack your bags."

The corners of her mouth twitching up, Vic bowed to Martha and left the Master's lodge. They'd accepted her. Tomorrow, she would be a Logkeeper.

She didn't even glance toward the Isle as she walked home. Laughter and firelight filtered across the water, but Vic had no interest in going out there, especially when she saw Henry on the beach with his boat.

She tried to hurry past unseen, but he called her name. Even if Henry didn't stink like legumes, he would still be pudgy and greasy, Vic thought as he huffed up the short distance between the water and the road. "Vic," he gasped, "aren't you going to the Isle?"

She snorted at him. "What for? Rolling around in the bushes with teenagers is *not* something Logkeepers do."

"Come on. We're missing the fun."

"Martha's making me a Logkeeper. I have to tell my father the good news."

He blocked her way, eyes rolling over her spindly frame. "Come with me, Vicky. It's not like you're going to get any other offers."

Skinny Vicky, short and icky. A taunt the girls in Ourtown chanted whenever Vic passed. Her throat closing, she dug her fingernails into her palms and pressed her lips together, trying to hold in tears.

Henry reached for her elbow. "Come on."

She jerked away, stepping quickly down the beach. "You won't shame me into rolling with you! I'll be a Logkeeper tomorrow. Then you can't treat me like this."

"You'll be an ugly old hen tomorrow," he cried as she ran down the beach.

When she reached Belfast's Point, she climbed the rocks, tearing her skirts, until she could see the breakers. Ourtown nestled against the cliff as if waiting for a tsunami to come and drown it. In the shallow bay, ribbons of red light and white adorned the wavecrests, reflections of the bonfires and Elesendar's pale gleam. Vic wondered what the indigenous life of Knownearth thought when a new star entered their heavens and began rapidly crossing the sky, moving overhead at least three times most nights. Nearly three thousand years had passed since Captain Wong parked a United Mineral mining vessel with the registry LSNDR2237 in orbit around this world; two hundred generations since the Oreseekers came north, hunting iron and copper and other ores needed to repair the *Elesendar*'s disabled drives. They'd failed in their quest and for some reason had decided to settle these steppes, thousands of miles from where the *Elesendar*'s crew had disembarked. Her ancestors had preserved every record they could from their space travels and home planet, but they hadn't recorded why they never returned to their people.

She sighed, wondering if life as a Logkeeper would be as purposeless as the Oreseekers' quest. She could recite thousands of Logs from memory, but who cared if she remembered equations for the precise targeting of a wormhole if no one would ever use it? The waves whispered and shouted of other lands, where the rest of humanity still lived. Occasionally peddlers made their way up the coast, though the harsh winters turned most back before they made it to Ourtown. Still, they knew people lived in great cities far to the south, occupied forests and mountains, even mined precious iron the Oreseekers had missed. And on the high seas sailed the dreaded Caleisbahnin— merciless pirates and slavers who ruled the waves.

Vic wondered what such people would think of her. She'd spent her life training to be a scholar and teacher, but the other girls had teased her and the boys ignored her because she was weak as a jellybug and skinny as a totem. And Henry thought she would settle! As if she would ever consider rolling in the bushes with *him*.

> *"Your mother looked just like you at your age," Father says, eyes sparkling. "Don't worry, honey. You're not pretty. Pretty's a common thing, and you're not common. Beauty is something you acquire a taste for."*
>
> *"I'm not a pickle."*
>
> *He laughs and glances at Veronica's portrait. "Neither was she."*

Vic gazed at the stars, wondered which one was circled by Gamorrahs One and Two. Did they have a taste for beauty there? She shook her head. Why did that matter? She'd be a Logkeeper tomorrow, like her father before her and his mother before him. The youngest Logkeeper in Ourtown's history. Great things, Vic, she whispered. You're destined for great things.

† † †

The next morning, Martha bestowed the Logkeeper's sash in a brief ceremony quickly overshadowed by the hubbub of Festival, and Vic departed on her first journey as a Logkeeper.

As spring unfolded across the tundra, she traveled inland trails, camping in patches of purple spineflowers, sleeping in the corners of barns or, in the larger villages, by the mayor's hearth. Her duties—teaching the children their letters and mathematics, drilling the youths on the history of the Oreseekers—made her welcome most places, especially because she brought news and mail, an unofficial function she discovered as she left Ourtown and an old woman pressed a letter into her hands and asked her to deliver it to an old man in another town. By the summer solstice, her route brought her back to the chill winds of the coast, and she carried several letters for the residents of Cairo, nestled into a sea cliff like a little sister of Ourtown. Standing atop a bluff, Vic scanned the cluster of ironreed lodges through a swarm of gnats dancing in the golden light. Far bigger than the inland villages, the town boasted a fleet of fishing boats and a school and full-time teacher. As she came down among the lodges, townspeople waved cheerily at her yellow sash and pointed her toward the schoolhouse.

"You'll find Samson still there," said a woman slicing fish. "Don't let him bother you. He's a good sort."

Vic followed her gesture to a mud-caulked dome surrounded by verdant fronds and flowers. Chillenherb flared her nostrils. Strong stuff, she thought. Except for festivals, most people kept their cooking bland—as bland as the tundra.

She walked in the open door and announced herself, but no one emerged from the shadows. A closed door beckoned from behind the teacher's desk, so she knocked.

"Not now."

"I'm a Logkeeper," Vic told the voice. "The villagers sent me here. Where can I put my things and bed down?"

"Go to the innkeeper's lodge. I'm busy."

Chagrined, Vic wished she were older. Since she'd left Ourtown, she had more often come across suppressed chuckles than eyes wide with awe at the sight of her yellow sash. That upstart mayor in Hackensack had actually accused her of being an impostor.

Gritting her teeth, Vic demanded the teacher come out and greet her.

"I will soon enough. I'm in the middle of something."

"What could be so urgent that you won't greet your superior?" she asked, raising her chin.

Silence ebbed from the doorway. Vic stamped her foot— she would not put up with this. She turned the doorknob.

"Get back!" Samson cried as the door popped open and a draft sucked inside. Vic dove aside as light and heat burst into the schoolroom and then vanished with a thwump. Cautiously, she peered into the billowing smoke.

Coughing, a man stumbled out, black with soot. "What did you do that for?"

"I don't know." Idiot, she thought, that's a child's answer. "Why wouldn't you answer me?"

He looked around them as if the smoke said it all. Vic followed his gaze back into the room.

"What were you doing in there?"

Shaking his head, he walked out of the schoolhouse. "You can leave your papers here. Nobody's going to bother *them*."

The innkeepers prepared a hot bath for Vic as soon as she walked in their lodge. Well-fed and red-haired, the duo laughed and guessed that the soot on her face came from one of Samson's experiments. "He's always tinkering, that boy," the husband said.

The wife shooed Vic off to a curtained corner of the lodge and down a ladder to the cellar, where a clay bathtub steamed. "You want your clothes laundered, honey?"

Vic nodded and slipped into the tub, saying she'd wear her green dress. The innkeeper bundled her other clothes into the washbasin and busied herself with soaping and scrubbing. Vic lay still as heat eased travel-weary muscles. Spread across the water, her hair turned from sunset gold to deeper red as the water pulled it down.

"Such lovely amber hair," the innkeeper said, laying a pair of towels near the tub. "Bet the boys just fall all over you."

Vic blushed, and the woman smiled. "Don't worry, dear. Pretty's a common thing."

"My father always says that."

The innkeeper nodded. "Wise man. Now hurry and dress. You've arrived just in time for the Solstice Scoop!"

At the shoreline, boats tilted on their sides in the sand, shadows slanting across the beach to kiss the base of the cliff.

"While the tide's out," the innkeeper explained, holding her apron in the shape of a basket, "we all run out to the waterline and the men scoop up crabs and mussels while the women run behind and catch them in their skirts. Do they have Scoops in Ourtown?"

Vic shook her head.

The innkeepers whispered at each other, then the woman turned to Vic. "Go with Justin and he'll find you a partner."

Smiling wanly, the husband grumbled under his breath as he led her through the gathering crowd. "You there." He tapped a black-haired man on the shoulder. "Samson, you got a partner?"

Vic backed away when she heard the name and blinked at Samson's almond eyes when he turned.

He frowned. "I guess I've got one now." With the soot washed away, he was younger than Vic thought, perhaps only five or six years her senior. She edged closer.

"I don't bite. But next time a door is closed and you're not invited in, don't open it."

Vic narrowed her eyes but swallowed a retort. "So when

does the scooping start?" Shellfish scuttled here and there, waiting for the return of the sea.

"We'll wait until the tide ebbs as far as it'll go, then we'll run for it. The beach is steep; the water washes back pretty fast. You've got to be quick."

Vic fingered her skirt. "I can be quick."

"Just don't drop anything. Aren't you too young to be a Logkeeper?"

Someone whistled, and Samson clutched her hand and rushed down the beach alongside other couples. Whooping, laughing, the men grabbed and tossed, women dodged and swerved, everyone leapt over each other. Samson kept a steady stream sailing over his shoulder, and Vic managed to catch more shellfish than she missed. By the time the tide washed back up the shore, she and the teacher were laughing along with the rest, and Vic's skirt was as heavily laden as the others'.

"What do you do with all of it?" she asked as Samson led her among the cauldrons, sorting crabs and snails into different pots.

"Tonight we'll feast until everyone goes home too stuffed to sleep, and we can the leftovers for winter."

At the last pot, a few dungcrabs clambered over each other within the basket of her skirt. Vic grimaced. "These are foul. We don't eat them in Ourtown."

"We don't either. Let's throw them back in the next cove. They'll eat our nets."

At the far edge of town, the sand gave way to rocks. Shadows long, the water red, they scrambled over the sharp, glistening stones to reach another beach, then walked in the gloaming in silence. She'd never seen honey skin and almond eyes like Samson's. The Oreseekers filled their early Logs with tales of "vitamin D deficiency," a condition that had left many of her darker-skinned ancestors bent and crippled. No one remembered what had been wrong with those people, but now dark hair was uncommon, brown skin a rare throwback. She asked Samson where he was from.

He grimaced. "Here. I was born here. Just because I don't have pasty skin and round green eyes, don't think I'm not one of you."

Vic's cheeks warmed. "I was just curious."

Halting, Samson gazed out to sea. The waves rolled in, the crash and churn echoing off the cliffs behind them. Dipping into the ocean, the sun flickered around something, perhaps a boat out for a solstice cruise. "My mother was a Caleisbahnin," Samson confessed, and Vic's breath caught in her throat. "One winter my father found a Caleisbahn man washed up on shore, half dead. He took the man in and in the spring gave him a fishing boat so he could go home. Late that summer, the man returned and left my father the best boat he's ever owned."

"That huge green skiff? It's fantastic," Vic exclaimed. The boat had stood out from the others like a rosy in a bed of spineflowers. Most fishing boats were made of ironreed and looked as utilitarian as they needed to be, but this one was wood with a carved bow and a mast that spiraled high above the others, green paint glimmering amid the scuffed and patched hulls of the others. "And your mother?"

Samson sighed and began walking again. "The skiff was payment for the boat my father had given the man. But, by Caleisbahn law, he still owed my father his life—or at least *a* life. My mother was the other half of the payment."

Vic almost dropped the crabs wriggling in her skirt. "You don't pay debts with people."

"Here, we might as well let those go. We're far enough away now."

She looked back at the distant cliff. Another stone outcropping marched into the sea ahead of them, and she wondered how far the Caleisbahn sailor must have traveled to wash ashore here.

Samson shrugged. "Far enough you don't see more people like me."

Her skirts fell, and the crabs scuttled toward the waves like cows for the barn during a thunderstorm. Certain she had not said anything aloud, she stared at him. His face cracked into a grin, then he burst out laughing. "Vic, you Logkeepers spend years reading and rereading about quantum mechanics and space travel, but you don't know anything. My mother taught me mindspeech—the ability to Hear what people don't say. It's a common skill among her people."

"Who? Among slaves sold by pirates?"

His eyes narrowed, but his smile widened. "My mother was proud of what she was. Among her people, to be traded to pay a debt of honor is an honor in itself. She loved my father, but she never let me forget who I am. She taught me mindspeech and the history of Knownearth. That's where the rest of humanity lives: Knownearth. Where we live is called the Unknown on their maps. If other people have heard of Oreseekers at all, they only know *us* as slaves traded by pirates."

Vic shivered. Rumors of Caleisbahn raiding parties regularly filtered up from the southern Oreseeker settlements, and parents would use the threat of pirate slavers to frighten children into good behavior.

"No one else in Knownearth cares about the Logs either. The few who do think they're religious parables, not history. We have to stop waiting for somebody to show up and ask you to recite all those records you know by heart. If we would use that knowledge ourselves, think of what we could accomplish!"

"Your experiments?" she snorted.

"Yes. Ways to make freshwater out of seawater. Lighting that doesn't fill your eyes with smoke when you read in winter.

Why are our lives so hard, Vic? Our ancestors had all sorts of things to make life on these tundras easy, or at least easier. Why else would they have settled here at all?"

She shrugged. Samson echoed all the doubts she had harbored for years but been afraid to voice. *Ours is not to understand, but to preserve.* She had said that maxim so many times, she never thought about what it meant.

"A scholar doesn't just memorize as many texts as she can," Samson continued. "A scholar seeks understanding. We could be so far ahead of the rest of the world, but we're so mired in old knowledge that we've fallen behind. There's a country called Latha where all people speak is mindspeech, and it's no harder to learn than any spoken language. And then there are the cities. My mother said that Traine is gorgeous to behold. Spires that kiss the clouds, and all the different kinds of people in the world moving like a multicolored tapestry. Our lives are all gray."

Vic stood and began striding back toward Cairo. "I don't believe you. They'll come. Our lives"—she turned back and shouted at him—"my father's life and his mother's before him are not meaningless!" Her feet sinking heavily into the sand, she ran from him, from her doubts. How could the rest of the world have forgotten, when the Oreseekers hadn't? Three thousand years since the marooning. Her people hadn't forgotten—how could anyone else?

The surf blotted out the screams until she came around the cliff to Cairo's beach. The feasting tables lay jumbled together on sand strewn with boiled shellfish. Strange men carrying bludgeons stomped past the overturned cauldrons, heaving prone villagers into boats drawn up onto the sand. A raider guarding the boats shouted and pointed at Vic.

Samson grabbed her arm and broke the icehold of her fear. "Run!" He dragged her back over the sharp rocks and onto the other beach. Vic's feet pounded across hard-packed sand, spray flying as they ran through water crawling up the beach. Behind them, men shouted. Samson panted next to her, but in her mind she heard his voice, "If we can make it around the next cliff face, there's a cave where we can hide."

Her legs pumped faster, but her dress—the thick, multilayered skirts designed for warmth—caught around her shins and slowed them down. She paused to gather them up above her knees. Samson urged her on, and the cliff on the other side of the beach inched closer.

The pirate tackled her, his weight knocking her breath from her. Her mouth full of sand, she gagged and coughed, but before she could scream, his bludgeon rose up and blotted out the stars.

CHAPTER 2

TRAINE

The creak of planks beneath her, the sobs of the woman next to her, and the smell of fear and misery intruded on Vic's memories, pulling her back into the nightmare of the slavers' ship. As a Logkeeper, she had prepared for sickness, flood, even starvation. As a Logkeeper, she was supposed to *lead* in times of crisis, but what she could do now? Swallowing her fears, she sat up.

Startled by the movement, the woman next to her yelped, then clutched her arm, moaning. Vic asked her name.

"Ellen," the woman choked. "I don't recognize your voice. Why is it so dark?"

Vic patted the woman's shoulder, wishing for some comfort herself. "I'm Victoria, the Logkeeper," she announced. "Is the mayor here?"

Many feet away, someone cleared his throat and said he was Michael, son of Cairo's mayor. "None of our parents are here," he said tautly. "At least, I don't think so."

Other voices confirmed it—no one over twenty-five, or under twelve, had been taken. The older villagers and children must have been left unconscious on the beach—with the tide rolling in. Vic shuddered. "Have they told us anything?"

"No," Michael answered. "I wish Samson were here. His mother taught him their language."

As if the words were a prophecy, a hatch opened and blinding sunlight shafted into the hold, followed by a thunk and "oof." The hatch slammed shut.

"Who are you?" Michael asked while Vic blinked to clear the starbursts from her vision.

"It's me." Samson's voice. All talking at once, Cairo's youth crawled over each other to reach him. Vic hung back, her stomach grappling with fear.

Michael's voice spoke out over the babble, silencing the others. "What do they want?"

Samson stayed silent for a long time. Ellen began to whimper softly. "They're taking us to Traine," he said at last.

The city of spires that kissed the clouds. It sounded lovely when he'd described it before. Why did it sound so ominous now? Vic cleared her throat. "What will happen to us there?"

"I don't know." His voice cracked. Vic wondered if Samson did know but thought it too terrible to say.

Scuffling, people moved away from him. "Are they going to feed us?" a boy asked. "We were only sitting down to eat when they came."

No one answered. Vic shuffled backward on her knees, away from Ellen and her wailing. Wedged against the hull, she pressed wet cheeks to her knees and willed this to be a dream.

"How did they find us, Samson?" Michael's voice knifed through the darkness again.

Samson started to answer with a whisper, then stopped. When he spoke again, his voice was as strong as Michael's, but flat and hollow. "The captain of this ship is the man my father rescued. Apparently, his usual . . . supplies . . . had run dry. They had me on deck so he could find out about each of you and enter your names in his ledgers."

"And your name, Samson. Where was it entered?"

"It was the first one on the list."

"We have to escape," Vic said. Others murmured their agreement, but Samson laughed. The slow halting guffaws shut everyone up, including Ellen and Michael.

† † †

The journey passed in darkness, relieved only by snatches of light whenever the pirates dropped water and flatcakes through the hatch. Days stretched into a week, then two. In the beginning, Vic swallowed her fear and helped Michael and Samson distribute the food. She gave comfort, letting the boy, Freddie, sleep on her lap and Ellen cry on her shoulder. But the darkness and tossing of the ship wore at her resolve. She grew smaller, her mind shrinking from the creaking hull and misery. As the second week slipped into the third, she retreated to the edge of the hold. When Samson handed her a flagon of water, she drank. If Michael placed a flatcake in her hand, she ate. But she tasted nothing. The time passed, filled with cruel whispers and wishes the ship would sink and they'd be done with it. She almost smiled at the idea of a few cold gulps of saltwater, then oblivion.

When the bucking hull eased into a sloshing roll, she drew her knees up under her chin in disappointment. Hours later, the dull thuds and groans of the ship pulling up to dock jarred her out of her stupor. The hatch banged open. Burly sailors swarmed down a ladder, laughing and holding their noses. No one struggled as the sailors heaved them to their feet and fastened leather collars around their necks. Vic dumbly followed the others out onto the deck, where they stood blinking in the wan light of the setting sun while the pirates linked their collars together with a long rope. Above the wharf, the city climbed hillsides surrounding the bay, the spires indeed reaching for the sky. Vic shifted her gaze away from the towers and their leering red reflections.

When they walked down the rampart onto the dock, Vic kept her eyes on the ground, sickened by the whorl of color and sound and smells. Around them, hawkers held up fish and meat on sticks, musicians drew crowds at street corners, and people bearing great loads on their heads or backs bellowed for others to get out of the way. One of the prisoners ahead of her yelped, and Vic gasped when she looked up. Their heads held high, five nude men strode down the street, carrying a sedan chair. All wore leather bracelets around their ankles and wrists, and all were tied together by a line attached to a leather belt. The man in the front, however, wore a metal belt. Metal! Vic's eyes widened in disbelief.

The bearers stopped when they came abreast of the captives. A woman stuck her head out of the curtained chair, a glorious halo of black curly hair framing her dark face. She shouted something at the Caleisbahnin at the front of the line, and he smiled and waved toward the warehouse in front of them. Blowing the man a kiss, the woman disappeared behind the curtain, and the two groups moved on.

At the warehouse, they waited for some cattle to be herded in ahead of them. Great birds with sharp beaks pecked and nudged the animals along while calves called for their mothers. Under the feet of cattle and birds scampered little green lizards. The lizards woke Vic's awareness enough to notice the sweat trickling between her breasts.

In the warehouse, shadows bled heat like a furnace, and Vic fought to keep her knees from buckling. Shoving the captives along, the pirates led them into a room where a half dozen big-shouldered men glowered behind a man and woman who tapped pencils on writing boards. Ellen whimpered. Vic's stomach twisted.

The pirates uncollared the men first. As each captive was released, the woman felt his hair and arms and looked at his teeth while the man took notes. She spoke to each one, the language harsh and strange. Samson answered her in the same tongue. Frowning, the woman spoke to her partner, clucked her tongue and shook her head. Moving on, they pulled Freddie, the youngest, aside and made him turn around, then sent him out of the room with a guard.

The pair started down the line of women, performing the same examination—hair, teeth, shoulders, a few words. Next to Vic, Ellen sniffed and twisted the wedding band on her finger. Vic swallowed guiltily, thinking of all the times she'd wished the young woman would be quiet. When they reached Ellen, the examiner held her chin and stared into her eyes. After a moment, Ellen stopped crying and straightened up a little. She was a buxom girl with fine blond hair—just what the boys liked back home. Vic sighed, wondering if these people had found something special about her because they sent her off with another guard. *Will they find anything special about me?* As soon as the thought crossed her mind, she scolded herself. *Better they find you so useless they put you out on the street.*

The woman pulled some of Vic's hair off her shoulder, felt its weight and said something to the man. *"Amber girl,"* her father used to call her. Vic bit her lip to stifle a sob. *"But Father,"* she'd tease him, *"amber's nothing but dried up old tree sap with bugs in it."*

Pulling Vic forward, the woman held her shoulders and turned her around. She ran her hands down Vic's sides and murmured something. The man's voice echoed deeply as he wrote on his board. With a pat on Vic's cheek, the woman grasped the collar of her dress and yanked, tearing the material down to Vic's belt. Yelping, Vic fell to the ground, trying to cover herself, but two guards came over and pulled her up.

While the guards held her arms, the woman ran her hands over Vic's shoulders and along her belly, speaking all the while to the man. Then she cupped a breast and teased it erect with her thumb. The man spoke again, nodding. The woman laughed. Wiping the tears from Vic's cheeks, the woman forced Vic to look at her. This time when she spoke, Vic understood her. "Don't cry, darling. Your life will be an easy one."

The examiners moved on and a guard dragged Vic by the arm toward the door. She searched for a pair of eyes that would meet hers, but everyone looked away, their faces red. As they crossed the threshold, Samson's voice echoed in her mind: "I'm sorry."

At the other end of the hall, they passed into a small room housing a large clear vat full of orange jelly. The door clicked shut, and the man reached for Vic's belt. Screaming, she tried to pull his hand away, but he caught her wrists in one hand and tore away her clothes with the other, then hoisted her over his shoulder. Kicking, beating his head, she shrieked at him to let her go. Growling a little, he ignored her blows, carried her up a set of steps next to the vat, flipped her upside down, and forced her head into the jelly. Yelling, she pushed against the sides of the vat, but the orange stuff was cool on her cheeks. She swallowed some, a taste of spring and honey on her tongue. The guard shoved her down, her shoulders, elbows, and waist sinking into the goo, and she wondered what she had been so upset about. I'm still breathing, she realized with a yawn, then wondered if she were dying. Sunny, cool orange eased the pain in her head, melted over her thoughts, and lulled her to sleep.

† † †

Sunshine streamed through gauzy curtains. Vic blinked at the light, yawned, and stretched in the warmth. A green blanket.

White sheets, white furniture, white walls, a white animal's skin carpeting a white stone floor. The strangeness slapped her in the face, and she sat up. In the mirror across the room, a girl with shining amber hair and a jeweled band around her throat stared back. Her skin was like cream. "My face," she whispered, feeling her chin, once plagued with blemishes. Still staring at herself, she stood on the bed. Jeweled bands also circled her wrists and ankles, sewn on too tightly to remove. A metal band backed with suede fit snugly around her waist.

"Metal," she gasped. The Oreseekers had found so little they had been ashamed to return, while the people here used something so precious for decoration. The belt bore jewels of green and red and blue and small metal rings that tinkled softly when she moved. She wore nothing but these adornments. Her cheeks flamed.

Stepping off the bed, she pulled the spread around her shoulders. A pair of windows on opposite sides of the room let in light; a cross-breeze whispered through slots above the glass. Two closed doors faced each other on the remaining walls. One was locked, the other led into a bathroom, complete with a tub large enough to lie in, washbasin, and commode. Vic gasped when she turned a knob above the basin and cold water poured out of a spout. Only the Ancients had had running water.

Back in the bedroom, one of the windows overlooked a courtyard far below. A youth came through a gate with a pair of cows and took them into a stable while two women pulled greens and tubers out of a garden, loading them into a broad basket. A boy ran through one gate carrying an armful of half-plucked birds and disappeared inside the building below, downy feathers swirling in his wake. Everyone, women and men, wore brightly embroidered vests and trousers that billowed around their hips. A man rode through the gate on a long-legged, capering beast, and a boy and girl ran out of the stable to hold the reins while he leapt from the saddle. Vic wondered if the animal was a horse. All the mammals on this world had come with the crew of the *Elesendar*, but the last Oreseeker horse had died generations ago. Below, the man slapped the boy on the back and laughed. Blond hair waved away from a handsome face to the nape of the man's neck, held there by a silver ribbon. He waved a burly fellow over and pointed at something in the corner of the yard. Vic followed their gaze to a small scaffold. A man's corpse hung by his hands from the jib. As Vic stared, a bird fluttered down and pecked at an eye.

Eyes wide, Vic ran to the locked door and yanked on the handle, rattling and tugging. It remained fast. The other window overlooked the street and wouldn't open either. She banged on the glass, shouting at passersby, but none looked up. Some wore red and orange turbans that towered high above their heads. Others swept down the wooden sidewalks in great, billowing robes that hid the motion of their feet. An old woman limped by in rags, holding out her hand. Cartwheeling across the street, a child dropped a shiny stone in the beggar's hand.

Then there were those dressed only in jewels like Vic. Fully clothed men or women led naked girls like her, and boys and young men too, down the street by leashes attached to their belts. Her lip trembled as she watched, her fingers scraping at the glass. One couple passed, the clothed man carefully holding the woman's arm, her stomach swollen beneath a filmy white skirt hanging from her jeweled belt. When she stumbled, the man supported her, his eyes worried. She nodded and ruffled his hair, and they moved on.

Oh Martha, Vic whimpered, what am I going to do? For weeks she had shut out the nightmare, but the reality hit her like a sledge. Sold into slavery, she did not know the language, or how to escape, or even if escape was possible. The hanging man haunted her. What kind of people left the dead out so birds could peck out their eyes? Panic rose from her stomach like vomit. She ran around the room, pulling and banging on the doors and windows. Her breath short, her face hot, she threw herself at the outside door and wailed when it would not budge. Her cries filled her ears, and she crept to a corner, pulled the blanket over her head and wished again and again that it all was a bad dream. It has to be a dream, she said. Come on, Vic. Wake up.

She did not wake up. The sun dimmed, finally sinking past the tower across the street. As the shadows deepened in the white room, her tears dried. Her breathing eased. She waited.

At last, the outside door clicked open. The man who had ridden the long-legged animal walked in, carrying a tray. Vic's stomach grumbled at the smell of roast meat. "Hungry, my dear?" the man asked.

"No."

"I'm ravenous. Had barely a thing all day. Are you sure you don't want anything?" He locked the door behind him, slipping a key on a ribbon over his neck. He wore a robe held together at his waist with a large green jewel. A touch of gray and crow's feet marked him as her father's age. Sitting at the table, he piled meat and vegetables between two thick slices of bread. "I heard you thumping around earlier. Come dine with me."

Vic eyed the fruit and cheese, her stomach rumbling again.

"Join me, my dear. We're going to celebrate your arrival."

From the corner, she watched him eat. "How come I understand you?" she asked flatly. "I hear strange words come out of your mouth, but I know what they mean."

"I speak to your mind as well as your ears, darling. I thought one of your village-mates had the skill. Anyhow, don't worry. I'll teach you Betheljin before you need to speak to anyone else. We have plenty of time."

He ate as if he didn't want to swallow before tasting every flavor, leaving only a slice of cheese and a small red fruit when he came and sat next to her on the floor.

"I'd like to see you." He tugged gently at the bedcover.

She hunched over further, fresh tears spilling onto her cheeks. He gazed at her with deep indigo eyes, his teeth gleaming cruelly. She would have thought him handsome except for the hardness of that smile.

Brushing her tears, he chuckled softly. "You are young. It's almost a crime, except nothing's a crime in Traine if you have enough money to pay for it." Standing, he held his hand down to her. "Come to bed, love."

CHAPTER 3

POLITICS

Marble columns adorned the face of the brothel, a carpet skimming the steps down to the cobbled street. Ashel whistled softly at a brass knocker. Traine had twice as many thieves as slaves. How did the knocker remain fixed on the door and not carried off in someone's pocket?

Simlael rubbed his hands together. "This is what I've dreamt of since I was a lad, boys."

Bellin, face flushed red as his hair, held Ashel's arm. "You cannot go in there."

Exchanging a grin with Simlael, Ashel hefted his pouch. "I think I can."

"I'm not talking about the cost!" His eyes darting at passersby, Bellin leaned closer. "If you get into trouble—"

"Come on," Simlael snorted. "Leave the old biddy here."

"I just want to see," Ashel assured Bellin as he mounted the steps. "We'll meet you back at the Guildhouse."

A woman, clad only in strips of gauze tied to a ring round her neck, admitted them. Ashel's cheeks flamed at glimpses of creamy brown skin molded in luxurious curves. Since he'd arrived in Traine, he'd grown accustomed to mistresses walking nude through the streets—or, at least, he no longer feared the buttons might burst off his trousers. The buttons strained in their buttonholes now. "Maybe this was a mistake," he muttered.

Simlael cast him a scathing look as they followed the woman to a parlor furnished with silk-upholstered chairs and gleaming tables. Carpet thick as summer grass cushioned their steps, and damask draperies graced doorways leading elsewhere. Patrons garbed in silk and erinsheen chatted while gauze-clad youths strolled among them. Ashel and Simlael sat upon a vacant couch and took the wine offered by a green-eyed boy of twelve. Ashel's stomach flopped over, thinking what duties the boy might have. His mother's railing against Trainer debauchery rang in his mind as a girl the same age knelt before them and handed them cards discreetly printed with services and fees. "Anyone who pleases you." She gestured at the courtesans scattered among the patrons: mature men and women down to youths barely into puberty. They're not slaves, Ashel reminded himself. The courtesans belonged to a guild, just as he did.

"Well, I see one I like. Or maybe two," Simlael said, hopping off the sofa. "Don't know how long this'll take, my boy."

Ashel lounged back, examining his cuticles. "See you in ten minutes."

"Ha! I'll see you back at the Guildhouse." His friend put a finger alongside his nose. "Don't let Bellin's nattering stop you from having fun."

He gathered a pair of youths, waggled his eyebrows at Ashel, and followed them out. Sipping wine, Ashel watched the other patrons. One woman, her hair braided with silver twine, beckoned to a young man with sculpted biceps and thighs. Pulling aside the gauze covering his hips, the woman pursed her lips. With a curt nod, she glided out, courtesan in tow.

"You're a beauty," a woman purred, sitting beside him. Blue silk strips cascaded from the band of jewels round her neck. Dusky aureoles peeked through the gaps in her gown, and Ashel's blood rushed to his groin.

Do not act like a lusty bumpkin, he ordered himself. Imparting his best smile, he raised his glass. "Only one of many in this room."

"Let me tell your fortune."

His eyes fell on the card, but she covered it with her hand. "To serve the prince of Latha would be an honor, Your Highness."

He glanced after Simlael. "You know who I am?"

"Who you must be—two younglings come into my establishment, clearly Lathan by their dress and speech, or lack of it." She smiled slyly. "It's disconcerting, hearing voices in your head but not in your ears."

"I'll speak aloud then," he said in Betheljin.

"Oh Highness, your voice is as easy on the ears as you are on the eyes, but in this house you must do as you please."

"I'm pleased to continue listening to your deductions."

A contralto laugh turned the air a sultry red. Ashel's heart thudded, his palms moist as she leaned closer, her hand sliding up his thigh. "As I said, two Lathan younglings stroll in and one may be the comeliest youth I've ever seen. Considering my business, that's quite something. There could be only one conclusion. It's an honor to serve you, Your Highness. I'll tell your fortune upstairs."

Her hand pressed into his crotch, and the buttons of his trousers threatened to pop. His breath came in short gasps, and he had to swallow a yelp as the woman pressed against him. "No charge," she breathed.

Elesendar. His hand floated toward the gaps in her garment and those plump brown breasts, his lips hungered for the salty skin below, his fingers longed to glide along her thighs, he yearned to feel her hands reaching round his—

"I'm sorry, madam," he said, thrusting himself off the sofa. "I shouldn't have come." Setting his wine glass on a table, he reached for his pouch. "For the wine—"

"No charge," she said with a wry wink. "But come again, when you're ready."

Outside, the afternoon heat pressed upon him, and he considered heading for the docks and a plunge. The stink of dead fish and raw sewage might cool his ardor better than the water, but he'd never survive Simlael's ribbing and Bellin's disgust. Instead he turned toward the Guildhouse, choosing a path that led him past a warehouse sporting a mural of a woman descending to a valley full of erin. Three rams stood in front of the herd, their horns fierce in a brilliant sunset. Facing them, the woman clasped her hands in supplication. It was a mystery why this painting of a Lathan mountain valley should be here, in the richest, most powerful capital in Knownearth, but Ashel enjoyed the reminder of home, and he found something new each time he studied it. Today, a hint of white caught his eye, and when he peered closely, he saw the artist had included Elesendar's Shrine on a bluff overlooking the valley. "Samantha Farrak giving herself up," he breathed, then kicked himself for not recognizing the painting's subject sooner. He was studying to be a Loremaster, for Shrine's sake.

"Samantha Farrak indeed," a passerby said, halting beside him. Blond hair framed a handsome face, the man's skin bronzed from sunshine. The gemstones and thread of gold adorning his vest bespoke wealth; the brawny pair of guards, eyes flicking over the street, marked him as a Citizen. "Without her sacrifice," he continued, "the Erin Alliance would never have come about."

Ashel smiled to cover a tick of nervousness at the bodyguards' threatening glares. "But it would never have been drafted without Lieutenant Grossmont."

"A scholar of the Logs! Oh, but you're Lathan. Did you attend the Academy?"

"I'll be teaching there once I return home." Ashel relaxed, pleased to find one of Traine's first rank who cared about something more than profit.

The Citizen's blue eyes sparkled. "A fine institution, with a well-deserved reputation for excellence. Are you headed to the Minstrels Guildhouse now?"

At Ashel's nod, the man declared he had business in that direction, and they walked together, talking of the mural's artist and how various influences on art, architecture, and music crisscrossed between nations. Ashel felt he'd found a kindred spirit and welcomed the arm the Citizen placed on his shoulder. When they paused in front of a silversmith's, the man pointed at a silver flute in the window. "Have you ever seen its like?"

Ashel's lungs emptied of breath. That single instrument probably cost more than three months' provisions for the entire Lathan army.

"Gold in the morning, pink in the evening," the Citizen quoted an old poem. "The spires of Traine deny the shame of her people."

"Those lines were penned two hundred years ago to protest the Betheljin monopoly on metal ores," Ashel said as they resumed walking.

His companion smiled. "You do know your history! Some say it's still true. What do you think?"

Ashel glanced at the bodyguards, then squared his shoulders, determined to honor the man with an honest opinion. "I've found many glorious things here, sir. I don't begrudge the Citizens their wealth, but you have slavery and crushing poverty too, and a society founded on the backs of the starving and the despised will collapse, sooner or later."

"Ah, but in Latha, the Guilds guard their capital as closely as the Citizens watch theirs."

"My nation's war with Relm has lasted a long time. The Guilds are weary of the cost."

The man's smile sharpened. "Well said, young man, and here is the square. I hope we meet again. Farewell."

When Ashel entered the Guildhouse, the apprentice on door duty told him Jovial wanted to see him. He knocked on the Guildmaster's office and pushed open the door at her call.

"What have you been up to? Bellin stomped in here an hour ago and declared he'd just witnessed the unraveling of Latha's moral fiber."

Ashel clenched his fists. He'd thought Bellin had outgrown tattling to the masters. "We were studying Trainer culture, as instructed."

Jovial raised an eyebrow. "In a brothel."

He offered an innocent smile. "It's a well-regarded profession here. The Commissar has brothel-lords on his council."

"And when I found you dicing away your passage home, you reminded me the gambling dens play a vital role in Traine's economy. Bellin is right that you should take more care. Remember where you are and *who* you are, Ashel. Traine may be a neutral capital, but the Relmlord keeps a home here—you could run into him anywhere, any time. And after the Guild swore we could protect you without a boatload of guards, the last thing I need is to be forced to inform your parents that the Relmlord has had you snatched off the street and is holding you for ransom." He started to protest, but she waved him to silence. "You're performing tonight at the Commissar's."

An impish thought produced a grin. "What'll you do if the Relmlord is there and has me snatched out of the Commissar's parlor?"

Jovial glared at him. "The Guild used to cane journeymen for cheek like that, prince or no."

"Luckily I apprenticed in more benevolent times." He sobered. "You know the only reason the Commissar asked for me is because I'm a prince who sings. I'm no more than a novelty to him."

"Be that as it may, you're going." The corners of Jovial's mouth tilted upward. "The Commissar pays well. You might even earn enough for a cabin on the ship home, instead of a hammock in the hold."

As midnight approached, Ashel changed into the ceremonial robes of the Guild, hesitated, then slung the spun crystal sash over his shoulder, declaring his status as a Lathan royal. A novelty indeed.

Jovial waited for him downstairs, her hair done in elaborate curls sparkling with crystal dust. Glintil shell shimmered around her throat and at her ears, and a jeweled brooch held her cloak about her shoulders. She smiled as he came in. "Try not to look so uncomfortable. A minstrel must use everything to his advantage. If being a prince gets you a gig, be a prince!"

In the Commissar's palace, a butler led them into the largest hall he'd ever seen. Crystal chandeliers hung from a lofty ceiling covered with mirrors. Lamplight reflected on a floor blazing with red and gold silk. Elaborate costumes bedecked the guests, from chandelier-bumping turbans to an emerald gown with a train so long two yawning children had been employed to carry it.

The butler's voice echoed across the babble, announcing them: "The Minstrel Jovial of Alna, Master of the Guildhouse in Traine. The Recorder Ashel of Narath, Prince of Latha."

Jovial led him to a sitting area where courtiers surrounded a sharp little man. "Commissar Parnden," Jovial said aloud in

Betheljin, asking Ashel in mindspeech to put on his best rustic-prince face, "your invitation came as such a pleasure! May I present his Highness, Prince Ashel of Latha."

Ashel bowed and offered his hand. An enormous diamond strapped to the Commissar's forehead seemed to crush his neck into well-padded shoulders, so the man looked like he was drowning in orange silk. Parnden clasped Ashel's hand, his grip soft and his grin malicious. "How is your lovely mother? I was schooled in Latha, you know, and miss the sight of her. But here you are, her very image, if she were a fine young man, that is. Here, sit with me."

Hiding revulsion behind his stage smile, Ashel accepted a glass of wine while Jovial excused herself to oversee the musicians. Halfway across the room, she dipped her knees to a tall, blond Citizen—the art connoisseur from that afternoon. The Commissar smiled devilishly at the man's approach. "There's someone else who attended your Academy and knew your mother and father. You ought to meet."

Ashel stood, his gut twisting with foreboding.

"We met this afternoon." The Citizen dipped his shoulders and offered his hand; his grip might have broken the bones of someone who had not spent years stretching for chords on a harp. "And now we've run into each other again, just as I hoped."

"Ah, you know each other already?" Parnden sniggered. "And yet the watch reported no trouble today."

Ashel cursed himself for the biggest fool in Knownearth. *Snatched off the street.* That pair of bodyguards could have stuffed him into a carriage before anyone noticed. "We weren't properly introduced. Lornk Korng, I presume?" His heart quailed at the lecture he'd receive from his mother for acting the rube in front of the Lord of Relm. And like a buffoon he'd told Latha's enemy that the Lathan Guilds were tired of paying for the war! Elesendar's Shrine, it was lucky his father hadn't made him the Heir.

The Relmlord flashed white teeth at him. "Pleased to make your formal acquaintance. How are your parents?"

"Well. The Lathan border expands every day."

Lornk laughed. "By fall we'll have regained our rightful lands. Perhaps by winter we'll have won through to Narath. I haven't dined at the Manor in"—his eyes rolled over Ashel—"twenty years? Certainly before you were born."

Ashel returned a tight smile. "Olmlablaire is something to behold, I hear. I look forward to the day when its bannerpoles bear Latha's flag."

Jovial came over and rescued him. Nodding to the Commissar, he walked to the dais and picked up his harp. His great-grandfather, a master minstrel, had carved it and won the heart of Latha's Ruler with it, so becoming her consort. This harp, Ashel thought. Music, not politics. The notes drifted into his mind as he sat. When they assembled themselves, he began to sing.

His voice had settled into a baritone a few years before, and he reveled in its power as the audience's contempt for a rustic prince from a poor country turned to admiration. Even the Relmlord bent forward, indigo eyes staring intently. In response, Ashel shifted his selections to heroic sagas about Lathan heroes overcoming great odds. He sang of Kara, Knownearth's greatest wizard, and of how she defeated the beast that rose out of the sea. He sang about Saelbeneth, his ancestor and leader of the Council of Wizards that went to the fabled Direiellene to defeat the evil sorceress Meylnara. Casting a dagger at the Relmlord, he sang of the founding of the Erin Alliance, and how Samantha Farrak sealed the bargain with her death. Snuffling, the emerald-clad woman dabbed her eyes with a silk handkerchief, an action echoed by others around the room. And Ashel reminded them all that Elesendar chose Latha as the home for His newborn children. Latha was the birthplace of humanity, and their spirits returned to Latha when they died, to be reborn as cerrenils in the forest of Kiareinoll Fembrosh. Ashel's chest filled, his voice broadened when he saw Elesendar shining through a window, adding His light to that of the candles. Good timing, said the showman in him.

When he finished, the audience stood enraptured, the applause slow to begin, but soon clapping and cries slaked his thirst. The Relmlord's scowl convinced him he'd won a battle in their war, and he gladly answered Citizens' questions about the Academy and how often it accepted foreign students.

"See, Ashel," Jovial teased, "you love the glory."

The hours passed, and the ensemble played country reels mixed with stately waltzes, the courtiers dancing as gaily as Lathan villagers at Landing. When golden dawn shone through the windows, the courtiers and other musicians retired, leaving Ashel and Jovial alone with the Commissar and Relmlord. Jovial curtsied to them, and Ashel returned the bows of the two men. As he turned to leave, the Relmlord grasped his hand.

"Sometimes I forget why Latha is so important," he said. "Tonight, you reminded me. Farewell, Your Highness, and give your mother my love."

Ashel's eye twitched, his sense of victory unraveling. Nodding again at the Commissar, he strode to the exit, Jovial hustling after.

"I thought you weren't interested in politics," the master said when they reached the square.

"Do you believe in evil?" he asked, suppressing a shiver as he thought of the Relmlord's last words: *Give your mother my love.*

She pursed her lips. "I believe in misunderstandings."

CHAPTER 4

AN EASY LIFE

Blood pulsing in her ears, Vic paused in the doorway to look back at Lornk. The key, swinging slowly on its ribbon, brushed her thigh, mimicking his fingers. He lay still on the bed, his breathing as slow and steady now as it had been when she dared untie the ribbon from his neck. Shutting the door softly, she exhaled, outside for the first time. A month or more had passed—she wasn't sure. She no longer measured time by the setting sun, but by Lornk's comings and goings.

Wan light bled from beneath the door. The stairs, open on one side to a well of blackness, descended the square tower through air thick as pitch. By the first turning, the light was gone. Her toes scraped across wooden steps, seeking the edge of each riser as her hands crept along the outer wall. Her ears strained for noise of pursuit, but she heard only her own tense breathing and the slow scuffle of her feet. At the second landing, she gulped back a whimper and fought the urge to climb the stairs and crawl into bed before he missed her. The dead man she'd seen hung out for birds to feed upon had been his last mistress, a term applied to the slaves—male or female—whom Citizens kept for pleasure. Would Lornk kill her for trying to escape, hang her in the courtyard as bird fodder?

She swallowed, clenched her fists, and pressed on. At the third landing, she wondered how heavily guarded the courtyard would be. A bodyguard patrolled it each night, but if she stuck to the shadows, she might be able to get to a little door she'd noticed. If that led to the street . . . Shutting her eyes, she took a breath and held it. *See if you can make it that far.*

At each landing, doubts and fears loomed. She forced herself to move through them, down the next flight, but they followed her, gnawing at her resolve, weakening her knees. What would he do if he caught her? How would she get out of the courtyard? Where could she find clothes? Would anyone help her? Did she *want* to leave him? Finally, legs shaking, she felt cool stone beneath her feet. A line of pale starlight leaked across the floor. Biting her lip, a cry of relief or joy caught in her throat, she trotted toward the gleam.

His footsteps banged on the stairs behind her. Yelping, she dodged, but he grabbed her elbow and flung her against the door. The wood was smooth and cold on her cheek and belly; he pressed himself against her, sandwiching her between his prison and the freedom outside, crushing her with his weight until she could hardly draw breath. His silken robe brushed her calves as he wedged his hand between her legs, long fingers pressing, teasing. She closed her eyes, swallowing whimpers, and her head seemed to grow in the darkness. Short, gulping breaths echoed softly. His fingers lit a fire; his cock, dancing across her backside, stoked the flames. Tears spilled as her hips tilted toward him and the black fire in her loins rose to her throat. The key clinked on stone, Lornk stood back, and she dropped to the ground, her head pounding.

His voice turned the air red. "Never forget I am a very light sleeper. I *let* you get this far." Wrapping her arm in one hand, he picked up the key and carried her back upstairs; she flopped against him like a rag doll as they ascended.

In the room, he dumped her on the animal skin. "Kara," he barked, "what are you?"

She had learned the answer to that question early. Shaking, she pressed her forehead against the white fur, whispering, "I'm yours."

Silk hissing, he draped his robe over a chair, then stood beside her. His feet and toes were long, the muscles of his calves graced with soft hairs. "I didn't hear you," he menaced.

But you did, she thought. She did not have to speak for him to know her mind. She had once wished he would bring a knife with her meals, and he had laughed until tears ran from his eyes. *I lead a nation at war, girl! Do you think you could slice me open so easily?* Now she gulped and raised her head a few inches. "I am yours, my lord."

"That didn't sound as if you meant it."

A shiver ran down her spine as he knelt and his hand encircled her neck, his thumb against her windpipe. She kept her eyes on the floor, studying the angles made by his knee and foot. "Once more," he commanded.

She cleared her throat, sure if she didn't her voice would crack. "My lord. I am yours."

Wordlessly, he reclined on the rug and pulled her head down. As she took him into her mouth, his musk filled her nose and throat and she considered biting, but the grip tightening around her throat pushed the thought from her mind until sweet and salt burst in her mouth. When his desires were sated, he scooped her up and laid her on the bed, his face pensive as his fingers skated over her hips and belly. Her skin grew hot as if burned by the sun, and she trembled as his hand migrated into the nest of soft hairs between her thighs. With his thumb, he pressed and eased off, pressed and eased off. Her breath fell into his rhythm as if he worked a bellows, slowly stoking desire in her heart and submission in her limbs.

Trembling, she asked, "Why don't you just finish it?" A month or more she'd been locked in this room, and his cock was still just a threat, or a prize she'd yet to earn.

"My mother was a bliss addict," he said, adding a circling motion that sent waves of lava to Vic's eyes. Over her gasps, he continued, "She'd smoke it in the Roost. That's a slum on the north shore of this city, populated by thieves and brigands and escaped slaves, most of whom are Oreseekers, like you." Vic's ears twitched at mention of her people, but each press of his thumb ratcheted her hips upward while her breath still matched the rhythm he set. "My mother smoked away more than half the Korng fortune. That was no easy task, but she was diligent and committed to her cause." Blood boiling toward a climax, Vic gnawed on her lower lip as a moan leaked out. He pressed once more, the circling motion achingly slow and she teetered on the edge—

He withdrew his hand. She collapsed onto the mattress, quivering, her head aching as heat receded. His thumb brushed the tears leaking into her hair. "I want you to crave me the way my mother craved bliss," he purred. "Your body does already, but your mind does not. Does it?"

She swallowed, unsure of the answer he wanted. "I'm yours, my lord," she said meekly.

He smiled softly, with a sort of relish. "No, not yet."

† † †

He never struck her. He didn't have to.

The first days, she wore the green bedcover as a robe and did not take it off when asked. When he came, she crouched in a corner, holding the spread around her like a shield. Her throat constricted as he approached, and she heard herself gibber in fear when he knelt down and laid his hands on her shoulders.

Murmuring sympathetically, he would wrap his arms around her, stroke her hair with the palm of one hand, and gently pull the spread away. His hands would caress the tension from her shoulders and belly with clinical skill. When at last she relaxed in his arms, meek and quiet, his fingers would stray below her waist. And when he left an hour or two later, she would lie beneath the sheets, weeping at the yearning coiled in her loins.

One night he stood in the doorway, frowning as she cowered in the corner. "Are you going to take that off?"

Wondering if he would leave if she refused, she slowly shook her head.

He took one step inside the room. "You try my patience. Are you sure of that answer?"

Her stomach muscles clenched at the color of his eyes—bluer than the midday sea. But she nodded, hoping he would leave her alone.

Slamming the door, he strode over and tore the cover away. She screamed, and he shoved her back into the corner and threw the spread over her head. Peeking, she cringed as he pulled sheets from the mattress and flung them at her. He tore down the curtains and swept the heavy skin off the floor and dropped them on top of her. Pressing them down, smothering her cries, he asked if she wanted to wear them all. Flailing, she tried to push him off. But he pressed the linens onto her face, and her struggles weakened, her head ached, and her eyelids grew heavy until all went black. When she woke up, she lay on a bare mattress with the dawn bleeding through a naked window.

He brought breakfast that morning, put it down on the table, and motioned for her to join him. She remained on the bed, glaring from behind her knees. Finally he sighed and asked, "What are you, Kara?"

"My name is Victoria of Ourtown, and I am a Logkeeper for the Oreseekers."

He raised his eyebrows and cocked his head at her. Then he smiled secretly and shook his head. "Wrong. You're mine. You belong to me. What are you?"

Above the smile, his eyes blazed like glaciers in the sun. Her stomach knotted, she crept backward on the bed. "I'm your mistress?"

"Today you're less than that." He towered over her. "What are you?"

"I don't know. Please don't hit me," she screamed as he raised his hands. He seized the little table beside the bed and flung it at the window. Glass crashed. He grabbed her and shoved her across the shards to hang upside down. Crying, begging, bleeding, Vic reached for the window sill, but he shook her by the ankles, yelling the question over and over. "What are you?" Below them in the street, passersby looked up and hurried onward. "What are you, Kara?" He let go of an ankle. "I'm yours," she sobbed finally. "Just yours." So the litany began.

† † †

A few days after he broke the window, a pair of shears lay on the tray when he arrived with breakfast. Eyes locked on the porcelain blades, Vic clutched her tresses and shrank into the corner.

"Come here," he demanded, swiping a chair from the table and jamming it down in the middle of the room.

"Please don't," she begged as he picked up the scissors and snapped the blades together. "Please, my lord. Please, no."

His fingers drummed on the chair back, his eyes glacial blue again. Tears dripped onto her feet as they paced slowly toward the chair, onto her knees when she slumped into it. Tugging a lock taut, he warned her to hold still. The shears opened, and the hair sprang free of the slicing jaws. She let him tug and cut the hair to chin length, but hoarse sobs clogged her throat.

When amber littered the floor, he knelt beside her and tugged her chin round to face him. The anger had melted from his eyes, and they shone sympathetically. "Why do you want to hide yourself?"

"My hair was the only thing about me people ever admired," she admitted, swallowing another sob. "It was the best part of me."

"Oh, my dear," Lornk cried. "It was the least part of you! You have bewitched me, Kara, and not with your beauty. Never be ashamed. I won't permit it."

Her hair was not all he took. From her mother's death when she was four, Vic had clung to her father's side, learning about the world through study—first his, then her own. When Lornk left her alone, she wondered if her mother had not died so early, would she have followed her path instead? And if her ambition had taken her along another route, would she have ended up here?

By town legend, Veronica had sampled Ourtown's men like a chef after spices before she finally chose Theodore. She announced her pregnancy when she won the mast-scaling competition at Festival, brandishing the trophy in triumph. So many children were lost to the cold and the hard life that most expecting women retired from the boats or the fields to indoor duties, but not Veronica. She still sailed with the other fishers at dawn, and when winter came and Vic was born, the ice, not the child, kept her off the water.

Vic had fuzzy memories of sitting in a hammock slung between the mast and the prow of Veronica's skiff, listening to her describe how the wind would reveal itself in the whitecaps on the water's surface. She could almost see her mother's face, lively in the sun, her auburn hair dark with sea spray. She remembered watching her parents dance around the bonfire at Festival, her mother's small, strong body reined in by her father's arms. And the two of them grabbing her and swinging her between them, up and down, back and forth, spinning.

But all these memories could have been just pictures her imagination had made to color her father's tales. She did remember the sad looks of the townspeople after the fever took Veronica, how their heads shook as she drew in on herself, became shy of the other children's games, and turned for solace to Martha's libraries. Most Logkeepers apprenticed when they turned eleven or twelve. When Theodore took Vic to Martha's lodge, saying he'd taught her all he could, she was eight.

Now her hands ached for the cool sheaves of Martha's books. The first weeks in Lornk's tower, she spent the days copying out all she remembered of the Logs onto the table, her fingertips writing an invisible record across the wood. But summer's heat soaked through the walls, shimmering from the table, the mattress, the glass in the windows. Over time, her thoughts smoldered away, leaving lethargy like ash. She lay on the bed, gasping at the whispers of air sifting through the slats above the windows, waiting for him.

Sometimes as he approached her, his hands, his head, his arms and legs would grow to a gigantic size, and as time passed, she felt herself grow smaller, to the size of a doll who sleeps until the child plays with it and gives it life. The light through her windows dimmed whenever his key turned in the lock, the door opening like the world turning toward the rising sun. Eventually the breeze through the slatted windows cooled so she shivered when she slept alone, and she began to welcome his warmth. She began to address herself as Kara. And then one morning, she surprised both of them by smiling when he brought her breakfast.

Setting the tray on the table, Lornk sat down and draped an arm across her shoulder. "Kara," he exclaimed, "are you happy to see me?"

She nodded, tears streaming. Her body, enlivened by his touch, leaned into him. "Yes, I'm glad to see you, my Lord," she said.

"Oh my dear, not nearly as glad as I am to hear that. Now go wash your face."

"Will it be today?"

He kissed the top of her head. "You're not ready yet. Not today."

Standing and walking toward the bathroom door, she felt her muscles groan in disappointment. Her anticipation for him strong, she had to wait a long time to relax enough to use the toilet. *I want him*, she admitted, beginning to weep again.

When she came out, her face and hands clean, he had gone, taking her breakfast with him. A cry of frustration bit out of her, and she threw herself on the bed, clawing at the mattress.

He didn't come again for two days. "Hungry?" he asked her, poking his head in through the door.

Eagerly, she pushed herself to the edge of the bed and nodded.

"But not for me. Let's see if I can change that." Another day passed before he returned, bringing a vase filled with flowers and a tray of cheese and fruit. She tottered toward the table, smiling softly.

He fed her each bite, breaking off tiny bits of cheese and placing them in her mouth, his fingers lingering on her lips. Gratefully, she kissed his fingertips. When she reached for the fruit, he shook his head and peeled it for her, placing each section in her mouth, watching her intently as she chewed and swallowed. "Three months to the day," he said, when she'd swallowed the last piece.

Coughing, she met his eyes. Three months? Summer long gone from the Oreseekers' land by now, her father would be expecting her home. Clearing her throat, she moved back to the bed. What would Theodore do when snow closed the roads and she still had not come? Her shoulders began to shake, and she gulped back a sob.

Raising an eyebrow at her, Lornk sat back, splaying his hands wide and examining his fingernails. "Do you love me, Kara?" he asked casually.

She blinked at him. He had just taken her father from her, as he took her clothes, her hair, her self. Her head shrank into her shoulders, while his eyes grew larger, bluer as he watched. "You want me to have nothing but you," she said, her voice clearer than she would have thought.

He laughed softly, stretching his arms out, then twining his fingers behind his neck. "I told you once—I want you to crave me. Why do you think that is?"

"So I'll obey you."

"Oh, I've had your obedience for months. What I want now is your devotion. The day may come when you will have the world in your hands, and I want you to hand it to me, without reservation."

She gaped at him. "What does that mean?"

He laughed softly. "I want you to know what's expected of you, so you will rise to the occasion. But that's a discussion for another day. For now . . . come here."

She shook her head, wincing at her audacity. "No. Not today, not willingly."

"What?" He stood, towering. But his voice was light, almost playful. "What are you, Kara?"

Averting her face, certain he would finally strike her, she met his gaze from the corner of her eye. But she did not answer him. *I am nothing.*

Sighing, he grabbed the flowers and stepped toward the door. "I've probably spoiled you. I'll have to change that."

CHAPTER 5

PLACES

A knock startled Vic awake. Drawing her knees under her chin, she rubbed her eyes. Lornk never knocked. "Hello, may I come in?" A voice as deep but less self-assured than Lornk's—a stranger. She looked around for somewhere to hide. "Are you awake?" A youth perhaps a year or two older than her poked his head through the door. He stopped short when he saw her cringing on the bed. "Can I come in?"

What is he doing? she wondered, craning her neck to see if Lornk stood behind the boy.

He stepped across the threshold. "I understand your name is Kara. Please call me Earnk. My father asked me to look after you while he's gone—what's wrong?"

Vic scurried to hide behind the bed, shaking her head furiously. "He's gone?" she croaked, eyeing the open door.

"He didn't tell you?" The boy rolled his eyes. "Oh, well. He'll be gone a month or two. I'm supposed to take care of you. Are you hungry? You look like you could use some sun. How long have you been with us?" He sat on the corner of the bed and waited for an answer, blinking his father's indigo eyes at her. He spoke like Lornk, both out loud and to her mind, but his speech seemed . . . smoother . . . than his father's. Earnk

47

had Lornk's golden hair, but his face was longer and his frame shorter and more slender.

"Where's your mother?" she asked suspiciously. It had never occurred to her that Lornk might have a family.

"Dead." His eyes hardened. Flinching, she slid toward the bathroom. He stared at her, his lips tightening with menace, then softening into a frown. "You weren't born in Traine, were you?"

"I don't even know where Traine is."

He nodded. "There're so many dialects in the city—I didn't think. Where are you from?"

She shook her head. "North. It's much warmer here."

"That will change. Summer's over."

A shiver rippled down her spine in memory of the night before, the coldest yet. Would she be allowed clothes when it grew colder? She continued edging toward the bathroom as he watched her, his gaze as intent as his father's. Suddenly flushing, she wished he would go away.

"Do you want to get some air?"

Her eyes darted to the outside door, left open on the dark stairway. "I can leave?"

"The garden and courtyard are all right, but you shouldn't leave the house. You're too valuable to get lost in the streets, and Traine's not an easy place to find your way. Even I've gotten lost on my way home from school."

"School?" Books, she thought, with longing.

He shrugged, a closed smile curving his lips. "The only time I come home is when he's away." The nonchalance of his voice, as if he weren't telling her anything personal, surprised her. Starting suddenly, he touched the bare mattress. "Where are the bedclothes?"

Swallowing, Vic glanced at the door. If this were some trick . . . "He took them."

"Do you want them back?"

She hesitated. The boy's question was earnest, puzzled—not calculated, as if he were luring her into something. Slowly, she nodded.

"I'll have someone—"

"Never mind," she blurted.

"What's wrong?"

Her voice caught on the answer. But he must also have been able to hear her thoughts because he sighed and sat down again. "Why are you afraid? No one but my father can touch you. Hasn't anyone else come by before now?"

She shook her head. Frowning, he went to the door, flexed the handle, told her it was no longer locked. "I'll be back later with the linens." As the latch clicked, Vic ran and put her back against the door, then sank to the floor, her fingers raking through her hair. *I've spoiled you. I'll have to change that*, he'd promised. Now she feared his return more than when he had left.

† † †

Earnk felt his way down the dark steps, his thoughts muddled. She was young, though boys and girls younger than her waited outside cafes all the time. Yet he had never seen anyone scared like her before, except his mother. The last year of her life, Mother had huddled in the corner, whimpering. She'd gone mad, everyone said. Earnk stumbled on the stairs, shaking his head to free the clinging memory. Richelle had been proud to be Lornk Korng's mistress, especially as he never married. But the last year of her life, that pride had withered into shame, and shame into madness.

"Maybe Father's new mistress will tell me why," he muttered, thinking of her wide green eyes and quivering hands.

Light and noise burst through the open door at the bottom of the tower. Bodyguards and servitors, just rising to their morning duties, clapped him on the back as he passed through the courtyard, welcoming him home. They expected an easy month while Lornk was gone and his son was in charge. Discipline already slack, Earnk stopped and cast a round of dice with the grooms, grinned, and ruffled a boy's hair before heading toward the kitchen.

He found Elsa in the pantry. "Where are the bed linens?"

She nodded toward a closet. "What do you need them for?"

"Father's mistress doesn't have any."

"That man." Elsa smiled and shook her head. "He brought them down some time ago and asked to have them laundered. You mean he hasn't returned them to the poor girl? He's so forgetful."

Negligent, you mean. "Well, here they are, curtains and all. Why hasn't anyone been up to see her?"

"Oh, his lordship said she was from a savage place with no civilized ways. He didn't want anyone to laugh at her because she didn't know how to use a fork. She's quite good for him. He needs a hobby."

"She's an expensive hobby if she's not bred in Traine."

"True. But you know your father's whims. He does care for her though. I think she reminds him of your poor mother. He grieved for Richelle too long."

Grimacing, Earnk shook his head. "Right. I'll take these upstairs now."

"Why don't you let me? I haven't seen the girl yet."

"She's very timid."

Elsa waved her hands dismissively. "That's nothing a friendly face won't cure. I hear she's from the north, where my grandfather—your great-granduncle—came from." She sighed. "The stories he would tell. All these fables about great ships falling from the sky. Nonsense, but delightful."

"Let me go up for now. I don't think she knows anything about ships. I'll bring her down later."

"You're the master for now." She patted the sheets in his hand, then winked at him. "But careful, dear. Don't grow too fond of your father's toys. Don't play with her either."

"I'm well aware of the consequences, Elsa."

He gathered some fruit and sausages from the larder and took them with him back to the tower. On the way, he stopped at the library and picked up a few picture books. It was time this girl started learning Betheljin.

When he had stumbled with full arms back up the stairs, he had to knock again because the girl had shut the door. He waited a minute, then called to her. Finally the latch clicked open. As he elbowed his way inside and dumped his load on the table, the girl peeked at him from behind the door, her eyes like emeralds.

Uncomfortable under the intense stare, he threaded the rod through the curtains. One window was missing a glass pane—something to have fixed before the autumn storms blew in. While his attention was on the drapes, she crept over and took a sheet from the pile, then lay down on the bed beneath it.

"I brought you some breakfast," he said when the curtains were up.

"Thank you," she croaked.

"I also brought some books—"

The eyes peeped out. "Books?"

He raised his eyebrows, not expecting her interest. "I thought I could show you the pictures and tell you how to say them. Not everyone has mindspeech in Traine."

"Show me." She sat up, head and shoulders emerging from the sheet, careful to keep the rest of her body covered. Earnk had never heard of such modesty—even Relmans seemed more sophisticated than this girl. He sat beside her and opened one of his childhood favorites. "Man, woman, chair, table, bowl, spoon. You try."

She pointed and repeated his words, then named other objects in the picture. "Cookie, bread, tray, plate. Read me the story."

"What?"

"Please." Her eyes had softened to a brownish hazel, weighted by long dark lashes. "Don't think the words to me. Just read it and let me follow the pictures. That's how I'd teach the children to read at home."

He blinked at her. "Teach? You can read?"

"Of course." Eyes flashed at him, then fixed on the ground.

"It's about a cookie that comes to life and runs away," he began unsteadily. Somehow she had made him feel like the savage.

"Hmph."

He grinned. Modest and brash at the same time. "You don't want to run away."

"I don't know. Read the story."

He read that story and all the others. She asked him to bring more and let her keep these so she could study. "Your alphabet is quite similar to ours, and I think I can remember what you named things."

"You learn quickly."

"Your father taught me a little."

"What other words do you know?"

She flushed and Earnk felt his own face grow hot—prying into his father's privacy was a mistake he would not wish to make in front of him. "Are you sure you don't want to go walking?" he stammered.

Her face turned toward the outside window, and hope rippled from the blink of her eyes down to the corners of her mouth. Then her expression hardened. "I wish you'd bring me more books."

Fascinated, he sat at the table, nibbling at her breakfast. "So, you were a teacher?"

Startled, she turned back to him, her eyes wet. "I was . . ." She swallowed, then looked down at the bands around her wrists. "I *was* a Logkeeper."

"You collected firewood?"

"No," she snapped, her eyes flashing green again, her face flushed with impatience. That look alone confirmed she had been a teacher of some sort—he'd seen the same on his own instructors when he taunted them. "I traveled around the villages, teaching our history, among other things."

He nodded. "You mean you were a recorder. Can you sing?"

"I know some songs, but I'm no singer." Leaning forward, she spoke more loudly, with greater confidence. "The Logs are our history—and yours too. Our ancestors came from Earth on the mining ship *Elesendar*. We weren't supposed to end up here, but there was an accident."

Earnk laughed. "You're a heretic! I'll have to try that one out on my friends next time we discuss theology. Elesendar an accident!"

Now she glared openly at him. "Logkeepers preserve the Logs and the data banks so that someday the people on this world can go home."

He suppressed another guffaw. "To the stars? Why don't your own people go?"

"If you haven't noticed, there's precious little metal on this planet." Beneath the sheet, her hand tugged at her belt. "We chartered ourselves to preserve the Logs—the rest of you are responsible for figuring out a way home. Instead, you waste your time"—she waved at the room—"indulging yourselves."

Blood pounding suddenly in his ears, he stood. "I have things to do."

† † †

Vic watched him charge out, her heart in her throat. This boy's open face and clumsiness, so different from Lornk's grace and veiled looks, invited her confidence. Lornk would smile with all his teeth bared, like a koot before it bites. Earnk had a gentle mouth. Lornk's eyes stripped her like a gale; Earnk's gaze ruffled her like a spring breeze. She could still smell his spicy-earthy cologne, and his voice, reading, echoed in the room. The food lay frazzled from his nibbling. She shook her head, trying to clear it. *It's only because he's the first one I've seen who wasn't* him. A book lay open next to her on the bed. Her heart sighed. Books. *Like water in the desert,* she thought. No. *Like, like*—similes failed her. The Oreseekers had nothing that compared with books, although she imagined that chocolate, the delicacy of the Ancients, might. The Ancients had described one bite of that food as a metaphor of life: hard and bitter followed by a softening in the mouth to a final sweet lingering. Some of the books transcribed in the Logs would linger in Vic's mind for days, their hardness, their bitterness often the source of their sweetness. She sighed. It felt like a lifetime since she'd thought about such things. This boy had appeared and Kara had vanished.

The door stood open. She thought again that Lornk could be waiting outside, testing her loyalty. *Even if this weren't a trick,* she thought glumly, *where would I escape if she ran?* For all she knew, that pirate ship might have taken her off the planet and put her among the stars. Someplace where people already had a taste for beauty. Her own dreams mocked her.

Standing up on the bed, she looked at herself in the mirror. Really looked. Her eyes had avoided that wall for the past three months, but now she threw off the sheet and stared at the reflection. Touching the jeweled band at her throat, she thought of all the other mistresses she had seen walk by on the street below. Why couldn't she muster the same pride? A vision of

Lornk's tongue licking his lips gripped her stomach, and she sank to the bed again. She had never been good at anything physical, and she certainly had never kissed anybody, not even—especially not—greasy Henry. So why would Lornk, or the trader who'd picked her, have thought she would be good at this? This boy Earnk acted as if she ought to enjoy it, and that woman at the warehouse had said she'd have an easy life. The people from Cairo who'd been taken with her—what awful things had happened to them? Did they toil in a mine somewhere or push oars in a galley? It seemed likely Ellen and Freddie had been sold as mistresses too, and poor Freddie was only a boy! Did they suffer rape and degradation from masters even more cruel than hers? She supposed things could have been much, much worse, but still . . . her fear of Lornk, and, worse, her *craving* for him—the shameful desire to accept him and her place with him—was the hardest thing she'd ever known.

Lost in thought, she didn't hear the voice in the doorway. A woman bustled in with a soft smile and kind eyes that rooted Vic to her seat. Gray hair waved loose over her shoulders, and her vest bared large, well muscled arms. Oreseeker men would have appreciated that physique. She spoke, something about Vic's breakfast.

"No," Vic answered, signaling that she didn't want the food taken away yet. Nodding, the woman took a yellow sash from a pocket in her trousers, unraveling it in the sunlight.

"Where did you get that?" Forgetting to be shy, Vic moved to take the sash. It wasn't hers. "This is a Logkeeper's sash. It's very old."

The woman laughed and kissed Vic on the cheeks, then began talking rapidly and pointing at the ceiling. She took Vic's hand and started toward the door, still laughing and talking.

"No! No, thank you," Vic managed in Betheljin. She retreated to the table, and pointed to the food, excusing herself.

With a frown, the woman shrugged and left, leaving the sash in Vic's hand. Reverently, she laid it out on the table, bits of the fragile wool clinging to her fingers. Once again she wondered if the day's events were part of an elaborate trap leading up to a punishment for defying Lornk. "I don't care if it is," she whispered, laying her cheek against the wool, feeling she'd just regained a small part of herself.

† † †

Earnk hesitated before opening the glass cabinet. His father had never forbidden him the books inside—on the contrary, Lornk Korng would have been pleased to find his son thumbing through the leather-bound diaries and Ancient volumes. But Earnk's shoulders crept toward his ears, hoping to muffle Mother's contralto laughter as she and Father exchanged verses from these books. Shaking off the memory, he pulled open the cabinet and took out one of the older volumes, a Log of the Ancients, written in their obtuse, vowel-heavy language. The same one Kara spoke.

"I'm having the east tower sconces filled with oil," Elsa said, coming into the library. "It's a wonder your father hasn't broken his neck, climbing those stairs in the dark."

Earnk ducked his head to hide a grimace, his fingernails digging into his palm. "Do you know where these came from?" He held up the one of the diaries.

She smiled. "Those belonged to my grandfather. Your great-grandmother put them in here. He told me his fables were written inside them, but no one ever tried to read them except your mother and father. Pappy was gone by then."

"How come you never learned?"

"Come now. I was to learn to cook, not study old books. I like a good story, but my ears are better than my eyes."

"Kara talked to me about going back to the stars."

"I knew it." She clapped her hands together. "I know you told me not to, but I couldn't resist seeing her, and she didn't seem that frightened. I took my grandfather's sash, and she went wild over it."

"Do you think she could read these books?"

"Could be, dear. Let her finish eating and then go up and ask her. Perhaps I should come with you."

"Are you that curious?"

She pressed her lips together, cocking an eyebrow. "You know I love you. But after I've seen her, I'll warn you again. I know you. See that you don't get too close."

"I'm not stupid, Elsa."

"I know. You're clever enough to think you can get away with something. Don't even think about it, love. After his last mistress, your father's been a little suspicious of everybody. He'll know, believe me."

"And how do you know?"

"Don't be flip with me. You're not the master yet."

"That isn't what you said earlier."

"I was humoring you. His lordship tells me things nobody else hears. That girl's a virgin until he can trust her. Don't let anything happen that could hurt either one of you."

Earnk's cheeks flamed. "Nothing's going to happen, and you don't have to chaperone us. I know my place."

"Good. I hope she knows hers."

"Nothing will happen."

† † †

When he went back to Kara's room that afternoon, Earnk found the rest of the curtains up and the bed made. Even with the draperies, sunlight blazed off the white walls and furnishings, blinding him after the walk up the dark stairway. The bedspread glowed like a patch of lawn found clear after the first snowfall. Verdant, alive, doomed.

He expected to find Kara hiding under the bed, but she surprised him by being seated at the table reading one of the books, wearing nothing but what she ought. When he came in, she looked at him with glistening eyes and puffy cheeks. He asked if she'd been crying.

"This story is so sad." She held up a picture book that had been one of his favorites.

"That's a happy story. The king finds his lost love."

She shook her head, her frown telling him he was a fool. "That isn't what the pictures say. Look at this woman being turned into a bird. Her expression is rapturous, as if that's what she's always wanted. And here on the last page, after the king disenchants her and is taking her to his castle, she looks sad, and they're so old. By that time, what difference did it make?"

"The point is that they found each other, no matter how long it took."

"Maybe she didn't want to be found."

He shook his head, cleared his throat. "Elsa, the woman who came up earlier, thought you might know what these are. She said you recognized the sash."

Kara glanced down at the yellow wool in her lap. "How did she get one of these?"

"It was her grandfather's."

"How did he get here?" He could almost taste the bitterness in that question.

"I think he was found adrift by some traders. My great-grandmother bought him and let him keep his things."

She swallowed. "You're his great-grandson?"

"My family came from a formal arrangement."

She peered at his books, saying nothing. But her thoughts

were loud as anyone's who didn't know mindspeech, and he Heard glimpses of a man defying tradition and setting out on a boat alone with some valuable artifacts. Kara sighed. "Are those his Logs?"

He brought them to her and sat while she thumbed carefully, reverently, through the pages. "These are the personal logs of the first officer. They detail a visit to Jupiter, another planet in the crew's home system." Her voice trembled. "These have been missing for generations—hundreds of years. Charles the Fool did not take these away with him. Where did they come from?"

"They were in the same cabinet with the books Elsa's grandfather had. We thought all of them were his."

"There are more?"

"A whole cabinet."

She looked at the window, clenching and unclenching her fists. He sensed sudden determination building up inside her like a brick wall. "Take me to them."

Earnk smiled. She was like a wounded bird stretching her wings for the first time in weeks. And he suddenly thought that he might become her friend, and that would be enough to make sure his father could never trust her. *I won't touch her, Elsa, but he won't have her either.* "Come on. I'll show you the library."

Chapter 6

Customs

She read avidly, up at dawn and in the library pouring over the Logs. She didn't share her hmms and uh-huhs with him, so Earnk Listened in on her thoughts. What he Heard astounded him. She actually believed the stories of ships that flew through space, on board which people had lived, worked, loved. He kept asking questions about the books, pulling her out from behind that brick wall. A good storyteller, she related many of the log records to him, sharing her theories about the sabotage of the *Elesendar*. At night, he took her up on the roof and had her point out the Gamorrahs and the constellation from whence the *Elesendar*'s crew had come. The first week, instead of teaching her Betheljin as he'd intended, he found himself learning from her as they scanned the Logs together. He looked forward to the dumbfounded look on his Classics teacher's face when he returned to school. But the more time they spent together, the more Elsa would drop into the library at random, patting Kara on the head and frowning harshly at him.

Within a few weeks, she settled into the household, no longer blushing when she bumped into someone in the hall. She would walk in the garden and ask the gardener in broken Betheljin what herbs he was growing and when the vegetables would be ready for harvest. She joined the household on Enddays to watch the bodyguards wrestle. She spent evenings with Elsa, telling her stories of their ancestors, her Betheljin improving each evening they spoke together. The day the clockmaker came to tune the floor clock, she watched his work so avidly and asked so many questions that he took the entire mechanism apart to show her how each gear drove the others. So long as no one mentioned Earnk's father, she seemed happy. And the library became her domain. After she had read through all the Logs, she moved on to studying Betheljin, picking it up far quicker than he had learned Relman with formal instruction at school. Then she announced one day that the library was a mess and she was going to reorganize it. Now genuinely wanting to be with her, Earnk didn't hesitate to offer his help.

"Why do you have a copy of this book about rocks?" she asked as they were sorting, holding out a large tome with a picture of a granite slab on the front.

"That's the Relman Stonemasters Guild Creed. Go ahead and put that in the non-Betheljin pile."

"Why do you have it?"

"My father rules Relm—that's where he is now. The war's heated up, and he was needed there."

"Oh." He Heard her wonder if Lornk had stolen the throne.

"It was a peaceful succession, I promise you! The Relman people love my father. The Lathan war has lasted a whole generation. They've been fighting as long as I've been alive. All that time, Father has defended the border and made sure trade never suffered." Beckoning her over, he dug an atlas out of the piles and made space on the table. "This is Relm here in the south. You can see it's got no seaports because these mountains in the west are impassable. Relm used to send its goods through Lathan ports, but when the Lathan Ruler closed the border, my father negotiated overland routes through Semeneminieu here in the east, and trade has boomed since."

"Semmen-emmen-what?"

He laughed. "Semeneminieu. Just say Semeana plains; everyone will know what you mean."

She gave him a quizzical look. "Relm is landlocked, but Traine is a port city."

He grinned and pointed to it on the map. "It is. See, it's the capital of Betheljin, up here."

Her eyes measured the distance between the two nations. "That must be thousands of miles!"

"About five thousand."

"Your father couldn't travel that far in one or two months."

Earnk chuckled, enjoying her consternation. "He can and does. He goes to Relm nearly every day. The only reason he's been gone so long now is that his Council needed him in Re—that's Relm's capital, here on the plains." He directed her attention back to the map. "But my father rules mostly from Olmlablaire, up here in the mountains. People also call it Lordhome."

She arched her eyebrows at him, a look he'd come to recognize as an expression of ignorance she blamed upon him, not on herself. "Five thousand miles? How is that possible?"

"I'll show you." Happy to teach her something, he clambered over the piles of books and shoved some volumes aside on a shelf, revealing a small wooden knob poking out of the paneling. "This will let you into a room behind these cases."

"A secret room?"

"Not secret to anybody who lives here. Do you want to see it?"

"Can I?" The question was suspicious, not curious.

He pulled out the knob. "Come on."

A section of the bookcase swung back, revealing a smooth granite passage lit by sconces. As they descended, he told her how the servants kept the sconces lit all the time so Lornk wouldn't have to fumble in the dark for candles. Her steps hesitated at the mention of his father, but as they went deeper, her shoulders straightened and she bowed her head. The ramp leveled out, and the passage widened before ending abruptly, forming a circular room carved from the bedrock beneath Traine. In the center of the floor, a black metal knob angled out of a white porcelain sconce. Around the knob, slots spoked between blue gems. Kara walked around the Device, glanced at him, then knelt down and pointed at the knob, resting in the southeastern slot. "What is this?"

"The Device. That's how my father can keep two houses five thousand miles apart. Don't touch it—you could end up in Relm."

As if stung, she jerked her hand back. "How? Who made it?"

"I always thought it was wizards' work, but nobody knows for sure."

Kara harrumphed. Why a girl who believed their ancestors came from *space* refused to accept the documented facts about wizards was one of the mysteries he liked about her. "What happens if the knob is in one of the other slots?" she asked.

"Oblivion. None of the other slots will take you anywhere, but you'll disappear from here. It's a death I'd rather not think about."

Kara bit her lip, her fingers lingering near the Device. "I'd think about it," she whispered.

Swallowing, he glanced back toward the library. "I thought you were starting to like it here." Those green eyes shot daggers at him, then faded to hazel, and her glare smoothed over. He couldn't eavesdrop at times like these; her thoughts were too jumbled.

"I do like some things."

"Do you like me?"

"I might if you called me by my real name."

"The name we gave you is your real name now."

She shook her head. "My name is Victoria . . . Vic, to my friends."

He grabbed at what she offered before he could figure out what it was. "I'll call you anything you like if you come out with me tonight."

She stood, her hands hugging her shoulders. Whenever visitors came to the house, she would quickly disappear, retreating to her tower. Clearing her throat, she raised her eyes and asked, "You promise not to call me Kara anymore?"

"Yes. Vic. There's a fair outside the Commissar's palace tonight. I'd like to buy you some winter clothes."

"Clothes? I'm allowed?"

"It snows a lot in winter. You'll need boots and a coat. Is it very cold in the north where you're from?"

"The tundra's probably already frozen by now," she said sadly. "I'll be glad when it gets truly cold here."

Their eyes met and he smiled. "It will. Soon." Then his smile faded. After my father gets back.

"Do you think I'm beautiful?"

The question ambushed him, and he stuttered his answer. "You're very appealing."

But not beautiful, he Heard her think in response. His fingers reached for hers—the first time he'd ever touched her. Static jolted up his arm, and his heart lurched. "I cannot say you're beautiful. I cannot even think it. I'm not allowed. We all have our place"—drawing his fingers out of hers was like drawing aching muscles out of a hot bath—"and mine is to be nothing more than your friend."

She stared at him, eyes blinking back toward green, glanced

at the Device, then turned and started up the ramp. "I don't think you can even do that."

"Will you still come with me tonight?"

She did not turn around. "Do I really have a choice?"

Unable to answer her aloud, he shook his head.

Back in the tower room, Vic watched the milk peddler make a late delivery across the street, but her mind was stuck on the secret room under the library. When Earnk had so nonchalantly shown it to her, she had expected to meet Lornk there, as if the son was presenting her—tamed—to the father. She was certain nothing that happened in Lornk's absence was done without his blessing. He'd put her on a very long lead, perhaps to show how pleasant her life might be if she gave him what he wanted. *I have your obedience. I want your devotion.*

Could she give it to him? All his servants had—grooms, bodyguards, housemaids, cooks all venerated their master. Elsa revered him, seemed to bear no resentment that they shared a grandmother but Lornk had inherited a kingdom while she labored as his housekeeper. Earnk alone betrayed discontent, but just now, in the library, his eyes had shone with admiration as he described his father's reign. Earnk bore his father's face, his hair and eyes, but was in every way smaller, more human, more humane. Softly, she cursed the boy. With the curtains and bedclothes, Earnk had restored her dignity. With books, he had restored her intellect. With her name, he had restored a life she'd thought lost.

When Lornk returned, he'd take them away again, unless, perhaps, she gave him what he wanted. *Your devotion.*

A sob welled up from her belly, her eyes filling with tears, but she bit back the grief. This is *my* life. Not Lornk's.

I am . . . Her thoughts paused. The litany was so familiar, she could not complete it without "his." I *am* his. She felt herself—Vic, the girl Earnk had resurrected—slipping down a hole, leaving nothing but the craving of Kara. For nearly a month she'd slept alone in this room, and she missed the smell of him, the heat of him, the press of his skin to hers in the night. Shame surged up her throat, revulsion for the part of her that was eager for his return.

Slowly she rose. Elsa's workers had lit the lamps all the way down and the door at the bottom stood open, letting in light and chatter from the courtyard. It was no longer the dark place where Lornk had caught her that night, yet every time Vic touched the door, her heart would jump to her throat. He might have killed her here. That night he had shown her how her very breath came and left at his command. *I want you to crave me.* Elesendar, but she did. Shivering, feeling ill, she hurried across the courtyard and through the kitchen door, slipped through the servants' dining room to the hallway. A solid red runner led down the marble floor past the library. She paused, looking back at the white stone walls, the hallway empty except for the floor clock, ticking off miracles as the interlocking brass gears turned in time with the pendulum swing. How many marvels had she found within this house? Not enough, she decided, and went into the library.

Stacks of handwritten quartos, piles of printed volumes teetered all over the floor, narrow walkways between the heaps. Earnk was gone, had shut the door to the secret room, even replaced the books in front of the switch. She reached up behind them and quickly pulled the little knob out. When Lornk came back, she knew in her bones she'd fall to her knees and give him whatever he wanted, lest he lock her away again. Panting, heart beating wildly, she felt loathing churn in her belly, not for him, but for the clockwork doll he'd make of her.

The bookcase swung back; she clenched her fists and ran down the passageway. Oblivion, Earnk had said. A protest gibbered in her stomach, but she clamped her jaw shut and moved forward. Oblivion was better than life as his toy.

At the bottom of the ramp, Elsa squatted over the knob, holding a letter. Vic skidded to a halt.

The housekeeper trundled up, tucking the letter inside her vest. "My dear! How did you get in here?"

Thwarted, Vic sat on the cold stone floor, suddenly unable to swallow her tears. Elsa kneeled beside her and put an arm around her shoulders. "What were you going to do?"

Vic pressed her forehead to her knees. "I want to die, Elsa."

"No, you don't. Let's go up and I'll make you some tea."

Shaking her head, Vic gulped back another deep sob. "He's coming home soon, isn't he?"

Elsa squeezed her shoulders, but her voice was firm. "Now listen, miss. Don't you blame him for what those pirates did to your village." Surprised, Vic raised her head. Elsa's mouth was grim, her resemblance to Lornk sharp. "He treasures you like silver."

A clockwork doll made of silver, a fragile thing that would tarnish if left out in the air. "I can't let him own me."

"Anyone who loves you owns a part of you. The secret is to own a part of him."

"By loving him?"

Elsa nodded. "As Earnk's mother did."

"And that worked so well for her," Vic spat. "Did he kill her outright, or just neglect to feed her?"

The slap came fast and stinging. Vic stared at the housekeeper, heat spreading from her jaw to her eyebrows. Elsa's lip quivering in anger, she shook her finger. "He loved Richelle as he loved his life. Now, he has opened his heart to you, and you should cherish that gift; he doesn't give it easily."

Standing, arms akimbo, her eyes blazed with the same glacial fury as Lornk's.

Elsa escorted Vic up the tower stairs; by the time they reached the top landing, she had resumed the manner of the kindly housekeeper and promised to send some hot water for a bath. After the men brought up the steaming urns, Vic let it grow cold before she slipped into the tub. Shivering, she hoped to freeze her tears and brace herself for the future.

When Earnk arrived near sundown and fastened a chain to her belt, she managed to gulp back her protest and accept it. He offered an apology anyway. "We have customs. The crowds will be thick and I don't want to lose you. It's for your own protection."

Glum, she followed on his lead out into the street for the first time. Immediately, the crowd swept them down steep hills toward the wharves. Silks and animal tails tickled her skin as they hustled their way forward. Colored lanterns hung overhead; banners flapped from drainpipes and cornice stones. A woman danced by them and grabbed Earnk's neck, kissing him before teetering on. Everywhere people swirled in laughter and abandon, every face wearing an eager smile. After a long walk down switchbacking avenues, they entered an enormous square seething with color and music.

Every few steps a musician stood with pipes or harp or guitar or a poet heralded the passersby with tales. As the barrage of color and sound assaulted her, Vic forgot herself and began to smile. Grinning, Earnk pulled her out of the way of a passing troupe of jugglers. "Let's find the weavers. I know you don't want to stay long," he said drily.

In the cluster of crafters' booths, boys and girls bearing bolts of cloth or strips of leather hawked their way through the crowd. Young people danced by, rattling bells in their faces, trying to entice them into this booth or the other. Earnk pointed to a sign showing a strange creature with large horns shedding its coat, and they went inside. She'd almost forgotten the precious privacy clothing provided. As she tried on one cloak and another, she bit her lip to stifle the longing to hold one around herself and walk free. But even the choice of color was not hers. "I think the gold one suits you best," Earnk said, and paid for delivery.

After a visit to a cobbler, Earnk bought them skewers lined with succulent meat, followed by a dish of sweet iced cream. A minstrel strolled by, her voice clear and lovely but her language strange.

Earnk gave the young woman some crystal stones. "She's a Lathan minstrel."

"Isn't Latha the country your father's fighting?"

"I can still admire them."

A roar went up some aisles away. Earnk said people were dancing in the center of the square. "Would you like to go see?"

At her nod, he clasped her hand and pulled her toward the noise, but as they passed a brewer's stall, someone called Earnk's name, and they slipped through the throng, across the walkway to the beckoning young man. "Come, have a drink with us," he said.

"Friends from school," Earnk whispered, pointing to a bench outside the stall. "Wait here. I won't be long."

"I can't come with you?"

"Silly law. You're not allowed in. I'll only be a few minutes."

He handed her the other end of the leash and went over to his friends. The one who'd invited him smiled and nodded at her. "Where did you get her?"

"She belongs to my father."

With that sour reminder, Vic sat. People jostled past, fascinating her with their clothes, their hair, their shapes. The mistresses on their leads all held their heads up, smiling at the admiring glances. One of them sat beside her while his master and her friends went inside the brewer's stall. The boy's glossy black hair hung past his waist, covering his lap as Vic's had done once. She couldn't help staring at a cock much smaller than Lornk's, but just as lively. When his black, almond eyes looked up at her and he grinned, her cheeks grew hot.

"Come with me," he whispered in Betheljin, tossing his head at a space between booths.

On his third mug, Earnk looked as if he planned to stay a while.

"Why?" she asked the boy.

"They'll be there a long time."

Feeling like an errant child, but relishing a chance to *choose*, Vic tiptoed with the other mistress into the space between tents. Bushes and canvas screened them as the boy touched her arm and ran light fingers up it, making the hair stand on end. Her stomach tightened.

"I should get back now." She forgot to speak in Betheljin. The boy's grip became suddenly strong and he pressed her hips to his. Vic yelped and slapped him, pushing him away.

"Save it for your master then," he spat. "He won't want you soon enough."

"I hope you're right," she cried as she ran.

Back at the brewer's, more people had gathered around Earnk's table, all laughing and toasting. She let the crowd sweep her toward the center of the square. There, on a stage erected before the gates of an enormous palace, musicians played a reel. Couples, threesomes, people alone skipped in circles and threw their hands above their heads. The dancers spun wildly, running into each other and knocking one another down. But hands pulled the fallen back on their feet before they could be trampled, and everyone laughed. Vic grinned softly, remembering the fish scoop.

"Would you like to dance?" The question sounded entirely

in her mind, not in her ears at all. A tall young man stood in front of her, hand extended. Dark eyes danced beneath heavy lashes. Teeth dazzled white against light brown skin. Her breath frozen, she looked around, thinking he could not have been speaking to her. Then she pointed to herself and shrugged her shoulders. "It'll be fun," he said, beckoning with long fingers.

"No, thank you," she mumbled at last, backing into the crowd. The young man gazed after her, hands twitching at his sides, then shrugged and moved off. Vic watched him from a safe distance. His dark eyes glowed in the torchlight; his hair glistened in tight black ringlets; his laugh inviting as he watched the dancers—she had never seen anyone so beautiful. When the reel ended, he made his way to the stage while a woman called to the crowd for their attention. Getting a white harp from a stand at the back of the dais, he stepped forward as the woman announced, "Ashel, Recorder of Latha."

He sang in the strange language she'd heard earlier, his voice ringing deep and clear with profound emotion. The words unintelligible, the ballad still spoke of safety and home and never being ashamed again. As Vic watched, his eyes scanned the audience, resting on one and another, pausing on her, moving to someone else. The murmurs of the crowd died to a whisper, then silence as the song continued. Nearby, a large, flamboyantly silked woman placed her hand over her heart and sighed. Piqued, the blond mistress beside her rolled his eyes, but the minstrel's pure voice drew the mistress's gaze back to the stage. Then the singer's tone changed and his voice sank with despair. Tears ran down his cheeks even as Vic tasted the salt on her own lips. Enthused stomping and congested cries greeted the song's end. Vic stumbled away, feeling as lost as she had her first day in Traine.

When she got back to the brewer's, Earnk sat on the bench, alone and fuming. As soon as she emerged from the crowd, he swiped up the chain at her belt and waved the ringed handle in front of her face. "Do I have to fasten you where I leave you? Where have you been?"

"I didn't think you'd miss me."

Grabbing her arms, he shook her. "You've embarrassed me. Do you know what that means to be snubbed by a mistress?"

"You're drunk."

Snarling, he tugged her after him, back up the steep hills to Lornk's palazzo. It was a long walk, the silence broken only by Earnk's mutterings. When they finally reached the top of the tower, he shoved her in her room and locked the door. Throat tight, eyes dry, Vic hid all the way under the covers and tried to pretend she was safe.

The next morning, she woke at dawn to find Earnk reading at the table, breakfast and flowers next to his book.

"I need a bath," she said.

He nodded at the door, eyes bloodshot. "Please go ahead." Hoping he'd leave, she took a long time in the bathroom, but he was still there when she came out.

"I didn't mean what I said last night."

She glared at him. "Don't take me out again. Next time I won't come back."

"I thought you'd become comfortable with . . . who you are."

"I hate who I am! I'm your father's *slave*, and I hate it. I hate myself."

He looked away. A warbler cried from the roof. Children shouted at each other on the street below. Vic tore at a piece of bread, aware of how noisily she ate with a nose full of tears.

"You can't hate yourself," he whispered. "You can't because you're loved."

She scowled. "Elsa told me. He loves me and it's a great gift. I'm so honored, I'm repulsed."

"I'm not talking about him." Earnk twisted his napkin. "Vic, I love you."

She put down the bread and stared at him. "You can't. You said you can't."

"I do."

"What about your father?"

"My father," he spat. He reached across the table and grabbed her head, spilling the juice. Pulling her toward him, he kissed her, then came round the table and took her in his arms. At first when his tongue pushed past her teeth, she was too surprised to do anything, feel anything. But the kiss catalyzed her anger into desire. A flame suddenly flared in the pit of her stomach, and she trembled as he tugged her head aside and kissed her neck. She wanted to go limp in his arms, wondering if she loved him back. Lornk could make a black fire erupt in her head, but she'd never felt this warmth in the pit of her stomach before.

"Wait," she breathed, his mouth hot on her shoulder. "Not here. This is your father's place."

He stopped. "So let's go to ours."

They went down the stairs, talking nervously, as if they could keep the waking servants from guessing what they were going to do. "We really should finish cleaning up the library."

"Oh yes. A terrible mess."

"Books all over the floor."

They walked very fast, barely keeping themselves from running. "Why don't we put the books on wizardry in with the other craft books."

"You think so?"

"It was a craft once, with apprentices and everything. It really did happen, you know."

In the library, they locked the doors and closed the curtains. "What about the Device?" Vic asked, her eyes fixed on the wall hiding the secret passage.

Earnk bent down to kiss her neck. "It's too soon for him to be back; it takes time to travel to and from Re." He opened his robe and pressed against her belly. His lips setting her skin aflame, Vic quivered with the anticipation and the defiance. "I'm going to die for this," he whispered. "I love you."

"Just kiss me," she gasped, clutching his neck. If Lornk killed her for this, so be it; the clockwork doll would never breathe for him again. Earnk's mouth tasted sweet and cool. His hair smelled like fresh grass. She ran her fingers through it, thick and soft. A shaft of sunlight would set it ablaze. "You're like a summer day," she marveled.

"And you are beautiful, Vic." He swept the books from the table and lifted her onto it, brushed his lips against a nipple, his tongue teasing. Sparks shot through her blood as he pulled the breast into his mouth. His cock strained within his pantaloons, and Vic tugged at his laces.

"Elsa said . . ." He pulled back, eyes earnest. "I don't want to hurt you."

Her breath short, her blood on fire, she opened her legs. "You won't."

"This explains a lot." Lornk's voice cut through their ardor, and they sprang apart like errant children. Their lord sauntered in, dangling a key from a finger. Vic's breath froze as his glacial eyes passed over her. "When I came home last night, I asked Elsa why my library was such a wreck. She said you'd taken it upon yourselves to catalog it. Now I see why the reorganization has taken so long."

"It's my fault," Vic stammered, stepping in front of Earnk.

"I'm sure it is, my dear." He took her by the scruff of her neck, pulling her head backward. "Don't worry. You'll survive."

"Don't hurt her." Earnk's voice quavered. Lornk backhanded him across the face. "My son," he snarled. "You know the price of betrayal."

Vic backed away as Lornk struck Earnk again, and again. Earnk stood still, his fingers gripping the edge of the table behind him. Whimpering at the bloody gash over his eye, Vic sank to her knees. Earnk's gaze followed her. I love you, he said silently, the words distinct in her mind. The father's next blow sent the son sprawling across the table. Her fear crystallized, Vic sprang up and grabbed Lornk's arm. "Stop it," she screamed. "You're killing him."

He smiled at her, the rest of his face smooth, calm. "That was my intent." He struck her. Reeling backward, Vic fell across a stack of books and banged her head on the edge of a bookshelf. Stunned, she grabbed at the bookcase, pulling books out as she scrambled to stay on her feet. Her knees gave out, and her fingers grabbed at something cold and hard, pulling it out. The false bookcase swung back, and she fell headfirst into the passageway behind it. "No!" Lornk cried, as she rolled down the ramp. She struggled to her feet, dazed, and heard him tripping over the books above, trying to get to the passage. Head pounding, she stumbled toward the Device. Lornk yelled for her to stop. He wouldn't kill her; he'd lock her up and strip her bare again, tinkering with her will until once again the clockwork doll breathed and blinked for him alone. The black knob jutting from the floor gleamed, inviting her to oblivion. Lornk's hand stretched toward her, his face contorted, not angry, but scared. "Not yours," she mumbled, then dropped down and shoved the knob into the southernmost position.

† † †

"No!" Father screamed, his hand passing through empty space. Earnk struggled down the ramp, wiping blood out of his eyes. Lornk spun round and grabbed him by the throat. "Did you show her this?"

Earnk shook his head. "She found it," he lied. He glanced at the knob, and his blood went cold. "Where—"

His father released him, snarling, "To Latha"—then, choking—"to her death."

PART 2. SMELT

CHAPTER 7

ASYLUM

Pins and needles rippled from Vic's toes to the roots of her hair, and she sucked air like the drowned. In the wake of the tingling, polished stone pressed against palms and knees. Pale orange light bled through tall windows into a long hall, dark beams supporting a lofty ceiling, two pair of doors at opposite ends, and a shallow well carved into a granite dais surrounding a black knob and gemstones identical to the Device below Lornk's library. With a strangled squeal, Vic scrambled out of the depression. Vision reeling, she probed the ache at the back of her head, wincing as her fingers found a tender mound. A moan leaked through clenched teeth, and one thought echoed: Where?

A pair of doors burst open and she dodged behind a tall, broad-backed chair set in front of the Device. A boy of eight or nine dragged a teenage girl into the room. Another girl, younger than the boy, tugged the teen's silken robe the other way and shot fearful glances toward the dais supporting the chair and Device. Behind the trio marched a portly old man wearing a tooled leather jerkin, thumping the butt of a spear on the floor as he gestured for their attention. The children shouted in a strange language, excited tones rattling the windows while the teen yawned at the man's exhortations. As they came closer, Vic realized the man and the teen didn't open their mouths when they spoke, and she remembered the handsome minstrel who had asked her to dance—was it possible that had only been last night? With a wealth of black curls framing a lovely brown face, the young woman could be the minstrel's twin.

"Highness"—the man's silent pleas crystallized in Vic's mind—"no one is permitted in the throne room without—"

"What in Shrine are we doing here?" the teen asked the boy, silencing the guard with a raised hand.

"I told you, we summoned a genie." The boy pointed at the dais. "There she is. Behind Uncle's throne."

The younger girl screamed, the older one gasped, and the man flipped the point of his spear forward and leapt onto the dais. Vic yelped and covered her head with her arms.

"Gaston, stand down," the teen commanded, pushing past the guard. With an oath, she flicked the knob back to the center of the spokes. "It's closed," she said to the guard. Then she touched Vic's shoulder with gentle fingers. "Did you come from Lornk Korng's house?"

Cheeks aflame, Vic nodded.

"It's closed," the young woman said again, her eyes on the Device. "No one else can come through," she continued silently as she untied her sash and shrugged out of her robe. "No one can follow you." She laid the garment over Vic's shoulders. "You're safe now."

Hot tears rolling down her cheeks, Vic poked her arms into the sleeves and tugged blessed fabric around herself, then let the young woman's graceful words and gestures coax her out from behind the throne.

"Timny"—the teen rounded on the boy, dropping her gentle manner like glass—"you did this, and now you can go inform the Ruler."

Freckles stood out as his face paled. "Send Gaston."

"Gaston has to guard *her*." She pointed at Vic. "Now, go!"

Timny hesitated, his face full of protests, but the girl took another threatening step toward him, and he dashed toward the door.

Hefting his spear, the guard searched the corners of the room with his eyes, finally landing a suspicious glare on Vic. "She could be an assassin, Highness. It'd be just the sort of devious thing the Relmlord would do, sending a slip of a girl to murder you and yours. I could tell tales about the mischief Lornk Korng pulled the king into when they were boys."

Stomach churning at the thought of Lornk's youthful hijinks, Vic sank onto the dais. The remaining child crept toward her, eyes wide. "Are you a genie?"

"No, I'm just a girl." Vic wiped damp cheeks. "And I'm really scared."

"My aunt is really scary," the youngster confided. "But if Uncle comes down, it'll be all right."

"Where am I? Latha?" If she had arrived in Relm, Lornk would have followed, or somebody would have sent her straight back to him.

The girl nodded and pointed at the teen. "That's my cousin Bethniel. Her father is Ruler."

"I guess that makes you a princess." Vic tried to smile, but it faltered.

The child gave a solemn shake of the head. "She is, but I'm not. Only the Ruler's children are titled prince or princess."

The door banged open again and a half dozen men and women rushed across the room to surround Vic, spears lowered. Another man and woman—surely the Ruler and his wife— strode behind them, alarm and fury plain on their faces, while Timny dragged his feet at the rear of the procession. "How did this happen?" the king asked.

"Stand up," Bethniel hissed, tugging Vic to her feet. "Timny and Cimba were playing with the Device," she said aloud, "and they let her through."

"So I heard." The king glared at Timny. "Gaston, how did they get into the throne room?"

Flushing, the guard looked down at the floor. "There's no excuse, Majesty, but an old man has business to attend to at dawn, if you take my meaning." He cleared his throat at the blank stares. "The type of personal business that can't wait, but which takes a while."

The king's chest rose and fell, lips flat under a red mustache. "Olivet"—he turned to a man with elaborately decorated leather armor—"adjust the duty roster." While the men conferred, the queen pushed past the guards. A multitude of beaded black braids clicked softly as she towered over Vic, lip curled in distaste. Woozy, Vic fought to stay upright under the regal glare, but she staggered when the queen's hand shot out and grabbed her arm, shoving the sleeve aside to reveal the gem-studded leather bracelet.

"She's just a girl, Mother," Bethniel protested as the queen pushed open the robe's collar and thumbed the choker.

"You're his mistress?" Entirely silent, the words rang clear in Vic's mind.

Regaining her balance, Vic nodded and fixed her eyes on the floor.

"Do you want to be?"

Vic looked up into intent black eyes. "N-no," she stammered.

"You will address my husband and myself as Your Majesty. Tell me your name."

Vic's mouth opened for the letter K, but she bit her lip and said, "Vic. Victoria of Ourtown, Your Majesty."

The queen's eyebrows shot up and she stepped back as if stung. Then stern composure rippled into place, and she turned her glare on Timny and Cimba. "Since you two are such early risers, you will help the scullions for an hour before school and two after. Starting now!"

The children fled, and the queen took Vic's head in her hands and looked in her eyes. Swallowing terror that this woman might snap her neck, Vic winced as long fingers grazed the knot at the back of her head.

"She's an Oreseeker by her name and language," the queen announced. "And she's concussed."

The king signaled his wife to step aside and offered his hand. Vic's palm hesitated toward his, but when he clasped her fingers, his were warm and dry. His red beard and pale blue eyes, so like her father's, made her eyes well, and she struggled to breathe, her throat thick.

"I'm Sashal of Narath," he said aloud, speaking the Oreseeker's language. "This is my wife, Elekia of Reinoll Parish. Welcome to Latha."

† † †

"Stay awake, now." A hand shook Vic's shoulder, and she peeled open bleary eyes. She sat propped in a bed, garbed in a white shift with long, loose sleeves. Bethniel sat beside her, holding a bowl of porridge. "Are you hungry?"

Bile climbing her throat, Vic shook her head.

"The healer said not to let you fall asleep, but you keep nodding off. What do you like to do?"

Vic frowned at the silk coverlet and down pillows. "Why—"

The princess grinned. "We don't get visits from injured genies every day. Selcher, will you take these things and bring something for our guest's headache?"

A sour-faced woman stepped out of a corner and took the porridge. Vic hadn't noticed her until she moved.

"Playing hide-and-seek with her is a misery," Bethniel said drily. "Do you like card games? Music? I'm a lousy singer, but you should hear my brother. They call him the Crystal Voice of Latha. Not a moniker you'd expect for a prince, but even my parents couldn't deny the gifts Elesendar gave him." As the princess prattled on, Vic heard that deep clear baritone that had spread enraptured silence over the square like butter. Seeing his visage in the girl sitting beside her, mortification heated her face and clogged her throat. As pressure built inside her head, the princess's voice sank beneath her awareness . . .

An acrid scent jabbed the passages of Vic's nose, and she jerked awake.

"Sorry!" Bethniel capped a bottle. "I'm boring you into a stupor!"

"I'm trying to stay awake, Your Highness."

"Oh, let's be friends. Call me Bethniel." As Vic stared, baffled as to why these people were being so generous, the princess's smile fell away. "I can't imagine how strange this is for you. I promise, we're good people." She guffawed. "We rather pride ourselves on that—being *good*."

"You've been incredibly kind—"

"Oh, piffle. If we're not nice to you, you'll put a genie's curse on us."

A smile pulled at Vic's lips. "That'd be a nice power. So is mindspeech. The people who had it in Traine, they spoke with their thoughts and their voices. But you use only your thoughts?"

Bethniel shrugged. "We do use our voices when we get excited. You heard Timny and Cimba yammering earlier. And we always speak aloud on formal occasions like funerals and on Landing Eve, to honor Elesendar."

"The ship?"

The princess gasped. "You're not a heretic, are you?"

Vic shrugged. "My people know the Logs to be literal truth. It was a real surprise to find they'd been turned into a weird religion by everyone else."

"The Logs are parables Elesendar provided to guide us through the forest of life," Bethniel retorted. "Latha is the birthplace of humanity, you know."

Vic sat up. "It's where the *Elesendar*'s crew settled, I'll give you that, but you don't really believe people are born from *trees*, do you?"

"Not *now*," Bethniel said testily. "But Elesendar's children were. Come here." She pulled Vic out of bed and across a soft green carpet to a window. They stood on the third floor of a house larger than Lornk's palazzo, built not of stone but of whole logs. In a vast garden, cobbled paths wound through verdant lawns and hedges, arbors and flower beds arranged in geometric designs. "That's a cerrenil." Bethniel pointed at a tree dominating one of the beds. A massive white trunk supported limbs adorned with green leaves turning to gold. "We call them the old mothers. The first humans came from them, and when we die, if we've led a good life, we are reborn as one of them."

Vic raised a skeptical eyebrow, but her head ached too much to argue, and the view beyond the garden wall pulled her attention back outside. Under a sky ribboned with clouds spread an ocean of green and blue foliage broken by an island of peaked roofs. Crowned with something that caught the sun and scattered it over the city, a dome stood high above the other buildings. "It's beautiful."

"It's the Kiareinoll," Bethniel said reverently. "The city is Narath, and that dome is the Senate, but the forest is called Kiareinoll Fembrosh, and it's our *home*. How old are you?"

"Almost sixteen."

"You have another year before you go in. Everyone goes into Fembrosh the summer after they turn seventeen. That's how we know our path—what we're meant to do in life. Ashel—my brother—he came out talking music, music, music, which ended all notions of him doing anything related to *governing*. I went in this summer, and I started clerking for the prime minister the day after I came out."

"You work as a clerk?"

The princess laughed. "The Eldanion royals don't do a thing but throw parties and race horses, but in Latha everybody *works*, even the Heir to the throne."

Vic looked down at her fingers, spread wide on the windowsill. "I *was* a Logkeeper among my people. That means I preserved—studied—the Ancients' writings, and I made sure people remembered where we came from."

Bethniel's eyebrows rose. "Shrine, you're like a heretic Loremaster! Well, the Academy has the largest collection of ancient writings in Knownearth. I'm sure you could study with our Loremasters . . ." Grinning, she knocked her elbow into Vic's. "Although *they* make sure we don't forget we came from Fembrosh."

The door opened on the queen and Selcher, who placed a tea tray on a table. "We'll take those bands off, unless you want to wear them," Elekia said snidely.

Vic shot a glare at the queen, but shrank from her regal glower. Eyes downcast, she said, "I'd like them off, Your Majesty."

Motioning her back to the bed with a white-bladed knife, Selcher ordered Vic to bend her neck. The blade slid between choker and skin. After a few sharp tugs, the maid handed the leather strip to the queen.

Elekia examined the gemstones and dropped the choker in Vic's lap. "He spared no expense on your adornments."

"I didn't want them." Vic offered a wrist to Selcher.

"How long were you his?"

Vic cringed at the ice in the queen's mindvoice. "Four months. It's been almost five since I was taken from—"

"And how did you escape?"

I love you. She choked as she saw Earnk's bloodied face, heard his last words. Had Lornk killed him? A wristband dropped into her lap, and Selcher began sawing at the other. Tears splattered on gemstones and leather. "He and his son were fighting, and I . . . ran to the Device while he was distracted."

"Did you know what it was?"

Ire stirring at the queen's callousness, Vic scrubbed her cheeks as the second wristband came off. Selcher slipped her knife under an ankle band. "I was told if I pushed the knob to one of the other spokes—not the one to Relm—that I would . . . die."

"Lie down on your belly," Selcher said, slicing through the second ankle band. She arranged the covers over Vic's legs and buttocks while she pushed aside the nightshift to expose the belt.

Bethniel gasped. "Is that—"

"Bronze," Elekia said. "The Relmlord always liked to flaunt his wealth."

Selcher's fingers fumbled around the clasp of the belt. "I think it's soldered together."

"So you were trying to kill yourself? Why?" Elekia demanded.

The sheets under Vic's cheek were wet, but her face burned with growing anger. "I couldn't stay . . . his," she answered tightly.

Elekia yanked the covers away and shoved the nightshift to Vic's neck. "I see no bruises," she said over Bethniel's protests. "Was he unkind to you?"

Rage flaring, Vic rose to her knees and tore the shift over her head. "He *stripped* me down to nothing, nothing but the slave you see and despise." The three women gasped and stepped back as Vic continued. "It's easy to despise the wretched, Your Majesty, and to think we want what we have and deserve what we've got. Well, I didn't deserve to be taken from my homeland and sold to a man who broke me into pieces so he could remake me into someone *I* despise." Her heart lurched as she thought of Earnk's bloodied face and earnest eyes—she'd left him. Had Lornk killed him? Voice shaking, she continued, "Someone weak and cowardly, and yes, I decided I'd rather die than be what he made me."

Trembling, Elekia blinked rapidly. Vic felt strangely ashamed, not because she'd just told off her host, but as if she'd struck an unjust blow. In a moment, Elekia's lips shifted back to a sneer and she turned to Selcher. "Check the belt again. The joining may have weakened in the Device."

Selcher's cheeks blazing red, she bent over the clasp again. It popped open the moment she touched it. With a look of confirmation at the queen, she handed the belt to Vic.

"You'll catch cold like that," Elekia said as she sailed out, maid in tow.

Vic pulled the nightshift back on, her head emerging to find Bethniel staring at her.

"No one speaks to Mother like that," the princess said.

Shivering, Vic pulled the covers up to her chin. "I'm sorry. You're all being very kind, and I—"

Bethniel shook her head, eyes shining. "Oh, no, don't apologize. You're an inspiration!"

†　†　†

Healers came with potions and probing fingers and pronounced Vic recovered a day after her arrival. Tailors came with measuring tape, cloth, and pins made of bone and returned a few days later with skirts and dresses, tunics and wide-cut trousers, all with necklines that covered the collarbone and hemlines that fell to the ankle. Vic relished the silky texture of the erinsheen fabric, grateful to be clothed but also delighted by weaves that felt comfortable whether the day was warm or cool.

She took meals with the royal family, fumbling with the sticks they used to eat. Elekia's eyes turned hard whenever they crossed her, but Sashal asked questions about her homeland, jested with the children, and teased smiles out of everyone, even his wife. In the garden, Cimba and Timny taught Vic to use a wooden mallet to send a ball through hoops stuck in the ground, then roped her into endless games of hide-and-seek.

Bethniel took her shopping in Narath, and they would inevitably meet someone known to the princess. Curious eyes would rest on Vic, whom Bethniel would introduce as an asylum-seeker from Traine. Before any questions probed too deeply, the princess would turn the conversation toward some other concern. Bethniel's friends were mostly concerned with fashion and revelry. Vic struggled to appear interested in their shallow frippery, but she didn't mind it. Boredom was a balm after Traine.

The princess introduced her to serious people too. "Victoria of Ourtown," a rheumy-eyed old man said one day. "That's an Oreseeker name." Bones creaked as he sat down and folded gnarled hands on their luncheon table. "Shifted the search from iron to refuge, did you?"

Surprised and pleased to hear her own language sound in her ears instead of her mind, she smiled. "I suppose so, sir. You speak like an Oreseeker. Are you—"

The man offered his hand. "No, I'm born a Lathan. Dalborn of Cabanarl."

"Vic, this is the Harmony. He heads the Loremasters in the Minstrels Guild," Bethniel said. "Vic is a sort of loremaster among her people."

"Are you a Logkeeper?"

Her smile broadened, and she sat straighter. "I was. I heard you have many of the Ancients' writings in your library."

"We do indeed. Come see whenever you like. In fact"— he exchanged grins with Bethniel—"we're always looking for talented scholars to join the guild. I'll arrange some assessments."

Vic flushed, excitement mixed with apprehension. "You should know, I'm what you'd call a heretic."

Standing, the man clasped her shoulder. "Oh, we don't mind an atheist or two in the ranks. You keep us honest." He left with a wink at the princess.

"Well, wasn't that lucky, meeting him," Bethniel said with one of her sly smiles. "Elesendar must have put him in our path."

Vic spent three days taking written and oral exams. On the morning of the fourth, Loremaster Laelin, a young woman who delighted in speaking the Ancients' language, left Vic to wait in her office while she fetched the senior Loremaster who had reviewed the scores. Vic fidgeted on the edge of her seat, her eyes leaping from jumbled bookshelves to music scores littering the desk. The door creaked, and Laelin bustled in, leading an older woman who gazed around the messy office with distaste.

"Victoria, this is Loremaster Silnauer," Laelin said, moving a stack of papers off her chair.

"You have an impressive knowledge of ancient history." The older Loremaster settled behind the desk and pulled a page of notes from the stack she carried.

Vic leaned forward eagerly. "I couldn't believe how many original logs you have in your collection here. It's a Logkeeper's dream."

The woman looked through the pages, lips pursed. "Your knowledge of the rest of world history is abysmal, however. Modern languages and music were equally poor." She stopped on a sheet. "Ah, mathematics is adequate."

"She did very well in mathematics," Laelin said. "I gave her that test along with Ancient poetry."

Silnauer raised her eyebrows, and the younger woman looked at the floor as the older continued, "Geography, deplorable. Natural philosophy." She tutted over the page. "This sheet is full of heresy."

Vic bristled. "The Harmony said—"

"The Harmony said we were to offer you a place. You may join as a novice apprentice."

As Vic blinked in consternation, Laelin protested. "But that would put her in with the youngest children. Surely given her existing knowledge, a senior apprenticeship—"

"You are too far behind to merit a higher position."

"I'll catch up quickly." Vic stood. "I was a Logkeeper at fifteen."

Silnauer's lips tilted in scorn. "How quickly did you learn your craft in Traine? You had a master of some renown, or so I hear."

Vic's cheeks stung with mortification. "What have you heard?"

"Enough to know what sort of person you are. In my view, we already have too many deviants in the guild." Silnauer looked pointedly at Laelin, who flushed scarlet. "And I also see no place for heretics within an institution designed to revere Elesendar. Nevertheless, I have been told to offer you a place, so you may join as a novice apprentice. Or the Courtesans in Alna might admit you at a more senior level."

†††

After the humiliation with the Loremasters, Vic noticed how Bethniel's girlfriends cut their eyes at her, how young men leered and elbowed one another as she passed. Conversations died when she entered shops and restaurants; whispers and sniggers buzzed in her wake as she left. As autumn turned the cerrenils red and gold, she stopped going into Narath and found refuge in the manor's kitchen, helping Timny and Cimba with the chores they still did in penance. While the children were at school, Vic hid in her room, reading or studying the pattern woven into the carpet. At first she thought it only an expanse of green leaves, but each day she noticed more details—human figures and strange beasts hidden in the foliage—until she realized it depicted a battle between people and giant, triangular-headed monsters.

Loneliness set in, no less than she'd felt in Traine. Here she could come and go as she pleased and endured nothing worse than the queen's glare across the dinner table. Bethniel was always friendly and kind, but Vic couldn't help wondering if the princess secretly felt as other Lathans did: that Vic was a deviant slut.

She found some solace in the manor's library. Smaller than Lornk's, it still contained more volumes than she had seen gathered in one place before Traine. She learned to read Lathan, fluency growing day by day. Some reading brought her to realization that the monsters woven into her bedroom rug were Kragnashians, the indigenous species with whom Captain Wong had first negotiated landing rights for the *Elesendar*'s crew. An atlas reminded her of Earnk—Bethniel had told her he'd been seen in Re, clerking for the Relman Council, not only alive but back in his father's good graces. Glad he lived, sorry she'd never see him again, she traced the route north to the border of her homeland and wondered how far the gemstones and bronze belt could take her.

The idea smoldered as the weather turned chilly and

winds stripped away foliage. Each supercilious eyebrow from Elekia, each frivolous anecdote from Bethniel, every half-heard whisper from the manor's servants and visitors stoked Vic's desire to return home. Late one afternoon, she gathered her courage and went to Sashal's study, where she found king and queen conferring over a stack of documents. Putting down his quill, Sashal overrode Elekia's dismissal and invited Vic to sit.

"I've been thinking about something Bethniel said when I first came here," she said. "She told me that everyone in Latha works . . . but I don't. Not since the Loremasters—"

"You should have taken their offer," Elekia said curtly.

Vic bit back a sharp retort. Instead, she said, "It was clear I wasn't actually welcome, Your Majesty."

"Not everyone knows their path before they begin to tread it," said Sashal. "But the world contains a forest of opportunities."

"That's just it, Majesty. I already knew my path . . . before. I'd like to return to it."

"And you'd like us to send you?" the queen asked scornfully. "What should we do, hire a ship to take one girl home, somewhere in uncharted territory thousands of miles away? How should we should finance this journey? Latha is a poor nation defending itself from a tyrant—a fact you should appreciate all too well."

Vic swallowed angry tears, determined not to cry. "The gemstones and belt would help pay for it."

"Those would buy you a fine cabin on a merchanter bound for Traine," Elekia snapped.

"Vic," Sashal said, casting his wife a reproving glance, "the gems and belt are very valuable, but not enough, and the monarchy cannot spare the funds to pay for such an expedition."

"I was a Logkeeper at fifteen," Vic muttered, rising to go. "I'll find my own way home."

"Wait." Sashal looked at Elekia, and both nodded after a fleeting, silent exchange. The king pulled a page off his stack and handed it to Vic.

A Bill of Care

Herewith, Sashal of Narath, Ruler of Latha, and his consort, Elekia of Reinoll Parish, declare and decree that the minor Victoria of Ourtown shall henceforth be known as a ward of the Lathan Royal Household and shall be entitled to the privileges and bear the responsibilities thereof.

Vic stared at the decree, reading the lines over and over, wondering if she misunderstood. Perhaps she hadn't attained the fluency in Lathan she thought.

"It means what you think," Elekia said, as curt and cold as ever. "The king is willing to make you his ward."

"If you're willing," Sashal added. "I know you have a family, but we are offering you a home."

"Why?"

"Elesendar brought you to us," he replied. "Don't you wish to know His purpose?"

Eyebrows creasing, she shook her head. "I don't believe in your god."

"Nevertheless," Elekia said, her tone suddenly mild. "By providence or chance, you're here."

"Come look at something." Sashal stood.

They walked to the throne room, where he pointed to a tapestry hanging floor to ceiling behind the dais. "Has anyone told you this story?"

Vic shook her head. A seascape woven in blues and greens, the tapestry seemed out of place in an inland capital. It showed a dark woman standing on a bluff facing a tentacled monster emerging from the ocean. Lightning shot from the woman's hands toward the creature while its tentacles threatened to engulf her.

"Sometimes destinies befall us, and sometimes we make our own. This woman was an orphan who endured terrible suffering at the hands of a rich and powerful man. But she had a genius for understanding the writings of the Ancients that made her the greatest wizard the world has ever known."

"A wizard." Vic couldn't keep the skepticism from her voice. Just as in Traine, an astonishing number of library volumes depicted the exploits of wizards, nearly all of them shelved under "History" instead of "Fable."

"They're uncommon now"—the king winked at Elekia—"but in Kara's time, you couldn't swing a stick without hitting one."

Vic's breath froze. "What was her name?"

"Kara of Alna. She lived and died eleven hundred years ago, but her legend has inspired uncounted songs and stories."

"What are you, Kara?" Lornk's voice purred as the ghosts of his fingers encircled her throat. His thumb on her windpipe, she couldn't breathe. Her knees buckling, her vision darkened with each strangled gasp until all went black.

Her own coughing woke her. She sat on the dais, Sashal's arms supporting her, Elekia kneeling beside them, patting Vic's cheeks.

"She's fine," the queen said, standing.

Shoulders hunched, Vic slid away from Sashal. *"He* called me by that name."

Royal eyes darted to the tapestry. "Lornk always had a wicked sense of humor," Elekia said.

"Is it true you were friends?"

The queen bristled, but Sashal smiled sardonically. "We were. He is . . . seductive. You must have seen that. We were as close as brothers, and I loved him more than my actual brother, in truth."

"Then he revealed his villainous disposition," Elekia spat.

The king took Vic's hand. "I know you want to return to your father, but until that's possible, please consider this your home, and stay."

She looked from king to queen, at faces taut with the same pain she felt in the sinews of her knees, in her belly, in her heart when she thought of Lornk. She didn't know what he'd done to them, but she knew they understood what he could do. Would her father, if she made it home? She might receive his sympathy, but probably the mayor's daughters and too many others in Ourtown and the surrounding villages would treat her as Silnauer had—a vile, ruined thing to be despised. Standing, she bowed her head, then met their eyes. "Thank you, Your Majesties. I'd like to stay."

CHAPTER 8

THE KIAREINOLL

A double rap and a creak pried open Ashel's eyes. His head aching, he peeled the blankets off his face and found his father watching him, two steaming mugs in hand. "Your Majesty!" Ashel sprang out of bed and stumbled as fire lanced behind his eye. "How did you get in?" he asked, rubbing the afflicted temple. Silnauer had imposed strict rules about visitors in the journeyed minstrels' quarters.

"A king can go anywhere he likes," Father said, wrapping an arm around Ashel's shoulders. "I brought you some tea." Chuckling, he tipped a flask into one of the mugs and handed it to Ashel. A whiff of harlolinde flared the nostrils. "Don't make a habit of this." Sashal topped off his own mug. "And don't tell your mother."

Grinning, Ashel took a sip. His throat closed at the first sting, but the heat of liquor and tea together oozed past his tongue and soothed the ache in his head. "Hair of the dog," he quipped in the Ancients' tongue, raising the mug.

With a smirk, Sashal cast an eye over the empty bed. "You keep on with the benders, son, and you might wake up one morning with a wife."

Ashel's cheeks flushed as he felt the press of the brothel-lord's hand on his thigh. "I'm waiting for the right woman, sir."

"Just choose her carefully before she chooses you. A prince can't afford to be hooked for life to a wine-soaked urge."

Ashel smiled, more amused than affronted by the warning. "I visited the grandest brothel in Traine and left with my virtue intact."

Father sobered. "More miraculous is that you met the Relmlord and left with your skin intact."

Ashel nodded, his own humor fading. "The Commissar introduced us. He seemed disappointed we didn't come to blows. Is that why you're here?"

"I'm here because my son's been in Narath for several weeks and hasn't come to visit his family. Your mother wants to see you, but she's too stubborn to come down here. Make it easier on all of us and go home for a few days."

Gut clenching, Ashel sank onto his mattress. "I don't want to be interrogated, Father."

"The longer you put it off, the worse it will be. She's fuming that you didn't come straight to us the moment you passed the city gates."

"I have classes to teach," Ashel protested. "I can't simply shrug off my duties to please her."

"Your obligations aren't keeping you from carousing at night. Such an energetic young man can easily walk between the manor and Narath in the mornings. Your sister does it daily."

"How's Beth liking the Senate?"

"Ask her that yourself when you go home. Today. Ruler's orders." Father's smile split his beard again. "There's a change in the household you might find interesting."

Still leery of his mother's judgment, Ashel relented. "After my classes are finished, I'll go up."

† † †

Trepidation grew with every step up Manor Hill, and a solid lump of iron lodged in his belly as he came in sight of the intricate mesh of logs surrounding the manor. More decorative than protective, full of gaps and easy to climb, the wall wouldn't keep out a determined harrier, much less a conquering general. But Narath hadn't been attacked by wizard or army for a thousand years. And so a nation at war had a lone trooper guarding the gate to the home of its Ruler. She stood as Ashel approached, admitted him with a smirk. Ashel sighed. The guard probably knew a royal harangue awaited him.

Hefting his bags and cases, he tramped through the snow-dusted grounds, past the cerrenils lining the road. As soon as he entered the house, servants swarmed to take his cases. He laughed in their embraces, knowing their greeting would be the warmest he'd get.

"Ashel!" Except Bethniel's. His sister charged headlong down the hall and tackled him with kisses. "It's been so long," she cried. "Elesendar, how are you? Mother's been beside herself, worrying about how much money you've lost at the gaming tables."

"Thanks, sis. And how much of the national treasury have you spent on clothes?"

Bethniel took his arm and prattled about the latest gossip, asking questions about Traine, and never giving him a chance to answer as she led him to the solarium, where sunlight blazed through glass and crystal yet failed to dispel winter's chill. His mother stood in the middle of the room, debating how best to save her herbs while servants carried braziers here and there at her direction. Locks bright as autumn leaves caught his attention, and a pale girl somewhat younger than Beth flushed scarlet when she noticed his gaze. Not a servant—her erinsheen gown was too finely tailored—and not the first manor visitor drafted into a chore. Ashel flashed her a sympathetic smile and turned his attention to the queen.

"Your Majesty," he said, formally and aloud.

She gave him a cold kiss on the cheek. "My prodigal son. You've come on your father's orders, not your own recognizance. Am I right?"

He clenched his teeth. She always knew exactly what he was thinking—a Listener couldn't do better against an unshielded mind. "I came as soon as I could, Your Majesty. I have teaching duties now."

"Of course. But it's been more than half a year. We missed you at Landing."

"I was on assignment in Traine."

A brazier clattered, and the bright-haired girl apologized for the ceramic shards and glowing coals scattered across the floor. Servants rushed to the mess, and Bethniel pulled the stranger toward him.

"Ashel," she said, "this is Victoria of Ourtown. Vic, this is my brother, Prince Ashel. He likes to pretend he's not one of us and spends all his time hiding in the Minstrels Guildhouse."

"Your Highness." Eyes on the floor, the girl took his offered hand, her cheeks still blazing.

He studied her narrow face, his eyes drawn back to her hair, the color of sunset. Certain he'd seen her before, he couldn't place her among Beth's friends. "I think we've met, but I'm sorry, I don't remember where."

Vic straightened her shoulders and raised her head a little. "It was in Traine. You asked me to dance."

He shook his head, smiling. "Forgive me. I can't believe I could forget dancing with anyone so lovely."

Mother cleared her throat. "Ashel, tell me about this meeting you had with the Relmlord."

The color washed out of Vic's cheeks, and she stepped back. "I think I'll take a walk," she mumbled and darted out.

"Who is she?" he asked.

Bethniel glared. "Elesendar, Mother. Do you have to taunt her every chance you get?"

Ashel looked between princess and queen. "Who is she?"

"Mother never stops testing her. It's wildly unfair, and I'm ashamed to have had any part of it today."

"Who is she?" he grated.

"The Relmlord's mistress," Mother snapped, as if he should have caught that already. "And how in the Shrine did *you* meet *her*?"

He remembered then. One of his last nights in Traine, he worked up the nerve to speak to one of Traine's beguiling underclass. "I talked to her at a fair. My interest was purely academic."

"Academic," Mother scoffed. "So you danced with her?"

"She turned me down."

Bethniel barked a laugh, then clamped her mouth shut at their mother's sharp glance. Elekia tapped her fingers on her arms, then sat. "Well, go on. Tell me what happened at that idiot Commissar's party."

The debriefing went better than he expected, and his mother even laughed at how the Commissar's courtiers had wept at tales of Lathan heroics. When he was done, she nodded in satisfaction and returned to berating the servants over the braziers. Skipping over, Bethniel grabbed his arm and dragged him from the room. "Now tell me the good parts. Is Traine totally scandalous?"

"If you've had a Trainer mistress living here, you should know better than me. What is she doing here?"

"She came through the Device. It was purely by accident; Cimba and Timny opened the thing and Vic just happened to go through at that moment."

There's been a change in the household you might find interesting. He frowned. "And Mother and Father let her stay?"

"Well, we got for free what the Relmlord paid a fortune for. It's a thorn in Korng's side, isn't it? Father even made Vic his ward. And she is like a little sister who needs to be taught everything—how to talk, how to dress, how to live. I like her a lot, except she always has her nose in a book, which I'm sure *you'd* like about her. She knows an awful lot about ancient history, and the Harmony even asked her to join your Guild, but Silnauer was very rude and insulting, so she declined."

He snorted. "Silnauer's a master of rude and insulting, and she's been causing all kinds of grief since she took charge of training."

Bethniel waggled her eyebrows. "Oooh, there's an idea. Go commiserate with her. She'll feel better, knowing she's not the only one."

Somehow his sister had steered him to the side entrance. Through a window they could see Vic strolling through the bare allenver. Ashel backed away from the door. He saw her, standing alone and naked in the crowd, and blood rushed below his belt and into his face. Shrinejump, what had ever possessed him to speak to her? She must think him the worst sort of lecher. "I can't right now," he stammered. "I have to unpack."

"Coward," Bethniel cried as he turned and rushed down the hall. His sister went out, letting in an icy gust. He shivered, glad of something to cool his blood.

† † †

When Bethniel hailed her from the doorway, Vic hurried toward a grove of cerrenils and the arbor beyond them. A frigid wind cut through her garments, but she relished the smell of winter blowing down from the mountains. She wanted to see the whole world carpeted in snow, wished it could cover her memories and make them clean.

Following her, the princess called Vic's name aloud, a strange thing in this land where no one spoke. Vic hardly thought about the silence now, or how oppressive it had been those first days here.

"Vic, don't make me start Listening for you!"

Grimacing, she ducked out of the arbor. "Stop hooting like an old hen. What do you want?"

Bethniel blinked at her. "You don't have to snap at me." She unleashed her sly grin. "You never said you'd met my brother."

"I didn't know it was him," Vic lied. "He seems nice, surprisingly."

Bethniel's eyes hardened, but then she sighed and plunked down on a bench, tossing heavy black curls out of her face. "I'm sorry Mother threw the Relmlord in your face again."

Vic stared at her, jabbed a toe into the yellowed turf, fighting between raging at her friend and sighing along with her. "None of you have the slightest idea what he made me."

Bethniel looked up, startled.

"No, I'm not a spy. I'm not an assassin. I'm . . . nothing. It's like . . ." She searched for the words. "It's like he peeled back the layers that made me a Logkeeper—everything I was that I wanted to be and cared about—and left a . . . a lump of something, something raw and . . . tainted."

"Tainted—no. Vic, I hate Silnauer and those awful things she said to you. Ashel says no one likes her at the Guild."

"Maybe she has a point," Vic said, shame heating her face. "Maybe I should go to Alna and, and the Courtesans. At least I'd be among other heretics."

"Now wait," the princess said firmly. "First of all, stop being ashamed of something that wasn't your fault. Secondly, if you did decide to go to Alna and join the Courtesans—and I'm not saying you should—you should make that choice with pride, not shame. We inlanders aren't as free with our . . . selves . . . as the people in

Alna, but the Courtesans are a respected guild and all Alnans—Courtesans, merchants, fisherfolk, and heretics too—are citizens of this nation. And so are you. My father made you his ward, and that makes you my sister. Whatever path Elesendar intends you to walk, you'll walk as one of *us*."

Vic gaped at the princess, the pressure of tears building behind her eyes. "Why do you people want me?"

Bethniel gazed at her, shaking her head, then her lips split into a teasing smile. "Shrine if I know. You're a bit weird, you're puny, and you're only interested in books. And you think I'm a silly flibbertigibbet, which may be true but is still very insulting, so I can't figure out why I'd want you as my friend, or my sister, but I do. I guess it's Elesendar's will." She stuck her tongue out with the last sentence.

Vic's mouth quirked. "I think He just revealed you're not as foolish and shallow as you pretend." The humor faded as quickly as it rose, swamped by the useless emptiness that had plagued her for months. "I'm still lost, Beth. I need help."

The princess stood. "I'll talk to Mother—now don't groan. She's not as *bad* as she pretends to be. We'll help you find your path. I promise."

† † †

Morning light danced through the lace curtains when Elekia barged through Vic's door. "My daughter says you need help," she said curtly, as if that had been only too obvious for too long.

Replacing her toothbrush in the holder, Vic spat in the basin and wiped her mouth. "Good morning, Your Majesty," she said tightly. "I'm still dressing—"

"Look at me." Elekia spoke aloud, and as if she had cast a spell, Vic turned her head, raised her eyes, and faced the queen. They stared at each other, Vic's gaze tracing the fine lines around the woman's eyes and mouth, the arching, perfect eyebrows, the small mouth with its full lips. In her youth Elekia had surely been even lovelier than her daughter, and everyone called Bethniel Narath's greatest beauty. Vic stared, knowing the beauty masked the woman, wondering if she was sad and bitter or just spiteful and mean. Then she wondered what the queen saw in her eyes, her face. A scared kid? An assassin? Both?

"What do you want?" she managed to say, though she felt like the words had to swim through frozen jam.

Elekia raised an eyebrow. "Be still," she said. People whispered that Elekia had supernatural powers. Vic scoffed at the thought she was a witch.

"Wizard."

"What?" Vic shook her head, suddenly free to blink her eyes, move her hands. Off balance, she clutched at the dresser.

"You remind me of my sister. Richelle had green eyes like yours and was headstrong like you, though you've better manners."

"Richelle." Vic gaped. "That was—"

"Earnk Korng is my nephew. Not many know that. The king knows, of course. My children don't." She spread dark brown fingers in front of her, and a sad smile graced her face, easing the severity. "Her skin was as pale as yours, and she had hair like the sun on a rainy day. She wasn't my blood sister, but my parents reared her as their own, and I couldn't have loved her more if we'd shared a womb. The head and the heart, we used to call ourselves. She was the heart."

"Why are you telling me this?"

"She was my heart and Lornk Korng took her from me. Not by force—he persuaded her to live . . . that life. It hurt more than if he had torn my actual heart from my chest."

"Is that why you took me in?"

"In part." The queen strolled across the carpet, studying the battle woven into the leaf pattern, then considered Vic from the center, where two red-haired figures faced one another. "You want to know your path. I think you'll find it in the Kiareinoll." She angled her head at a pack left by the door. "I've brought what you'll need."

"I don't understand," Vic stammered, suspicious of the queen's abrupt confidence as well as her intent. "You want me to . . . go into Fembrosh? I'm only sixteen."

"You're only sixteen, and it's winter. And you have no idea what awaits you. Yes, I want you to go into Fembrosh and find your path. People go at seventeen because that's when most are ready. You're ready now. You can do this now. You will do it now."

"Your Majesty, I . . . appreciate the confidence, but . . . " She looked at the cold gray clouds hanging over the garden. "Camping in winter doesn't hold much appeal."

"I think you have metal in you, Vic, but only Fembrosh can divine the alloy. Dress warmly." Elekia paused at the door, her face lined with a deep frown. "Richelle never went into Fembrosh. Maybe if she had, she would have resisted Lornk."

The latch clicked behind the queen, and Vic stared at the pack, heart pounding. What could a trek through snowbound forest give her besides frozen toes? The coals in the hearth hissed, and her eyes fell on the book she'd planned to read that day. A day spent in comfort, doing nothing. A nothing doing nothing. *She would have resisted Lornk.* Vic's skin pebbled over, her cheeks heating as she remembered not the thumb on her windpipe, but the one pressed between her thighs. The cajoling whispers, the promises of adoration, the enthralling pleasure that had held her suspended for hours. Her throat swelled with revulsion for the clockwork doll in his tower.

If he'd done the same to Richelle . . . Sinking to the floor, she thought of Earnk, the humane reflection of his father, still mourning a mother long gone. Clerking for the Relman Council the way Beth worked at the Senate. Heirs to rival domains, living parallel lives. Cousins. Enemies. *Whatever path Elesendar intends you to walk, you'll walk it as one of us.* Standing on trembling knees, Vic went to the washbasin and scrubbed her face. "Time to find the path," she said when the tears were erased from her reflection.

† † †

She stopped in the kitchen for breakfast, where Kachel, the manor's chef, cloaked her in his beefy arms. He liked to use his voice when he spoke, and Vic liked sitting at his scarred and pitted work table, watching him juggle spoons and pots, beakers of oil, and flagons of wine while he told her funny stories about his boyhood, when he was a scullion in the royal kitchens in Eldanion.

"What breakfast can I make for you? Elekia put you on gardening duty?"

"I'm going out into Fembrosh for a few days."

His eyes fell on the pack slung over her shoulder, and he paled. "In winter?"

"Oh, I'm from the north. It's fine."

His lips moved as if to voice a protest, but he kept his thoughts quiet and turned back to the stove, a construction of stone and brick and thick porcelain, and dished out a bowl of hot cereal. While Vic ate, he peeked inside her pack, muttered to himself, and disappeared into the pantry. While he was gone, Selcher swung through the doors, laughing at something. She clamped her mouth down upon seeing Vic and hustled over to the pile of table linens next to the ironing board.

Kachel bustled out of the pantry, his arms loaded with cheese and bread and dried fruit, and began cramming food into the pack.

"Kachel, I'm not going on a four-month trek!"

He gave her a worried look, and turned to Selcher. "Do you know about this?"

Selcher looked sharply at the chef, then at Vic. Her eyes widened. "In winter?" A reproving glare flattened her eyebrows and lips. "Damn foolishness. She'll need another blanket." Shaking her head, she bustled toward the door. "You better find her a bigger pack," she admonished on her way out.

Ashel came through the door on the backswing, his gaze following the housekeeper.

"Your Highness, there's hot cereal on the stove and milk in the crock by the window," Kachel said, hurrying out. Ashel filled a bowl for himself and sat across from Vic. "Good morning."

She nodded, her mouth full, mortified. Bethniel's friends traded sniggers and leers about Vic's former life, but the prince had *seen* it.

"Where were they off to?" he asked.

"I'm not sure. I have to be going." She gulped the last of her cereal and looked at the pack spilling over with food. Elekia had promised she'd packed what Vic would need. Shaking her head, she pulled out the overflow, leaving it on the table.

"Where are you off to?"

She wished her hair weren't tucked into the damn cap. She felt as if her cheeks were going to burn off. "A walk."

Before he could comment on the thundering noise her heart was making, she left, feeling no less relieved than the day she escaped Traine. The air in her chest loosened once she left the manor gates. Down in the city, she lingered at an open market, watching the ordinary people barter over late-season fruits and dried meats. A trio of apprentice minstrels practiced dance tunes in the doorway of a jeweler, and a couple of jugglers tossed burning brands back and forth. Vic dropped a few crystals in the performers' pots, then made her way down the muddy streets, past the timbered houses with their empty flower boxes, across the bridge over Kiareinoll Creek, and finally out of the city.

A quarter mile down the road, the forest grew around her like a curtain, and a tickling plagued her stomach. "What in Shrine are you doing?" she muttered, hefting the pack, suddenly wondering why she trusted Elekia enough to walk alone into the woods without even checking the supplies she'd been given. Going into Fembrosh. All she knew about the Lathan rite of passage was that you camped for two or three nights in the forest and when you came home, you were an adult. "And you camp in summer, when you're not likely to die of hypothermia," she grated, wiggling cold toes. "Half a year away from home and you've lost your mind. Your brains are utterly addled."

But perhaps that was the point? To order her thoughts, to find herself again. Three days without anyone judging her or demanding her attention or gratitude. Three days *alone*. In the north, breath froze and tinkled to the ground as ice crystals. Here, snow barely dusted leaves and stones, like sugar on Kachel's cakes. "It's like a spring day back home," she assured herself. "You can do this. Maybe it will help, maybe it won't, but it won't harm."

She climbed the embankment and passed the first tree trunks. Brambleberries and hoarsgrout gathered beneath bare branches. Tiny creatures scurried through leaf litter. Gizzards hooted, now near, now far. Leafless branches twined into gloomy tunnels, shafts of sunlight painted vibrant pictures of moss and mushrooms, golden leaves, the ghostly trunks of cerrenils.

Cerrenils, she snorted. The old mothers who bore humankind when Elesendar came down from heaven. What rubbish! Bethniel insisted the trees could move at will. She insisted they had wills! Fantasies about wizards fighting monsters, fairy tales about angry trees tearing up greedy farmers' fields. All because the trees had the peculiar trait of lowering their canopies at dusk. In daylight, the limbs reached for the sun and could support a horse. But at night the crowns collapsed, each branch as supple as a vine. Vic had explained to Bethniel, Timny, Katchel—anyone who would listen—that the phenomenon must be due to diurnal changes in xylem and phloem distribution. The hypothesis made perfect sense and could be easily verified by a few experiments, but that horrible Silnauer had declared the same clear, scientific reasoning heresy. No wonder the people the Oreseekers left behind never made any progress fixing the *Elesendar*'s drive, when they spent their time making up this nonsense about walking, talking *trees*.

At least I have some sense, Vic thought as she made little piles of rocks pointing the way back to the road. She noted landmarks and made her signs, her feet carrying her deeper into the woods. Her calves began to ache, but the wind tasted like snow and whistled like an Oreseeker pipe. When she had set out from Ourtown, the youngest Logkeeper in history, she'd been so confident of conquering that little bit of the world, so sure everyone would be so grateful she kept the Logs for them. How many weeks or months would have passed before she realized people sat through her lectures so she'd deliver their mail?

"I never had the chance to find out!" she shouted. A surprised hoot and flap of wings were her only answers. Her throat suddenly tight, she sat in the crook of a root, aching to weep, but her grief and longing were too deep for tears. She pictured her father stirring the coals of his fire, his eyes fixed far away, on memories of his wife and the little girl who used to laugh as they swung her between them. She wished she was a Listener, one of those Lathans whose telepathy was so strong they could know the thoughts others tried to hide. If she were, she would reach out to her father, send him love and comfort. "I'm all right, Father," she whispered. "It was bad for a time, but I'm all right."

As she nestled in the cerrenil roots, the pressure faded behind her eyes and the rush and burble of water tickled her thirst. Following the sound, she found a glade golden with fallen leaves and ringed with cerrenils. A brook cut through the clearing, water sparkling in the noon sun. Somehow she'd walked right through morning tea; Narath must be leagues behind her. Belly hollow, she opened the pack, spread a blanket over the mulch, and dug through the provisions. Bread and cheese, some dried fruit, a bottle of brandy, and something wrapped in cheesecloth bearing a note: *Eat at noon the first day.* Shrugging, Vic settled onto the blanket and unwrapped a piece of cake.

Spicy sweetness burst in her mouth. Surpised and delighted, she took another bite, and another, devouring the cake as if she hadn't eaten in weeks. Brook water, cold as snow, washed it down. Sated, she reclined on her elbows, eyes darting between the branches crisscrossed above to the burbling water. Across the stream squatted a cerrenil, leafless branches heavy with fruit, looking very much like a peddler woman. As Vic stared, the tree leaned toward her. A few fruit bounced onto her blanket. With a guffaw, Vic thanked the tree and sipped some brandy. The sun warm on her shoulders, the ground swam up at her.

Warm, green air wraps around trees stretching for a sky bluer than Lornk's eyes. Tall shadows glide through showers of light and shade, pursued by warriors. They scramble over twisted roots, jabbing pikes into the shadows, then turn on each other. Screams of pain, shouts of glory echo, while the weeping rage of a red-haired woman sings in woeful counterpoint.

Grass blades pricked her cheek. Above, a red sky washed into purple. As Vic blinked and stretched, turf crinkled under boots and shoulders. The blanket! She sprang up, staring around the clearing. Blanket, pack, brandy, food—all gone. The bloody creek was gone! In the gloaming, she hunted for her things, for a slope she might have rolled down in her sleep, for the prankster who'd carried her from the glade and dumped her here. Wherever here was.

Her eyes scanned the last bit of red in the east. Narath lay the opposite way; the road was south. She couldn't camp without provisions, not in winter. Shrine, why had she so readily trusted Elekia and blithely walked away from comfort and warmth? Muttering more curses, she headed southwest, knowing she'd come to either Narath or the road leading there. Or a farm—farms surrounded the city, forming a patchwork through the forest. She'd studied enough maps to know the Kiareinoll didn't become truly wild for a hundred leagues around Latha's capital.

The wind cut through her cloak, the fierce tang of a coming storm raising a shiver. Snow flurries slipped down, and the breeze whispered her name, "Vic. Vicky. Victoriaaaah."

"Nonsense," she muttered, rubbing her ears, then stopped, transfixed. Veins of crystal pulsed over an outcropping as broken clouds swept past Elesendar. Cerrenils arched above the rock face, branches drooping across it like hair. Drawn to the silver glow, she touched the rock. Her hand sprang away from unexpected heat, then pressed against the stone, soaking up the warmth. The veins seemed to brighten at her touch. I'll come back and look at this in daylight, she thought. In daylight and warmer weather.

Turning, she ran smack into a flaccid cerrenil limb. The trees did look like old women with unkempt gray hair. Shaking her head, she pushed past the limp boughs and into the night-gripped forest, feeling her way up a hill. As she reached the crest, a gale howled over, tumbling her into a thicket. Brambles tore at her cloak, ripping fabric. "That's better," a deep, leering voice hissed. "Let me see you." The trees shivered. "Slut," scolded a crone's voice, and the cerrenils shook their heads and cackled.

She dragged herself free of the thorns, fought off twiggy fingers that grabbed her, wheezing in a nasty caricature of Silnauer. "Promising student? Stupid girl, look where your ambition got you, whoring yourself to the first man who drops a compliment." Martha's voice hissed, "You can't come home, Vic. Go find your path among the people who've forgotten us. Just like you."

"I didn't forget!" she screamed, but the haggard trees wheezed and cackled and pulled her deeper into their domain. At last she spilled down a slope and found herself on her back, staring at the granite outcropping, its crystal ribbons still throbbing with light. She crawled toward the rock, feeling her way across crackly brown grass to a mossy hollow at the stone's base. With an exhausted gasp, she rolled beneath the overhang. The wind gusted, suddenly ghostly with heavy, wet snow. Vic cringed against the warm granite, shivering with sobs or cold—she wasn't sure.

Hunger awakened her. The cerrenils stretched their boughs toward the yellow sun, snow piled around their trunks like heavy skirts. Her blanket lay atop the drifts, and within its folds nestled an armload of cerrenil fruit. The pulp bitter, it still soothed her empty stomach. Her chewing loud in her ears, she stopped eating to listen. The air still, the forest ebbed silence. When she stood to go, her footsteps crackled on the snow like lightning.

She resumed the southwest course, followed by stillness. Today she marched easily through the trees, the underbrush always in the distance. Yet when she had walked until the sun rose and sank again to kiss the tops of the trees, and she hadn't seen so much as a poacher's hut, she realized her trip into Fembrosh wasn't done. Not yet.

"What was in that cake?" she muttered. Trudging on, she came to a brook gurgling through a deep cut in the snow, small crystalline boulders jutting out of the drifts. She found some fallen evergreen branches, laid them down for a bed, and tied the blanket to some drooping cerrenil limbs for a tent. The pinking clouds to the west meant more snow, but tonight the old mothers offered her shelter. The wind started again just after sundown, humming softly this time, bringing snow like feathers.

She slept. And dreamed again the shadows in the trees, moving as smoothly as boats over still waters. The massive trees swayed in a great wind, and the image shivered into an icy bluff. Beyond that next rise lay Ourtown. Ocean salt filled her lungs and she stopped for a moment, breathing deeply. It was good to be home.

Something whistled behind her, and she ducked and spun round. A long stoneknife swept toward her stomach. She jumped back; the knife wielder cursed and rushed forward, weapon high. She caught his hands, tried to pry his fingers off the hilt. Taller and stronger, he grabbed her wrist and they wrestled for the knife. Her nails bit into his hand, drawing blood. He spat on her and pressed the knife toward her heart.

"Who are you?" she gasped.

He grinned like Lornk, his eyes blue, his hair yellow. "Die, Lathan," he said aloud, and she realized her words had been silent.

As they struggled, her foot slipped on a patch of ice. She fell, and the knife arched downward, slicing past her head, curving back into the man's belly. Groaning, he collapsed. His blood stark on the snow, he choked, and the light faded from his eyes.

She woke to a glade dusted with sunshine and the last golden cerrenil leaves. A soft breeze lifted snow and leaves into the air, revealing something dark—a leather-bound handle. Her stomach knotted. Digging through the drift, she found a stoneknife like the kind Relman soldiers used. "Die, Lathan," he had said.

Gazing at the weapon, she thought of Richelle. *Maybe she could have resisted Lornk.* "My name is Victoria of Ourtown," she said in mindspeech, wishing he could Hear that thought across the thousands of miles separating them. She grasped the hilt of the knife, turning its blade in the sunlight, feeling it absorb the warmth. Lathans carried long crystal daggers that caught the sun and refracted it into their enemies' eyes, or so the songs said. She wondered how it would feel to hold one of those, to fight, to win a war against Lornk. Bethniel had called her puny, and soldiering was the last ambition she would have imagined. But her fingers wrapped round the hilt easily. A practice swipe felt *right*. During her dream, she'd felt no fear when the Relman attacked. If she faced Lornk? Would her breath stop until he wound the clockwork toy, forged from an alloy of terror and desire? Or would she breathe freely as a flesh and blood woman? She ran her finger along the blade, and red sprinkled the snow. Hissing, she sucked at the wound, and the tang of iron spread over her tongue. "My name is Victoria of Ourtown," she said aloud in Lathan. "And I am not yours."

A wind whistled through branches, and in its wake came all the sounds—hoots and chirps, scratches and scurries—that had surrounded her the first day. Vic walked in the direction of the breeze, and her eyes fell on an ankle-high mound of stones identical to one she'd made on her way in from the road. Another pile of pebbles lay ten feet ahead, and another beyond that. She stopped at a cerrenil, laid her hand on the white bark. "I don't know if you did this," she said aloud in her own tongue. "I don't know if you even know I'm talking to you. But thanks."

The noonday sun flashing on snowdrifts, Ashel shielded his eyes as he approached the manor gate. A good foot of snow had fallen since he'd last been up Manor Hill—a gig at the Harper's Wind had given him an excuse to sleep at the Guildhouse a few nights—and the tracks of horses and wagons no longer cut through to the gravel. At the gate, Gaston rose and flashed a row of wooden teeth. "Good day, Your Highness! Did you hear about the Alnan barmaid and the Caleisbahnin? When he tipped her, she tossed it back and told him to bring a bigger sword." The old guard slapped his knee and hooted, and Ashel chuckled all the way to the manor. Selcher took his satchel at the front door, imparting her usual scowl. "The family has already sat down, Highness."

In the west dining room, white hazed through a crystal wall that kept out the cold no better than an ill-chinked poacher's cabin. In spring, the garden hues would fuzz together like watercolors sold on the streets of Cabanarl, but winter and summer vied in discomfort—why his mother would choose to dine here was as mysterious as every decision she made. Still, Bethniel's laughter warmed the room as Father told a story about a fat Erin merchant. Their cousins giggled, and even Mother chuckled, a sight so rare Ashel stopped in the doorway. His mother, when she wasn't scowling, outshone every woman in the world, including his sister. "You're late," she said when she caught him staring.

"I came as soon as morning classes were over. If I had a horse, I could have gotten here sooner."

"The royal stables are for royal business. But if you spent less on ale and dicing," Father said, eyes twinkling, "you could buy your own."

"A man has to have his priorities," Ashel replied, taking his seat, "so I guess I'll always be late for lunch." Everyone laughed, including Mother. More at ease than he'd seen her in years, she traded playful gibes with Father, hardly scolded Timny and Cimba, and even complimented Bethniel's handling of some minor crisis in the prime minister's office. The meal passed like he imagined they had when he was very young, before the war began. That thought he squashed before his mother caught it. Nothing could spoil the mood so quickly as an argument between his parents about the war.

A draft of cold air and wet wool brought all eyes to the doorway, where the girl from Traine stood, her clothes hanging in tatters, her cheeks hollow and white as the snow outside. "I never saw the trees move," she said, teeth chattering, "but weird things happened."

"You're back early!" Mother and Bethniel sprang out of their chairs. Dread erupted in Ashel's stomach as Mother called down the hall for a special tea and Bethniel swung a quilt off a rack and wrapped it around Vic's shoulders. She ladled soup into a bowl while Mother settled Vic in a chair and fetched a spoon and napkin for the girl herself! "Did you find it?" Elekia asked, adjusting the quilt around her shoulders.

"I think so," Vic replied, stuffing soup-soaked bread into her mouth.

Ashel had to swallow bile before speaking. "Mother, what have you done?" He looked around the table. Father kept his eyes on his own soup; the children stared at Vic in awe. "Beth, what's going on?"

His sister refused to meet his gaze and ran out, promising to check on the tea.

"Ashel," Mother clipped at him, "tell Selcher to ready a hot bath and warm Vic's bed. Remember going into Fembrosh? You slept for a week."

The rest of the afternoon, his mother and sister wrapped themselves around the girl like a shroud while Father fled questions, claiming business at the Senate. Ashel wandered over the manor grounds, kicking at snow drifts, furious with them and with himself for not realizing what was happening the other morning. He'd been too busy trying to start a casual conversation and prove himself a worldy sophisticate, easily chatting with the Trainer mistress, instead of the rube who couldn't stop ogling the girl he'd once seen naked. He'd been so focused on his shame, he hadn't seen her danger, and so hadn't stopped it.

Late that afternoon, he found queen and princess in the solarium, plotting like two witches over a brew. "Just what did you hope to accomplish?" he asked. "She could have died."

"Calm yourself, Ashel. You sound like an indignant husband."

"Mother, she could have died. A city girl, with no woodcraft? Have you seen how much it's snowed? What did you hope to prove?"

"First, she's from the frozen north and is probably better able to survive a winter storm than you. Second, she needed to be tested. Fembrosh has passed her."

He rolled his eyes. "Superstitious twaddle."

"Vic's going to join the army," Bethniel said.

Ashel's mouth dropped open. "You're insane."

"She saw it," his mother said. "She brought back the talisman." She picked up a narrow stone from the table. With a long, leather-bound hilt, it curved to a razor point. "She said she found this stoneknife beside her when she woke from a dream in which she fought a Relman. Selcher was there when she told the story; she didn't lie."

"You can't do this. She's barely older than my apprentices."

"Fembrosh has judged her."

"Mother, the Kiareinoll is just an old wood! Sending her out there during winter was folly and making her take up the dagger because of a drug-induced dream is ludicrous."

"I see." Elekia folded her hands primly in her lap, but a corner of her mouth urged toward a smile. "And did you think your dreams of cerrenils singing to you were folly? You said that you wished you could have stayed longer, listening to the music of the trees. You claim you found your destiny in the fallen limb of a cerrenil that curved into the shape of a staff. What if I had said that a prince becoming a minstrel was ludicrous and made you study to become a king?"

"That's different. I knew what I wanted when I went into the Kiareinoll. Look at Bethniel. She didn't dream anything, just came back complaining of bug bites and ruined boots."

"You weren't even there!" Bethniel retorted, but their mother's hand silenced her.

"So you used the Kiareinoll to make your father and I let you remain with the Guild?"

"I didn't say that." She had him. He cursed himself for trying to argue. She always found a way to turn his points against him and open gaping wounds with them. Growling, he left them for a tankard of ale at the Wind.

Chapter 9

Freedom

Olivet eyed Vic skeptically. Behind him in the training yard, a few guards sparred with practice daggers. "How old is she?" he asked Elekia.

"I'm sixteen," Vic said, straightening her shoulders and trying to stand taller. "I learn fast."

Shaking his head, he strode over and grabbed her biceps and squeezed. Vic winced, thinking of the examination in Traine, and Olivet let her go and spat. "Look how she jumps," he said. "If she can't stand to be touched, she'll make no trooper. Besides, there's no muscle on those arms. We take farmers, miners, even weavers. People who have *worked*, put some strength in their limbs. This one would be squashed like a bug."

"Did you go into Fembrosh?" Elekia asked, frowning at the spittle slowly melting into the snow.

He nodded. "Yes, and I saw myself a deacon in the Bankers Guild. But I couldn't do the math. Our dreams don't always point toward our destiny, Your Majesty."

"I know I'm not strong," Vic interrupted, "but my mother was an athlete and a fisher. I've never tried to—" She waved at the guards fighting, gulping at their legs slogging through the muddy snow. Some of those drifts would come up to her waist. "Give me a month to learn."

Olivet met her eyes, scowling, then looked at Elekia. "She won't last a week."

Elekia nodded. "I think she will."

"And if she doesn't?"

Elekia looked down at Vic, her eyes and smile hard. "Then she will have to find her own way."

Vic stared. The queen had trapped her now—become a trooper or don't expect any more charity from us. So much for Elekia's confidences and kindness. She looked again at the guards. A pair of them were on the ground, rolling through mud and snow, groaning, straining to gain control of a single bundle of reeds held between them. One was a woman, a foot shorter than the man above her. The man abruptly wrestled the reeds out of her hands, raised them, then swung them down and laid them across her throat. "Give me a month," Vic repeated, forcing her voice to sound determined.

"One month. All right. But she lives in the barracks with the other troopers, starting today."

† † †

A spoon banged on a hollow pot, and Vic blinked her eyes open, listening to the grumbles of those rising around her. Her limbs heavy as wet straw, stiff as frozen ironreed, she struggled to roll onto her side, push herself up. For two days, she'd done nothing but run to Narath and back and stand in the training yard, raising a spear over her head, again and again, and again.

"It'll be worth it, you know," Margren said from the next cot, grinning as Vic groaned toward standing.

Vic nodded, unable to straighten her arms or legs all the way. "I'm sure."

The woman laughed, shaking long, straight brown hair out behind her, then quickly plaiting it into a tight bun at the base of her neck. Vic envied the hair, remembering when her own hung to her waist. She envied Margren's prowess with dagger and bow, too. "It'll be worth it, trust me," Margren said, patting Vic's shoulder.

That morning in the training yard, Olivet came over while Vic struggled with the spear and showed her how to use it to stretch her shoulder and arm muscles. Then he moved off to correct the stance of a man sparring against a thick log with rungs stuck out at odd angles. For two weeks, that was all the direction she got out of the marshall. But over that time, a firmness began to form over the bones of her arms, and her legs recalled the strength they had known walking over the steppes. Her body embraced the rigors of training as if it had finally remembered her mother's defiant laughter while she wrestled sail and tiller against wind and waves. On the run down the switchbacks to Narath, Vic forgot about Lornk, even about her lost life as a Logkeeper and focused on putting one foot ahead of the other. She learned to revel in the speed—the power—as the slope pulled her legs down, and on the way up, she found solace in the labor of keeping breath and steps together in an even rhythm.

Evenings, Vic sat in the mess, at the edge of a table Margren shared with the other officers in training, listening to their stories of weird happenings in the Kiareinoll, feeling tolerated but not quite welcome. Then one night Olivet stopped by and told her to report at the manor's gate before dawn. They all looked at her as he left, Margren grinning. Jaslin, a broad man with a scar ripped from the corner of his eyebrow to the base of his ear, reached across the table and knocked her on the shoulder. "Olivet sees something in you."

Blinking at them, Vic shook her head, her shoulder throbbing. "He doesn't think I'm fit for this."

Margren rolled her eyes. "No, he does. You'll be an officer by the time the summer campaigns start."

Vic dropped her bread. "What?"

They glanced at each other, Jaslin's blue eyes dancing in the lamplight. "You knew this was an officer's training camp."

"Yes, but—"

"You don't want to be an officer?" Margren asked.

"I don't have any experience. How can I be?"

Jaslin shrugged. "You're from the royal household."

Her face suddenly hot, Vic excused herself from the table and left the mess. The troopers' barracks lay on the western edge of the manor grounds, on a hillcrest overlooking a small prison. She watched the prison guards walk the ramparts, silouettes cutting across lights that flooded the field around it. Prisons. Choices. Her breath steamed in the night air, her anger growing at Elekia. That woman taunted her with the illusion of freedom but never gave her a choice. An officer? She had not become a Logkeeper at fifteen because she was Theodore's daughter or Martha's apprentice, and she refused to accept a commission now because of a piece of paper naming her the Ruler's ward. Marching to the manor, she thought about how she had traded one prison for another. Well, this time she would free herself for good. At the rear of the house, she stomped through the screened porch and yanked open the kitchen door. Kachel stopped her as she swiped her feet on the mat.

"You can't visit tonight, Vic," he apologized. "The family is hosting some Senators."

These people with their silent speech, their secret motives, their incomprehensible hospitality to her. What motivated them to push her into officer's training when she only intended to join their army as an ordinary trooper? Her mouth opened, but she shut it with a frustrated sigh, unwilling to release her ire on the chef. "Can I at least talk to Bethniel?" she asked.

He shook his head. "She's the Heir."

"Shrine's bitch," Vic cursed. Bethniel always complained about having to attend state functions, no matter how tedious, how mundane. Vic cursed again.

"But Ashel's in the house tonight," Kachel offered, with a disapproving frown at her language. "He isn't invited to the dinner either."

Surprised, Vic raised an eyebrow but shook her head. Whenever she saw him, Ashel was kind and discreet, but his height and grace and beauty still awed her, made her feel even smaller and cruder than she felt around his sister. "No, I won't bother him." Her anger deflating, she turned to go.

"Elesendar, it's cold in here," the prince said, entering from the hall.

Vic froze in the open doorway. "In or out, Vic," Kachel called. "If my fowls cool before I serve them, the Ruler won't be able to free the Weavers Guild of senatorial review."

Vic looked back sheepishly. Ashel had his nose in a pot; Kachel arched his eyebrows and vigorously nodded for her to come all the way inside. Her cheeks burning, she stepped onto the plank floor and pushed the door shut behind her. Ashel stood, white teeth dazzling. "Hello."

Kachel drew a chair out from the table, poured her a mug of tea. "Vic came by to keep me company, but I've got to ready the tubers now, so will you amuse her, Ashel?"

"Gladly." Ashel pulled a cookie out of a jar and sat at the table. "How can I entertain you?" A maid came in, uniformed in black with a white collar, and took a tureen from the warming oven next to Kachel's stove. He whispered some instructions to her, then dumped a bowl of sliced tubers into a pan on the stove and began whistling while he sprinkled them with oil and spices.

Vic sidled toward the table and sipped the tea. "You don't have to entertain me. Kachel's amusing enough."

Ashel grinned as Kachel's whistling grew louder. "How is your training going?"

Vic shrugged, glancing at the door, hating his attention on her. "All right."

He leaned across the table, his eyes concerned. "That didn't sound convincing. What's wrong?"

Shaking her head, she looked down at her fingers in her lap. "Nothing," she began, but her frustration overcame her embarrassment. Her eyes shifted to the ceiling. "I didn't know they wanted me to be an officer," she blurted. "It isn't fair that I'm down there with people who've worked for that. I haven't even tried to be a soldier yet."

"Oh"—Ashel nodded knowingly, crossing his arms—"that. Royals are entitled to commissions. I'm a captain, not that any fieldmarshall in his right mind would give me a patrol."

"But I'm not a royal."

Ashel exchanged a smile with Kachel. "You're a royal ward."

She grunted. "Right. I think your mother regrets that decision."

"Oh, I think my mother has other regrets, like her eldest being a frivolous musician instead of a serious prince." He frowned deeply, imitating Elekia, then softened his lips into an encouraging smile. "What would you like to do?"

"Go down to Narath and sign up as a regular recruit."

"Have you told Olivet that?"

"No."

"Well, there you are. You've been to Fembrosh, which means you make your own decisions and your parents or your fosters can't make them for you."

"Done!" Kachel shouted, tossing the tubers up and arching them into a tray waiting in his right hand. "Ashel, would you go ask the maids if the party is ready for the next course?"

Assenting gamely, Ashel rapped his knuckles on the table and flashed his brilliant teeth at Vic before leaving.

"Did you get your answers?" the chef asked.

"Yes, I have."

That night, she went to Olivet's cottage and told him she wanted to transfer to the army's main training camp in the southern Kiareinoll. Smiling, he shook her hand, looking at her for the first time since she'd met him. "Come back in two years," he promised, "and I'll make a damn good officer out of you." Afterward she lay in bed, trying to imagine what it would be like to hold a dagger. To use it. "Margren?" she asked into the darkness.

"Yes," the woman replied sleepily.

"What's it like to kill someone?"

Blankets whispering, Margren sat up, her profile black in the starlight leaking through the shutters. Vic swung her legs onto the floor and continued speaking when Margren didn't answer. "I've killed fish and mussels and fowl for dinner, and bugs of course. Every time, a little part of me hurt—a finger, a rib, something. I haven't liked killing."

"I've liked it," Margren said, her mindvoice soft so that Vic barely caught the words. "When my dagger sinks into a Relman's back, and his blood is warm on my hand." She raised her fingers to her mouth, as if tasting the iron in blood, her voice dimming into silence. After a pause, she went on in a hoarse whisper. When Lathans spoke of the dead, they spoke aloud. "When you see your brothers thrown together in a heap, their throats cut as if *they* were fowl, and your mother lying face down in the hay with a stoneknife stuck in her back, you get . . . Well, you need to take it out on somebody. My youngest brother was three years old. That anger does not die."

Vic rested her chin on her knees. Could her anger compare with this woman's? She felt it, rolled in the corner of her mind, seething at Lornk like a bundle of molten iron waiting to be forged into a weapon of vengeance. She thought of her father, not dead but thinking she was, grieving beside his books and his small fire in their lodge. Had news of Cairo reached Ourtown, or did he imagine her body lying beneath the snow, the victim of a summer snow squall or the prey of the few ruffians who wandered the steppes? Instead, Victoria the Logkeeper had died in a white room in Traine and been reborn as Kara, a creature who woke to Lornk's light, not the sun's. Vic hated her, the sniveling coward, the clockwork doll, who had moaned and sighed at Lornk's command. Kara was his. "But my name is Victoria," she whispered. Elesendar, let it be true.

† † †

In the morning, she went to her room in the manor and gathered her few belongings, stuffing the stoneknife she'd found and the gem-studded leather bands and choker into a bag. Heart thudding, she fished in her bottom drawer and drew out the bronze belt. Its rings clacked softly, and her throat closed on the memory of Earnk's paternal gaze as he leashed her like a pet. Earnk had treated her as a slave no less than his father. If Lornk hadn't walked in on them, would that have changed? That morning in Traine, Earnk had declared his love, but he'd made no promises to free her. "You have to free yourself," she whispered.

She wrapped the belt in a scarf, took the other things, and went downstairs to the dining room, where she found Olivet breakfasting with the royals.

Sashal's gaze fell on her when she entered. "Vic! Olivet told us you don't want a commission. You're entitled to one."

She flushed. "Thank you, Your Majesty. I—it doesn't seem fair, or right. I have so much to learn."

The king smiled, coming round the table to embrace her. "Elesendar blessed us the day you arrived." As the smooth fabric of the king's doublet rubbed her cheek, she had to blink fast to dam tears.

When he released her, she looked at the others. "I came to say goodbye and thank you." She went first to Cimba and Timny. "Thank you both for letting me in." Smiling and giving each a hug, she handed Timny the stoneknife and Cimba the bracelets. She pulled out the choker and anklets for Bethniel. "Thank you for your friendship, Beth. I'm sure a jeweler can turn the gemstones into something pretty for you."

Eyes shimmering, the princess stood and squeezed her tight. "Be safe, Vic. I'll miss you."

Coming to stand beside his sister, Ashel offered his hand. "Good luck."

Her face hot again, she shook it. "I'm sorry I don't have anything for you—but I'm grateful for your advice."

He beamed, his arm around Bethniel. "It was my honor."

Eyes flicking to the king, Vic went to the queen and handed her the silk-wrapped belt. "Thank you for everything—for harboring me, my clothes, my board, everything." Elekia arched an eyebrow. "Maybe you can . . . sell that," Vic added.

Elekia looked inside the scarf and shot a glance at her husband. "These gifts are wholly unnecessary."

"I want to repay you all."

Sashal put an arm around her shoulders. "There is nothing to repay, Vic. This house is your home, now and always. Take care at the front, and we'll see you when you have leave."

† † †

Mist, orange in the rising sun, straggled between copses, peeling away, then massing toward them. "I can't see anything, can you?" Devanna, her lookout partner, asked.

Vic shook her head, her stomach so tight she thought she'd be sick if she spoke, even silently. A geilmor spine jabbing her thigh, she shifted her weight on the branch. She'd spent the winter training in woodcraft and killing, but no one had taught her how to sit comfortably in a tree with spikes for leaves.

"I've been thinking," Devanna chattered in a nervous whisper. "After a year, I think I'll train with the healers. I know our patrol has one, but when you and I lead our own, we'll need somebody. I already know so much about herblore, and of course we've had our training in field aid, so what could be so hard about learning the rest?" Her mindvoice buzzed on over the creaks and groans of artillery being primed. Devanna had turned up at Narath's recruiting office the same day as Vic, and they'd trained together all winter. For their first battle, their captain had assigned them lookout duty and sent them to this copse on the far left flank of their division. Last night the Lathan campfires had stretched across sparsely wooded hill crests for a mile, and a league off, Relman fires mirrored the Lathan line. To shore up their courage, their patrol mates had told them tales of narrow escapes and daring deeds, and the captain had made them each take a swig of harlolinde. The acid sting of the liquor still a sharp memory in her throat, Vic listened to the ratcheting of catapults. The mist muffled and deflected the noise; it seemed to come not from the archers' column but from the opposite side of the copse. Trees blocked her view in that direction.

"I'm going to the other side," she signed with her fingers, worried there might be Relmans close enough to hear—or Hear. Startled, Devanna stopped talking and nodded, then peered toward the battlefield. Vic stepped down the branches winding around the tree's trunk and slipped deeper into the stand. Mist dripped from geilmor spines, the drops cold on her neck. The trees screened out the noise, offering sanctuary from a battle not yet begun. Stepping toe to heel through fallen needles, she passed quickly and silently to the opposite edge. There, an abrupt rise in the ground—an earthwork thrown up in some ancient war—screened the field. Suddenly worried that no one had stationed troopers on top of the rise, she climbed it on her elbows.

As her eyes peeked over the crest, a shout preceded the thud of a dozen catapult arms into their frames. A volley of rocks and flaming oil arched over the copse toward the Lathan ranks. Screams erupted from the far side of the geilmors, and Relmans whooped as they charged past their own artillery and up the hill in a surprise attack on the Lathan flank. As the catapults released a second volley, Vic scrambled toward the trees. Relmans crested the rise behind her as she ducked into the copse. Smoke and the crackle of burning wood drifted toward her. "Devanna!" She twisted under branches and slipped across the carpet of needles, Relmans crashing through the woods. From above, a third cascade of rocks rained down, torching the branches around her. Vic dodged forward, too scared to cry, even as she found Devanna lying face down in the grass, her clothes and hair scorched, her head turned at an impossible angle. Tumbling to her knees, Vic shook Devanna's shoulders. Her friend's head rolled unnaturally. Mist and smoke curtained the field, but shouting, screams, the thwack and thud of artillery sounded all around her. Vic climbed to her feet and dashed toward the knoll where the marshalls had stationed themselves. Surely they knew by now the Relmans lay off the left flank? What if they had troops off the right as well? Should she run straight there? She couldn't head toward her patrol's spot in the line. That would lead Relmans to a rear attack. Her steps slowed as she debated, shouting and the thump of feet loud behind her. To her surprise, she understood their commander—not his words but his meaning—as he yelled orders: a few should follow her while he led the main group toward the line. Shelving the realization that she had learned enough mindspeech to Hear the thoughts of those who didn't have it, she sprinted off to the north, away from the lines and away from the marshall's knoll. All of you follow me, she thought at them, please, follow me.

The Relmans closed the gap behind her. Now, her heart echoing through her ribs, she pushed her legs faster than she'd ever run before. Her feet flew over the grass, leapt over rocks jutting up in her path. She watched the ground for harrier holes, the mist curling back a few yards ahead, limiting her view. She dared not look behind her, knowing they followed close enough to see her, afraid to see their faces stretched with the effort of running, angry, ready to kill. Her hand landed on the dagger at her waist. That morning, Devanna had poisoned her blade; Vic had not. Devanna. Elesendar take her, Vic prayed. A ship, not a god, but blinded by fog with Relmans closing, Vic figured a prayer couldn't hurt. Elesendar, take her, and give me strength and speed.

She could not outrun them. They were close enough she heard their breathing hard but steady. Her own breath shuddered out of her chest, her heart weakening from the extended sprint. As her stomach clenched with a cramp in her side, her right hand closed on the dagger, freshly gummed to give her a grip on the quartz hilt. Could she use it? Don't think about it, she ordered herself, drawing the blade out of its sheath, whirling suddenly around and swiping at a Relman reaching for her neck. He twisted out of the path of the blade, slipping on the grass but rolling back to his feet. A woman bore down on Vic, her own weapon raised, her face a mean grimace. Vic parried her blow, kicking at the woman's ribs, but the woman grabbed Vic's boot and yanked her off her feet. Before Vic could roll away, the man flung himself across her, laying his stoneknife over her throat. In the pause before anyone spoke, Vic saw that only these two had followed her after all.

"Tell me why I shouldn't kill you," the man panted.

Vic gulped air, trying to fill lungs pressed into the ground by the man's weight. His knife scored a line stinging with sweat and blood across her throat. Now her tears came, leaking down the sides of her face.

"Lathans bring 'em down here young," the woman spat. "Look at her. She's almost a baby."

With a heave, the man pulled himself off Vic, flipped her over, grabbed her arms and held them behind her. The woman's foot stepped on Vic's buttocks, holding her still. The turf smelled rancid, soggy from the mists and rain. "You got any twine?" the man asked.

The woman laughed. "You after that bonus? We're in a full battle, not some hunt and strike. We don't have time for you to be bringing in prizes."

"Orders are, look for young girls, take them alive."

"Sick Trainer business," she growled. "I don't know about foreigners running our country, Mel." Fear and bile rising in her throat, Vic gagged.

Mel yanked Vic into a sitting position, untied the laces at the neck of her tunic and pulled them out, using them to tie her hands behind her. Vic's bladder and bowels hurt, her stomach lurched, her whole body shaking with spasms. "I don't like this," the woman complained. "Look at the poor thing, sick with fear. It'd be kinder to kill her."

Mel leered, bringing his face in close to Vic's, his hand holding her head steady. "She's sort of pretty. Do you think I'll get extra if she's pretty?"

"Mel—" the woman warned.

Mel drew his hand back and brought the hilt of his stoneknife down. Vic felt herself jump when it hit her, then felt nothing but blackness.

CHAPTER 10

THE TASTE OF BLOOD

Cold air and blank faces. The light around them dim and brown, Vic walked with her captors toward a Device surrounded by dank stone. Sharp images of black chairs and red tapestries kaleidoscoped to a blur of blue, green, and pink and back again. Rough twine biting into her wrists, her shoulders ached. Tremors shook her knees and ankles, and she could not walk without the help of those beside her. Towering over her, they had square shoulders and hips, neither male nor female. Gray cloth covered their faces and bodies, stretching over their noses and the hollows of their eyes. From hidden mouths, they buzzed at each other in a language she could not understand, the words almost beyond the range of her hearing. Stepping onto the Device, they stood her on the dais. Without their support, she almost fell. One of them bent down and twisted the black, shining knob on the Device. The world hazed into beige, her skin tingling with a million pinpricks. Then she stood in the cellar beneath Lornk's library, where he waited, arms folded across his chest, eyebrows cross. The gray forms were left behind; only he and she faced each other.

"I've been waiting," he scolded, walking forward, revealing a steel blade. Her knees still weak, she trembled as he approached. Lowering her eyes, she clamped her mouth shut to guard against screaming. He grasped her wrist, and electricity jolted up her arm as he cut her bonds with the knife. She stood silent, her legs finding strength as warmth spread from her loins toward her face, like blood rising toward a blush. Lifting the fingers of her left hand, he pressed his lips to her knuckles, his eyes still flashing. "What are you, Kara?" came the question.

She knelt at his feet, tugging the laces at her neck. "I am yours, my Lord." Pulling her tunic over her head, she raised her eyes and smiled shyly. "I've missed you."

She jerked awake, heart racing. A thong drew her ankles toward her wrists, fingers and toes tingled, knees and hips and shoulders ached. Wet, trampled grass scratched her cheek. A fire crackled behind her, warmed her back, cast wild shadows as troopers moved around it. Elesendar lay just above the horizon, sinking fast. The sky deep black, the constellations told the time: a few hours before midnight. Groaning softly, another Lathan lay nearby, large feet and tanned hands struggling weakly in bonds like hers. She twisted her head around, trying to see if there were any others.

"Marshall," a deep voice called, "the girl's awake."

Footsteps approached from behind, then hands grabbed her arms and pulled her up. Kneeling beside her, a woman peered at her. Her deep brown skin was caked with mud and blood, and a bandage wound over wiry red hair. "What is your name?" she asked silently.

Vic swallowed. "Victoria," she said. Perhaps Lornk had never paid enough attention to remember her real name.

The marshall glanced over at the other Lathan. "That one

got himself captured trying to rescue you. Taking you put us at a big risk. Will you make it worth our while?"

Vic shook her head. Would they kill her if she said no? That dream was true—if she faced Lornk, she would fall at his feet, beg his forgiveness. "I'm just a rookie. I don't know anything." Death had to be better.

Nodding, the woman stood. "Stupid waste, in my opinion," she said to no one in particular, then sighed. "But orders . . ." She moved toward the fire. "Somebody cut this girl loose and feed her. She's no danger to a flea."

Another woman came over with a canteen and bread. Releasing Vic, she gave her a sip of water, then led her closer to the fire before handing her the loaf. Munching with dirty hands, Vic listened for some hint of their plans, but the Relmans said little. A few lieutenants came to the fire with reports. Nodding toward the Lathans, the marshall led them out of sight. Other troopers quietly diced while a sentry disappeared from the circle of firelight, reappearing a few minutes later. They camped on the crest of a hill, other fires dotting nearby hilltops. Behind her, the other Lathan prisoner groaned again. He'd tried to save her. Vic looked at her bread crust, suddenly guilty that she'd eaten while he remained bound. The marshall came back, and Vic stood, her hand raised. The other Relmans rose, eyes wary, but the marshall signaled them to relax and smiled kindly at Vic.

She waved at the other Lathan. "Do you have any food left?"

The marshall's smile faded, her eyes narrowing. "We can't untie him."

Vic hung her head. In Traine, she had learned that humility was sometimes useful. "I could feed him, if you'll let me."

She snorted, but patted Vic on the shoulder. "Gabrin," she called. "Bring some water and bread for the other prisoner. And watch them closely."

Cursing, a man tossed his dice to another trooper, grabbed a canteen and a loaf, and strode over. He handed Vic the food, then roughly tugged the Lathan onto his knees, turning him so he faced the fire. "Maynon," Vic breathed, kneeling next to him. She'd met him just two days ago, when she'd been assigned to his party. Blood caked his eyelashes and cheeks. He stretched his shoulders, his mouth sour. Vic lifted the canteen to his lips, tipping it slowly.

"Give me a drink, girl. Don't trickle it in like milk for a baby," he growled.

Stung, Vic raised the canteen sharply. Water spilled down his chin and splattered on his trousers. Spluttering, Maynon jerked back. "Do you want to drown me?"

"I'm trying to do you a kindness," she snapped back. "If you don't want it—"

"I don't want to be trussed up here like a fowl for roasting. Never should have come after you."

"No, you shouldn't have." Vic felt the blood rush to her ears. "I'm sorry."

Maynon sighed, rolled his head around, stretching his neck. "I almost had that bitch with you, and I coulda taken that whoreson. But she suckered me." He raised his eyes in the direction of the wound in his forehead. "How's the other rookie?"

"She's dead."

Maynon spat, scowling. "Sorry, kid." He aimed a shoulder at the loaf in her hand. "Break some of that off for me, will you?"

Smiling ruefully, Vic tore a piece of bread and put it in his mouth, then gave him some more water, careful not to spill it this time. The Relman set to guard them paced back and forth. As he chewed his second piece of bread, Maynon hooted at the guard. "Hey, what does the Relmlord want with this little twig?"

A leer split the trooper's scowl. "Some Trainer orgy. We've orders to capture the young ones like her alive."

"Shut it!" the marshall barked from the fire. Frowning, the man paced away from them.

Blanching, Vic felt sick. Could Lornk really be looking for her among all the Lathan army, or was this bizarre plot a coincidence? How many girls? She knew exactly what he would do with them—surely telepathic Lathans brought good prices on the markets in Traine. "We have to escape," she whispered to Maynon.

He stared at her, caught halfway between laughing and spitting again. "Of course. As soon as I'm untied, I'll leap up and cut all their heads off."

The guard's footsteps sounded behind her. Vic tore off another piece of bread and stuffed it in Maynon's mouth. Her back shielding her hands from the Relmans, she signed to him, "We have to try."

They developed a plan, Vic signing, Maynon asking for bread if he disagreed, water if he assented. When he had finished the bread and water, Vic stood and rubbed her knees. Maynon eyed her enviously as he rolled back onto his side. Elesendar would rise again in four hours. Four hours of darkness, another six in Elesendar's meager light, then dawn. If Relmans killed her this night, so be it, she thought. But her gut tightened, on the edge of nausea.

She pretended to sleep, watching the other troopers nod beside the fire, their voices fading into snores. The marshall disappeared, assigning someone to guard Vic and Maynon before heading for her tent. A sentry patrolled the camp, her steps measured like those of someone counting to infinity to keep awake. An hour passed, then Vic sat up and signaled the woman guarding them. "Um, excuse me, but he needs to . . ." She mimed a man urinating.

The guard glanced at Maynon skeptically. "You his mother? He hasn't said anything."

"I can Hear him thinking about it. He's got to go really bad."

The woman yawned. "Let him piss in his pants. It won't hurt him."

Vic turned away, shrugging. "All right, but we're all going to have to smell him afterward."

As Vic sat down again, the sentry came into camp. Their guard frowned and called her over. "The big Lathan has to take a leak. Can you take him for a lap?"

"I'm not helping him," the sentry warned.

"I've been trussed like this for hours," Maynon complained. "You let me take care of business, I'm not going to run off—too sore."

The women debated while Maynon taunted them, asking if they were afraid because he was a man. Finally, the sentry walked over and cut his ankles free, then stood back as he struggled to his feet. She refused to untie his hands, arguing with him as they descended the slope of the hill. Vic settled herself close to their guard, her muscles tense as she closed her eyes, trying to breathe in the same rhythm as nearby troopers. A minute ticked by. Five troopers asleep, the guard drowsy, she hoped. The woman's weapon was sheathed on her right side, farthest away from Vic. A left hander. A reluctance to kill flitted in her gut. But that dream, her smiling at Lornk, the warmth in her loins, froze the guilt, twisted it into loathing. She would not be his.

Now. Heartbeat echoing in her ears, she took one slow, deep breath like someone sighing into sleep. Then she jerked her legs up, slamming her toe into the Relman's nose, shoving the spike of bone into her brain. A squishy crunch, like a bug crushed underfoot. Vic winced at the noise, her ribs hurting. That pain is Kara's, she thought. Kara the coward. Another soldier stirred on his blanket, blinking toward them. Vic swung herself free of the woman's body, grabbed the stoneknife from her belt and threw it at the man's face. He screamed, the knife jutting under his clavicle. Vic flung herself at him, landed with her knees straddling his chest, pulled the knife out, and rammed it into his throat. The other troopers climbed to their feet, shouting. She dodged a thrown blade, dove at the grass, and rolled down the slope. Looking for Maynon, she skirted the crown of the hill, relying on the darkness to hide her tracks, hoping the troopers would run straight down. Instead, they spread out. One ran down the grass directly ahead of her. Dropping to the ground, Vic held her breath until he was below her, then sprung at his back and wrapped an arm around his shoulders. He roared and grabbed her thigh to fling her off. But the stoneknife caught his throat as he tore at her, and he collapsed as she hit the ground beside him. Vic sprinted forward, hearing Maynon hiss her name. She dropped down into a little hollow at the base of the hill, screened from above by a thicket.

"The sentry?" she gasped, cutting his hands loose.

"A few swift kicks, my girl. How many for you?"

"Three." They broke out of the hollow, running across a flat expanse of grass at the bottom of the hill. Maynon puffed beside her, his strides limping, then grabbed Vic's arm and tugged her down. The beam from a hooded lantern swung over them. Maynon grimaced, his face almost black in the darkness, his blood an ugly shadow. "My knees are sore," he grumbled.

"We'll never make it back to the Lathan lines tonight," Vic whispered.

"Brilliant deduction."

Suppressing a growl, she looked toward the Relman fires. At how many campsites did other girls lay bound, ready to be taken to Lordhome and Traine. "Look," she said suddenly, her voice assuming the authority of a Logkeeper. "All this business capturing young girls is because of me—"

"What?" Maynon scoffed. "The Relmlord have a personal vendetta against *you*?"

"You can do what you want tonight," she went on, "but I'm going to try to rescue other prisoners. The Relmlord will sell them in Traine, and I wouldn't wish that on my worst enemy." Not even Kara.

Maynon lay speechless. He looked at the fires, at the stars, his mouth grim. "Madness," he muttered. "Crazy insanity." Then he eyed her. "Wish I'd looked the other way when I saw those two hauling your ass off the field. But since I can't sit by a fire with my pipe, I might as well help you."

Vic smiled, but a lump blocked her throat. Swallowing hard, she pointed across the grass. "If we head for that gully—"

"What gully?"

She blinked at him. "The one on the map. We're about a league south of the battlefield. There was this string of hills like a necklace, then this flat area—"

"You memorized all that?"

Shouts echoed across the grass, lamps bouncing among running figures. "We need weapons, Maynon. Can we ambush them in the gully—is that a good plan?"

"As good as any, kid."

They sprinted, diving and lying still whenever a beam rippled their way. Reaching an embankment, they leapt down, splashed into water, then ran downstream, hoping the burbling creek would wash footprints away. In a stand of trees, Vic hid behind a curtain of exposed roots while Maynon grabbed a heavy stone from the creek bed and swung himself into some overhanging branches. They waited, hoping their pursuers would split into small groups when they reached the stream. Orders echoed toward them. Minutes later, a pair of troopers ran along the rim of the gully, a third splashing through the stream, lamps flashing on the water. Vic pressed herself deeper into the shadows, her breath still in her throat. As the man in the creek passed beneath his tree, Maynon dropped on top of him, knocking him facedown in the water, and slammed his rock into the man's skull.

The other Relmans leapt at Maynon, and Vic sprang from her hiding spot and stabbed one in the back, the razor sharp stone sliding easily through the woman's ribs. Maynon sparred with the other, water flying around them in black droplets. The woman fell, coughing blood into the stream; Vic swiped the bow off her back, yanked her quiver free, and climbed the embankment. Arrow nocked, she took aim, but Maynon already had the third trooper down.

Stripping the Relman weapons, they doused the lamps and sprinted toward the center of the Relman line. In a copse, they paused to catch their breath. Vic's ears pricked, and she held her breath, signaling Maynon to quiet his own gasps. Jeering laughter filtered through the leaves, voices egging each other on. Muffled whimpers and choked screams punctuated the glee. Vic knew that suffering; even if Kara had submitted to Lornk, Vic never had in that room in Traine. Ears burning, she hissed, "I thought Relmans were supposed to be just as prudish as Lathans."

Maynon's spittle thwacked against a fallen trunk. "Rape's a killing offense, but folk still do it."

Stealing toward the noises, they stopped outside a circle of firelight. A Relman man and woman lounged near the coals, giggling while a third, trousers pushed to his knees, pressed himself into a dusky woman, gagged and stripped, each hand bound to an ankle.

"Think of it as training, honey," the woman taunted.

"Training for Traine," the watching man said, laughing.

Cold rippled from the roots of Vic's hair, encasing her heart in ice. Her fingers tightened around the hilt of the stoneknife, then loosened, sure of their grip. The shadow of Lornk's hand encircled her throat, and her nostrils flared at the rutty stench pervading the campsite. Never, she promised herself. Never his. Striding into the circle of light, she jabbed the stoneknife through the ear of the woman, leapt over the fire, and rammed the blade through the eye of the man, then straddled the rapist, pressing the knife edge against his throat.

"Pull out—gently," she whispered. He complied, eyes rolling between her and his dead companions. "Maynon, I want him bound like her."

Maynon's eyes were just as big as the rapist's, but he stepped over to the captured woman. "You'll need some twine." Cutting her loose, he pulled off his tunic and gave it to her, then tied the Relman hand to foot while Vic kept the knife at his throat.

Once he was bound, Vic went to the Lathan woman. "What's your name?"

Shivering, she huddled within Maynon's tunic. Her eyes darted between Vic, Maynon, and the Relman, then she pressed her lips together and answered. "Silla of Pilagg. I was with the Thirty-second. Can I kill him?"

Vic shook her head. "I need him to give a message to the Relmlord." Facing the Relman, she said, "You caught the wrong girl. But if you had got the right one, do you have any idea what he would have done to you?"

The man's eyes flicked to Silla, then to his shriveled privates.

"He might have started there." Vic smirked, tapping the blade against her palm. Ice still enveloped her heart, but she felt a heat in her loins she hadn't felt since those last moments in Traine. "In fact, he might still. Maynon, hold him down."

"Vic—"

"Hold him!"

Silla strode over and pushed the Relman into the dirt. She pressed her palms into his shoulders, Maynon's tunic falling over his face. "Enjoy the view, asshole," she grated, giving Vic a grim nod.

Maynon grabbed the man's legs, and Vic sliced open his shirt, handing Silla a swath of fabric to force between his teeth. "I hope they find you in time," she said as she cut. Shrieks muffled, the man jolted and bucked, but her comrades held him. "I almost wish I could be there when the Relmlord sees this. I hope you're still alive, so he can tell you what your punishment would have been, had it been me you found. Knowing him, he probably won't tell you—he'll show you."

"You're the one they wanted?" Silla asked over the man's gagged scream.

Vic pointed to the name carved into the man's bloody chest. "That's what he called me."

"Kara. Like the wizard."

Vic shrugged, then read aloud the message she'd cut into the man's skin. "I raped a girl I thought was Kara." Standing, she touched her tongue to the blade, relishing the iron. "I really hope you're still alive when your comrades find you. If you are, when you see Lornk Korng, tell him Victoria of Ourtown will *never* be his. She's a Lathan now."

CHAPTER 11

WORK OF THE DAGGER

"You've done good work, Captain. I congratulate you." The fieldmarshall sipped his tea. "It's an ugly business, what Relmans do with prisoners."

"Yes, sir, it is," Vic replied. Command had called it a miracle when she, Maynon, and Silla had walked into Summerquarters with ten other troopers. More than four years had passed, and in that time Vic had lost count of the Relmans she'd killed, but not the three hundred and two Lathans she'd saved from the auction block. Relmans had found good money in the sale of Lathan slaves, and now they tried to take anyone, man or woman, strong enough for the mines or comely enough for the mistress mart. An ugly business, worthy of Lornk, and one she'd dedicated herself to fighting through the two years spent as an ordinary trooper and one as a lieutenant. In the year and a half since she made captain and got command of her own patrol, she'd doubled her tally of rescues. She smirked to herself, thinking how Lornk had wanted her devotion, and she'd given it to him after all. "I'd like to rest my troops for a few days," she told Henrik.

He swallowed more tea. "You can have one night. The Relmans are up to something. We've got massive troop movements headed in this direction." He tapped a map. "I need you to scout it."

"I will, sir. I'm a man short though. Can you find me another?"

Reluctantly, the marshall let go of his warm mug to shuffle through the papers on his desk. "Some rookies were released from training last week. Don't scowl at me, Captain. You did very well on your first mission. I'll let you take the best of them. Coastman named Geram. He's a crack archer."

Vic smoothed the frown out of her mouth. "Thank you, sir. I'll go find him."

The wind knifed through her cloak when she stepped out of the fieldmarshall's cabin. Shrugging the fur up around her ears, Vic headed through the trees toward the archers' quarters. The tents and cabins were all hastily assembled and in poor repair. Tired of trade embargoes, Lathan merchants wanted the war over. They'd get their wish all too soon if the Senate didn't boost army funds. As it was, Lornk's forces, better manned, better equipped, had pushed the border ten leagues deep into Lathan territory. This year, Command feared, he'd push it halfway to Erin.

That thought stopped her, and she put her hand on a tree to steady herself. For every prisoner she saved, every Relman officer she killed, it seemed like Lornk added another squadron of troopers. At this rate, his army would roll into Narath in another two summers. Boisterous laughter burst from a nearby cabin. She shivered, determined to find her new man and get back to her own quarters. This winter was too damn cold.

Coming out of the archers' cabin, a lieutenant gave her a look just a hair shy of a glare and saluted. "I'm here for Geram of Alna," she said in clipped tones. "Is he inside?"

He nodded. "He's just packing up for you."

"Packing up? He was only just assigned."

The lieutenant grinned tightly. "He Heard you coming for him. Use him well, Captain. We don't get many of his kind down here."

Vic sighed and cloaked her thoughts. Another Listener. The army recruited them as counselors, meant to help troopers deal with the "horror of war" and all that rubbish. In her early days, one had shadowed her on every assignment, and their reports had seeded a creeper of suspicion and innuendo that still wound around her, sparking vile rumors about how she got promotions. Loremaster Silnauer wasn't the only Lathan to jump to conclusions about Vic based on those three months she'd spent in Lornk's thrall. Prudery and jealousy stirred an ugly pot, and a lot of other officers didn't believe the Relmlord's mistress deserved a command in Latha's army, much less was capable of one. Vic smiled to herself. They should ask the Relman fieldmarshalls she'd killed under the noses of their guards. They should ask the Lathan prisoners she had brought home. Three hundred and two Lathans could vouch for her.

Shrine, what was taking so long? An archer, a Listener, and a rookie from Alna, a sea town more than fifty miles from any forest, much less the Kiareinoll. Useless and dangerous in one package. Her feet sunk into half-frozen mud, and ice bled through boot leather and wool socks. Grumbling, she flexed her toes to ward off the cold. The door finally sprang open for a stocky man juggling a pack and bow. She put her hands on her hips as he saluted her, dropping the bow.

"When you're ready, fisher."

He nodded, flashing white teeth in a dark brown face. "I thought you might be in a hurry."

She snorted. "Some Listener. No, take your time. I enjoy standing in the freezing wind waiting for my troops to get their shit together."

His gear sorted, he stood waiting for her to lead the way.

"You don't know already?" she asked. "I thought by now you'd know where my party's housed, how much ale we have, and my grandmother's pet name for me. You lead the way, trooper."

The sun sinking into a cloudless dusk, Silla and Maynon slipped into the dell where the Dagger camped. Vic had lost touch with them for a few years—Silla had been transferred to desk duty in Narath after her rescue, and Maynon had been promoted and assigned to another party—but when Vic received her captain's laurels, he'd turned up and offered himself as her second, and Silla had herself transferred back to the front, claiming she'd only been waiting for Vic to have her own patrol.

"We counted fifty tents," Maynon said, "two wagons, a marshall's canvas, and a cabin."

Vic nodded. "Good work. Thrusher, you and the others get back to Command and tell them what they're up against here. Maynon, stay with me to do some mischief."

Maynon's grin brightened, but Geram rose from his place near the fire. "I don't think that's a good idea, Captain."

Vic blinked at him. Someone laughed, a muffled chortle. "Why?"

"As the captain, you are too valuable to risk losing to the Relmans. The regulations clearly—"

The party's laughter cut him off. "Querkle, they call us the Dagger," Vic said. "What do they call me?"

"The Blade, sir."

"Why do you suppose that is, Geram?"

"Because you're the one who strikes deepest, I know. If you insist on staying here yourself, you should at least have someone with you who can protect you."

Maynon bristled. "What was that, fishlicker?"

"Ho, Maynon, settle that when we're out of Relman earshot. I think Geram means his Listening."

The rookie nodded. "Even Relmans can think quietly. But I can Hear them."

Vic took out her dagger and cleaned a fingernail with the tip. Maynon's pride would be hurt, but his ego needed it sometimes. Besides, he *was* her second, and she'd been reprimanded more than once for leaving the party without an officer in charge. "OK, let's see what you can do. Maynon, you're my best, but you Listen about as well as I do. With ten score Relmans in that camp, I'd like to avoid fighting while I can."

His smile gone, Maynon nodded. Later that night, he settled his blanket next to hers. "I don't like you heading off with some Alnan cad who doesn't know a tree from a bush," he whispered, nodding at Geram, asleep in his bedroll.

"Still trying to save my ass?" she teased.

"You still need it," he grumbled.

The next morning, snowshoes bound to feet, the party left for Winterquarters while Vic led Geram in the opposite direction. "Hope you don't mind being cold," she said as they searched for a cerrenil where they could hole up without the benefit of fire. He shrugged, but the shrug turned to a shiver. Vic chuckled to herself. If she'd brought Maynon, he would already have been whining about his toes and nose. "At least you have a beard," she would crack back. "Look at me, bare-faced to the wind, and I don't complain like a toddler to his mommy." Geram walked beside her, clearing his throat from time to time as if he wanted to say something, but he kept silent until she bent down, dug into the snow, and pulled up a few drerwood leaves. In her pack, she carried some of the Dagger's special poison—a sulfur clay she would plant in the Relman commander's tent when Henrik's companies attacked. She needed drer leaves to wrap the clay and for fuses.

"Aren't you afraid carrying explosives on your back?" he asked when she told him to look for more leaves.

"No. You have to light it, fisher. I do *try* to keep my pack away from campfires."

He nodded solemnly. "I'll remember."

They found a cerrenil with a good view of the Relmans' camp and used their snowshoes to dig out a cave beside the trunk, lining it with evergreen bows. Vic pulled a book from her pack, climbed the tree, and settled in. Geram followed her up and looked toward the camp, shading his eyes against the sun.

"Don't tell me you're farsighted as well." She peered at him over the pages of her book—*A Treatise on the Origins of Mindspeech*. She'd picked it up from the Winterquarters library after Geram joined the patrol.

"A little." He laughed quietly to himself. "It helps when you're a useless archer."

She swallowed her irritation and hid behind the *Treatise*. She'd hoped the book would help her learn how to defend her mind better against his like, but the first chapters droned nonsense about Elesendar endowing Lathans with the gift of telepathy because they lived in the Kiareinoll, His chosen land.

The afternoon dragged. They watched clouds roll in over the mountains, glad of the snowfall, cover for their tracks. Darting through the fat flakes, a pair of warblers harried Vic until she moved to another branch, whereupon the leathery birds squeezed through a hole in the trunk. As dusk fell, Vic shut the book and watched one fire after another spring into view. Soon the Relman campsite winked at them like the many-faceted eye of a terpwe.

"What's a terpwe?" Geram asked.

Vic huffed and swung out of the tree. "It's a big, bird-sized insect that lives in the north, in your Unknown. Will you please stop that?"

"I can't help it," he said. "An unmuffled thought to me is like a spoken word. I can even Hear the Relmans over there." The cerrenil's branches going limp in the failing light, he rode down and stepped smoothly off onto the snow. Vic frowned at his acrobatics, then unfolded her bedroll and crawled inside the cave to spread the blanket over the boughs.

"Don't try to impress me, Geram," she said, coming out and settling next to him on the snow.

"Just trying to keep up, Captain."

She looked at him out of the corner of her eye. His face was shadowed, but his voice had been earnest, not flattering. In the week since she picked him up at Winterquarters, she'd watched him move about the woods with an ease few rookies had, showing a deftness with bow and dagger that put the lie to his clumsy act when they met. She reached over to her pack and pulled out a flatcake for herself and one for him. "How long have you been in the army? Two years? Five?"

He hesitated as he took the cake from her, then his lips curved back from those very white teeth. "They told me I wouldn't be able to fool you."

The skin around her eyes tightened suddenly. After all she'd done, the bloody marshalls had set another Listener on her. And this one had the audacity to tell her straight out what he was. She should have known. "Why?" she grated.

"A Blade has two edges, sir."

Her hair bristled at the nape of her neck. "After all this time, they're still afraid I'll betray them? A Blade has two edges? I have more reason to hate the Relmlord than any of those fat bastards in Narath who've never even seen him!"

He shushed her, his hands urging calm. "They know that. You've had more opportunities to betray them than they could count back to me in the briefing. But . . ." He cleared his throat; he probably wasn't supposed to say this much. "They're worried your early experiences left you . . ."

"What? Mad?"

"Captain, all those years ago, why did you escape from the Relmans?"

"What kind of question is that? Isn't it *normal* to try to escape from your enemies? Wouldn't you have escaped, had you the chance?"

He looked out toward the Relman camp. Far to the east, the sinking sun still caught the leading edge of the cloud bank, turning it pink. The clouds deepened to purple as they watched, Vic fuming.

When Geram finally answered her, the air was black with shadows, and snow whispered around them. "They sent me to watch you because your missions are getting too risky. The division counselor thought she caught a hint of a death wish in you, and they assigned me to find out its strength, and treat it if I could."

"She was wrong," Vic answered hollowly. "I don't want to die." But Kara—she squashed that thought, scuttled it away before she could finish it and he Hear it.

"Why did you escape that time you were captured?" he asked again.

She didn't want him to know, but it was as if he were drawing the words up from a deep well in a bucket, and once it reached the surface, he would see the answer before she could turn the bucket over and dump it away. "I wasn't ready to face him."

"The Relmlord."

One curt nod.

"And now?"

"I'm not his anymore." She hadn't felt Kara's longing in a long time. "I'd like to spit in his face so he knows it."

"And you want to get captured again so you can do that?"

"That question is even stupider than asking me why I wanted to escape. I don't want to be captured. I *do* want to be the one who takes Lordhome. I'd like to see him grovel at my feet. That's what I want, Lieutenant."

"What makes you think I'm an officer?"

"Please. All army shrinks are officers. Go tell Command that's why I've tried so hard to rise so fast. Make them promote me to fieldmarshall and give me five battalions I can drive straight across the Relman plains and up to Lordhome." She crawled into their cave. "You take first watch, fisher. I'm going to bed."

† † †

"She's unpredictable, unstable," Marshall Huron had told him. "Watch her close—but if she finds out your mission, beware. You might find yourself trussed up and left in the middle of a Relman camp." A soft guffaw leaked out of Geram's throat as he thought of that last warning from Huron. He'd half believed it, after everything they'd told him to expect. He did not expect her to pick him for a shrink so fast, but after a week in her company, he could see he'd have more success being honest about his mission than trying to trick her.

What he'd seen the past week also put the lie to gossip that she had seduced half of Command to rise as fast as she had. He hadn't seen her in action yet, but Vic framed herself in sharp elbows and the curled sneers of a committed soldier, not the welcoming curves and willing smiles of a seductress. Whatever she'd learned as a Trainer mistress, she'd squashed and locked it away so well she seemed blind to the passions roiling within her own party. He snorted softly, thinking of Maynon and Silla. Like most inlanders, that pair cloaked their passions in prudery, but Geram would lay odds they'd consummate before winter ended. The question was, would they declare it? Among inlanders, a first bedding was a wedding—a mad custom that had half the nation trysting in secret. And two thirds of the military, since marriage was forbidden among combat troops. Geram smiled, glad to be from Alna, where people passed under the arches to wed with a Loremaster to bless them. In Alna, you went into marriage sober and with your eyes open.

He shivered and dozed through his watch, rocking himself with his hands and knees drawn under his cloak and blanket, his feet numb. A month from the solstice, twenty hours passed before dawn. The first time they traded the watch, Vic yawned and stretched but was out of the snow cave and alert on her blanket in the course of a minute. When she woke him for his second watch, he took longer. Settling himself under the swaying cerrenil boughs, Elesendar peeked over the mountains, beginning His second quest across the sky. He'd start a third before dawn. In the dale below, most of the Relman fires had died, leaving only a circle of watch fires that winked as the guards passed. The world eerie and beautiful like the reefs off Ildrich Duin at night, the snow reflected the starlight, sharpening the shadows moving softly in the breeze. To keep awake, he pretended the snow drifts were whitecaps and he and his uncle were racing for the Flag, as they had done just before he'd left to join the army. He imagined the spray slapping him in the face and felt the halyard rip through callused hands as they jibed around the first buoy and the wind caught him off guard. Uncle Arnan shouted and Geram pulled on the line, laughing at the sea splashing across the deck. He had daydreamed that memory so many times he could smell the brine and hear the luff of the sail as it searched for fresh wind.

He could hear his uncle's voice yelling—aloud in the excitement of the race—for him to go to the bow and reach out for the Flag. "I'll handle the sail and the tiller, boy. Get me that flag before you go." The sour reality was that he hadn't been able to stretch far enough and take the Flag, and before they could come about for another pass, Larame's skiff had swooped in and won it. But in the daydream, his fingers stretched the extra inches and snagged the red silk from the wind's grasp. In the dream, when they got back to the harbor, his uncle banged him on the shoulders and bought him a tankard with their prize money. In reality, Uncle Arnan had shaken his head and apologized that he hadn't gotten the boat close enough to the buoy. Geram had bought the tankard that day with an advance on his pay.

Whimpering cries from the cave brought him to the present. Vic was dreaming, and he caught glimpses of stone walls and cold hands. This he shut out. Dreams were too private. Like stuffing wool in his ears, he closed his mind to hers and Listened for Relmans instead. He could just catch snatches of their spoken conversations, could just Hear about that one's new baby nephew, or that other one's losses at dice. But Vic's cries cut through his concentration. Awake, she was sobbing quietly. He coughed, and the sobs stopped. A moment later she came out and sat beside him.

"Do you dream of him often?" he asked after a minute.

"Is that the shrink asking or just insidious curiosity?"

"Both."

"I don't need therapy, I need revenge," she snapped. A moment later, she asked sarcastically, "And what made you join up? Patriotism?"

"Yes." Patriotism, and a sour ending of things with Ideigin, but the captain didn't need to know about Geram's failed love affairs.

"You're Alnan!"

"Yes, I'm Alnan. And Alna is part of Latha."

"Barely," she scoffed. "Your Senator is undermining everything we're doing out here. The Relmans are winning because of him."

Geram raised his hands in protest. "I'm as loyal to the monarchy as you are, Captain."

"I don't fight for them."

"You fight for revenge."

"Damn right." She unplaited her waist-length hair and began to comb it, grimacing and tugging on the tangles while he watched the fires in the distance. He Heard nothing but her frustration with her hair until she startled him with a question.

"How do you Listen?"

He raised an eyebrow. "I've never thought about it. I just do it."

"I've been reading this book," she hinted. He had seen it and chosen to ignore the taunt. When he refused to acknowledge it, she changed her tack. "When I first came to Latha, actually in Traine too, people would Hear my thoughts without my projecting them. Were they Listening?"

"No. You don't really project your thoughts now so much as you hide them. You must not have known how to hide them then, and that's how people knew what you said."

"That explains why I couldn't lie at first."

"You probably started to learn how to hide your thoughts as soon as you felt others Hearing them, though I'm no linguist. Maybe your book—"

"Useless crap," she spat.

Grinning, Geram explained what he could. "Most people, even Lathans, tend to think in complete sentences, or at least in words. Anyone with mindspeech can Hear those thoughts, but the thought you have before you utter the words with your mind voice—only Listeners can Hear that in someone else's mind."

"You mean that flash of meaning that your mind voice takes and shapes into words."

"Yes."

"So you're a Listener, because you can hear those thoughts?" Grunting, she moved back into the cave. "Wake me when your watch is over."

The snow began again during Vic's watch and lasted through the morning. She moved them farther south, taking advantage of the weather to scout the area all the way round the Relman camp. Cerrenils, evergreens, geilmors stood around them like sentries, passing them from glade to grove. Breezes whistled softly in the branches above them, a ghost's moaning punctuated by the crunch of snow falling from tree limbs. After scouting the Relman perimeter, they found a tiny cave at the base of a pile of granite boulders within shouting distance of the camp sentries. Hidden by a dense stand of trees, the hollow was close enough that Vic thought they could sneak past the guards that night. This was the kind of stunt Geram had been ordered to prevent if he could, but her eyes dared him to stop her when he told her so. "Command has never complained when I've stabbed from behind before. I don't understand what their problem is now."

"They can't be sure you'll take adequate measures to protect yourself."

"That's why I brought you, Geram. Aren't you adequate?"

He had to clear his throat at that. They huddled inside the cave together for the rest of the afternoon, speaking very little. Now and then he caught wisps of her unworded thoughts: a stoneknife sweeping down into a belly, a hand caressing a naked hip, an explosion of fire through an open door. He sensed nothing of her emotions as she remembered these things—that was his one failing as a Listener. All too often he couldn't tell how people felt about their thoughts, only that they had them.

At sunset, they dined on flatcakes the captain pulled out of her pack, apologizing for the handfuls of snow needed to choke them down. After they ate, they diced and shared stories, finding an unexpected kinship in both being orphaned, and her ideas about Elesendar being a spacefaring vessel reminded him of the heretics who would gather in his aunt's tavern. As they talked, clouds rolled in again, bringing pitch darkness.

"Snow's going to start soon," Vic said. "Let's go."

He crawled out of the cave after her. The air was frozen still. When the clouds broke, it would be ice that fell. They padded from tree to tree, passing easily in the darkness through the sentry lines. More than a few Relmans still gathered close to their fires, and Geram Heard Vic's longing for that warmth as they flitted among the surrounding tents. Smoke filling his nostrils, he too felt the agony of a starving pauper outside the baker's.

Vic navigated them around the perimeter first, counting tents and fires. Geram envied her clean chin as his week-old beard gathered icicles. Circling deeper, they finally came across a rough shack next to a large tent crowned with the Relmlord's banner. "I'm surprised Fembrosh permitted that," she muttered, touching a knot, still oozing sap, on the green wood. Geram shook his head. She didn't believe Elesendar was a god, but she thought trees could move. He would have reported that as delusional, except most of his superiors also believed the forest had powers. "Is it guarded?"

He Listened, then shook his head. "Three or four people are sleeping inside, but no one guards the door." He paused a moment. "A trooper is walking toward us from around that pavilion."

She nodded and they circled to the front of the cabin. Very gently, she put her hand on the knob and tested the door for squeaks. It scraped against the frame, but, opening the door slowly, she kept the sound to a whisper. Geram had to admire her skill. "Stay here," she ordered, and he caught something in her thoughts about large, clunky men. Sighing, he crouched down in the shadows by the doorway while she slipped inside.

The patrolling guard came around the side of the building. Covering his eyes with his hands, Geram peered at her through his fingers. She hummed softly to herself, hugging her cloak around her. Geram aimed a quick message to Vic to stay inside, but otherwise didn't think at all. The woman yawned, but her eyes flicked around and came to rest on the spot where he crouched. As she stepped closer, he concentrated on nothing. He projected nothingness into her mind. She blinked, stepped back, then crossed the space between the cabin and the marshall's tent, moving out of sight. With a whisper, the cabin door opened, and Vic stepped out.

Her eyes were wide and glowed dimly green, even in the darkness. She shivered and waved him to follow her with ghostly hands. He Heard no thoughts from her as they dodged back to their cave, and they moved so quickly he felt warm when they crawled inside, but Vic shivered uncontrollably, her jaw clenched.

"What's wrong?" he asked. She answered him only with sharply swallowed breaths. He wrapped his blanket as well as her own around her. "What did you see?"

Shaking her head, she grabbed his hand. Hers felt like a claw of ice as she clung to him. She said nothing, but he Heard over and over, "Don't leave me. I need you."

CHAPTER 12

TWO EDGES

Inside the cabin, the air was toasty warm, thanks to a lot of mud caulk and one of those stone furnaces the Relman marshalls hauled with them. The fire's glow cast dim light over several figures snoring under blankets. She wound carefully through the sleepers to a table at the far end of the room. A quill pen, some books, a map, and several large sheets of paper lay on the table, the light too dim to read anything. Her hand strayed across the table as she debated whether to take the papers. That sort of theft was folly—better to leave no trace she'd been here.

As she crept toward the door, one of the sleepers stirred. A blanket fell away from a rising head and shoulders, and Vic leapt toward the figure with her dagger and a silent curse. Slamming a hand over his mouth, she plunged the blade into his stomach. So much for no trace—Huron would have her hide, and Geram's too. She yanked the dagger out, aimed for his neck to finish him.

"Kara," he gasped.

Her hand froze and her eyes met his. In the dim red light, dark blue irises looked black, blond hair gray. He moaned that name again, eyes closing as blood welled from his belly. Heart pounding, she sheathed the dagger, covered him with his blanket. At the door, she waited until the Relman guard's footsteps faded, then slipped out and led Geram back to the cave.

She had never moved so furtively or so carefully out of an enemy's camp. But when they reached the cave, her body began to shake. She wanted to tell Geram she wasn't cold when he wrapped the blankets around her, but her thoughts were glaciated. She squeezed his hand, trying to thank him for his efforts, and then she didn't let go. As her teeth chattered and spasm after spasm shivered down her back, Geram took her in his arms and asked her again what had happened. She couldn't answer him. He finally gave up and fell asleep.

He woke when the first rumbles of thunder outside mirrored the whimpers coming from her throat. As the wind outside began to howl, her first scream echoed through the cave. The first crash of lightning shattered the crystalline box in which she'd locked Kara, the clockwork doll. As ice burst from the clouds and sheared through the forest, grief exploded within her.

† † †

The first night in Traine, when she didn't take his hand, Lornk's smile had deepened, growing sadder and kinder. He had picked her up off the floor, pulled the bedcover out of her grasp, and declared, "In time, you'll be the envy of every mistress in Traine."

The next morning, he brought a damp cloth from the bathroom and mopped the salt from her cheeks. "I shall call you Kara," he whispered.

A new tide of tears rising, she had swallowed and shook her head. "My name is Victoria."

"Such a treasure you are," Lornk had exclaimed. He knelt beside the bed, took her hands, kissed her on the forehead. "I'm the luckiest man in the world, Kara." So he took her name and gave her a new one.

Thereafter, he told her each night how her skin shone like Elesendar, every morning how her hair shimmered like the dawn, every afternoon how her eyes glowed like dewed grass. What the world thought of her ceased to matter because he became her world. So he took her shame and gave her beauty.

When her memory stumbled over passages of the Logs she had known as well as the streets of Ourtown, Lornk showed her the tenets of passion, and she proved herself an adept pupil—as quick an apprentice to Lornk as she had been to Martha. She knew when he wished her to approach him, when he wanted her to lay quietly while he explored the terrain of her skin, when to create, when to wait. So he took her profession and gave her a vocation.

When she was alone, she often imagined walking with him through the city's streets, saw herself at his side, her chin up in the same air of pride she saw in the mistresses who passed beneath her window. The pregnant mistress she had seen the first day walked by at the same time nearly every afternoon, her master always doting, glowing with pride. The woman grew huge, walked more and more slowly; then they disappeared. Some weeks later, Lornk called her to the window and pointed to the couple, out for the first time with the baby.

"Would you like that?" he asked her, draping an arm over her shoulder.

The woman, clothed in red and white silk, no longer wore jeweled leather around her neck or wrists. Beside her, the man carried the child in his arms. Both nodded and smiled at everyone they passed. Vic looked up at Lornk, unsure whether he meant the baby or the woman's freedom. He watched the couple enviously, a wistful frown on his lips. She felt very acutely the pressure of his hand on her shoulder, the strength of his fingers, the tendons in his forearm, his biceps. She felt that strength pour into her, course with her blood through her heart to the tips of her fingers and toes. The ghost of an ache swept through her womb, and she imagined herself presenting him with a tiny form, snowy down on its head, chubby fingers clutching the air. In return he would clothe her in silk, open the gates of his home so she could leave as she chose, return to him and their child when she wanted. Among the Oreseekers she had never imagined herself a mother, only a teacher. As she'd never expected to have it, she never thought to want what he offered. Trembling, she leaned against him and wrapped an arm around his waist. "Yes," she said. "Yes, I would like that."

He smiled and squeezed her shoulders, bending down to kiss the top of her head. "Then you shall have it. But not now. You're too young, too small yet. It might hurt you. We'll let you grow a little."

There were other times when he spoke of their future, promising a life filled with love, with devotion—not only hers to him, but his to her. She indulged in the visions he fed her, and they slid down her throat like well-aged liquor, harsh at first but seductive as she grew accustomed to the flavor. Then he left, taking the bottle with him.

† † †

"I truly wanted to die that day," Vic said as the thunder faded. She described Lornk's return, the fight in the library, the flight toward the Device and its promise of oblivion. "I was scared of what I'd become if I stayed with him, but sometimes I wonder if I was also scared of losing his . . ." She gulped, unable to say it.

"Love?" Geram asked.

Shuddering, she nodded.

"What happened in the cabin?" Blood rushing past her ears, Vic bit her fingers to keep from screaming. "Deep breaths," he told her. "Slow breaths. Let me Hear it if you can't tell me."

Drawing air in slowly through her nose, Vic pulled clenched fingers out of her mouth. She took one, two, three, then a fourth breath before she found the strength to speak. "I killed him."

"Who?"

"Lornk Korng. He was in the cabin. I didn't know it was him until my knife was in his belly. I killed him."

Geram let out a long, slow breath himself. "You're sure?"

She nodded. His blood had poured over her hand; she tasted it on her fingers. She hadn't slit his throat, but blood had welled from his belly. Fat Lathan crystal daggers made gaping, ugly wounds. He had to be dead. He had to be.

"This could mean the war's over," Geram whispered.

Vic rolled over and grasped his collar. "You don't understand. I killed him." Her voice caught in her throat and rose in pitch as she said the words out loud. "I killed him." Letting him go, she curled up in a ball. "I killed him."

Geram had never seen anyone so broken. Command had assigned him to watch over the captain because they thought an Alnan could grasp the mind of a Trainer mistress. But inlanders never understood that for Alnans, desire and love flowed in separate currents, and Alnans charted their romances as consciously as a sailor chooses his tack. Vic, like too many inlanders, had been caught by those currents and drowned. He felt her reaching out to him, begging him to drag her back to land, but right then, another urgency overcame his concern. The Relmlord was wounded, possibly dead. And hundreds of Relman troopers camped within shouting distance.

"Vic—Captain," he grated, shaking her arm. "We have to leave now. Before they find him. When they do, they'll comb this area like a husbandman looking for fleas. The storm's over; we've got about four hours before dawn." He paused, wrestling with the fear gripping him by the throat. "They're not going to overlook this cave."

She lay with her hands over her ears. "Vic," he dug his fingers into her shoulder, "I don't want to die in a Relman prison. The war could be over now, but that won't stop them killing us if they find us, or worse."

"I can't," she whispered.

Now he was the one taking deep breaths, beating back panic. "Captain, I need your help to get out of here."

He felt the knots in her shoulders suddenly relax. Wordlessly, she rose to her knees and started packing the blankets away. She was so silent that he'd have thought no one was there if he couldn't feel her next to him in the cramped space. Still, her hands moved, preparing to leave. He guessed that if she'd been alone, she would have stayed here until they found her. Geram relaxed a little. He at least wouldn't see the dungeons in Lordhome.

As they crawled out of the cave, a warbler's cry shattered the frozen air. Their breath dusted the front of their cloaks with tiny crystals of ice. Skirting the Relman camp, they walked north and east. The storm had stripped away limbs twice as thick as his thigh, scattering them like twigs. Thunder sounded far to the east, and the wind carried the groans of dying trees. Vic slid over the branches and through the bracken like a nymph. Stumbling after her, Geram panted with the effort of keeping up. If he lagged too far behind, she would stop and wait, dancing from foot to foot. But she never reproached him, never looked at him at all, but kept her eyes focused on a tree or rock far ahead of them. He still Heard nothing from her, and he wondered if she went mad, if he'd be able to Hear it.

Dawn broke, the sun peeking briefly between mountains and clouds, painting the landscape a dusty red. Vic dropped them down into a gully and drew rations out of her pack. Geram's fingers frozen, he had trouble holding the flatcake. Vic ate hers quickly, consuming without tasting, her eyes bright green. The snow, glowing in the dawn, had more color than her face. Removing a glove, she thrust her bare hand into a drift, ignoring the jagged ice around her wrist. Blood stained the handful of ice crystals she pulled out; her stare silenced his protests. Bile rose from his stomach, as bitter as it had been when he hadn't caught the flag for his uncle. She had saved him from a Relman prison, but he'd failed to save her.

She didn't let them rest long. The sun disappeared above the clouds, the light turning gray and dim. Geram imagined the Relmans waking to find their lord, a wound shaped like a Lathan dagger in his belly. Would they think the assassin one of their own, or would they immediately suspect the Blade? If so, they'd waste no time fanning northward. Or perhaps the Relmlord's death would throw them into confusion, and they'd still be in chaos when the Lathan companies found the camp.

They moved. His thighs shook every time he put a foot down, his knees jelly. Vic looked more and more like a ghost. But they moved steadily north. At the end of the first day, they passed out of the storm's path and found a village road. His ankles felt like they'd shed ten-pound weights on the flat surface. Trotting forward, both ignored their fatigue. Still, the trees passed slowly on either side. Geram imagined Relman voices erupting behind them, a shower of arrows, a fall, capture.

When Elesendar rose, Vic stopped them to rest. Geram tried to stay awake, to talk to her, but she refused to answer him and he dozed fitfully. Before midnight, they were moving again. Elesendar shone in a cloudless sky, just touching the tops of the trees. Around them, the woods pulsed with magic.

Woodscent filled Geram's nostrils, giving him strength. A nightwing hooted them onward. He felt the forest urging them home. Then he Heard Vic's thoughts echo his. She believed the Kiareinoll wanted them to live. Color appeared in her cheeks.

Close to dawn, a Lathan scout dropped out of a tree onto the road in front of them. Geram saluted and explained they had come from the Relman camp and needed to see Command immediately. The scout directed them up the road, saying they would find the marshall's camp two leagues farther on.

The sky glowed like a bright blue gem when they walked into Marshall Huron's tent. Scowling, he demanded Vic tell him why they had left the Relman camp early.

"The Relmlord is dead," Vic said, taking a steaming cup from the hand of a shocked aide.

Huron's jaw dropped open. "How?"

Vic looked at her tea. When a minute passed in silence, Huron growing redder by the second, Geram cleared his throat and stood at attention. "The Blade killed him, sir."

"Lieutenant"—Huron turned on him—"you were supposed to prevent these antics! How did this happen?"

As succinctly as he could, Geram told him Vic had figured out he was a counselor, not a green recruit. Then he described how they had gone into the Relman camp to become acquainted with it before the Lathan troops arrived, and how Vic had entered the cabin, found the Relmlord there, and killed him. "We came back as fast as we could, sir."

Huron's eyes shifted from one to the other during Geram's story. Vic stood silently drinking her tea, her face white, her eyes as green as a cerrenil in spring.

"Captain," Huron snapped at Vic. "Are you sure he's dead? Are you even sure it was him?"

Vic looked up, her eyes glowing with—what, hope? Geram cursed his skill that he couldn't Hear feelings. "It looked like him." She paused, one corner of her mouth creeping up, her eyes on the ground. "It smelled like him. I sunk the knife in his belly. He was still alive when I left, but bleeding out."

"And you didn't finish him?"

"No, sir," she replied in a small voice.

Huron grumbled, then called for his aide. A large brown hand swept open the tent. The face familiar, Geram cocked his head as the officer winked at him. But the captain's grin faded as Huron told him their story.

"We've got to move double time, now," Huron barked. "I want everyone ready in twenty minutes. See that these two are sent back to Winterquarters." The captain signaled Geram and Vic to follow him outside, where he relayed Huron's orders, then grabbed Geram and squeezed him in a massive hug.

As he struggled for breath in the laughing man's arms, Geram wracked his brain to put a name to a face. "Geram, my boy," the man said as he released him. "I hardly knew you with that ice-caked beard. Last time I saw you, you would have been proud to have a single hair on that chin. How are you?"

Geram smiled. "I'm sorry, but . . ." He saw something of his aunt around the man's eyes. "Cousin Drak? Aunt Celina speaks of you all the time. I'm sorry I didn't recognize you."

Drak bellowed with laughter again, guessing little Aunt Celina said of him was good. "Well, come on now, I've got to find transport for two heroes back to Winterquarters."

"Heroes?" Vic asked.

"Of course. If the Relmlord is dead, the war's over."

Vic's face turned a shade closer to her eyes. Her hand over her mouth, she fell to her knees, retching into the snow. Geram tasted the bile in his own throat again. This failure was more bitter than the flag. Far more bitter.

† † †

Back at Winterquarters, the healers nursed the cold out of Vic's limbs, but they couldn't put color back in her cheeks. Geram told her how Marshall Huron's troops had caught the bulk of the Relmans fleeing south, but the senior officers had all escaped, and there was no sign of the Relmlord. The Relmans didn't surrender or call a truce, but everyone figured Relman command would soon collapse. When people talked of this in front of her, Vic turned to the wall and hugged herself. Neither Geram nor any of the other counselors could Hear anything from her. No one but Geram understood why she behaved this way.

Fieldmarshall Henrik came to congratulate her after Huron's troops returned. She saluted him and stood at attention while he gave a speech praising her boldness, then nodded silent thanks when he placed a leather thong bearing a tiny crystal dagger around her neck. After he was gone, she pulled the dagger off, threw it against a wall and screamed until the healers forced a mixture of slotaen and harlolinde down her throat. They had to keep her drugged for days after that.

Geram waited for new orders, but none came. He bunked with the Dagger but no longer pretended to be a rookie—camp gossip moved too fast for that. Maynon glared at him, spat when they passed each other on the grounds, and Silla always had murder in her eyes. The pair visited Vic each day, bringing back the same report: no, she didn't recognize us; no, she didn't speak. Maynon spent hours sitting next to her bed, sporadically rasping camp gossip at her. The day after Henrik's visit, Geram met the lieutenant coming out of the infirmary. His eyes and face were red, his hair teased so it stood on end. For once, instead of spitting, Maynon shrugged hopelessly.

"Can't you do anything for her?" he asked.

Geram hung his head. "No. I—"

"Then what good are you?" Shoving Geram off the path,

Maynon stomped off. Anger surged past Geram's ears, but he had been asking himself the same question since they'd left the Relman campsite.

Every time Geram visited Vic, his breath choked around a lump in his throat. After she recovered from Henrik's visit and the healers stopped drugging her, her eyes acknowledged him, but he couldn't coax any words from her. This was not the same woman who had scoffed at his woodcraft and led him dancing around the Relman camp, thumbing her nose at him and his orders from Command. Grief stifled the strength that had gotten them out of the camp, that had brought them home. If he held her hand and Listened very hard, he caught mumbling echoes of incoherent cries, but he Heard nothing he recognized as the trooper they called the Blade.

"You said you hated him," he said one day, hoping to provoke some—any—reaction. "You should be rejoicing he's dead."

For once Vic looked at him, her eyes clear and gray. "I did hate him," she said defensively.

The drowner's hand, reaching for help. Geram seized on that thought to yank her free, but she pulled him into the morass.

> *His nostrils swell with the scent of soap and sex. A black mattress, bare of bedclothes, stands upon a black stone floor. Books lie everywhere, stacked into precarious towers, discarded in jumbled piles. A breeze riffles exposed pages, every one blank. Hearing a clank and whine, he turns and finds Vic, bald and naked, crouched atop a mound of brass gears. Geram's eyes pop at the profusion of jagged metal. As he climbs toward her, the gears slip beneath his feet, rip his hands. Vic watches him, her lips taut, eyes wide. Her feet and hands buried in sharp metal, her skin is ribboned with cuts.*

"Why are you here?" he asks.

"Have to find the key," she mutters, rooting among the gears. "He took it. He took it with him."

"What key?"

"There may be a copy." Digging deeper, she turns away from him, revealing a bronze belt, studded with gemstones and small, tinkling rings. The belt clasp is a keyhole, and through it Geram sees a multitude of gears ticking and spinning under her skin.

"Captain, come away from this place."

"Have to find the key."

The gears begin to slide out beneath him. He climbs in the opposite direction, knees and hands churning through the clatter of metal. "Vic," he shouts, but she sifts through the jagged discs, mumbling about the lost key. He lunges for her, as he had lunged for the flag, stretching to make contact with her fingers. "Kara?" he cries, and her eyes swing toward him.

"Captain, Lieutenant." A gruff order brought the infirmary back into sharp focus. Dazed, he stood and saluted Marshall Huron. Automatically, Vic copied the gesture from her bed. "We just heard," the marshall continued. "The Relmlord survived."

Vic's eyes swiveled up. "What?"

"The official report from the Relmans is that he took ill while in Re—our people confirm he was wounded, but they think he'll recover. You took a big risk, Captain, and it turned out to be for nothing."

Geram felt the scene shift in Vic's mind, the gears melting into the infirmary. Color blooming in her cheeks, she sat up, wrapping her arms around her knees. "Not for nothing, Marshall," she said slowly. "It would have been better if you'd caught the Relmlord yourself, but once your companies attacked, he probably still would have had time to escape, no matter what I'd done."

The marshall's face turned red, but he kept his voice steady. "I've talked to the fieldmarshall, and he and I agree you should take leave. You may go as soon as you're able, Captain."

Glancing at Geram, Vic actually smiled. "Thank you, sir. I will be sure to come back by spring. I assume my party may go on leave as well?"

The marshall grumbled, but agreed the Dagger was no good without the Blade. Huron's bluster failed to drown a voice like a father indulging his most talented, but troublesome, child. "Lieutenant"—he signaled to Geram—"you'll be reassigned tomorrow."

"Marshall." Vic leaned forward, looking sidelong at Geram. "My party's a man short without the lieutenant. Do what you must with him now, but I think I'll be lost without him when I return."

His fingers drumming his belt, Huron looked from one to the other, grumbling about paperwork. "Captain," he barked finally, "if you pull another stunt like trying to assassinate the Relmlord without orders, I'll see both you and your counselor thrown in the stockade for it. Lieutenant, you have leave as well."

Vic raised her hand in salute. "Understood, sir." After the marshall left, Geram sat beside her again, Listening, but she brushed the air between them and laughed. "Stop eavesdropping, Geram. Go home to Alna, and I'll see you in spring."

CHAPTER 13

DEEPER THAN DUTY

His father's breath was a thin rattle, the heavy scent of slotaen masking the stench of pus and bile. Earnk stared out the window of the barge, watching the water creep up the timbered sides of the lock. Moss and vines coated the upper reaches of the walls, and in the near distance stood the blue peaks of the Lorn oc Re. Another week or two would see them home, in Olmlablaire.

Not Traine. Earnk hadn't been to the city of his birth in more than three years. After he finished school, his father had apprenticed him to one of his allies on the Relman Council, and since then Earnk had lived in Re, learning everything he could about governing. In that time, he'd come to love Relm and its straightforward people. He'd decided never to return to Traine.

Then, three days ago, his father had arrived in Re flushed with fever and angrier than Earnk had ever seen him, save the day Vic escaped. Earnk had a barge ready to take him up to Olmlablaire, where Lornk could return to Traine through the Device. He hadn't expected his father to ask him to come along.

"The Relmlord should pull the big weeds and lop off the stray limbs," Father said suddenly, bringing Earnk's attention back to the stateroom. "Let the Council untangle the day-to-day snarls of governing." Pallid and sweating, his father raised himself onto an elbow and sipped water laced with harlolinde. In the frigid air of the cabin, he wore only a nightshirt, damp and soiled with seepage from his wound. A pile of furs and quilts had slipped off the bed onto the floor.

"What's more important?"

Father took a deep breath, then appraised Earnk's boots and shoulders. "What do you think? You can't see the garden if it's overrun."

Nodding, Earnk looked out the window again. The lock had filled, the gates opening. Before long they were moving upstream again. The oars made a regular thump against the hull. Along the shore of the canal, long, slender branches twined together, forming a solid curtain of blue-green leaves that stretched twenty or thirty feet to hang hair-widths above the water's surface. A dark spot, a wallowwood bush up the river, approached more and more quickly until it flew by as the barge came abreast of it. Absorbed in the passing countryside, Earnk was startled by a sudden wheeze from his father.

"You know who did this to me?"

He did not turn around. "Yes."

"Do you still think you love her?" The question was lightly asked, when before, every word had ached.

Earnk's head swiveled to face his father. Lornk was grinning, his teeth and eyes cloudy, his face now shining with fever. Clenching his fists behind his back, Earnk shook his head. "Of course not. I've—that was an infatuation." He cleared his throat. "You know how it is sometimes in Traine."

"It's too bad I couldn't send you to school in Latha like my mother sent me. You might have learned to appreciate something other than your father's belongings."

"I know my duty—to Relm as much as you. Count on it."

"I'd like to." Father's smile relaxed, followed by Earnk's shoulders. "But can I? You're your mother's son more than mine."

His jaw quivering, Earnk looked out the window again. His father's breath wheezed faster, but irregularly, like laughter. The memory of his mother's mad fingernails itched across his face as he beat down remorse and anger. Outside, a bargeman went by, the top of his red cap bobbing over the sill, his breath fogging the view as he walked past. It had been midsummer the day his mother threw herself down the tower stairwell. But the blood on the tiles steamed just the same.

"You have her softness," Father panted. "She reminded me of a spring rain." He sighed, drawing Earnk's eyes back toward the bed. "You know the light ones like we get in the Kiareinoll. 'Nothing which we are to perceive in this world equals the power of your intense fragility . . .'" he quoted one of the Ancient poems he and Mother used to read to each other. Collapsing back onto the bed, his hands waved above the quilt like a conductor's, his eyes rolling past the ceiling to the wall behind him. "'. . . rendering death and forever with each breathing.'"

Death and forever. Along with the blankets, his father had knocked most of the pillows onto the floor. Earnk picked one up and sat in a chair next to the bed. Lornk's eyes rolled from the ceiling to his son's, and he smiled in the middle of his recitation, his eyes still glassy, his hands raving.

When word came that his father had been wounded, the Relman Councilors had listened earnestly to Earnk's opinions while they waited for news. "You've a fine model in your father," Allosard had whispered to him. "If Elesendar takes him to the trees, I've no doubt you'll fit his mold." Digging his fingers into the plush of the pillow, Earnk leaned toward his father. If he bore the title Relmlord, what would he do? Negotiate a peace treaty with Latha? Sell the Citizenship in Traine? Would Elsa be happy living in Relm?

Would Vic? Earnk pressed his knuckles deeper into the

pillow as his father reached the end of the poem. "'. . . deeper than all roses. Nobody'"—Lornk's voice rose triumphantly, his neck arching back, his hands straining toward the ceiling—"'not even the rain, has such small hands!'"

His father fell back, eyes shut in exhaustion, fevered body shivering. The pillow hovered above his febrile eyelids, sinking closer to his face. Earnk's hands shook, his fingers crushing the stuffing. Expelling a breath, he slid the pillow under Father's head, picked up the blankets and covered him to his chin. If he finished the job Vic started, Earnk would destroy any chance the Relman people would one day accept the Blade as their First Councilor.

CHAPTER 14

HOME

Drifts hid the fence, white undulating over the Cobblestone's garden, swirling up around the laundry pole. Beneath the cauldron, mud coated the firepit rack and Vic's boots in a thick, warm paste. At least my feet are warm, she thought, dropping another chamberpot into boiling suds, chagrined she was paying for the privilege of choking on other people's stinks instead of curled around a book in her room at the manor. "You really have gone mad," she muttered. "Or you're the biggest coward in Knownearth." When she had arrived at Narath's gate two weeks ago, she thought how Elekia would react to the news that she'd failed to kill Lornk, and she asked the gate guard to recommend an inn. Helara, the Cobblestone's owner, had the tilted eyes and jet hair of a Caleisbahnin, but despite that, Vic had liked her from the moment they met. Her manner with guests warm, she was stern and demanding with her staff, though not unkind. Sensing a kindred spirit, Vic quickly developed a rapport with her host, and, with little to do during the day, she was soon volunteering to help. Helara threatened to start paying Vic rather than charging her for all the work she did around the inn—laundry, washing dishes, scrubbing floors—but Vic was glad to do it. "I want to wash the blood off my hands," Vic blurted one afternoon when Helara scolded her for washing the windows. After that, Helara found chores for her to do.

Lye and shit stabbing her nostrils, eyes watering, Vic snorted. Chamberpots? "That's a bridge too far," she grumbled, "but you've no one to blame but yourself." That morning, Helara had complained about the service guild contracted to clean the pots, and Vic had volunteered to wash them. Helara protested; Vic insisted, and in an hour she stood in the backyard, her nose frozen and her feet sweating. She wished for once, when Helara had rolled her eyes, the innkeeper had decided that Vic's time was better spent checking the numbers in her ledgers.

Frozen steam and breath crinkled the handkerchief over her nose, and she yanked it down and reminded herself to be glad she had a warm place to piss at night. Taking a pair of wooden tongs, she fished another pot out of the boiling suds and scrubbed the clinging bits with a brush before dunking it in the rinse water. As each porcelain moved from the pile of dirty to clean ones, her urgency to finish the job grew. Wiping her eyes on her sleeve, she tossed the next pot into the cauldron.

One of the inn's windows shattered, raining glass into the garden. A stoneware tankard tumbled across the snow, followed out the window by bellowing laughter and Helara's angry screeches. Vic shrugged. Since she'd arrived, another window, two paper partitions, four goblets, and six chairs had been broken. And the Cobblestone was considered a quiet inn. After a minute, a woman wearing the black and gold of a minstrel stumbled out the back door and across the yard. Giggling, she swung a hand down after the tankard, missed, then reached for it again, this time falling face first into the snow. "Help," she cried, laughing so hard she choked.

Sighing, Vic stepped toward the minstrel but froze as a tall figure staggered down the back steps of the inn. Ashel. Vic thought of her smudged face, the hair straggling out of her cap, and the mask slung around her neck instead of covering her nose. Turn around and hide, she urged herself, her feet rooted where she stood. Ashel approached, blinking, staring at her. "Vic," he said slowly, "is that you?"

"Uh, no." She tugged the mask back up. "I'm just the serviceperson, uh, cleaning, ah . . ."

He straightened. "I'm not that drunk. Melba, am I that drunk?"

The minstrel flopped onto her back. "No. But I am."

"What are you doing here?"

Vic sighed, feeling like a cat caught with the cream rather than a drudge cleaning chamberpots. "Hiding, I guess. They put me on leave until spring. I didn't want to go to the manor."

Ashel nodded. "My mother would never look for you here, that's for sure. I won't tell. Come on, Melba. Let's pay for the window before the innkeeper swipes me with that broom again."

He helped the other woman stand and sent her back toward the door with a pat. "Can I come see you when we're both in better shape?"

Vic ducked her head, her cheeks tingling. "Sure. Why don't I meet you somewhere?"

"The Harper's Wind, tonight?"

She nodded and, after he left, doubled her pace with the pots.

† † †

"I feel silly," Vic said as Helara's daughter braided a ribbon into her hair. "I should just wear my uniform."

"I sent your sweaters out to be rewoven," Lora replied. "The only suitable thing you have is what you're wearing."

Vic looked at her reflection. An apprentice tailor, Lora had convinced Vic to buy two bolts of erinsheen and commission three new dresses, even though she hadn't worn a skirt since entering the army. Vic stared in awe at the quilted gown made of auburn fabric. Silk streamers from Lora's scrap bag flowed from the wrists up the sleeves to a neckline that left Vic's shoulders bare. She watched as Lora hung the braids in loops at the back of her head, shivering as the girl's hand brushed against her neck.

"Cold?"

"No. Just a bad memory. Maybe I should cut it off."

"This hair? Elesendar, if I had hair like this, it'd be down to my ankles!"

"You have beautiful hair." Lora had her mother's thick black hair but with curls that must have come from her father. With creamy brown skin like the princess's and exotic eyes like Helara, the tailor had a lot of suitors.

Lora put her hands on Vic's shoulders. "All done. It's not every girl cleaning chamber pots who gets asked out by a prince. Have fun."

Vic swung her cloak round her shoulders. "It's not like that. I've known Ashel for years. We—we're friends, sort of."

"If you say so." Lora clasped her hands behind her back and winked.

Cheeks warming, Vic remembered that the longest conversation she'd ever had with Ashel had been the night before she joined the army. She stepped toward the door, the sweeping skirt an awkward drag. "I should wear a uniform. This feels weird."

"No time to change." Lora pushed her out the bedroom door and down the steps. "Now, you know the way?"

"Everyone in Narath knows the Wind." She paused on the steps, her belly twisted in knots. "Maybe you'd like to come?"

Lora's eyes brightened as she put her hand over her mouth. "Are you kidding? Let me ask Mama if it's all right."

Helara's scolds echoed off the kitchen hearth while the scullery boy mopped up fish and pottery from the floor. Lora's beaming faded at the squabble, and Vic had to catch hold of the tailor's hand to keep her from retreating back up the stairs.

Helara glanced at them, then looked again, her frown softening. "Vic, you look lovely. Didn't I tell you my daughter was the best tailor in Narath?"

"Yes, you did. As part of Lora's reward, I'd like for her to dine with me at the Wind tonight—if you don't mind her patronizing the competition."

Helara's eyes sparkled. "The Wind? Paugh! That's no competition to me. Let old Barnerd have those minstrels; let them break his windows. I serve far better Eldanion than he, and everybody knows it . . ." Arms waving overhead, Helara continued her tirade of Barnerd's flaws into the common room.

"How fast can you change?"

"Like the Wind." The girl's grin returned.

"Well, hurry before she realizes she didn't say no."

†††

Ashel slipped through the stage door, stamped the snow off his boots and hung his cloak on an empty peg, an odd tickle of nerves in his belly. The memory of naked hips and small pert breasts blossomed in his mind, and he groaned softly into the fabric of his cloak, blood rushing to his face and below his belt. "Stop it." The last time he'd seen Vic had been at Cimba's Nine Day party, two years ago. On that occasion, and the few others they'd attended together, Vic had never left Bethniel's side, and his sister's urgent gestures of invitation drove him to seek wine on the other side of the room. As the years had passed, his audacity speaking to Vic at that fair appalled him more and more. Citizens killed their mistresses for even a hint of betrayal, and he'd blithely strolled up to one and asked her to dance. What a selfish, stupid thing to do. He was still mortified. So why'd you ask her here? he wondered. Because I was drunk and caught off guard. And why had she agreed to come? That question stirred the nerves in his belly.

"Do you want to go on tonight?" the stage manager asked as Ashel came out of the cloakroom.

"Is there an empty slot?"

The manager scowled. "The Guild cut Winder's sets last minute and left me with dead air for half the night! I got him on the bill under his kid's name, but she's only an apprentice and they won't let her do more than one song. So I've got time to fill, if you want it."

"Why'd they cut him?" People thronged the streets when they heard Winder's tenor curling through town like a mischievous mist, tickling the women behind their husbands' backs. Ashel wondered if the master minstrel's dalliances had caught up with him.

"Dunno, but it's wrecked my schedule."

"I'll take a set," Ashel said. "Let me see who else is in the house and we'll help you out."

He wove through the wings, patting backs and giving silent encouragement to waiting performers. On stage, a magician turned card tricks to raucous laughter from the audience. Ashel ducked onto the floor and made his way to the bar, where he found Melba and Simlael and told them about Winder.

"Fools," Melba spat. "He brings more revenue to the Guild than anyone."

"A purge is coming, mark my words," Simlael said, angling his cup at them. "Ever since Silnauer became Harmony, the ethics board has been ruining our lives."

"What say you in your defense?" the Harmony asks, folding her hands. The Loremasters to her left mirror her stern gaze, but the Melody and other Master Minstrels on her right shift in their seats, eyes on the table.

Ashel swallows. "I have none." He feels the pull of a sultry smile, the whisper of "sweet prince" in his ear, the surge of his heart as one throw of the dice leads to another, the crystal piling higher, the lure of the courtesan's fingers guiding his hand to another toss, and then the shattering, scrambling, falling sensation as time and again the dice land wrong side up. Meeting the stern gazes of the ethics board, he prays for Elesendar's mercy. "I will bear any penance you dictate, but I ask the Guild for a loan against my wages to pay the debt."

Silnauer confers with the other members of the board, then stands to deliver judgment. "The board agrees your exemplary record warrants some leniency. We will not demand a penance, although this incident will be noted in your records and your masters exams postponed another year so you may attain the maturity required for the post of Loremaster—or Master Minstrel," she adds as the Melody clears his throat.

"And the loan?" he asks.

"You need not concern yourself with that. The Senate will banish the gamerunners from Lathan soil."

"I'm taking a set. Melba, will you back me?" Ashel asked, shoving away that bitter memory. Thanks to one drunken evening in Alna, he was a twice marked man: a stain on his Guild record and a bounty among the Caleisbahnin. The gamerunners may have been banished, but he still owed them ten times his annual salary, with mounting interest. He dared not leave Latha, or even vist a port city, until he found a way to pay the debt.

Melba poked him in the ribs. "I thought you were meeting the Blade tonight."

"She's coming here?" Simlael asked, handing Ashel some ale. "You have to introduce me."

"I'd tell her to come armed, if I were introducing her to *you*."

"He wants her for himself." Simlael winked at Melba. "Will the Blade be the latest in a long string of aborted cuddles, or will you finally find release?"

Ears hot, Ashel took a swig of the ale. "Vic is my sister's friend and my parents' ward. She's family, nothing more."

"Tell that to the bulge in your trousers."

"Shrinejump, Simlael. You need to go home to Alna and get yourself laid so you'll stop acting like an ass for a month or two."

"Oh, sweet, virtuous prince. Saving himself for his One True Love. Will she be soft, or will she have an edge?"

Fuming, he turned to Melba. "Are you going on with me or not?"

His oldest friend cut her eyes at the usher weaving through the crowd. "Looks like the One is here. And yes, I'll back you, if you back me. I'll go see who else I can round up." With a wink and a grin, she slipped away.

"She's just my sister's friend," Ashel called after her.

While Simlael chuckled into his ale, Ashel downed his and took a note from the usher. On it was written the box number where the house manager had seated Vic. He crumpled it into his pocket and went backstage.

By the time he and Melba had sorted their set list and lined up their accompanists, Winder and his daughter Wineyll were taking the stage. Forehead beaded with sweat, Winder beamed as the audience leapt to their feet. Wineyll's smile just as broad, she bowed alongside him and raised her flute. "Let's go out front," he whispered to Melba, and they slipped into the house and squeezed past jammed tables while Wineyll played the first bars of "Wizard's Last Embrace." That melody had been written for a soprano to sing, but Wineyll's tonguing was so lithe the lyrics could almost be heard in the flute's music. Ashel had tutored the girl when she was young, had played in ensembles with her, but had never heard her embrace a tune so well. Keeping time on a drum, her father opened his mouth, and the sweetest tenor in the Guild washed over the audience. Bittersweet sorrow raised a lump in Ashel's throat, and his gut ached with lost love. Tears spilled over Melba's cheeks, and sniffles and gasps swept through a floor filled with off-duty guards and troopers, teamsters and miners, all hard folk wiping cheeks and noses on their sleeves. Ashel blinked at the duo in awe. He'd never *felt* music like this.

"It's Wineyll," Melba sniffed. "She's projecting."

Wineyll's Listening, and the pranks she pulled with it, had netted her more reprimands than any apprentice in Guild history, but Ashel had never heard of a minstrel using the talent to move an audience. "That's clever stagecraft," he said, scrubbing his cheeks. "It's brilliant, actually." Winder sang about missed opportunities, Wineyll's flute answered with regret and longing, and he thought of Vic, sitting in one of the galleries above the floor, listening to this. Did tears run down her cheeks? "Just my sister's friend," he muttered. But his feet backed toward the exit. Touching Melba's shoulder, he signaled with his eyebrows he was going up.

In the box, he found Vic with her elbows on the railing, a girl around Wineyll's age swooning beside her. Ashel watched them from the doorway as the flute wove the soprano's lament around the tenor's pleas. As Wineyll descended into a throaty interpretation of the wind, Winder slowed the tempo on his drum, letting his last note of grief fade to silence. Below, a few scattered claps exploded into approval, and Vic brushed at wet cheeks.

Clearing the lump out of his throat, Ashel said, "You didn't cry when I sang that two years ago."

Vic stood, sunrise-colored braids looped over cream-colored shoulders. "Ashel, you sang it beautifully. But this was different somehow."

"Your Highness," Vic's friend giggled, curtsying. Vic introduced her, and the girl slipped past him into the hall, winking at Vic as she left.

"Be careful," Ashel called after her. "Pretty girl like you could end up wedded to a minstrel before she knew it."

Laughter echoed back to the box. "My mother would kill me if I ever brought one of you louts home."

"She's my innkeeper's daughter and my tailor," Vic said as Ashel took Lora's seat.

"Fine work she does too." He pulled his eyes out of the shadowed edges of her neckline. She's *family*, he reminded himself as forcefully as he'd told his friends. "So what was different about Wineyll and Winder's interpretation?"

She coughed. "I don't know music, but I liked how the flute took the soprano's part; it left more up to your imagination as far as what the woman was saying. It made the man's part more poignant, I guess."

Ashel leaned forward. "I agree completely. Did you notice how Winder kept the tempo slow, giving Wineyll time to wind her flute around his song? That way, when the crescendo comes, they can play the passage allegro—that's not the way it was written, mind you—"

"It was very pretty, Ashel."

"I'm sorry." Elesendar, don't bore the woman! He sat back and offered a sheepish smile. "Is it strange for you, hearing that song?"

She looked at him askance. "Why would it be?"

He chuckled. "You, Captain, have a famous wizard for a

namesake." She paled, tiny freckles standing out on the bridge of her nose, her eyes suddenly very green. Shrinejump, this conversation wasn't going well. Within a minute he'd bored her and angered her. This was as tricky as talking to his mother! He continued tentatively, "Victoria of Ourtown was a member of the Council of Wizards who fought Melynara in Direiellene. That song is about her affair with another wizard named Thabean. She's saying goodbye to him so she can go back to her husband."

The color in her eyes dimmed toward hazel, and her lips spread into a bemused smile. "That is absurd."

He laughed. "It's a mystery how an Oreseeker ended up on the Council. But it's a historical fact a woman with your name fought in that war."

"And had a lover and a husband. She was busy."

"Well," he admitted, "I suspect an overly romantic minstrel made up the love triangle."

"Not to mention the part about the wizards."

He snorted. "How long have you known my family?"

"Five years."

"And you've never seen Mother's wizardry?"

She raised a dubious eyebrow. "Your mother is not a witch."

"No, of course she's not a witch, casting spells and brewing potions; that's the stuff of fairy tales. But"—he grinned—"she is a wizard."

"Those rumors are outrageous, Ashel. I'm surprised to hear you repeat them."

He poured himself some wine. "You've really never noticed? I'll admit, she's discreet, since wizardry is outlawed in Latha, but it *is* an open secret. Everyone at the manor knows. Watch carefully when she eats. She sweeps the crumbs off the table without touching them."

"She does not."

He laughed. "She does. She gave me a thrashing once when

I was a boy. She never touched me, but my backside was just as blue."

Eyebrows drawing down, she frowned. "Now that I think about it, there have been times when your mother . . . Oh, why the Shrine not? I thought the idea of moving trees was mad before I'd been to Fembrosh—and now I'm thankful for any help the Kiareinoll gives in the field. I'll watch for those crumbs next time I dine at the manor." Her lips tilted. "What was the thrashing for?"

He grinned. "I cheated on my Nine Day Maze." Her jaw dropped, and he continued. "Father found the map I'd made. He was so furious he delayed the ceremony until the gardeners could redo the maze. Mother"—he grimaced at the rage that had bled from her eyes—"was furious I got caught."

She stared at him a moment, then burst out laughing. Her tight reserve evaporated as her delight stirred his own. They shared more wine and gossip, then watched people step to a reel on the floor below. Vic wore a wistful frown, and he wondered if he asked her to dance whether she'd refuse. But a tightness around her eyes prompted the question that had nagged him since that afternoon. "What are you hiding from?"

She bit the corner of her lip. "Your mother? You know how she is—"

"Does Bethniel know you're here?"

"No."

"Why not?"

Her shoulders began to shake, her hands covering shimmering eyes. She struggled to master herself, but tears spilled past her fingers. "Every day since we found Silla, tasting his blood was all I thought about. I imagined myself dancing on his corpse. And instead I folded up and wanted to die."

Ashel's heart stuttered. The conversation had veered into a place far beyond his ken; Guild politics and Heralds' gossip were the worst problems he ever faced. His mind raced through excuses to go back downstairs. But you *asked*, he chided himself. Swallowing the exit lines, he sat still as a jumbled narrative spilled out: an illness at Winterquarters, an unexpected camaraderie with someone assigned to spy on her, an undeserved medal for bravery. Her story, confused and agonized, netted his sympathy and pulled him into an intimacy of truth. As he crossed the threshold, his breath came easier and his heart beat freely again. He moved his chair closer, patted her hand, asked questions in the same level tone he used with apprentices frustrated over a complex piece of music, leading her to pull the threads together.

Finally she revealed the heart of the tale: she had stabbed but failed to kill the Relmlord. "Why couldn't I?" she asked, meeting his gaze with bright green eyes. "I've killed hundreds of people, and every time, I imagined they were him. Why couldn't I actually kill him when I had the chance?"

"I'm so sorry," he said. "I wish—"

"And I was so, so hysterical. Geram was right—I should have been rejoicing when I thought he was dead. I hate him, Ashel. No one could ever understand how much."

"Mother." He reached toward a loop of bright hair, but put his hand over her fist instead. "Mother hates him that much. You should go see her."

"Ugh." She wiped her eyes. "That's the last thing I expected to hear from you."

He drew back, his chair squeaking on the polished floor. "Even I'll admit she gives good advice sometimes. She told you to go into the army. I thought that was a mistake, but now you're famous. Laelin even wrote a song about you: 'Exploits of the Blade.'"

"Yes, well"—she chuckled weakly—"my fame pales compared to yours."

"That reminds me." Ashel looked down at the jester on stage. "I'm on after this slouch. Can I walk you home later?"

"If you don't mind Lora coming along."

Ashel pointed to a knot of young minstrels surrounding Vic's friend on the floor below. "I think she'll find her own way back."

Vic exhaled a breath and smiled. "She hasn't been to Fembrosh yet. Helara would never forgive me if I didn't personally see her home."

Disappointment deflated his lungs, but he covered it with his stage smile. "I'll bring friends as well, then." He paused on the box threshold. "If you want to talk more, about anything, you know where to find me."

† † †

The turned page sliced the air, a soft echo of a weapon unsheathed. Vic's ears twitched, but her eyes devoured the type, scanning quickly across the spread, until the next page slid past her nose. The bell on the common room door jingled, a single figure entering the periphery of her awareness, but her attention remained glued to the book.

"Is it good?" Ashel loomed over her chair, eyes sparkling.

Cheeks warm, Vic marked the page and closed the cover, waving him into a chair. He'd mentioned the book during the walk home from the Wind, and that morning she'd borrowed a copy from the Academy library. "It's a pleasure to read."

"Really? Usually Loremasters are the only ones interested in the Ancients."

"I was a Logkeeper. It's sort of the same thing as a Loremaster, without the music." She tapped the book. "But honestly I haven't read so cogent a history of Landing. Even the religiosity doesn't bother me; you've got an unusually light touch with that, for a Lathan." She leaned back, crossed her arms. "Whatever possessed you to write it?"

"Elesendar called me to do it," he said, and laughed when she blurted an apology, her face hot. "In all seriousness, I'm a recorder. It's sort of the same thing as Logkeeper." Elbows on the table, he rested his chin in a palm. "But with music."

"How long until you're a full Loremaster?"

His smile faltered. "Another year or so, unless I decide to finish my Master Minstrels instead. I can't do both. The Guild makes us choose."

"That's a shame. I'd no idea you were as talented a scholar as you are a singer." She glanced around the empty common room, eyebrows quirked. "Why are you here?"

His teeth brightened the room again. "We'll be playing music at my house tonight, in case you want to stop by."

Eagerness pinged up her spine, and she sat straighter. "I don't play."

"We need an audience to keep us honest. Besides, there'll be a few Loremasters there. You can debate religion with them."

Her gut seized. "Will Silnauer be there?"

His head jerked back as if she'd punched him. "Shrine, no."

Relieved, she nodded. "I'd love to come." A glance at the clock on the mantel brought her to her feet. "Now, however—"

"Not more chores?"

She shrugged. "The glaziers replaced that window you broke, and I promised Helara I'd clean up the dust, plus there're still bits of glass—"

He flourished a shallow bow. "Then I should help. Lead the way, madam."

They fetched brooms and mops and a bucket of sudsy water from the kitchen, passed Helara, frowning in her office, and set to work in the rear parlor. Vic asked how they managed to send a tankard through the window. Ashel flushed, blamed drunken horseplay, and focused on his mop as she swept up glass and sawdust and dumped them in the crackling fireplace. Water splattered on her calves; she turned to find the prince assiduously mopping the floor beneath the new window. Frowning, she took a rag to clean the sills and felt the lash of droplets against her thighs.

"Ashel!"

He chuckled. "It's a very splashy mop."

"It's a very careless mopper."

She returned to her task, watching him out the corner of her eye. Softly sniggering, he flicked the mop. Leaping clear of the spray, she grabbed the bucket. "Do that again, you'll have this over your head."

He pulled his shoulders back and raised an eyebrow. "Captain, you forget yourself. I am a prince of Latha."

"And you forget who you're dealing with, Your Highness."

Humor playing around his lips, he raised the mop. Water dripped, threatening. "Perhaps I want to test myself against the Blade."

She tried to scowl, but a smile broke through. "Don't do it."

He wiggled his eyebrows and jerked the mop. She ducked under the droplets, tossing a cascade that splashed onto his doublet. He thrust the mop; wet strands squelched into her sweater, but she twisted around the handle and leapt, tipping the bucket over his head. Roaring, he caught her midair, pinned her arms, and hauled her through the hallway and out the back door, where he tossed her into a drift. Spitting snow, she hooked her leg round his ankle and sent him tumbling backward into a crystalline puff, then jumped astride his torso, pinning his elbows under her knees. Choked laughter plumed from them both as Helara's screeches rang out the back door, ordering them inside.

Vic rolled off the prince and gave him a hand out of the drift. "Never go against the Blade, Highness."

"I think I did pretty well," he said as they climbed the steps. "I achieved my objective."

"What was that?"

"To see you laugh again."

CHAPTER 15

FAMILY TIES

Midmorning sun bright through the windows, Ashel pushed against the tide of students and apprentices heading to their next lectures. Some hailed him as they passed, many girls batting eyelashes or giggling with downcast eyes. The attention assuaged his ego; in his own lectures that morning, distracted students had passed notes and whispered together, and all his usual tricks had failed to hold their interest. By his fourth class, he gave up and simply wrote three questions about the founding of the Erin Alliance on the board. While the class scratched out answers, he spent the period staring at the lectern and grumbling about the extra work for himself. He and Vic had planned a picnic that afternoon, and now he'd have to cut short their time. Perhaps she could help grade the essays, he thought with a smile.

In the refectory, Laelin and Simlael sat beneath a window, but a dark-haired girl sitting by herself, staring into a mug, commanded his attention. He collected his tea from the server and took a seat across from her. "Wineyll, how's your father?"

The apprentice pasted on a smile. "Oh, he's fine, thanks. The Guild is letting him stay in the Guildhouse. We're grateful for the Melody's generosity."

His gut twisting, Ashel clasped her hand, wishing he had realized the other night he was witnessing Winder's final performance. The ethics board had expelled the Master Minstrel for his indiscretions, and the Guild had lost a legend. "That show sealed his legacy, you know."

"He needed the acclaim," Wineyll said, her eyes shimmering.

I'm so sorry, he thought, knowing she would Hear it.

"And he's sick," Wineyll said, her mindvoice too crisp to be Heard by anyone but him. The girl's anguish squeezed the air out of his lungs. "The healers say he's only got a few months, so why they couldn't just let him pass in honor . . ."

Elesendar. Winder's expulsion obviated the Guild's obligation to pay for his treatments. The miserly cruelty shocked Ashel and kindled his anger. "Anything you need," he whispered, "let me know."

With a nod and silent thanks, Wineyll stood. "I'm late for a class."

Finding his tea bitter, he fetched himself some honey and moved to sit with his friends. Simlael slid a yellow paper topped with Heralds' scrollwork off the table onto his lap, and the students' preoccupation that morning became crystal clear. Gritting his teeth, Ashel asked, "What does it say this time?"

Laelin frowned in sympathy as Simlael passed the pamphlet to him. His eyes scanned the page, anger twisting in his belly. The copy led with the news that Vic had tried and failed to assassinate Lornk Korng, then it speculated on how the war might escalate, ruining any chance for peace. That was bad enough, but it also called Vic "the unsullied Trainer whore" and claimed she was the monarchy's weapon in their personal feud with the Relmlord, while Ashel—a wastrel shielded from scandal by the monarchy—caroused in Narath rather than fight at the front. For three paragraphs, the Heralds railed against his privilege and cowardice. With an angry guffaw, he pushed the paper back across the table. "It's nearly the same as last time. Do you suppose they keep a plate with the type already set?"

Simlael crumpled the paper. "Trash."

Laelin nodded, then stood to go. "There's a debate at the Miller's Wheel tomorrow evening. We'd love for Vic to come, if she's free."

He nodded. "I'll let her know."

Ashel waited until the Loremaster left, then whistled softly. "She's got it bad." Ever since the night Vic and Laelin had hotly debated the origins of Fembrosh's powers, Laelin found every excuse she could to be near her. It was painful to watch the Loremaster toss so many lines and fail to hook her fish, but Vic seemed oblivious to Laelin's advances.

"She's not the only one," Simlael chortled.

Ashel looked sharply at the other man. "Don't you dare try anything—"

"Me?" Simlael laughed broadly, his eyebrows twitching. "I'm talking about you, dundlehead." Ashel blinked at him, his gut cold and warm at the same time. Simlael went on, "I know, she's your sister's friend and you're just making sure she's not lonely. Well, where is Bethniel, if they're so close? Why are *you* over at the Cobblestone, mopping floors of all things?"

A wry chuckle in his throat, Ashel looked out the windows at the blue sky. "We're both banned from doing any more chores there."

Simlael's grin faded. "Just be careful."

"And what does that mean?"

His friend sighed. "I'm sorry I mocked you that night she came to the Wind. I didn't expect you'd actually fall in love with her—"

"I haven't!"

"You're doing a fine impression of an enamored man, then. Just don't get yourself on a tack toward marriage. You're going to end up broken on a shoal somewhere."

His ire rose again, mixed with incredulity. "She's just my sister's friend," he growled and headed toward the door. Perhaps it was a good thing after all that he had those papers to grade.

† † †

Cold seeped from the snow-covered ground, through the erinsheen quilt, his cloak, and then his leggings and breeches. Numb toes wiggled in his boots, and he blew on his fingers, rubbing them together while he waited for Vic to move one of her few chess pieces. Her chin propped in her palm, her mouth quirked in concentration, she lay stretched out on the blanket, milk-colored neck and clavicle visible through the gap in her cloak. Her hair cascaded over the quilt, a river of fine-spun amber. He crossed his arms, resisting the urge to reach across the chessboard and touch that hair, so like the dawn. Instead he looked over at Kiareinoll Creek, flowing nearby. A fallen tree strained the water clear of its burbles and rushing, combing it to stillness like the pause between movements in a grand lay, or the spread of her hair across the quilt. His eyes drifted over the smooth flow of amber, lingered on the lines of her collarbone, and his breeches suddenly tightened as he thought about the rest of her. Suppressing a groan, he cursed himself.

Vic's mouth seesawed back and forth a few times, and with an oath and grumble she sat up and conceded the game.

Chuckling, Ashel relaxed and snatched his king, bobbing it up and down while he said aloud in a raspy voice, "I accept your surrender, madam."

She frowned, raised her queen, and had it reply in a haughty, full-throated voice, "Next time we shall not be vanquished so easily." A smile tugged at the corner of her mouth, her eyes flashing green. "It is embarrassing how often you've beaten me. I'm the bloody Blade!"

He grinned, and she ducked her head, her hair falling between them. "Don't do that."

"What?"

Snorting, she peeked from behind the amber cascade. "Dazzle me with that smile. I'm not some student of yours."

His grin vanished, classroom whispers sifting his thoughts.

Head still down, Vic packed up the chess set. "We are not playing this again until I've gotten some pointers from Bellin."

He heaved himself off the blanket and found a flat rock on a beachlet clear of snow. Tossing it, he counted four skips before it sunk.

"Ah. A new challenge!" Vic squatted down to sift through the stones. Her rock jumped in three wide arcs, and a little fish flashed out and back into the water with an angry plunk.

They took turns, growling and laughing as they competed for skips and distance. Ashel had the advantage of height and strength and reach, but she knew how to pick the rocks that suited her. They exchanged advice on technique and discussed their preferred rock shape and heft. Ashel told her how Dalborn, the old Harmony, had taught him to throw with his left and right hand both, to build dexterity, and she described twilight walks along the shore of Ourtown with her father, tossing stones into the cold northern ocean. The third time her stone skipped past the point where his had drowned, he said he wished he'd never shown her his secrets.

Chortling, she elbowed him in the ribs. "Maybe it's because I'm used to plucking at bow strings instead of harp strings."

His grin froze, and his rock plunked into the water.

"Oh, Ashel." Gently, she rested her hand on his arm. Her eyes glowed like summer grass; her hair drifted from her shoulders in the breeze. Her usual mask of gruff disdain dropped, revealing sympathy. "You know I didn't mean it like that." Then she snorted bitterly. "I'm just an unsullied Trainer whore. Don't listen to me."

Her touch set off a symphony of voices, of flutes, of drums, and the noise echoed through his blood to match the rhythm of his heart. Swallowing, he looked across the creek at a grove of old mothers, and Winder and Wineyll's song swelled out of memory—an aria destined to become a dirge. Gazing at the warding trees, listening to her voice but hearing only song, he could no longer deny the truth his friends threw at him.

"Are you all right?" she asked.

He shook his head. No, he was definitely not all right. His heart had taken that tack toward marriage Simlael had warned him against. "I've got those essays to grade," he said, gathering up the bread and cheese still on the blanket. Dundlehead, he cursed himself. She was the bloody Blade. She was the bloody Relmlord's mistress! Those two shoals alone were danger enough.

Vic helped him stuff everything into the basket. "I'm no whore, Ashel," she said tightly, "and you're no coward. The Heralds write what they think will sell their pamphlets. It's all nonsense and nobody believes it."

He let her think the pamphlet explained his silence while he swept the blanket into a roll and started back. She dashed after him, taking two steps for each one of his, her skirts catching on brambles. Grumbling at the snags, she asked him to slow down. "You can't risk being captured. Imagine the political advantage that would give the Relmlord."

He stopped and grabbed her wrist, gripping it so hard he felt her pulse quicken. "How about his personal advantage of capturing the Blade?"

She blinked, then jerked her arm free. "What's your problem, Ashel?"

"I don't—oh, never mind. I have to get back."

They walked most of the way in silence. He called himself a fool, argued with himself. Whether or not she acknowledged it, Vic's heart belonged to the Relmlord. He'd studied enough ballads, operas, lays, and sagas about love and hate that he could recognize it in a real person. Is this why I've fallen for her? he wondered. His friends all mocked him for having the pick of Narath, but he couldn't have Vic. No different from Laelin, he had spent every moment he could with her, and she laughed at every compliment as if it were a joke. She had no more interest in him than she had in the Loremaster. Idiot. How do you stop listening to a song this beautiful? Wool in the ears? All the herds in the Lathalorns wouldn't have enough to block out this noise. Ashel, Prince of Latha, what an ass.

As they approached the east gate, he didn't want her to think he was angry with her, and he certainly didn't want her angry with him. "Will you come over tonight?" he asked. "I'll make us dinner."

To his relief, she grinned. "I don't know. Sounds pretty risky to me."

"I've been taught by the best."

"Kachel's taught your sister too. I've killed Relmans with her flatcakes."

He laughed. "*I* can cook—"

"You put them in slingshots, you see," she chuckled. "Command ordered a wagonload of them for the spring campaigning—"

"Vic, I can cook. Let me prove it to you."

With a final guffaw, she agreed and they parted at the next corner. Thank Elesendar, the music was gone from his head.

He had bought his house the year before with his own money saved from salary and gambling. It was small—only the kitchen and parlor on the ground floor, a bedroom on the second, and the attic, where Bellin lived. The other man's rent had paid for the maid and the cook since the Caleisbahn gamerunners wiped out Ashel's savings. Bellin sat in the parlor, a half dozen books spread over the sofa and floor. "Where's the maid?" Ashel asked, groaning at the scarves tossed across the sofa, the socks strung up by the fire, the dishes from that morning still on the table.

"Day off," Bellin said from behind one of the texts.

"I have company tonight. Can you help me clean up?"

Bellin's eyes peeped over the pages. "Vic?"

"She's coming over for dinner," he replied casually.

Bellin dropped his book. "You're cooking?"

"I *can* cook."

"I know you can cook. But you *don't* cook, except when you're courting."

"Not true. I made dinner for Melba a month ago. Can you at least take those things up to your room?" Ashel started piling the dishes together, his cheeks hot.

Bellin gathered his books. "Melba doesn't count. Vic's trouble, Ashel."

"You're prejudiced."

"I don't mean that. Being kidnapped by Caleisbahnin wasn't her fault. But you could never marry her."

Of course, the first time Bellin and Simlael agreed on anything, it was on *this*. Ashel carried the dishes into the kitchen, angry at them both. "We'll have to wait till she's out of the army."

Bellin cranked the hand pump to put water into the cauldron. "She's a trooper. Elesendar, she's the Blade. Do you think she'd want to leave the army?"

Ashel shrugged. The music he'd heard by the creek had already answered that. "People change their minds about what they want to do all the time."

"She dreamed of war in Fembrosh, you told me. That's her destiny."

"She dreamed of Kragnashians too. She could decide to become a merchant tomorrow." They hauled the cauldron over to the hearth and hung it above the fire to heat the wash water. Bellin dropped the dishes in to soak and they went back to the great room.

"What if she's killed?"

"I could be run down by a teamster tomorrow. Just take your books upstairs, please."

Just before dusk, he chopped up the vegetables and started the tubers boiling. Their regular cook came in with two fish in a bucket; he thanked her, told her they were perfect, and sent her home. Making popping noises, the fish sucked air at the surface of the water, suffocating. "Know how you feel," he told them grimly, then rolled out the pastry dough and layered in the vegetables and spices. He was just snagging a fish by its gills when the knocker sounded. Damn, he thought. Why aren't troopers ever decently late?

At the front door, Bethniel swept in, kissing him on the cheek. "I can't go home tonight," she cried, collapsing on the sofa. "I can't listen to another word about Fensin from Mother. It's not my fault he went to Relm! He came back today, and he was incensed about Vic almost killing the Relmlord. He called for a Senate hearing to find out if 'the monarchy' has been plotting secretly behind the Senate's back, while of course he's been secretly plotting behind *our* backs. I think the whole scheme was to get back at Father for making him take me on as clerk, and to punish *me*, he ordered me to distribute copies of that *vile* Herald's pamphlet to all the Senators—"

"I saw that pamphlet too, but . . . I'm having company tonight, so maybe we could commiserate another time?"

His sister took her arm off her forehead and sat up. "Oh

Ashel, what they said about you was completely ill-founded. And Vic—the gall to call her that! Speaking of Vic, we heard a month ago that she was given leave, but we haven't heard from her. She left Winterquarters with some lieutenant who comes from Alna, and Mother thought maybe she went to stay with him, but I just can't believe she'd go there. Of all places— Alna? But you'd think she'd at least write to us . . ." Sniffing, she looked toward the kitchen. "Are those tubers? Are you cooking?"

"Yes. Really, sis, I'd love to hear all the gossip and state secrets, but I'm expecting someone."

"Who? Ashel, you only cook when you're courting."

Dismayed, he glanced out the window into the gloaming. Bethniel's eyes sparkled at him, determined to find out who was coming. "Nobody you know," he told her. "A minstrel, my friend Melba."

"Not the one who got you into that Caleisbahn mess? Mother'll have a fit!"

"That's one reason I don't live at the manor. Mother doesn't know who I see."

"Oh, I wish! The Betheljin Ambassador's son and I are courting, you know. He's really lovely, even if he is from Traine. But we always have to meet in the city." She prattered on while he peeked out the window again, thankful the street was empty.

"Beth, get out."

Huffing indignantly, she launched herself from the couch. "When I'm queen, you won't be able to throw me out," she teased, pulling on her gloves.

"You're not Ruler yet." He kissed her on the cheek. "Maybe Kachel will sneak you in the back way."

She laughed and he swung the door open. Vic smiled from the gate. Slamming the door, he grabbed his sister's hand and dragged her toward the kitchen. "Actually, before you go, maybe you can give me your opinion on the soup I'm making."

"She's here? Oh, come on brother, let me grace the girl with the hand of Latha's heir."

The knocker sounded again. Giggling, Bethniel twisted out of his grip and flew to the door. As the light from his parlor spilled into the yard, her jaw dropped.

Vic's mouth fell open as well, then shut as her eyes kindled green. "I thought you stayed out of your mother's plots, Ashel."

"Vic," he said aloud, hoping the sound of his voice would stop her, but she pivoted on her heel and strode out of the yard. Staring after her, Bethniel closed the door and turned on him.

"And just how long have you known she was here?" His sister's brown eyes smoldered.

He sighed. "How about dinner, sis? Somebody has to eat it."

Ice misted the air, dusting eaves and wagons. As Vic passed warmly lit houses and empty markets, the snow failed to cool anger boiling out of betrayal. Her fists twisted the fabric of her skirts. Stupid woman. What was she doing letting Lora put her in dresses and send her following Ashel like a cat after cream? His family may have sheltered her, given her a place, but they'd never welcomed her. Elekia had tested and insulted her from the day she arrived, while Bethniel had treated her like a prize to be shown off before friends. "Look what I found in the throne room one morning. The Relmlord must be crying over his coffers that we got for free what he paid hard crystal for." Bethniel had been Vic's first friend in Latha, but the past few weeks, Ashel had been the one to offer real friendship. Her laughter the day of the mop fight was the first eye-watering, breath-taking belly laugh she could remember since the fish scoop in Cairo. They'd laughed like that almost every day since.

Now her eyes stung with furious tears.

On the Cobblestone's porch, a couple of city guards, cloaks wet with snow, stamped their boots. Vic stopped, stomach aching as if she'd been kicked. Of course, now that Ashel had told his family she was in Narath, Elekia had sent the guards to find her. Why couldn't they leave her alone? She owed them nothing. Fresh ire boiling past her ears, Vic spun around and stalked toward the city's west gate. Years spent playing cat and gekko with Relmans had taught her to attack the enemy in his own camp while he's looking for you in yours.

As she rounded the last bend in the manor road and walked into the light of the guardhouse, a hulking figure stepped out to greet her. "The gates are closed for the night, miss," the guard said, waving her back toward the city.

Vic pulled off her hood. "It's me, Gaston. I've come to report to the Ruler."

Startled, the old man stood straighter and saluted. "Captain Victoria! Where've you been? We've been expecting you for weeks!"

Vic shrugged and asked him to open the gate. "No need to herald me. Kachel will let me in."

With a grin, he put his finger to the side of his nose. "You coulda been born a royal, Captain. Sneaking in the back way so as not to get your nose nipped. Tsk."

Clenching her fists under her cloak, she smiled coldly at him. "This snow'll nip your nose if you don't open the gate so you can go back inside."

"What, this dusting? This isn't cold. The ice storm of sixty-two, that was cold—"

"Open the gate, trooper," Vic said, resorting to orders. Muttering audibly, Gaston finally tugged at the winch.

Shivering, she drew up her hood and passed into the manor grounds. Yellow light in the manor windows painted a jumble of ghosts and shadows over deep drifts. She trudged to the back of the manor, then made her way carefully through the vegetable garden to the kitchen. The porch was shuttered for the winter, but the exterior door opened and a scullion came out with a load of wash water. Vic slipped past her and into the kitchen, moving as stealthily as she might through a Relman camp.

Stirring something on the stove, Kachel bellowed laughter, accompanied by the tenor giggles of a boy washing dishes. Silently, Vic ducked into the pantry, walked through the canned fruit, dried meat, teas, and table linens, and passed into the servants' quarters. From there, she made her way to the main hallway and the south dining room, where the family usually ate. That pamphlet was full of disgusting lies, but she did feel used by the monarchy, manipulated. She had joined the army to escape them, but Elekia sent her "counselors," trying to snare Vic into doing her bidding. Her face hot, she grasped the doorknob. Their control would end this night, she promised herself. *I am not their child. I am not their servant.* Taking a deep breath, she went in, planted her feet, and saluted.

"Well, I'm here."

Sashal's eating sticks stopped halfway to his mouth. Swallowing nothing, he put them back down. Elekia blinked at her. Sashal cleared his throat. "So you are."

They stared at each other until Elekia threw up her hands. "Vic, sit down and stop glowering at us."

"I've come to give my report, Ruler."

The king nodded. "Good. Have a seat." His eyes darted to his wife. "Please, Captain. I've been waiting to hear what happened for a month."

Never looking at the queen, Vic remained standing and briefed the king on the reconnaissance mission. "The Relmlord awakened when I was reconnoitering in the cabin housing his staff. I stabbed him before I realized who he was. Geram and I then made our way back to Winterquarters."

The king nodded. "Going inside that cabin was foolish and unnecessary, Captain. That Listener was supposed to stop you from taking such risks."

Vic cocked her head. "He tried, Your Majesty." Her eyes strayed to the queen. Elekia leaned forward in her chair, watching intently. "I didn't realize that his orders—" she ventured.

"I gave them." Sashal came around the table to take her hands. She flinched when he touched her, but once again saw her father in his red hair and pale blue eyes. Gulping, she looked away.

"Vic, you're as dear to us as our children."

Coming to stand beside her husband, the queen touched Vic's arm. "I didn't know he ordered a Listener to watch out for you, but I'm glad you're safe."

Vic jerked free of them. "Safe?" The colors of the room, warm browns, deep reds and blues, whirled in her vision. She looked from queen to king but could not see the details of their faces. "My only value to you is as a weapon!" *Unsullied Trainer Whore.*

"Captain"—Sashal drew himself up with a king's authority— "you have a duty. To me. As your Ruler. And you will report directly to me, especially when you've done something so stupid."

"Why? Why do you care? Other captains have only their fieldmarshall to answer to. You try to control me like *he* did."

"Vic." Elekia's voice slapped her ears. "You are an officer in Latha's army, and as such, you are the king's servant. He can order you to report or not as he pleases. Now come with me."

An invisible wall pushed her forward. "Don't use your witchcraft on me," she screamed, fury roaring in her ears. Her nose full of tears, she gulped air through her mouth, searching for strength. "I will not be controlled. You and Lornk are the same—"

Light exploded, and the floor swung like a pendulum, her skirts blooming around her. "Stop it, Elekia," Sashal said aloud. Vic's breath shuddered, a pressure behind her eyes building—grief and longing, dismay and shame.

"What happened to you?" The queen knelt, shaking Vic's shoulders. "I thought you hated him. What in the Shrine happened?"

A wail unfolded in her belly, and Vic shook her head, her hands thrashing the air between them. Hysteria clutched at her heart, a great sob of anguish beating at her throat. "Get Selcher in here," the queen snapped. A scream escaped as a high-pitched whine. Her fist pounded the floor. She wished she had gone back to the Cobblestone. This frontal attack had turned into a rout. Selcher was the cavalry for Elekia's side.

Thin, cold sunlight woke the colors of the carpet. From the angle of the beams, Vic guessed it was midmorning. Last night, she had screamed and rolled on the rug as the queen tried to use her power to make her stand. When Selcher came in, she put Vic to sleep with one arrow of a thought. She had always wondered if Selcher were a Listener. Now she knew.

A rustle of silk snagged her attention, and she rolled over to see Elekia standing by a chair in the corner. "How long have you been there?"

"Stop being sullen and tell me what happened," the queen said.

Vic snorted. "Ever the nurturer."

Elekia harrumphed and smiled like a cat, like Lornk.

They are the same, Vic thought again. Crafty, manipulative, powerful. The queen's face sobered, became almost kind. "You nearly killed the man you hate."

"I gave my report. What happened afterward is my business."

Elekia stared at Vic a moment, then gazed out the window. Dust danced in the sunlight surrounding the queen, but the woman stood with stooped shoulders. "The king and I want to thank you."

"For what?"

"The Relmlord was in the Kiareinoll to meet secretly with Fensin of Alna, who'd gone there to negotiate a peace treaty without the Ruler's consent. You put a stop to that."

Air huffed out of Vic's lungs. "Did Fensin escape?"

The queen smiled grimly. "The Opposition could talk his way out of a lupear's jaws. Yes, he's safe in Narath now. The Heralds are in his pocket, by the way. Every word they print comes from him. Remember that."

Unsullied Trainer Whore. Vic fingered the hem of her nightgown. "Where are my clothes?"

"In the wardrobe."

Only a pair of trousers and a sweater she'd left behind on her last visit hung next to her dress. "I'm surprised you didn't move me out of the inn."

Elekia's eyes stayed fixed on the view. "Where you stay while on leave is your choice." Another moment passed before she turned around. "But why didn't you come home? What were you afraid of?"

"Home," Vic scoffed, reaching for the sweater.

"Wasn't the revenge sweet enough?" the queen asked. "Were you upset you didn't get to gloat a little? You were bedridden at Winterquarters for two weeks. What happened?"

Vic pulled on the trousers and found a clean pair of socks

in a drawer. She felt Elekia's eyes trying to force hers to meet them, so she turned her back to the queen. "Why did you make Ashel trick me into meeting Bethniel?"

"Ashel knew you were in town? And Bethniel too? As if she wasn't in enough trouble." Elekia's fists clenched in preparation for a tirade, but she relaxed her fingers when Vic finally met her gaze. "I don't know what you're talking about. Ashel hasn't come up here since last fall, and my daughter didn't come home last night." Elekia's face smoothed over. "If my son has taken up subterfuge, I know nothing of it."

Last night, Ashel's door had opened, and Bethniel had stood there with her mouth hanging open, eyes wide. Ashel had had his hands out in supplication, his face defeated. Perhaps she should have waited for an explanation.

"Vic, please tell me," the queen asked again. "I won't scold. I just want to know why."

Last night, Selcher had deflated her emotions like a pin in a balloon. Drained, she resigned from the battle. "I wish I knew. It happened so fast. He could have been anybody, and I remember being very annoyed because there was going to be a corpse in that cabin that would spoil our plans." With a sigh, she shrugged. "When I saw it was him, I wanted to die myself."

Leaning on the windowsill, the queen gazed at the battle between wizards and Kragnashians woven into the carpet. Vic snorted softly, wondering if one of the wizards was her namesake. "If you had been captured in that cabin, it would have broken this family," Elekia said softly. She met Vic's eyes. "If you were killed in battle, we would mourn you. If you fell into Lornk's hands again . . ." She trailed off. "I dread nothing more."

Vic frowned in consternation. "Why?"

The queen raised an eyebrow, kindness melting into her usual scorn. "You yourself thought life as his mistress was worse than death, unless you've changed your mind."

With an angry sigh, Vic tugged on a boot. "Of course not, Your Majesty." *This* is why I didn't come back to the manor, she thought, clearly enough for the queen to Hear.

"Good," Elekia said crisply. "If you get another chance, make sure he's dead before you leave him."

A corner of Vic's mouth crept down. "I will."

†††

Pushing open Cobblestone door, Vic spotted Ashel and Lora, each with hands clasped around a mug. She froze, her feet yearning to turn and go round to the back door, but the pair looked up at the jingling bell. Her stomach climbing up her throat, she came inside. "I'm sorry I didn't let you explain last night," she said, looking at the prince's boots.

"Can I buy you some mulled wine?"

Lora excused herself, and Vic sat, a sheepish smile pulling at her mouth. "I should buy you a cup. I really am sorry."

He shrugged and leaned across the table to briefly squeeze her hand. "How did you come to find me not guilty?"

She laughed at the innocent way he rolled his eyes. "I thought I'd been routed last night, so I retreated right into the hands of the enemy—I went to the manor."

"Oh. How was that?"

She shook her head. "Not as bad as I expected. Your mother—she surprises me sometimes."

He nodded, his face haloed by the sunlit window behind him. Shrine, he's perfect, Vic thought. There had to be something wrong with him, but she hadn't seen it. Intelligent and beautiful and kind, he was more like a storybook prince than a real man. A barmaid brought them fresh mugs of mulled Eldanion and sighed as Ashel frowned at it. Vic echoed her, watching him wrap long fingers around the cup. Then he looked up at the young woman and flashed straight teeth at her.

"Thank you," he said aloud, his smile widening as the girl's cheeks flamed up to her hairline. The breath in Vic's chest came out in a huff, and she had to suppress a laugh.

"Elesendar, Ashel," she said when she had left. "I've never seen anybody flirt so profoundly well as you. With two words you've got that woman's head spinning."

"I'm only being polite."

She raised an eyebrow. "It's a good thing I'm leaving today. Helara has been complaining how you take the women's minds off their work."

"You're going? I thought you had leave until spring."

Embarrassed, she hid behind her mug, sipping. "I'm moving back to the manor."

"I liked having you down here in the city."

"Frankly"—she looked around the room for sight of Helara or Lora—"I'm running out of money. All the work I've done around here has cost me a good pound of crystal."

"Helara shouldn't have taken rent from you—"

"No." She stopped him. "I wanted to pay for the room. It's like your house—staying here was something of my own, bought with my own earnings."

"You could stay with me," he offered, so quietly she almost didn't Hear him.

"Ashel," she blurted, "you scandalous rogue!" She grinned so he'd think she was joking, but her cheeks blazed.

He laughed, his eyes sparkling. "My neighbors would be horrified. I know—you could dress up like a Caleisbahn dancing . . ." He stopped, his smile fading.

"Or like a Trainer mistress?" Vic asked, her skin tingling with cold.

"Shrinejump! I'm an idiot. I—"

"Forget it." She leaned forward and patted a hand twice the size of hers, but long and slender. Perfect. "You don't ever have to perform with me," she said.

He clasped her fingers. "You're a good friend, Captain Victoria of Ourtown. I suppose you'll need my help moving up to the manor."

"Your mother's unhappy you didn't tell her where I was."

He grinned. "She's always unhappy about something. For you, I'll risk her wrath."

CHAPTER 16

ELESENDAR'S LANDING

A soft rain falling, Vic unrolled her blanket on a bed of damp moss and sandwiched it between canvas to keep it dry. Around her, grass squelched as the patrol set up camp. Spring campaigns had seen them tramping through knee-deep mud, but the Lathans had pushed the border back to the edge of the Kiareinoll, thanks to an influx of funding that brought fresh troops and equipment to the front. Summer had brought rumors of a large enemy camp, but after days of searching, the Dagger hadn't found a single Relman.

As she fished in her pack for a map, a lock of damp hair fell across her eyes. Cursing, she mumbled about cutting it off.

"I wish I had a mulla for every time I've heard you say that, and yet that hair only gets longer," Geram chuckled.

"Why you don't cut it is a mystery," Maynon added, sauntering over. "I've been saying for years, a Relman could grab that braid." Grinning, he snatched the plait at the nape of her neck, yanking her backward. Vic flung herself sideways, pulling him off balance, and kicked his feet out from under him. His grip on her hair still firm, she rolled with him to the ground, jabbing an elbow into his belly. With an oof, he let go, and she sprang up and returned to her pack.

Freeing the map, she said, "Can't a woman complain in peace?"

Laughing, Geram offered a hand up to Maynon.

"I'd like to see you do better, fishlicker," Maynon grumbled.

Still chortling, Geram shook his head. "I know better than to touch the hair."

"Captain"—Silla emerged from the forest with an armload of firewood—"the logs will smoke in this rain."

Vic looked at Geram, and he shook his head, said he hadn't Heard any Relmans, same as the scouts hadn't seen any. "Go ahead," she answered Silla. "We may as well indulge ourselves."

Silla dumped the wood, catching Maynon's foot. Ignoring his complaints, she built the sticks into a little lodge over a pile of dry moss she'd scrounged from somewhere. "Damn rain," she muttered as the kindling smoked but failed to light.

Maynon watched over her shoulder. "Maybe if you blew on them."

"Maynon, you're full of useless advice," Vic said, preempting a round of curses from Silla. "Go patrol with Thrusher."

With a nod, the pair left, and Silla's shoulders relaxed. Seeing Geram chuckling, Vic went over and joined him beneath a large hoin frond he held over his head. "It isn't funny," she hissed.

"I know. But you should Hear them."

"Shame on you." Three days ago, Vic had caught her friends pawing each other behind a bush. Now they snapped and hissed like cats in an alley. The army would discharge them both if the affair became known.

"I told you this was coming. You should have transferred one of them last spring."

Vic poked at the glistening turf with a twig. "If I'm the Blade, Mayon's the hilt and Silla the crossbeam of the Dagger. They're essential."

"But you have me now." He grinned.

"Lot of good a fisher does me, in the *woods*."

He chuckled, and Silla's fire finally caught. "I'm going up there," Vic told them, pointing to a nearby hill. "Signal if anything happens." Atop the hill, she sat among soft scents of wild herbs and summer blossoms and gazed over a patchwork of glades, hoarsgrout, and granite outcroppings. The rainclouds rolled away and sun flashed on butterfly wings; a galer song danced along the breeze. Off to the west rose the blue peaks of the Lathalorns, to the south the golden shimmer of the Relman plains, to the north and east the blue-green carpet of the Kiareinoll. How might Ashel describe the beauty of the land where Elesendar conceived His children? Vic chuckled. *"Does it bother you that I don't believe?"* she'd asked him after a lecture he gave on the metaphor of Landing. He had loosed one of those heart-stopping smiles. *"Does it bother you that I do?"*

The sun setting on a clear sky, she strolled back down the hill and diced with Geram and Silla while a spit of harriers roasted over the campfire. Maynon and Thrusher still out, the Dagger chewed their rations while the sky filled with stars and Querkle told them a legend about a wizards' battle. Just as he reached the climax of the story, Maynon sprang into the clearing and threw the fire tarp over the pit. "A Relman company is camped not two miles from here."

"How many?" Vic asked.

"Thirty," Thrusher said.

"Do you think their scouts have seen us?"

"Probably."

"Did any see you?"

"Probably not." Maynon's teeth flashed.

Vic nodded. "Show the fire. Let them think we're still here, still comfortable."

They piled leaves under blankets and hid in the midsummer

tresses of the cerrenils. The old mothers' foliage provided good cover but left little room for pulling bows. It would have to do.

Geram said, "Listen."

The Relmans came as quietly as cats, surrounding the campsite for an easy attack. Whispers and thoughts died among the Lathans. For every Relman, Vic shook a branch. Other rustles echoed hers.

"The wind's come up," a Relman whispered. Another shushed him. Vic flashed hand signals at the troopers who could see her, knowing they would relay her orders around the circle of trees. Thirty against twelve. Elesendar, don't fail us.

A nightwing trill piercing the silence, the Relmans loosed a volley of arrows at the blankets, charging toward the fire and screaming like the mad. The Lathans' arrows showered down as the Relmans drew their stoneknives and pounced at the bedrolls. Eight fell. Three more went down in the second Lathan volley before someone pointed at the trees.

"The old mothers," she shouted. "They're in the trees!"

Relmans swarmed at them. A man scrambled up after Vic, dodging her arrows. Unsheathing her dagger, she jumped past him and landed on another Relman, shoved her dagger into the woman's neck. Blood gushed. Vic rolled off the body; feet slapped the ground behind her. She dodged. A stoneknife thunked into the turf, and the Relman cursed, rushing forward with another weapon in his fist. She felled him with a scissor kick, but he rolled back into a crouch as she sprang to her feet.

"Well, Captain"—he pointed to her insignia—"you're a sweet prize."

The fire hissing with spattered blood, Vic sized him up. He was big but moved as fast as she could. Lit with uncertain shadows, troopers wrestled and sparred around them. Voices cried alarm from the surrounding woods, punctuated by the thwang of bowstrings and the thunk of feet and bodies on turf and wood. Relmans sprawled in the grass, lay over logs, slumped against the trunks of trees. The Dagger sliced through them like a scythe through grain, but the man facing her looked sure of victory. Grimacing, Vic dove inside his reach, swiping upward. He laughed and leapt over her, catching her in the kidney with a boot. She somersaulted to her feet, grunting against the welling ache in her side.

Spinning round, she ducked his fist and jabbed her dagger at his thigh. Growling, he slipped backward, clutching the wound. She grinned at him, shifting from foot to foot. Redja and a Relman woman fell between them, hands around each other's throats. "You didn't bring enough troops to take me, Marshall," Vic said, eying the stripes on the man's sleeves. With a roar, the Relman rushed at her. Vic backed into a tree and held ground. He charged forward, aiming to pin her to the cerrenil. Her height allowed her to duck him, but he grabbed her braid and swung her toward the fire.

She tripped over Redja, just rising from the strangled Relman, managed to twist away from the flames, but caught her elbow on the edge of a rock. Lightning flashed up her arm, kicking the breath from her lungs. Before she could scramble up, Redja fell across her legs, his throat spraying blood, and the Relman marshall stood over her, wiping his blade on his trousers. Vic yanked her legs free, but his boot struck her in the jaw, knocking her backward with her arms flung wide. A boot stomped down. Bones cracking, her dagger fell from her grasp.

"I brought enough, Captain." His grin spread wide, then opened into a groan. Toppling forward, he landed on her broken arm.

Wheezing, she waved Maynon and his bloody dagger away, dragged herself up, and dodged out of the clearing. Her arm throbbed, pain swelling past her shoulder, stirring nausea in her gut, but she swallowed the bile, fashioned a sling out of her belt, and stuck to the cover of the cerrenils, dashing out here and there to stab a Relman kidney, slice a hamstring, kick a spine. As their numbers dwindled, the remaining Relmans ran for it, followed by half the Dagger through the black forest. Soon, all the Relmans were dead or fled. Of the Lathans, only Redja lay among the bodies on the ground. Querkle took his boots and weapons and packed them so they could be returned to his family. They didn't have time to bury him.

They moved south, in search of the Relmans' camp and stray enemies. Thrusher splinted Vic's arm while they marched, warning her the healers at Summerquarters would have to reset it. Her jaw loose and sore, she already tasted iron in anticipation of *that*.

An hour later, they fought another dozen Relmans fleeing southward. The Dagger quickly killed them all. When it was over, Vic sat and shook her head.

"What's the matter?" Maynon asked.

"Sometimes doesn't it surprise you how easy it can be?"

He shrugged. "Troopers lose their edge."

"Not us," Silla quipped. "We've got the Blade."

Vic's arm ached, her fingers numb, jaw swelling, mouth dry and sour. She wished she could spit. "It could happen to anybody."

"Captain," Geram said, taking her hand, "breathe in time with me." She looked at him, puzzled, but complied at a second urging. Geram grimaced, and the ache in her arm and jaw dulled to a shadow.

"What did you do?" she asked.

He massaged his forearm. "It's a long way back to Summerquarters, and the Dagger needs a sharp Blade."

"Captain!" Thrusher held up a large leather portfolio.

"What's this?" Vic asked as he handed it to her.

"Nothing much," the trooper said. "Just maps and orders."

Vic lurched up, her belly warm. "I expect they'll be wanting that back."

† † †

At Summerquarters, Command celebrated the Dagger's discovery and promptly ordered the patrol to take the original documents to Narath. A healer named Orlon went with them to tend Vic's arm. A slotaen shortage at the front left him with little to stop the flesh around the broken bones from festering, and she spent most of the trip in the back of a wagon, sweating and hardly able to raise her head until the fever finally broke a few days out of Narath. Then, sitting alongside the driver, she marveled at the crowd slowly gathering round them. Side roads like tributaries emptied travelers into a great river of wagons, horses, and people. Children ran freely, their parents laughing and even talking out loud, everyone heading to the capital to celebrate Landing. The Oreseekers celebrated Festival on the day commemorating the disembarkation of the *Elesendar*'s crew and passengers, but Lathans called it Landing, and claimed it was the day Elesendar descended from the heavens and joined with the old mothers to produce human children. As Vic watched the crowd, her thoughts turned to Narath, and she admitted an eagerness to see the king and Bethniel, Kachel and Gaston and Cimba and Timny. Memories of debates and music and wine with Ashel's friends fostered grins and guffaws. And thoughts of the prince himself brought an uncomfortable heat to her cheeks. Orlon's quizzical looks prompted Geram, Silla, and Maynon to exchange chuckles and winks. Vic told them to mind their own affairs and urged the driver to go faster.

As the sun sank toward the Kiareinoll one afternoon, they finally crested the last hill before the capital. Blue and yellow banners hung from gleaming ramparts and fluttered from flag posts. People, horses, and wagons jostled in a river of color. A group of Miners garbed in the yellow and red of their guild whistled a working song behind a contingent of Weavers bearing bolts of wool and chanting praise of the erin. Behind the patrol's wagon came a troupe of Tinkers who shouted and banged their tools in syncopated rhythm. The sun dazzled across the meadow before the gates, and as they drew closer, Minstrels lined the road, piping and drumming a welcome into the city. The patrol laughed and pointed, and Vic confessed she had never been in Narath during Landing. Every year she'd managed to arrange a patrol or volunteer for a mission. But as the driver slapped the reins and the horses at last drew them through the city gates, she felt she was coming home.

She sent the Dagger to quarter at the Cobblestone, then squeezed through packed markets and crowded streets to the city's west gate. At the manor guardhouse, Gaston sent a boy running for the manor while he enveloped her in a warm, damp hug. To her astonishment, Sashal and Elekia met her outside, before the front doors, each welcoming her with a kiss on the cheek. Bethniel squealed as she squeezed Vic tightly, and even Selcher smiled and welcomed her back with a hot bath.

Afterward, Bethniel sprawled on Vic's bed, updating her on every Senate battle and rumor that had come up since spring.

"Is there any intrigue you don't know about?"

"Not a one. Of course, the biggest news of the year is about you and Ashel."

Vic's skin prickled with goose bumps, her heart rattling in her chest. She kept her reply as nonchalant as she could. "If there were news about me, I think I'd know about it."

The princess giggled. "Says the woman who spent every free moment this winter with my brother."

"And he was surely sick of me by spring and glad to see the back of me."

"Well, I'm certain he likes seeing your backside."

"Beth!"

"Let's see. He cooked dinner for you. Twelve times, as I recall."

"I can't believe you kept track."

"And he took a troupe to the front. Of course it was all under cover of the Guild, and raising morale, but he was disappointed he didn't see you."

"I'm sure it was to raise morale. Ashel really cares about how we're doing in the war."

"Oh? And I suppose he told you that on one of your intimate little picnics."

"Is Narath always this crowded at Landing?" Vic asked, desperate to change the subject.

Bethniel slapped her forehead. "Elesendar, of course you don't know. You're going to be decorated. All this is for you, Vic—for the Blade and her Dagger. At Landing Eve, Father's going to give each of you a medal. A metal medal, mind you. Not crystal, metal."

"The map wasn't *that* important." Vic frowned. "The Relmans moved their main camps before we hit many targets."

"True, but even so, it's been a long time since we've had so many victories so close together. People danced in the streets. Even Fensin gave a speech praising the resourcefulness of the army. I wrote it for him, by the way, but I never expected him to use it. Father was very pleased, and Mother didn't criticize, so she liked it. But anyway, it's everything you've done. Father thought we should finally recognize it."

"Shrine."

"In three days, you'll be a hero, officially. Aren't you excited?"

"Overwhelmed." She thought of the soiled uniforms crammed into her pack. "What will I wear?"

The princess sprang to her feet. "Let's go shopping."

Vic grinned. "All right. But I get to pick the tailor."

In three days, Lora threw together a gown even lovelier than the others she'd sewn for Vic. Between fittings, Vic and the Dagger basked in the praise of Senators and guildmasters. She'd wanted so badly to see Ashel before she arrived, but now thoughts of him set her heart racing, and she kept too busy to find out why. Bethniel began to ask if she was avoiding him.

"Of course not," she answered once again on Landing Eve. She picked up a diamond-encrusted comb for Bethniel to position amid her curls. Catching her own reflection in the mirror, Vic smiled sheepishly at the sunset-colored hair twisted loosely over one shoulder—her one good feature. And Lora's gown, golden satin, smooth to her hips where it ballooned out over layers of crepe, was lovely. Hands on hips, she turned to admire the plunging backline and her own muscled shoulders and arms. A fingerless glove, embossed with gold thread, covered the splint on her arm. "Lora did a magnificent job, didn't she?"

Bethniel smiled, her skin aglow in the lantern light. "You're beautiful tonight, Vic, like autumn. All golden with the first touch of frost."

"Ha. Leave the poetry to the minstrels." Vic helped the princess adjust the comb. "But you look like a summer night."

"I like that! Summer at midnight, the witching hour." She winked. "So, Captain, Ashel is having dinner with us before we go to the ceremony."

Vic shrugged. "So?"

"So, so, so. He said that thing about autumn. I told him about the dress Lora was making for you, and he said, 'I bet she'll look like autumn—all golden with the first touch of snow.'"

"I thought it was frost."

"Ask him yourself." Bethniel giggled and danced toward the door. "He's in the garden practicing. You claim you haven't been avoiding him, so go tell him dinner's ready."

Vic looked at herself again and saw every angle that ought to be a curve. How could he want *her*? The woman in the mirror shrugged, her cheeks pink. She lowered her eyes and examined a thumbnail neatly trimmed at Bethniel's command. For five years she'd avoided any thought of romance, but since winter, she'd thought of little else but the strength of his arms as he flung stones into the pool, the warmth of his fingers when he touched her hand, the sparkle of his eyes when they shared conversation and mulled wine. Yet as she tried to imagine him clasping her in his arms, her skin remembered the brush of Lornk's fingers and embers sparked in the pit of her stomach. Covering her mouth, swallowing bile, she turned away from the mirror.

"Vic?" Bethniel touched her elbow.

"Sorry. Indigestion—shouldn't have bought lunch from a street vendor."

Bethniel stooped a little to look her square in the face, her brown eyes earnest. "All these years," she said, softly and aloud, "I've never asked what happened to you in Traine, but don't think I can't see it hurt you deeply."

"Beth, I—"

"When you first came to us, I could Hear you wondering why we took you in, what we got out of it. Well, I don't know why Mother or Father let you stay here, but I know when I saw you in the throne room that morning, I thought, this girl needs help, and *I* can give it to her. I don't get many chances to *give*, Vic." Shaking her head, she laughed ruefully. "In the end, I guess I haven't been able to help you much"—Vic tried to interrupt, but the princess held up her hand—"I think Ashel could, if you let him."

Sighing, Vic cast her gaze over the floral nap of Beth's carpet. On the dressing table, jewelry and perfume bottles scattered before the mirror, a casual disarray that bespoke the princess's frivolity. All these years, Vic echoed her, she'd never asked whether Bethniel wanted to be Ruler, never thought about the fact she hadn't been given the same choice as her brother. The sun slanted across the room and set a string of diamonds afire, shadowing half the princess's face. Frowning pensively, she looked like a woman who wanted to rule a nation about as much as she might want to drink briny water. But when Vic's eyes met hers, Bethniel grinned. "Go talk to Ashel."

He sat among the blooms in the rosen grove, tuning his harp and muttering audibly to himself. Dizzy in the sweet air, Vic stopped behind a bush to watch him. Black and gold robes looped over one shoulder, covering his left arm but baring sculpted muscles on his right. He looked like a mythical god of the Ancients, sitting with his harp under a flower-draped arbor. And what could a god want with a pitiful broken thing like her? Sighing, she stepped out. "I thought I was the only one in this country who thought out loud."

He jumped, the harp twanging, and then he grinned. "It's the habit of minstrels and doddering old politicians."

Waving back toward the manor, Vic quoted from a play they'd seen together that winter: "'Against my will I am sent to call you in to dinner.'"

Smiling appreciatively, he adjusted the clasp of his mantle. "You're not in uniform."

"No. Just my captain's laurels." She fingered the braided leather leaves pinned to her shoulder.

"This is the first time I've worn official Guild garb since I was in—for a long time. Only a few of us wear the minstrels' colors and the scholars' robes." He tweaked a troublesome string.

Vic nodded. "What'll you play tonight?"

His cheeks darkened. "A new song." He looked down and flexed a fist, then back up at her. "You inspired it."

She laughed. "Something martial about the Blade, I guess."

"Not really." He made space on the bench for her. "How long until dinner?"

"I think we have a little time." She joined him on the seat but couldn't lift her eyes from the grass spiking around her slippers. Into the stretching silence she said, "I'm looking forward to hearing you sing again."

His fingers swept across the harp strings, the music echoed by a galer nesting above them. They watched the sun sink a little lower into Fembrosh. "I've never seen . . . You remind me of fall."

Biting her lip, her face hot, she let her hair slip between them. "Fall?"

He wrapped the harp in its case and set it on the ground. "The first time I saw you, you looked like autumn after the trees are bare and the first snow has melted, leaving everything dead and muddy and hopeless."

"Oh, well, thanks." Heat spread to her ears. Why did she listen to Bethniel?

"Let me finish," he laughed. Taking her hands, he drew her around to face him, his voice as cool and deep as a Fembrosh glade. He spoke aloud, as all Lathans did on Landing Eve. "When you first came here, I wanted to show you spring would come. But you made your own spring. And tonight you're autumn again, but in all its glory—autumn that has felt the touch of winter but remembers summer still. I love that time of year, Vic."

His hands warm and dry, he searched her face with kind eyes under those lovely long lashes. Lornk had been golden and terrible; Ashel was dark and beautiful. Can I love him? she wondered. He leaned closer, his lips, like his eyes and hands, warmer and more generous than Lornk's. Her eyelids closed, and his mouth touched hers, but she shivered as she pictured herself sitting on that bench with a man, and the hair mixed with hers was blond. "Stop, please. I don't know if I can love anyone."

With a guffaw, he let her go and draped an arm over the back of the bench. "I'm usually better at this."

That salted the bitterness of her thoughts. "I don't understand what you see in me."

The sun slipped past the curtain of rosen. Ashel sat up straight, turned to her, then leaned back and sighed, his eyes melting into the deepening shade.

Taking a breath to steady the skipping rhythm of her heart, she shook her head. "It isn't you. It's me. All I've learned how to feel"—she paused, shivering again—"is . . . him. And I don't know how to stop feeling that." His eyes shone darkly. "I want to stop. I just don't know how."

Threading a lock of her hair through his fingers, he turned her face to his. "In Alna they say love is a choice, not a passion. Inlander custom is different." His eyes glimmered in the fading light. "But you're not an inlander, Vic. You have a choice."

"And you?"

He smiled softly, shook his head. "I've never been in love before. And now I'm trapped."

"You're not. We're not wed." Chortling, she slumped against the bench. "I never suspected you felt this way until half an hour ago. It isn't real to me."

Grabbing her head, he kissed her again, parting her lips with his tongue. Warmth ran down her throat, reigniting the embers in her belly. Her hands inched up his arms, her fists slowly uncurling, fingers pressing into lean muscle. Gasping, he held her tighter, his lips roving down her neck. Her blood tingled against the surface of her skin, heat spreading from the roots of her hair to her toes and fingertips, and when his mouth found hers again, she returned the kiss, a deep longing budding in her chest as his hand slid inside her gown and bared her shoulder. She teetered on the edge of desire, but golden snares laid years ago waited to trap her when she fell. Throat tight, she pulled away.

Groaning, he released her. "That was real. Don't tell me you didn't feel *that.*" Taking her hand, he kissed her fingers and knelt. "I'm not a fool, Vic. I know you went through something—I can only imagine what it must have been like. But you need to understand: I want to wed you, not merely have you, and not own you. As if anyone could own *you*! I'm a Lathan. We don't—I'm not a schoolboy, I'm a man, and I know what I want. I want you *as my wife.*"

Tears building, she exhaled a ragged breath. "This isn't about what we want, the way we want things to be." She looked at him, glorious in the twilight, and she felt small and crude and *used*. "It's about the way things are."

He stared at her, his chest rising and falling, then grabbed the harp case. "We'd better head in."

"Ashel—"

He stopped at the edge of the grove. "I'm sorry, Vic. Beth said—she gave me reason to think . . . You've been avoiding me since you arrived in town, and I should have taken the hint."

"Elesendar, Ashel. I just said this isn't about what we want. What woman doesn't want you?"

"You don't."

"I didn't say that. I need time . . . he insinuated himself into every part of me." She shivered, feeling sick. "I can't just forget him."

"Do you *want* to forget him?"

"Of course I do."

"Then you have to try," he said coldly and strode toward the house.

† † †

At dinner, Ashel acted as if their conversation, their kisses, in the rosen grove had never happened. He jested with his father, ate heartily, teased his sister. Dozens of meals had passed like this, except Vic couldn't look at him. She couldn't eat either, a stew of emotions boiling in her gut: shame, remorse, embarrassment, and a growing anger that he would expect her to simply *forget*. As soon as she politely could, she excused herself and rushed down to the city to collect her patrol, reaching the Cobblestone with her hair awry and her skirt muddied. Spotting most of the Dagger through the common room windows, she dodged around to the back door and ran up the stairs to Lora's room.

"He told you he loved you, didn't he?" the tailor guessed, brushing the hem of her gown.

"How could I answer him?"

Grabbing her by the shoulders, Lora forced her to look in the mirror. Behind Vic's shoulder, the girl's eyebrows were stern. "Yes. You could say yes."

A knock saved Vic from a reply, and Maynon poked his head in. "I thought I saw you sneaking round the back." He pushed through the door, followed by Silla. "We need a word."

Her stomach flopping over, Vic asked Lora if they could use her room. After the tailor left, she stared between her dearest friends. "You've done it, haven't you?"

Maynon handed her a pair of sealed envelopes. "Our resignations. We would have finished our tours and not declared, but"—he clutched Silla's hand—"she's pregnant."

Vic sighed, and the tears she'd held back since the rosen

grove spilled out. "I told Geram you're the hilt and the crossbar of the Dagger. The Blade won't work without you."

Maynon's grin was hard. "You'll make do with the fishlicker."

Silla pushed past her husband and clasped Vic's hand. "We expected you'd be resigning too, the way you've been pining for the prince the past few months. You know he's come here every day, looking for you." She cast a wry smile at Maynon. "And he's a lot better looking than that lout."

Vic forced her lips apart, trying to return their smiles. "He is, but you two both know I have unfinished business."

† † †

Cheering crowds lined the road, tossing flowers and laurels. The joy infectious, Vic's mood lifted as the Dagger rode in a procession of officials and guildmasters to the amphitheater's entrance. Once there, pages came forward and helped them dismount. Timny elbowed aside his sister to present his arm to Vic. Winking at Cimba, she ruffled his hair as she slid off the horse. "I've come full circle, Timny," she said.

"How so?" The boy's voice cracked from tenor to soprano.

"I would never have made it to Latha without you, and now I need you to get to that stage down there."

Timny blushed, smiling shyly as they started down a long flight of stairs leading to the stage below, where he escorted her to a wedge arranged for the Dagger. Center stage sat king, queen, and princess in a triangle, and beyond them the Senate leaders and the prime minister formed a third wedge.

Once they were seated, the guilds filed in: first the Miners and Weavers, followed by smaller contingents representing the minor crafts. After them came the Dancers, Jesters, and Minstrels. The Music led in her Guild with the black-and-gold-clad Melody on her right, Silnauer garbed in the Harmony's gray robes on her left. The Master Minstrels japed down the aisles, followed by the Loremasters, their gait almost as rollicking as their flamboyant guildmates. The journeymen came next, led by Ashel and Melba. Vic ducked her head, wishing she could go back in time and redo that meeting in the rosen grove— or avoid it altogether. But the final wave of spectators— apprentices from all the guilds—captured her attention as they came charging down the slope, shouting and tumbling to the grass below the stage. The audience roared in turn, egging on the children. Clapping his hands and waving the audience to cheer loud enough for Elesendar to hear, Sashal stood and walked downstage. Finally he motioned for silence, and when the noise had diminished to a few coughs, he spoke.

"Welcome, friends. Good Landing." The crowd's response thundered and echoed off the Lathalorns. "Thank you for sharing Landing with us. We have much to celebrate tonight. We are a strong and brave people." His hands clapped together twice. "Minstrels, show us why."

Acrobats tore onto the stage, juggling chairs and instruments. A fat man dressed to mimic a Master Minstrel threw up his hands and chased after them, shooing them here and there, moaning over this guitar almost dropped, that chair almost broken. He screamed as the acrobats somersaulted over an enormous harp and cried while they tossed stools and lyres and flutes between one another. As the audience laughed, Ashel walked on stage.

Vic felt the color rise in her cheeks. People cheered, and one of the acrobats brought the prince a dulcimer and a chair. When he sat, the audience hushed, and he began to play.

He did not sing. The audience took up the melody after he played the first bar, sending their thanks to Elesendar and the old mothers for their ancestors' lives, for their lives, for their children's lives. The people stood as they sang the second verse, the song swelling as their ranks seemed to swell. Vic sang with them, and when they were finished, she wiped her cheeks like everyone else.

"Some heretic," Geram whispered as they retook their seats.

Sniffing, she angled her head at Silla and Maynon. "You're my new second."

He grinned softly. "I know."

Ashel had not stopped playing, but he was kneading the melody into something new. A group of very young apprentice minstrels tiptoed downstage, stopping in front of his chair. He nodded once, and they began to sing.

> *Over the mount,*
> *There lies a place*
> *Where love has lasting grace*
> *And peace and joy go hand in hand,*
> *Over the mountain, in that land.*

Their voices spread like honey over the amphitheater. Each child sang with the purity of Lathan crystal. The lyrics praised Elesendar, calling for joy and justice and hope, and when a quintet of men and women joined their voices to children's, the song's expressions of faith became sublime. Ashel sang the last line of the refrain by himself.

> *Someday that's where I know I'll be.*

Slow to begin, the audience's enthusiasm rose like the refrain. Cheering grew louder and louder until the last line swept up through the levels and the crowd sang it over and over again.

> *Someday that's where I know I'll be.*

Sashal walked to center stage and waited while the audience grew silent. "I think we're there already," the king said.

"That's my father." Bethniel's mindvoice cut through the din of cheering.

"He's a good politician," Vic answered.

"He's a better father." Elekia clapped as they watched the king embrace his son.

Sashal began to speak again. "Never has there been so much joy felt by so many in the midst of such sorrow. Some of you have lost your homes. Many have lost sons or daughters, brothers or sisters. And many from the north and the west wonder what difference it makes if we give up a little land in the Kiareinoll.

"It makes a lot of difference. The Relmlord has gathered all the people in Relm against us. He will not stop with a little more land in Fembrosh. He wants our crystal."

A third of the audience, those dressed in red and yellow, stood and cried, "No!"

"He wants our wool."

Nearly a quarter shouted their denials.

"He wants our music."

The audience leapt to their feet, shaking fists and stamping.

"He will not enslave our children," Sashal cried.

"No!" came the answer.

"He will not have our Fembrosh magic."

"No!"

"He will not disrupt our harmony."

"NO!" Vic laughed at the deafening roar.

From offstage, Ashel caught Vic's eye. He smiled and raised his thumb. "Friends?" he asked in mindspeech.

Blushing, she offered a relieved smile. "Always."

Sashal introduced the next performance. "Many hundreds of years ago, a great number of sorcerers lived here. They did a great many works—some good, some evil. But as the Relmlord will learn, all power fades. As the wizards' days came to an end, they forgot how to control their power, and the last wizard died without knowing how or why he could make the rain fall on his garden while his neighbor's stayed dry."

Those on stage heard Elekia's harrumph, but she maintained an attentive smile.

"The greatest wizard in the history of Knownearth wrote down everything she knew before she died, but no one has ever found her Books of Knowledge. Her name was Kara, and I'll tell you of her life."

Geram squeezed Vic's shoulder, and Silla cast her a sympathetic look. "It's just a name," she told them.

As the king told Kara's story, dancers and musicians assembled on stage. When he reached the final chapter, he returned to his seat, and a dancer leapt downstage, swirling a large, filmy scarf to represent Kara's power. She and a man swayed and twirled, embraced and spun apart as the Melody led an orchestra of pipes and horns, stringed instruments and drums. Other dancers appeared as cerrenils and erin, and the lovers danced among them until the bass strings thrummed and the bassoons boomed a warning. The dancers froze. Drums rumbling, woodwinds trilled up a scale until offstage a woman screamed. The human voice startled the dancers into action. The erin stampeded left and right. The cerrenils raised their limbs up and down, trembling with uncertainty. Kara pressed a scroll into her lover's hands and led him behind one of the trees. He refused to hide there, so she bound him to the tree with her scarf.

The music ceased. Onstage strode a towering figure swathed in black robes. Its plaster head flamed with orange and red streamers; its teeth gnashed within a painted grin. The monster jabbed spindly arms at the apprentices seated in front of the stage, and the woodwinds amplified the children's screams. To banging drums and crashing cymbals, Kara fought the beast, hurling green streamers while it returned volleys of blue. They battled across the stage, swaying, leaping, entangling each other in the streamers until they lunged to and fro in a tug of war. At last both fell, exhausted, and the music throbbed down to a single suspended note. Wrapped in blue, Kara dragged herself to the monster and tore away the robe. A wizened old man tumbled out, grasped Kara's shoulders, and pulled her to his chest. Kara tried once to free herself from his embrace, then she and the man collapsed and lay quiet.

The scarf fluttered away from the lover Kara had bound to the cerrenil, and the music swelled painfully as he pulled her limp body away from her enemy. In anguish, he picked up the scroll Kara had given him and debated whether to toss her knowledge away or tear it up. The orchestra clashed in hateful dissonance, then slipped into a mournful dirge. The lover hid the scroll beneath the roots of the cerrenil and left the stage with dragging feet.

The stage lamps winked out, and only Elesendar lit the amphitheater. Applause erupted from the audience, and the king took center stage once more. "Lathans overcame the era of wizards," Sashal cried as stagehands relit the lamps. "We will overcome a single tyrant." He smiled and waited until the cheers faded. "Now we come to the night's purpose. Thanks to the resourcefulness of the troopers sitting on this stage, Latha has just completed our most successful campaign against Relm in two decades of war. Tonight, this brave patrol, known to you as the Dagger, and the Blade, their leader, will receive Latha's highest honor, the Brass Star."

He waved Vic and the others forward, and they came grinning and squinting in the stage lights. Timny and Cimba appeared, bearing silk pillows lined with the medals. Sashal held one out for the audience to see. And in the bare moment before their cheers renewed, Vic's ears caught the whirring of a Relman stoneknife. The cheers melted into shrieks as the king fell back with the blade in his throat.

Stunned, Vic shook her head to clear it, then ordered the patrol into the crowd. They jumped down, tripping through the crying apprentices, trying to chase a faceless assassin. Ashel tore to the king's side. Bethniel lay on the stage in a dead faint. Elekia shouted orders for the guards to contain the audience within the amphitheater. As her head swam between the dead king, the screaming onlookers, and the angry queen, Vic realized they'd never catch the killer. With no walls to climb or gates to pass, he or she could exit from any level of the bowl.

Sobbing hoarsely, Ashel hugged Sashal's body. Vic stepped toward him, but froze when he threw back his head and roared. How could she touch that grief? Elekia came instead and kneeled on the other side of the king, her eyes wet, her cheeks dry. Hushing her son, she held his head and stroked his hair. Bewildered by the queen's show of affection, Vic took the hands of the royal cousins. Cimba's eyes were huge with horror, her body trembling on the verge of a wail. Timny put an arm around his sister, but he looked as pale as a ghost. Walking slowly, Vic led them upstage where Bethniel climbed back into her chair. The princess's hands quivered in her lap. "The king is dead," she gasped. "Long live the queen?"

PART 3. FORGE

Chapter 17

Royal Choices

Dawn painted pale pink rectangles on floorboards as the scents of herbs and blossoms breezed through open doors. Latha's last Ruler, surrounded by cerrenil leaves, lay still on a table, his ginger beard and a high collar covering the fatal wound.

Ashel shifted on sore knees, looking at the ceiling beams to stretch a stiff neck. Hushed sobs had filled the long night's vigil, the last few hours punctuated by birdsong heralding darkness's slow retreat.

"Can I get you anything?" Vic whispered, a hand on his arm, her eyes bleeding concern.

Shaking his head, he looked down at fingers clasped into a double fist. Last night she had stood frozen in her shimmering golden gown, haplessly looking between the screaming crowd and the fallen king. Last night, she had shone bright under the shadows in the rosen grove and rebuffed his proposal. Now he reached for the deep longing that had put him on his knees, begging her to become his wife, and found a poisoned well. If he drank from that now—eyes squeezed shut, he shook his head. Vic didn't want him; she wanted *Lornk Korng*, the enemy who had surely ordered the death of the king she'd failed to save from an assassin's blade.

Those thoughts were unjust, but he couldn't stop thinking them. All through the night, while his sister and mother wept, he had prayed for release from this irrational fury. All night, as he watched Vic confer with guards and constables, relay messages, bring tea and solace, he had told himself his anger was misplaced, unfair. He'd repeated the scold like a mantra: there was nothing she could have done to save Father, and she didn't refuse you, she asked for time. Yet a kind of madness beat beneath his ribs, and the sound of that drum drowned out all reason.

"There's nothing I can get for you?" she asked again.

All you can give me now is more grief, he thought, standing. His mother and sister looked up with red eyes, and a skein of twine twisted round his heart, biting into it. "I can't just sit here any longer," he said, backing toward the exterior doors. The first-night vigil was supposed to last until the third hour past sunrise, but he couldn't kneel next to his dead father, breathing the same air as Vic for one more minute. "I—I'm sorry, Mother."

He wandered garden paths, gravel crunching underfoot, his ears fixed on that sound so he wouldn't hear the awful whir of that stoneknife, the thud of Father's body on the stage. In his belly, grief surged and roiled.

"Are you disappointed?" he asks, entering Father's study, still haunted by the visions he'd had in Fembrosh.

Father smiles and claps an arm around his shoulders. "My son became a man today!"

"Mother's unhappy I decided to stay in the Guild."

"Mother's always unhappy about something. I have this for you." Father sets a harp case on the desk, peels back the leather to reveal a white frame, intricately carved. "Your great-grandfather made it. My grandmother used to say it wasn't his voice that won her heart, but his hands." Father

winks and places his palms on Ashel's cheeks. "You are the
son of a king, but you're your own man, and you make your
own choices. I'm proud of the one you made today."

I failed him, he thought, punching down his grief. Sashal
had never asked him to step away from music and earn the
titles he had by virtue of his birth: prince, captain. Captain. He
stopped. What would Father have thought had Ashel chosen
to earn that? As long as he could remember, Sashal had fought
the Senate to ensure the troops held the line, no matter how
hard the Relmlord pushed, or how many peace overtures
he made. The war with Relm had been the central fixture of
Sashal's reign, and Ashel had mostly ignored it. Inspiration hit
as hard as a muse. Bloody and filled with fury, the spirit drove
his steps toward Olivet's house.

The housemarshall's eyebrows shot up when he answered
Ashel's knock. "Highness! I have nothing new on the search.
None of the guards or constables have reported any leads."

"I know. I'm here for something else. May I speak with
you?"

Olivet ushered him into his office, where Ashel declined to
sit as the housemarshall settled behind his desk.

"I want to activate my commission. How would I do that,
without being taken for a fool?"

Olivet raised an eyebrow. "That's a good question, Your
Highness."

"Vic joined as an ordinary recruit."

"She was only a ward; you're a born royal."

"So what can I do? I know nothing about battle. I want to
kill Relmans, not get Lathans killed."

Olivet scowled. "Is that what you want to achieve? This
about-face is wholly unexpected, to say the least."

Coward. Spendthrift. Wastrel. Black type on yellow parchment swam before his eyes, every accusation the Heralds had ever levied. *Dandy. Fop. Royal disgrace.* His father may have blessed Ashel's chosen path, but Ashel had seen the Heralds' pamphlets crumpled and torn in Sashal's fireplace. And he'd seen his father's disappointment too.

> *"I can't fix this," Father says, clutching the deportation order. "The Caleisbahn Ambassador is furious, with good reason, and I cannot ask them to release you from your debt. They'd demand too much in return."*
>
> *"I didn't want them exiled," Ashel protests. "I asked the Guild to loan me the money!"*
>
> *"How in the Shrine did you lose that much? It's more than a year's allowance for this entire household—a royal household!"*
>
> *Face burning, Ashel drops his gaze to his knees. "I had every intention of paying the debt myself, and all I needed was a loan from my Guild."*
>
> *Father shakes his head, eyes closed in resignation. "More times than I can count, you have made me prouder than any father could ask, but now and then you shrink that balloon with an unimaginably asinine choice."*

Was he making one of those now? He felt his father's blood scald his fingers, soak through his clothes, and seep into his bones, hot as fury. He knew running to the front was the last thing anyone expected him to do, and perhaps it was the last thing he ought to do. But last night's double loss had rent his heart, and now it was a raging beast, wild and hungry for blood. It's not Vic's fault, reason protested, but rage squashed that thought once more. "I cannot simply go back to my Guild and teach history and sing songs," he said aloud, voice shaking. "I know I'm a novice when it comes to war, but I feel Elesendar calling me onto that path, and I *need* to follow it."

Olivet peered at him, eyes considering everything from Ashel's face to feet. Finally, he nodded. "Cavalry. You ride well, and the cavalry units are large, with multilayered command. Even as a captain, you'd be carrying out orders, not giving them. It would give you a chance to learn—an apprenticeship, of sorts."

"And I'd see combat soon."

"Soon enough. Are you certain this is what you want?"

He searched his soul for doubt but found only fury and a need for satisfaction. "As certain as the day I came out of Fembrosh."

† † †

Bellin answered Vic's knock. In Ashel's parlor, she found Melba, eyes rimmed red, and Simlael, looking murderous. "He's upstairs," Bellin said.

Vic started up the steps, but Melba took her elbow, fingers digging deep. "You're the only one who can stop him. Do whatever it takes, will you?"

Wincing, Vic looked at the steps. "I'll do what I can."

The minstrel's grip tightened. "If I were you, I'd do whatever I had to, to keep him here."

Ears hot, elbow throbbing, she climbed the stairs. She had understood what Ashel's friends wanted when she received Bellin's message, begging her to come. *Trainer whore.* Near the top of the steps, she faltered, the sensation of Lornk's thumb on her windpipe, the iron of a rapist's blood on her tongue. That night five years ago, when she'd found Silla, she had chosen the path of war and vengeance and stuffed Kara away in a locked box. Since winter, the sensations and desires she had known in a white room at the top of a tower had begun to slip out, an insidious corruption of the blood that pulled her thoughts away from death toward—toward what? Why did *life* frighten her more than a battlefield packed with enemies? Why did she shrink from love to embrace hate? "What in the Shrine is wrong with you?" she muttered, tears brimming. Ashel, beautiful and kind and perfect, had professed his love for her, a broken, used, pitiful creature whose desire for another man infected her like a parasite. Ashel knew that and had offered to wed her anyway. Wouldn't *life* with him be a better way to purge that infection than more bloodletting?

"I don't know." Angrily, she wiped her cheeks dry. Shrine, she was the Blade, and she was gibbering in terror at simply going up a flight of stairs and talking to a man. A man who had spent the entire night's vigil glaring at her. She knew all too well the rage in his eyes, and she didn't want it to spoil him the way it had left her standing in a dark stairwell, unable to embrace life. Maybe it was time she put aside her own quest for vengeance, to keep him from pursuing his.

She found him sitting on his bed, staring at a harp case on the floor.

"I can't decide whether to take it. I don't suppose it'll be any use."

"Why are you going?"

His eyes drifted to hers. "You of all people know why."

Shutting the door, she leaned against it. "Please don't do this. You're not a warrior. You have no business going to the front."

His gaze sliced at her. "I said the same thing about you, when you went."

"That was different."

"True. Your father wasn't dead."

"And what good will it do him when you're killed? You haven't any training—"

"Beth and I both trained with Olivet. We're not completely inept. And I am a captain, Captain."

"You said yourself, no fieldmarshall in his right mind would give you a command."

"Then I'll find one not in his right mind."

"Don't, please." She sat next to him on the bed, her heart pounding. Elbows on his knees, he brooded over his harp. Lousy idea, to bring a thing like that to a battlefield—but she didn't voice that thought. Instead, she held her breath, remembering his kiss in the rosen grove, the heat that had run down her throat and into her belly, igniting embers she hadn't felt since Traine. She shoved aside memories of soft blond hair and thought of the caress of Ashel's smile, of his slender long fingers on her bare skin, and she opened Kara's box. Warm desire to join with *Ashel*—not Lornk, not Earnk—poured through her. Perhaps she couldn't love him, but she cared deeply for him, and in that moment, she *wanted* him. She picked up his hand, brought it to her breast. "We can—"

He leapt off the bed as if burned. "My father's dead, Vic. I have my own reasons to hate the Relmlord now. You're the least of them."

Her breath gushed out of her, desire twisting instantly into anger. "You'll get yourself captured or killed, and trust me, captured is worse!"

"There is nothing you can do or say to stop me," he said coldly. "And you can tell those three downstairs their trap didn't work. I leave at first light tomorrow."

"What about your father's wake?" Vic's throat tightened as she thought of Sashal's pale stillness. All through the vigil she'd kept busy with news and tea and the giving of comfort, staving off her own grief for the man who had welcomed her into his home and family. "And the burial?"

"My mother and sister can sing him into the trees as well as

I can. Goodbye, Vic."

At the door, she expelled a slow breath, dread quenching ire. "Wait one month. Command has ordered me to stay at the manor, in case the assassin tries again. But once my arm is healed, I'll be rejoining the Dagger. Wait for me, and we'll go down together."

His lips tilted into a sneer. "I hope you do a better job protecting my sister than you did my father."

Stung, she stared at him.

Turning his back, he moved the harp next to a full pack leaning against the wall. "Maybe I'll see you in Relm."

She slipped out, tears spilling down her cheeks, ears twitching as she remembered the soft whir of the stoneknife that killed the king. If she had looked toward the audience a moment earlier, would she have seen the assassin? Could she have intercepted the weapon? The stage lights had blinded them; crowd noise had stuffed their ears. Five years in Fembrosh had taught her that sometimes the arrow simply finds its mark. One foot on the stairs, she paused. What if a Relman arrow found Ashel? Cavalry fought on open fields. No cover, and no one to watch your back. But for the next month or so, the Dagger was short a captain. Chin up, she marched down the stairs, determined to write Fieldmarshall Henrik. If she couldn't stop Ashel, at least she could protect him.

Vic sat in the solarium, feeling useless, while Bethniel picked leaves off a geilmor seedling, muttering to herself. The world was upside down—Ashel rode for the border, and she was stuck here in Narath. The assassin had done his job; surely he was back in Relm by now, and there was no reason she couldn't be on desk duty at Summerquarters until the splint came off. The urge to head south pulled at her, but she knew Command wouldn't tolerate such a direct violation of orders. "I'm going down to Olivet's yard," she said abruptly.

"No, stay!" Beth cried. "I'm too nervous to be alone. I wish I'd gone to the Senate. Mother and Fensin both said I shouldn't be there for the vote, but the wait is driving me mad." She rattled through a list of supporters, and those she thought might vote against her election as Ruler, reminding Vic the throne passed out of families as often as it stayed within them, all at the whim of the Senate. "But of course now they want stability," Beth asserted, and Vic nodded. "We're at war. They wouldn't make a radical change, and Fensin promised I had his support. Of course, he's just doing that to curry favor, but still"—her eyes begged Vic's agreement—"it has to carry weight that the Opposition wants me on the throne, right?"

"They've made their decision," Elekia announced from the doorway.

Bethniel grabbed Vic's hand.

"Sit down," her mother ordered. "Vic, please excuse us."

"No." Bethniel tugged her back.

Shaking her head, Elekia examined the seedling. "They debated this for a long time. I'm sorry."

Bethniel's fingernails dug into Vic's palm. "Who?"

"I am Ruler now."

"What?"

"The Senate decided I should take your father's place until you are older."

"Father was younger than me when he mounted the throne."

"There was no war then."

"So you're my regent?"

"No."

"But you said you'll rule until I'm older."

"I will abdicate when you are ready. You must be patient and take this time to gather more wisdom."

"Wisdom? Older? I've worked for this all my life, and they take it away in two hours?"

Vic looked toward the doors leading outside, wishing she could sink through the tiles as Bethniel's protests rattled the glass walls and her mother's dispassionate replies froze the air.

"My father was murdered."

"As was my husband, and our king. But I didn't faint when it happened."

Bethniel threw her hands up. "Is that what this is about? My father was dead!"

"A Ruler carries on when the unexpected happens—"

"Unexpected!"

"When the horrible happens. You cannot let it affect you."

"Like you, Mother? You're saying I'm not queen because I'm not a cold-blooded bitch like you. You wasted no time after he was dead, did you? Well, now you don't have to rule from beside the throne any more. You never loved him. You loved his chair."

Eyes blazing, Elekia stood perfectly still, but Bethniel jerked backward, holding a hand to her cheek.

"Go to your room," the queen said.

"You cannot order me." Bethniel squared her shoulders as Vic recognized the force pushing at them. The princess's cheek turned purple as tears ran toward her chin. "No, Mother. I will not be compelled."

"Fine." Elekia unclenched her fists, and Bethniel staggered, suddenly released. The queen hung her head. "Vic, go with her to the tailors so she can buy some pretty clothes with her people's taxes."

† † †

Sputtering, the fire licked the air between Geram and Ashel. The Dagger's new captain sat still, tuning each string on his harp sweet, then making them all go sour. The noise would alarm any Relman patrols within half a league, but they were well behind the Lathan lines, and they'd as likely find a force of Relmans in Narath as here. So Geram didn't ask the prince to put the harp away. He didn't Listen to him either.

"He's torn up with grief and aches for blood," Henrik says. "Just lead him round the woods a few weeks. Keep well back from the front, and do not engage the enemy. When he's cooled off, bring him back here and we'll put him on desk duty where he belongs. And whatever happens, do not let him be captured. I will not have a prince of Latha captured or killed under my command."

The fieldmarshall's orders circled around Geram's head like flies, a stink of foreboding in his nose. Tension crawled along his skin, hissing whispers itching in his ears. The night before, loud thoughts of desertion had awakened him, and he had caught Thrusher trying to sneak away from camp. Now Orlon, the new healer, kept looking toward the trees, jumping at every hoot and rustle. Without their Blade, the hardened warriors of the Dagger had turned as skittish as virgins at a pirate's birthday party.

A harp string snapped with a nasty shriek. What sort of fool brings a harp to a battlefield? Geram wanted to strangle Vic for foisting this spoiled fop on them. Not one member of the Dagger wanted to babysit him, and no one trusted him. The patrol looked to Geram every time the prince spoke. Fortunately, he rarely gave orders and never seemed to care whether anyone followed them. He muffled his thoughts as well as a Listener, but what Geram Heard told him Ashel was as happy to be the

Dagger's captain as the Dagger was to have him.

The harp strings whined eerily. This far back from the lines, Relmans were as likely to be here as in Narath, but there were Relmans in Narath the day King Sashal died. It never hurt to be prudent. Clearing his throat, Geram rolled to his feet and went around the fire.

"Captain," he said. The prince stared at his instrument. "Captain." The word cracked out of Geram's mind, a Listener's whip. Ashel blinked and looked up at him.

"Yes, Lieutenant?"

"Could you mute the . . ." Like a scent borne on the wind, Geram caught a wisp of an unguarded thought. "Relmans are coming," he warned. The patrol staggered up, some climbing trees, others taking positions around the fire, every motion sluggish. Ashel laid aside his harp, fingering his dagger. Geram wanted to kick him but hissed another warning instead. "They're upon us!" Startled, the prince jumped up and slung his harp across his back.

Yelling, Relmans charged into the firelight, swarming out of the geilmors, their stoneknives like black teeth gnashing the air. Lathan arrows showered the campsite, but the Relman troopers rushed forward like a tide in the rain. "There's so many," someone cried. Thrusher leapt from a geilmor to plunge his dagger into the neck of a burly Relman, but another five buried him. Querkle took an arrow in the eye. Natchez dove beneath a man's legs and sliced at hamstrings, but a flung stoneknife thunked into his belly before he could stand. This is it, Geram thought sadly. He hadn't believed he would die in battle. A big Relman woman rushed him, trilling. Geram dodged her knife, slashing at her stomach.

† † †

Ashel thought only of hanging onto his dagger. It slipped in his fingers, soaking and warm as his father's blood. But music had made his fingers strong, and they tightened around the gummed hilt. Around him people shouted and cried, but he didn't hear them. He heard the grunt his father made as the stoneknife sank into his throat, the thud when his body hit the stage, the ting of a medal hitting stone.

A trooper fell into his arms and clutched at his shirt, leaving a bloody print. Ashel caught her killer from behind and slit his throat. A wild chuckle burbled out as he watched the man fall. Then the strings on his harp screamed and a stoneknife bit into his back. White hot with rage, he spun around.

"Interesting armor, Captain." A Relman marshall pointed his stoneknife at Ashel's chest.

"It's served me well." Ashel lunged. The Relman ducked, spinning out of range. Someone wedged a fat elbow beneath Ashel's chin, cut the harp off his back and pinned his arms. Laughing, the Relman officer turned back to the battle. Ashel roared at his captor, twisting and turning in the iron grasp as his captor dragged him through the trees and shoved him to the ground. His chin struck gravel. A heel dug into his back; twine wound around his wrists and ankles. His nose pressed into a patch of venner moss, the bitter scent cleared his head like a healer's concoction cleared a fever, and the screams of the dying filled the empty space.

The firelight fractured bodies into arms and mouths, the whip of hair, the slash of a boot. Nothing seemed whole. Everything fell apart.

An arm snaked around Geram's neck. He elbowed his attacker and bent forward, flinging the Relman to the ground.

Their eyes met before she rolled out of his reach and disappeared behind a trio locked together, arms entangled, knives slashing. Turning, he found himself alone in the center of the storm. Four Lathans lay still in the grass. Geram's temples echoed the pounding in his heart.

On the edge of the campsite, a Relman with arms thick as a ship's mast dragged the prince into the trees. A wiry man and burly woman trotted alongside, eyes darting for pursuers. *Whatever happens, don't let him be captured.* Idiot. Henrik let a green prince loose in Fembrosh with that stupid harp and tells *me,* don't let him get captured. Geram followed them out of the copse and watched from behind a tree as they bound Ashel hand and foot in a dry creekbed. Listening, he picked out the voice of the Relman commander from their memories.

"Daniy," Geram cried into their minds, "come here!"

"Watch him," the biggest one told the others. "Sorrel needs me."

"Now!" Geram shouted.

The big one jumped and dashed off. Slipping from behind the tree, Geram put an arrow in the woman's eye and another in the man's chest. A slice across the throat finished him.

"It's me." He knelt and cut Ashel free. "Are you hurt?"

Muffling his thoughts, the prince sat up, rubbing his wrists. Blood seeped from a cut on his back, but he took a stoneknife off a Relman and headed back into the copse.

"No." Geram held him back. "It's all over now." Ashel blinked at him. Geram shook him by the shoulders. "Listen. We have to run for it."

Within the copse, the shouts dwindled. "Now, Captain," Geram said firmly, drawing Ashel down the creekbed into a ravine, then pulling him into a run. They had almost reached the end of the channel when a Relman shouted behind them.

"Keep going," Geram urged and turned round with his

bow. A Relman loosed an arrow. Geram fired without aim, spun round and bolted after Ashel. A thunk and fire hit his thigh; he ran a few more steps before his leg collapsed beneath him.

Ashel skidded back to him, pulled him up and slung his arm over his shoulder. "Are you mad?" Geram asked. "Go!" Ashel hoisted him forward. They made it out of the ravine and turned toward the cover of another stand of trees, Geram clenching his teeth as he limped alongside the prince. "You can make it alone," he urged. "Don't be such a Shrinejumping fool!"

Relmans charged up behind them, catching Ashel's shoulders and swinging them around. The arrow twisted, squeezing white hot pain into Geram's blood. A Relman's kick sent him sprawling. The others surrounded Ashel, shoving him between them like bullies in the schoolyard. Ashel clenched his fists, his eyes inviting harm. As the tall, swarthy marshall came up with another pair of troopers, holding Orlon bound between them, Geram pressed his forehead into the gravel.

"So much for the legendary Dagger," the marshall said. "But you're not the Blade."

"No," Ashel said aloud, in Relman.

The Relman laughed. "No, indeed. But you'll do. Let's go."

† † †

"I hoped you wouldn't wake up before I did this," Orlon said.

Dazed, Geram propped himself on an elbow. "Did what?" Sunlight slanted through rough slats of green wood. From the opposite corner of the shack, Ashel stared at flashing dust motes. Shirtless, Orlon crouched next to a little fire beneath a boiling pot. Smoke and steam drifted out through a hole in the roof. "What are you going to do?"

"I wrangled some nevrel from the Relmans. This is going to hurt, but you'll lose the leg if I don't."

His thigh bulged around the wound, soaking a bandage with a yellow ooze. Dizzy and nauseated, Geram lay back. "I can't feel it."

"I put some har juice on it."

"I thought that was poisonous," Ashel said, his voice dark.

"Not if you know what you're doing with it."

Orlon's fingers grazed Geram's leg, unraveling a bandage fashioned from the healer's shirt. "The heat will cut through the har," Orlon said, pulling a blue-stained length of his shirt from the boiling pot. "But this should stop the infection."

"Why are the Relmans so generous?" Geram asked, eyeing the boiling pot.

"They lost their healer in the battle. I've been filling in."

"You what?" Geram hoisted himself up. Orlon tossed the steaming rag across his thigh. Groaning through clenched teeth, Geram lay back again.

"You wouldn't be alive if I didn't help them. You almost died last night."

"He would have been better off," Ashel grumbled.

Fury swept over pain. "I'd have been better off without a harp-twanging fool for a captain."

Orlon pressed another hot compress over the thigh, then wound the rest of his shirt around the leg and tied it off. "Are you hungry?"

"No."

A tiny door opened for the big Relman who had dragged Ashel off the field. "You." He pointed at Orlon. "The marshall wants you."

The healer stood. "I'll be back."

"You too." The Relman signaled to Ashel. They left Geram lying in the dirt, alone.

Struggling against the panic that had gripped him the night Vic stabbed the Relmlord, he forced himself into the daydream about the flag race, but each time he reached for the silk, it slipped from his fingers, and his uncle's disappointment burned through the daydream's happy ending time and again as the long hours wore out the day.

Light fading outside, the wood of the hut sagged, remembering life as a cerrenil. Chippers called as the sky, glimpsed through knotholes, turned red, then purple. In the distance, a gekko squawked. The door opened, startling him. He had to shake his head. In better times, no one ever surprised him.

Ashel shuffled inside. One eye was swelled shut, and blood from his lip ran down his chin. The prince curled up with his arms over his belly, his back to Geram.

"What do they want?" Geram asked.

Ashel cleared his throat. After a pause, he said, "They believe they've captured Latha's prince."

"Why did they beat you?"

"They want me to admit to it."

What difference does that make? Geram wanted to ask. But if Ashel insisted that he was not the prince, and Narath never let it be known he was missing, the Relmans might not have the victory they thought.

"What do they want with me?"

"You're supposed to corroborate my identity. Besides, if that leg heals, you're probably worth about five hundred mullas in Traine." Groaning, Ashel rolled over to face him. "Maybe you'll get lucky. I've heard that the Senate authorized funds for buying back as many Lathans as our agents can find, and afford."

Geram shifted, raising the bad leg. Fear twisted in his gut as he imagined himself in a mine.

"Actually, you'd probably be worth a lot more, with that trick you pulled on that Relman trooper."

"Any Lathan could have done that," Geram growled.

"Not to him. He has mindspeech."

The corners of Geram's mouth turned up a little. It had been so easy.

A star peeped at them through the roof. His stomach rumbling, Geram slid over to Orlon's pack. Inside he found a few flatcakes wrapped in leaves, a couple green fruits, and a cup. A water bucket sat next to Ashel. Gritting his teeth, he pulled himself up and hobbled over to the prince. He shouldn't care what happened to the other man now. He had himself to worry about. But Ashel had come back for him—he had to credit him with that.

The prince sat up and took the food Geram offered. "I'm sorry," he whispered. They sat together in silence, Ashel's finger tracing the rim of the cup. The prince coughed, a painful sound, then filled the cup and handed it to Geram. "How is your heart?"

If they had stayed for King Sashal's wake, Geram might have brought Ashel a glass of Eldanion and asked the same question. "How is your heart?" would have been the question asked by everyone as they handed each other wine and spicerolls, then taken turns telling stories about the departed. But neither Ashel nor the Dagger had stayed for the king's wake, and now Ashel quietly opened the door for Geram's mourning. The prince had been studying to be a Loremaster, Geram remembered. Not only historians, poets, and composers, Loremasters were Latha's spiritual guides as well. Geram looked down at the flatcakes in his lap. They weren't spicerolls, the water wasn't wine, but perhaps they would do for a wake. Geram raised the cup. "My heart grieves for Thrusher," he said, speaking aloud, as one did at wakes. "He came from Alna, like me." He told everything he knew about all the troopers who had died the night before. Maelev had dreamed of becoming a chef. Querkle had hoped to return to the Minstrels Guild. Banter wanted to have six children and farm her family's land on the west side of the Lathalorns.

His tongue and throat weren't used to talking, so he paused to rest now and then, hoping Ashel would take a turn and talk about his father. But the prince just listened. Then Geram laughed, remembering Natchez falling on his head when a cerrenil let down her hair quicker than he expected. As Geram went on, he sensed the rhythm of his stories echoing the cadence of Ashel's grief. He could Hear the cries in Ashel's heart grow louder, overcoming the anger that had muffled them. Geram called to those cries with his mindvoice, and they broke loose.

At once all of Ashel's guilt, anger, shame, terror poured out of him. He screamed, flattening Geram against the wall of the shack, the sound blasting his mind more than his ears. Dazed, Geram shook his head and sat up. The prince cackled, the sound rising hysterically, then billowing out and down as the lunacy left it. "I can't believe this," Ashel gasped between hiccups of humor, his eyes tearing. "It's like I've gone into Fembrosh a second time, but the visions have come from rotten cerrenil fruit."

"I wish it were a dream, Captain."

Ashel leaned forward. "Call me Sol. I'm just a minstrel now, no captain." He put his hand on Geram's shoulder. "Sing with me. It's almost dawn. Let's sing them into the trees."

Geram's voice was hoarse, but he sang. Even Ashel's voice was rough-edged tonight. They sang the dead back to their roots, back to the old mothers who were the mothers of all. In time, those who had died would be reborn under Elesendar's light, they hoped as saplings in the Kiareinoll who would live for centuries. As the last note faded, they passed the cup between them and hugged while the chippers fell silent and the morning stars offered their bright trilling calls to the dawn.

Exhausted, they lay down to sleep. Geram had hardly closed his eyes before the door opened and someone kicked him in the ribs.

"On your feet," the trooper told them. "Your healer escaped last night. You two are going to Lordhome."

Chapter 18

Ordinary Choices

Vic's eyes startled open at a knock. Her bedroom door creaked, and Gaston stood on the threshold. "Captain, you're needed."

She bolted out of bed, thoughts full of assassins' knives. "The Ruler is safe," he added quickly. "The housemarshall wants you to meet him in his office."

Stomach in knots, she pulled on her uniform, rebraiding her hair as she ran down stairwells and out into the cool night. A yellow glow stretched from Olivet's window across the path, and he ordered her entry before her knuckles rapped his door. When she entered, Orlon stood and saluted, and her heart seized. "Ashel."

"Command sent me straight here," the healer said. Deep shadows circled his eyes; he shook with fatigue. "It's been fifteen days since the ambush."

"Give us your report," Olivet said, signaling him and Vic to sit.

With a sinking heart, Vic listened to the story of the Dagger's demise. Geram and Ashel in Relman hands, everyone else dead. Her hands itched to grab Orlon's collar and shake him. She wanted to scream, "You were supposed to protect him! Why didn't you?" But she listened to the story in silence. Without her, without Maynon and Silla, the Dagger didn't work. It was that simple.

"How many Relmans?" Olivet asked.

"A full company, sir. They knew Prince Ashel commanded the party."

"It was targeted, then."

"I think so, sir. After we were captured, I saw my chance to escape and took it. I would have gone back for the prince, but there were too many guards. We'd never have made it. I reached Summerquarters three days later, and as I said, they sent me straight on here. They were marshalling a rescue party as I left, but the Relmans had a long head start. There wasn't a lot of hope."

Thanking the healer, Olivet sent him to bed down in the barracks.

"I thought he'd be safe with the Dagger," Vic breathed. "Henrik promised he wouldn't see combat."

Olivet frowned at her. "Spies must have infiltrated Summerquarters, since the Relmans knew where to find him. But *you* shouldn't have interfered with his duty assignment, and Hernik shouldn't have agreed with you. If Ashel had been assigned to the cavalry as he requested, sufficient troops would have been on hand to effect a quick rescue, and we wouldn't have lost our most valuable reconnaissance unit." Each word pounded a knot deeper into Vic's bowels. "What are you going to do about it, Captain?"

She stared at the housemarshall, heart pounding. "What can I do? They're too deep into Relm by now."

He raised an eyebrow. "You're a clever young woman. What would you do, if you had every resource at your command?"

A map of Relm unfurled in her mind. Vast plains filled with hostile Relmans separated Ashel from them now, and the high peaks of the Lorn oc Re protected Olmlablaire from the north—but perhaps not from the west. "I'd go around, through Kragnash."

One corner of Olivet's mouth tilted up. "As would I."

† † †

The first rays of morning painted the floor gold as a page moved along the passage, blowing out the lamps. Vic stifled a yawn while Olivet knocked on the queen's door.

Belting a silk dressing gown, Elekia looked more like a woman hosting a morning tea than someone just rousted out of bed. "Housemarshall. Vic? Come in."

"Apologies, Majesty," Olivet said. "We have bad news."

"Ashel." Elekia shut the door behind them and leaned against it, her hand trembling on the knob. But when they briefed her on the capture and rescue plan, the queen's dismay turned into a stabbing glare. "This is a ridiculous plan. It will take months."

"It might be winter when they reach Olmlablaire," Olivet admitted. "But it's the best chance of rescue, and"—he paused, gazing at the queen no less sternly than he'd stare down a fresh recruit—"it could end the war, Your Majesty."

"There's nothing to stop Korng from taking Ashel to Traine."

"He could hold him in Re too," Vic replied, "but Olmlablaire is most likely. We can arrive from the west, in secret, and infiltrate the palace to find out where Ashel is. If we have to go to Traine to get him, we can get there from Olmlablaire and send you a message via the Device. The Relman nomads trade with the Kragnashians. There must be a ford across Umbrachlorn Plu. Give me a company and I'll find it."

"You don't know there's a ford," Elekia objected. "This plan of yours is mad."

Vic hung her head. "Madder than letting him go in the first place? You must have known this could happen."

The queen sighed, but her mouth crooked upward a notch. "I've never been able to stop him doing as he pleased."

"Give me a company," Vic pleaded. "I'll bring him home."

Elekia's eyes flashed to Olivet and back. "You're only a captain."

"Her rank can be fixed," the housemarshall said.

Elekia nodded. "So it can. You will go, Marshall. Olivet, find her the best troopers you can." After the door shut behind him, the queen sagged into an armchair. Feeling like an intruder, Vic stepped toward the door, but Elekia beckoned her closer. "Don't go yet." With a shuddering breath, she cupped Vic's cheek. "My youngest, and the one who bears the heaviest burdens. I'm about to make them heavier."

Astonished, Vic grappled with the implications of that sentence.

Elekia smiled sadly. "You were right to refuse Ashel."

Vic's heart lurched. "What?" How did Elekia know?

"You were right to refuse him. You have business to settle first, and he needed to hear 'no' for once in his life." Her face crumpled into her hands, and a muffled sob leaked past her fingers. Yet when she raised her head again, she'd ironed the creases round her mouth and eyes into sad serenity. "The day you arrived, the same day you first called me out for my lack of grace, I knew there'd come a time when you'd bring me the butcher's bill for bargains I made when I was young. I hated your arrival, Vic, but I have never hated *you*. On the contrary, you entered my heart the day you entered my house. I know that's hard to believe, considering how I've treated you, but it's the truth."

Jaw slack, Vic stammered her thanks.

"And now the bill I've feared so long is due." She went to a chest and rummaged inside, pulling out a velvet-wrapped bundle. "I'm giving you two things for your journey. The first is precious to me: my daughter."

"Bethniel?" Vic shook her head, appalled. Since Elekia had taken the throne, Bethniel had spent every night carousing with the Betheljin ambassador's son and every day sleeping off a hangover. So far, Beth had done her sleeping alone, but Vic feared it wouldn't be long before they declared themselves wedded.

Elekia's mouth tilted sardonically. "She's embraced the fool's role too well lately, but my daughter has iron in her blood. She's almost as clever as you, and she speaks Kragnashian. You'll need a translator in the desert."

"There are others who can translate, Your Majesty. And this mission is as likely to fail as it is to succeed. Do you want to give Lornk both of your children?"

Her lips grim, eyes hard, Elekia pressed the velvet bundle into Vic's hands, then held her shoulders. "I have three children now, not two. I'm counting on the youngest to keep the other two safe. I know how heavy this burden is, Vic, but Bethniel *needs* to go with you into the desert. You musn't leave without her."

Vic stared at the woman who had held her at arm's length for half a decade. Over that time, she'd come to respect Elekia, even grudgingly admire her, but she bore no love for this haughty, cold schemer. And rarely had she seen reason to think Elekia even had a heart, much less allotted space in it for Vic. Suspicious of the queen's declarations, she looked at the velvet bundle. The fabric hid something long and hard. "What is this?"

"The second item. A sort of talisman." Elekia pulled aside a corner of the velvet to reveal a bronze dagger with a jeweled hilt. "Recognize it?"

Vic's eyes widened in horror, and she dropped the bundle. The gemstones she remembered only too well, and the metal . . . Her belly twitched at the pinches and tugs she'd endured from the belt as it sat snug around her waist in Traine.

"You gave me this the day you left Narath as an ordinary trooper, not the officer I'd wanted." The queen chuckled softly, then grew solemn again. "Elesendar knows I've done nothing but test you since the day you arrived. But you passed, Vic. This is your prize."

Trembling, Vic retrieved the dagger. Its blade was finer than any crystal; it balanced marvelously in her palm. An emerald at the junction of the blade and hilt glittered green as the bedspread in a white room. "The belt."

"I sent it to Traine to have it recast into a dagger. Only one smith in all of Knownearth makes blades this sharp."

"Thank you," Vic said, her knees weak. The dagger felt slick, and her throat closed at its touch. Would Lornk have died if she'd had this dagger last winter? She felt his clinical hands stroking her breasts and thighs. Bile surged up her throat.

Elekia took the dagger and wrapped it in the velvet. "Use it to have your revenge. Fight him with his own weapons, and make him suffer with them. He deserves it."

Vic eyed the bundle, swallowing the hysteria beating up her throat. "It's filthy. I can't. Crystal's clean." She sank onto the queen's bed, itching with the memory of Lornk's fingers.

"Don't look at it." Elekia pressed the velvet into Vic's hands. "Don't touch the metal. But when you get to Lordhome, cleanse it with his blood." The queen pulled Vic's chin up. Her fingers warm, they soothed the hysteria creeping across Vic's skin and up her throat. "You are my youngest child, who came to me almost grown. I didn't bear you, didn't rear you, but you're no less mine than the ones I nursed from my breast. I know you have the strength to do what you must, because you have *my* strength. Show it to Lornk. Then bring my son and daughter safely home."

Nodding, Vic stood and brushed wet cheeks. "I will."

She unwrapped the dagger in her room. Beneath her feet,

the battle between wizards and Kragnashians raged across the green wool. The creatures beckoned from her future, but in her lap, the dagger echoed the past. Her memories, Kara's memories, the hate and the love that had filled her heart when she'd lived in that tower, all of it clambered out at the sight of it. Ashel needed her now, but if she met him and Lornk together, who would she choose? What are you? the dagger asked. I'm yours, Kara replied, clockwork gears whirring, and Vic wept.

The clack clack of hundreds of looms echoed through the darkened streets of Erin. Nearly twice as large as Narath, the city sprawled through an alpine valley, surrounded by orchards and tilled fields and forest, the mountains themselves its walls. In daytime, crowds milled past half-timbered buildings standing four and even five stories high. The sun long gone, Vic walked through empty markets, her arms threaded through the elbows of Orlon and Drak. Orlon had been first to volunteer for the mission, and Drak had signed on the moment he heard his cousin Geram had been caught in the net cast for Ashel. The captain had learned to speak Kragnashian during his youth in the merchant marines, and so Olivet had made him Vic's command second. The rest of the company, clothed as merchants, had arrived in Erin and departed for Cabanarl in twos and threes to maintain secrecy while the Weavers made robes and tents suitable for the desert. The gear was ready, but now they waited for news of the Summerquarters rescue party, and spent most evenings round a tap, sharing stories.

"There she was," Drak said, chortling. "The hero who ended the war—or so we thought at the time—and she's losing her breakfast on my toes."

"I suppose I owe you a pair of boots for that," Vic admitted.

"A surprise attack from the Blade," Drak quipped, and Orlon laughed.

"Gentlemen," she said, "this information is top secret." The men vowed their eternal silence as the trio reached their inn. "I thank you both for another memorable night," Vic said as she pushed open the common room door. "See you at breakfast."

She froze on the threshold. Bethniel sat with a stranger near the fire, both brooding over tea mugs, while a pair of manor guards nodded greetings from another table. Curls knotted, cheeks smeared with dirt, the princess looked as if she'd ridden from the capital without a stop. Her companion, a pale girl with dark brown locks, looked just as filthy and tired. Something about the girl tickled Vic's memory, but she couldn't place her. She was too young to be one of Beth's silly friends. "We leave at dawn," Vic said. Drak promised to settle the bill with the innkeeper, then followed Orlon up the stairs.

Bethniel scowled. "Where have you been?"

"At dinner."

"I'm glad you have your priorities straight."

Vic glared back. "You're here with news?"

Chairs squeaked as Bethniel stood and the others followed. "I want a bath, but we need to talk first. Your room, Marshall?"

Upstairs, the stranger followed Bethniel into Vic's bedchamber. Vic wished she hadn't drunk that last pint of ale as she splashed her face in the washbasin and gulped a tumbler of water. "Who's your friend?"

"This is Wineyll of Narath. She's a minstrel. Ashel tutored her."

"Why have you brought her?"

"To prove that I'm worth the weight of my water in the desert. I know you don't want me to come."

"I don't know why you want to come! Ashel is bad enough, without you putting yourself in line to be captured or killed too."

"My mother ordered me on this mission, same as you."

"Can you tell me why? She didn't."

"I'm surprised you didn't ask her."

Vic flushed, thinking how Elekia had distracted her with surprising declarations of affection and the damn dagger that lurked at the bottom of her pack. "I suspect it was to get you away from that Betheljin cad," she retorted.

"He's not a cad!" Eyes smoldering, Bethniel sat down heavily. "I'm your translator and negotiator. Mother said you needed my help, not just talking to the Kragnashians, but gaining their aid. She received permission from the Center to cross their land, and guides are going to meet us, but we may need more help than that, and Kragnashians won't change a contract without more formal negotiation. And when you defeat the Relmlord, you'll need someone there who can make sure the peace treaty favors Latha. That'll be my job."

"And do you want it?"

"I need it," the princess said grimly. "The Senate took my birthright and handed it to my mother. They're not going to take it away from her, and she's not going to give it up until she's dead. It's what she's wanted her whole life."

"That's Fensin talking."

"It is, but not everything he says is a lie. My father wasn't Heir—did you know that? When my grandfather died, the Kragnashians threatened to suspend trade unless the Senate elected Father as Ruler instead of his brother. I *know* Mother made that deal. So the title Heir only means something if the Senate agrees to the inheritance. They didn't elect me Ruler because they believed I couldn't handle it. I need to prove I can, or when the time comes, the Senate will pass me over again, and the throne could pass out of my family altogether."

Vic crossed her arms, a beat of sympathy in her throat. "This could be a suicide mission, and being captured is worse than being killed, when it comes to Lornk Korng." She glanced at the girl sitting at the table, but this wasn't the time for reticence. "He broke me into pieces, Beth, and if I hadn't escaped, he would have put me back together the wrong way round. I'm terrified what he'll do to Ashel. I do not want him doing *anything* to you."

"Don't you think Mother and I talked about this? There's no reward without risk, not for me anyway. And if I'm captured, Mother's going to name Timny Heir. It's settled."

Vic sighed. "You still haven't told me why you've brought a *minstrel*." She turned to Wineyll. "What do you plan to do, sing the Relmans to sleep with a lullaby?"

"I play the flute," the girl corrected.

"The flute." Recognition dawned, and Vic remembered the girl along with the aching grief that had clogged her throat while Wineyll had accompanied her father in a heart-breaking ballad, the same one Ashel had said was about a wizard bearing Vic's name. Thoughts of Ashel and his peril washed away sentiment. "A flute's about as useful as Ashel's *harp*. How old are you? Fourteen?" The girl was only a hair taller than Vic, with eyes as wide as a harrier's.

"I'm sixteen and I've been to Fembrosh. Like you, I went early, Marshall."

"I doubt you went early for the same reason I did."

The girl glared. "My father died, and the Melody said I should be a journeyman and earn my keep, but you have to have been to Fembrosh for that."

"Show her," Beth interrupted.

Wineyll nodded curtly, and Ashel appeared in the room. Vic yelped and hopped backward, her stomach lurching. He wore his Guild robes and beamed at her, his eyes fixed on hers. Pulse throbbing, she tore her gaze off the image. "Is that wizardry?"

"Illusion. It's entirely in your mind. I can trick your brain into seeing what's not there." Ashel vanished, and so did the princess. "Or make you think you don't see something that is." Bethniel reappeared.

"Wineyll is the most powerful Listener in Latha." The princess grinned.

Vic blinked, agog. "This can't be a common gift among Listeners."

"I'm the only one I know able to do it."

"Can the Blade use an asset like that?" the princess asked.

Breath gushing out of her lungs, Vic nodded. "I could."

Beth's smile broadened. "See, I'm already adding value to your mission."

CHAPTER 19

COST OF TRUTH

Ashel sat where the guard pointed, his stomach twisting. A stone chair with massive arms like a throne, but without a back. As the guard strapped his arms down, he looked at his fingernails, black from yesterday's torments. Just don't break them, he prayed. My hands, my voice, that's all I am.

The guard finished and stood at attention. Ashel closed his eyes, unwilling to acknowledge the forge in the corner, the metal—Elesendar help him—metal tongs and pincers on the table. Not my hands, not my throat. His breathing measured out the seconds, then the minutes. He told himself the anticipation of the pain was far worse than the pain itself. He'd made it through yesterday, barely, but he'd made it. A tune nagged him, and he nearly laughed that music would spring into his head at a time like this, but he snatched at it and imagined it played by a full orchestra. A battle march, he clung to the brave, rising tremor of the strings as he might have clung to a flag on the open field.

"We meet again, Highness. I regret under less comfortable circumstances."

The song collapsed in dissonance. Ashel had hoped the Relmlord would never dirty himself with the filth of his own dungeons. That he wouldn't remember that night at the Commissar's palace, or how they'd stood together, admiring the mural of the Lathalorns. Thick blond hair still waved back from Lornk's forehead, silvered at the temples. His face was smooth as a statue's. Fearing the Relmlord would see the recognition in his eyes, Ashel ducked his head. "I don't know what you mean," he said.

"Oh, stop," Lornk said irritably. "This ruse might have worked if we hadn't met, but don't insult me by pretending it to my face."

"I'm not Prince Ashel."

Lornk snorted.

"We do look somewhat alike, I won't deny that. When we were apprentices together—"

"Highness, it's very simple. I have a document I want you to sign." The guard held the paper so Ashel could read it.

> I, Prince Ashel of Narath, wish for peace between the people of Relm and the people of Latha. I call upon my mother, Elekia of Reinoll Parish, elected Ruler of Latha, who came to her position through subterfuge and malicious intent, to end hostilities and withdraw all Lathan troops from Relman territory.

"You're mad to think the prince would sign that," Ashel said.

"Sign it and be my guest in Olmlablaire," Lornk replied. "Sign it and I'll arrange for the return of your comrade to Latha, unless, of course, you don't care whether he's a line in my profit ledgers."

Calm, Ashel thought to himself. Don't let him provoke you.

"Well, then. I'll leave you to think about it." On his way out, Lornk nodded at a young marshall who came in and sat in a chair beside the forge. Ashel's eyes darted after Lornk, then back at the young man. About Bethniel's age, he had burnished gold hair tied at the base of his neck, indigo eyes that spoke of summer skies or becalmed seas. Recognition jolted through him, his arms tensing in their bonds: Earnk Korng.

A woman, her eyes and mouth pinched, drew Ashel's attention away from the Relmlord's son. Yesterday she had spent hours Listening, patiently, silently working needles beneath his fingernails. Now she walked past Earnk and began arranging tools in the fire. Sweat trickled down Ashel's back.

The Listener signaled her readiness, and Earnk studied Ashel. He looked much like his father, but smaller, softer than the Relmlord—the human model to the sculpture. Every smile of Lornk's implied a threat; Earnk's face promised mercy. This frightened Ashel more than Lornk's cruelty.

"So," Earnk said, "you look exactly like the Prince of Latha and you're a minstrel too."

"Not exactly. I'm better looking," he quipped in Betheljin. His friends would have appreciated that sally, though as Ashel said the words, they soured in his mouth.

Stone-faced, Earnk scratched something in a notebook. "And you know who I am."

"But you don't know me."

"What can you tell me of the Blade?"

The question startled Ashel. He shrugged. "She's a hero."

"Do you love her? The Heralds reported a marriage was imminent."

Ashel squashed his feelings into a ball, wrapped them in indifference. "Heralds print whatever gossip sells their papers."

"She rejected you, then."

"I have to answer to her for the loss of the Dagger," he said tightly. "That is my only connection to the Blade."

"For your sake, I wish that were true. My father is jealous of his possessions."

Ashel struggled to keep his muscles relaxed, his face neutral, and said nothing.

"Well, we'll talk more tomorrow." Earnk called a guard and ordered Ashel returned to his cell.

A warren of chambers and passageways, the dungeons of Olmlablaire lay within a high hill that separated the upper and lower Olm valleys. They'd arrived on a crisp autumn day, the highlands already dusted with snow. Ashel hadn't seen daylight since the guards had hustled him and Geram underground. Back in their cell, light flickered through the hole in the stone door, a counterpoint to the ache in his temples. Torch smoke, human waste, the stale breath pounded in his head as a guard brought in soup and dry bread. Geram stared at the tiny candle on the tray and laughed. "Now they taunt us with candles and no matches."

Ashel offered the lieutenant a dry grin and a pair of stone chips from the floor. "In a cell cut from Relman flint, you ask for matches."

"I'd like to see you jibe around a buoy in fifteen-foot swells," Geram grumbled, lighting the wick.

Ashel chuckled and sopped the soup with his bread. Neither spoke again as they finished eating and went to sleep.

One hand clamped above Ashel's elbow, a yawning guard knocked on a wooden door and pushed into a small office lined with shelves. A tea tray sat upon the desk separating Earnk Korng from the door. "Join me, will you?" The younger Korng gestured toward the chair facing his desk. Next to the tea lay a pen, an inkwell, and the declaration. *Elekia of Reinoll Parish, elected Ruler of Latha, who came to her position through subterfuge and malicious intent . . .* Eyes avoiding the document,

Ashel took a cup of tea and accepted an offer of honey.

Earnk uncovered a basket of scones and held it toward him. "My cousin Elsa made these."

Grime gathered round Ashel's cuticles, traced the whorls of his fingertips. Hardly the hands with which to dine in refined company, but he took a scone. Butter and citrus melted on his tongue. "My compliments to Cousin Elsa."

"I thought we should share morning tea together," Earnk said. "Would you like some jam?"

Wondering at Earnk's purpose, Ashel spread some preserves on his scone. "Did Elsa make this too?"

"She did." Earnk took a bite. "What can you tell me of the Blade?"

His gut clenched, but Ashel leaned back in his chair and swallowed more tea. "We have a song about her:

> *The Dagger is tricky, sneaky and sly*
>
> *And the Blade is as sharp as a harrier's cry*
>
> *She'll tweak Relman noses and tickle their ribs*
>
> *And run a blade up their ass, she's a quick little nib*

Earnk scowled. "Clever, and in the Ancient's language too. Did you compose it?"

"No." He forced a grin. "A Loremaster named Laelin wrote it." He waved at Earnk's notebook. "You might want to write that down."

Earnk obliged him and scratched a note. "So many admire her?"

Ashel raised his eyebrows. "You do." He'd practiced this sort of game among Trainer Citizens and Eldanion nobles—he could almost enjoy *this*.

A hint of pink appeared above Earnk's eyebrows, but his expression remained chiseled. "Do you love her?"

Ashel spread his lips in a sly smile, covering consternation. Why did Earnk keep asking about Vic? Was it on his father's behalf, or his own? She never spoke of Earnk Korng, but now Ashel wondered if he had two rivals for her. "There's a song called 'The Wizard's Last Embrace.' Do you know it?"

Earnk shook his head.

"It's about a Relman wizard named Thabean, who loves another wizard named Victoria."

Earnk's eyebrows shot up, and he took a quick sip.

"They fought together in the War of the Council and became lovers," Ashel continued, a knot of satisfaction in his belly, "but Victoria was already married, and she returned to her husband."

"I see. I'll let Elsa know you enjoyed her scones, and we'll talk again tomorrow. Don't break anything," he added to the guard.

† † †

Ashel woke face down, a filthy blanket clenched between his teeth, the cell pitch dark. Last he remembered, he'd been curled into a ball, arms covering his head while guards kicked him. Each day began with tea and buttered scones in Earnk Korng's office and finished with guards beating Ashel senseless. On alternate days, the Relman Listener stuck needles under his fingernails. "Why are they doing this?" he groaned.

Geram shifted on his cot. "They've surely asked a ransom for the prince and must know who you are by now, by the Ruler's response."

"It doesn't make any sense," Ashel whispered. *Elekia of Reinoll Parish, elected Ruler of Latha, who came to her position through subterfuge and malicious intent . . .* The thought died, swamped by memory.

A narrow sliver of light spills into his room, broken by a furtive shadow. His sister darts to his bed and huddles against him, her hands over her ears. His tender backside makes moving hard, but he scuttles aside to make room and pulls the covers over their heads. Mother's voice lashes, Father's strikes. Words obscured by closed doors, each volley stings like a switch.

"I'm sorry, Beth," he whispers, hugging her tight. "I'm sorry they woke you." Sorry he caused this fight, and all the other midnight battles between king and queen.

"Sing to me."

In a shaky whisper, he begins a lullaby, and the melody proves a better shield against their parents than the blanket. Within a few measures, crystal notes, high and clear, wrap them both in a field of blue. Bethniel's head weighs heavy on his arm, and his tempo slows with each rise and fall of her chest. His voice trails off; his eyelids droop.

Father's shout jolts them awake: "Then why didn't you declare with him?"

His mind wandered through such tempests during the empty hours between beatings. His parents' rows, the servants' whispers, and the steely glares of Uncle Navael, who had been Heir when Grandfather Rivern held the throne. One memory spun into the next, every vortex leading to Lornk Korng's arm across his shoulders while they admired a silver flute hanging in a shop window.

Shoving that thought away, Ashel sat up and lit a candle. He laughed, though it hurt. "Every morning, when Earnk is serving me tea, he asks about the Blade. Every morning, that failure stands above everything else. Will she forgive me for what happened to the Dagger? For the things I said, before I left Narath. And if she did, would she choose me over them—

either the father or the son—as if we were all just sausages in the marketplace."

The cell door squeaked, and Earnk Korng pushed inside. Ashel's eyes darted to Geram, wondering why he hadn't given warning.

"Here." Earnk handed a jar to Geram. The door slammed behind him.

Geram opened the jar, his eyes popping at the whiff of citrus permeating the cell.

"Slotaen?" Ashel asked, glancing at his blackened fingernails.

Geram handed him the jar. "That's . . . generous."

"It is." Daubing some on each fingertip, Ashel replaced the lid and put the jar under his cot. His gut twisted with foreboding; the healing salve was a boon, but one sure to come with a price.

Earnk swallowed the night-chilled air like medicine while Elesendar disappeared behind snowcapped peaks. Gravel crunched on a road that wound through orchards and forest, then vegetable gardens, stretching between Olmlablaire's prison and the palace itself. Long evergreen needles swept toward the ground, and the whorling limbs of the geilmors cast dim, tormented shadows on the roadway.

The wind cut through his cloak, and he longed for his bed's warmth, though not for sleep. While he still lived in Re and worked with his father's Council, he'd relished dreams of Vic's smooth skin, soft breasts, and salty flavor. He'd indulged in fantasies of reconciliation, in which his father's death enabled a truce between Relm and Latha. As the new Lord of Relm, Earnk would seal the peace with a marriage: Victoria of Ourtown, known as the Blade, ward of Latha's Ruler, would become his wife and

Relm's First Councilor. All these dreams faded last winter, when Vic nearly killed his father. After they'd returned to Lordhome, Lornk had put Earnk in charge of the dungeons. Now, he woke each night, twisted into sweat-soaked sheets, thoughts drenched with echoes of Vic's screams. He used to dread news of her death. Now he prayed she would be killed rather than brought here, but all Relm's troops had standing orders to take her alive.

Would she choose me? Earnk's nightmares had only grown worse when gossip about Vic and Prince Ashel reached Olmlablaire, and after meeting the prince, Earnk's last hopes withered. Bruises and scabs marred Ashel's handsome features, but neither the beatings nor Vendrael's needles had damaged his composure. At tea each morning, the prince greeted Earnk courteously and deflected his questions.

> *"Shall I sing it for you?" the prince asks.*
> *"Sing what?"*
> *"'The Wizard's Last Embrace?' I can do both parts. You have to hear it to appreciate it."*

Each day the prince brought up that song. Was it a hint he and Vic had married but not yet declared? It was common in Relm for couples to keep trysts secret until a child was on its way—perhaps Lathans did the same. *Would she choose me*? That question could mean Vic hadn't chosen anyone, or the prince feared she might leave him for another. Which could it be? And would she choose me? Earnk thought.

Pale gray washed out the stars as he saluted the guards at the palace gate, passed swiftly inside, and climbed the flights to his father's suite. He found Lornk in his nightshirt and robe, a roll in his mouth and a note in his hand. In the bedroom, a maid tucked the coverlet around the mattress, her hair tousled and skirts askew.

"Prince Ashel still insists he's a common soldier," Earnk said. "I understand the queen's emissaries have agreed to parley?"

Sipping his tea delicately, Lornk waved his hand between them. "Yes, but I want to move forward. Our gift arrived yesterday. Did you see it?"

Suppressing a gulp, Earnk nodded. All his life he'd witnessed his father's wrath, but the plans for Latha's prince astounded him. "They appear to be the proper size."

"Did you check on the slotaen stocks?"

"There should be enough. I gave them some before I came up." A lump clogging his throat, Earnk ventured, "Is it wise to martyr him?"

"This isn't about martyring him."

Earnk willed the blood to stay out of his face. "I know you're angry about him and Kara—"

Lornk laughed. "That? No, no. This is about curbing his will to mine. I'm going to take away his most precious possession, and then I will give it back. I regret we lack the time for subtlety, but by the end of this, Ashel will be as loyal to me as you are— and then that other matter won't be a concern. Just as it's not with you."

Earnk nodded, his face devoid of emotion.

"But I have other news." Grinning, his father held up a sheet of fine linen. "Read this."

You put the dagger of revenge in my hands. Now I send its blade to cut out your heart as you carved away mine.

Rosenwater wafted from the page. "What is this?"

"The crafty witch sent it through the Device to Traine."

"Why?"

His father smirked. "Elekia likes to send me nasty notes. We corresponded quite a lot when we were young." He quirked an eyebrow. "What do you think it means?"

"Dagger, blade." Earnk's heart lurched, and it was all he could do to keep his voice steady. "I suppose it means Vic—Kara—is coming."

"Exactly. Once I've got her back, I'll take a holiday, and let you run things here. I expect the Council will be pleased with that."

"So will I," Earnk said weakly, turning to go.

"You do know the prince is your cousin?" Lornk asked.

Earnk froze.

The tower room smells funny, and Mother sits in a corner, her face pressed to the wall, her skin very dirty, her scalp torn and bleeding. The eyes that turn on him shimmer. "What are you doing here, you little shit?"

He gulps and holds up the pastry. "I—I brought your favorite. Father—"

"He doesn't love you. He never did." Like a stalking cat, she crawls toward him. "Do you know you have an aunt?" His mother's mouth, once the source of lullabies and kisses, twists into a snarl. "My sister is a queen. And I'm a fucking slave." She pounces and knocks him down, her fingernails raking his cheeks. He screams; she screams louder. Footsteps pound on the stairs. The door bursts open, and someone shoves his mother off him.

"I told you to never come up here!" Father barks.

"He doesn't love you," Mother wails, back in her corner. "He doesn't want me."

"Of course I do, darling." Father wraps his arms around her, stroking her head. "You're my heart." Over Mother's shoulder, he glares at Earnk. "Stop sniveling and get yourself cleaned up."

Lornk placed an arm around Earnk's shoulders. "It's important you know you have Lathan relations. We're all family! And don't worry. Everything is coming together, just as we planned. When the Lathan campaign is over, we can turn our efforts to Betheljin. The Citizenry despises Parnden. Once I've ousted him, Relm will be yours to rule." Smiling, he returned to his breakfast.

Mumbling his thanks, Earnk stumbled over an ottoman on his way out. Relm would be his, but Vic would be back in his father's thrall. And where did the prince of Latha—his cousin—fit in Lornk's stratagem?

The slap of ice water jerked Ashel awake. Dripping, gagging, he was yanked from the cot and shoved to the ground and kicked. A pair of guards hauled him to his feet and hustled him down the corridor. The interrogation room throbbed with heat, a stone forge heaped with glowing coals. In the midst of the coals rested a pair of metal gauntlets.

His eyes locked on the orange-blue glow, his knees gave out from under him. With curses and grumbling, the guards dragged him over to a stone chair and bound him there, thick leather bands across his ankles, wrists, biceps, and chest. His hands dangled over the edges of the arms, a mockery of freedom. When he finally tore his eyes from the forge, he saw Lornk and Earnk Korng had come in, their Listener behind them. Another guard brought over two wire cages shaped like hands from the table. A sound, a growl mixed with a wail, leaked out of Ashel's throat. Together, the Listener and the guard pried his fists open and fitted the wire cages around them so his hands jutted straight out from the chair arms. He strained against the bonds, yelping hoarsely while the Korngs watched calmly. The Listener returned to the forge and heaped the coals over the gauntlets.

"The Commissar still teases me about the night we met," Lornk said. "Growing up, did you perform for your parents and their guests? They must have been the envy of Latha."

Dry air scraped his tongue. "My family are farmers."

Lornk shook his head. "Come now, Your Highness. I'm about to take away your most valued possession—your talent. To stop me, you need only stop this silly charade and sign this simple document. Your mother has agreed to negotiate a ransom, and she wouldn't do that for some hack minstrel who merely resembled the prince. All I'm asking is that you acknowledge the truth."

"No." His heart fluttered like a trapped bird as the Listener fished a gauntlet out of the coals. He reached for the distraction of music but heard nothing but the coursing of his own blood. The Listener brought the thing, glowing yellow-red. Encased in the wire mesh, his fingers cringed at the heat. Drops ran down his nose—tears or sweat, he didn't know.

Lornk flowed over. "These gloves were made especially for you. A very expensive gift." The Relmlord nodded and the guard lowered the open gauntlet to hover above Ashel's hand. Heat singed his hair; the stench hit his nose. "I'll start earning that back soon enough with the sale of your companion." Two more guards brought Geram into the room. They'd taken his clothes and put a leather collar on him, like a Trainer mistress. The Listener dropped the glove onto Ashel's hand. Skin searing, he howled.

A moment later, the hot agony dimmed, and Ashel glimpsed Geram clutching his own hand, his face contorted. Then the guard snapped the gauntlet closed, and Ashel's palm burned with renewed vigor.

Lornk laid an arm around his shoulders and whispered in his ear, "You don't have to lose the other hand. Sign the paper, Ashel."

"I can't," he moaned.

"Why would Elekia hate me so much she'd start a war, Ashel? Have you ever thought of it? And why is your *younger* sister Heir? Haven't you wondered?"

He shook his head, sobbing. Even with Geram shielding him, his feet jerked and strained against their bonds, his body shuddering. They were bringing the other glove. "Please, no."

"I want to stop this. When I think how your voice might have graced my courtyard, my solarium, my dining hall. What did Elekia do to gain her throne, Ashel?"

He rolled his head around to look at Lornk. "She wouldn't—"

"What wouldn't she do? She was the loveliest girl I've ever seen, you know. And as sharp witted then as she is now. But a horse breeder's daughter cannot hope for much, even if she is queen of the Academy."

"No!" Geram cried. He grunted at the thud of a guard's club but went on. "He lies. I know he lies."

Lornk shrugged. "Do you wish me to sell your companion to the most perverse brothel in Traine? Do you want to lose your other hand? Or do you want to come to Olmlablaire and live in a manner worthy of your heritage?" The second glove hovered, threatening.

"My father," Ashel panted, "is dead." The top of the gauntlet slammed down, and he shrieked, his hips twisting off of the seat.

"Are you sure?" Lornk whispered in his ear, somehow making him hear above his own screams. "It's not too late for slotaen to save your hands. Tell me your name. Tell me why your mother hates me so much."

He wanted to die. Lornk's voice buzzed in his ear, nagging him to confess, but it was Lornk who was confessing the last truth Ashel wanted to hear. "She would have been First Councilor of Relm, but she set her sights even higher." Geram spoke in his mind, begged him to believe Lornk lied. Yet the memories that had swarmed during the long hours of his captivity urged him to trust the Relmlord's word on this, if nothing else. If he kept refusing, what would they do next—cut out his tongue? If Father had made him Heir and the truth had come out . . . The truth. *Gained her position through subterfuge. Set her sights higher.* Cutting through the agony came the sensation of hot blood soaking his robes, of Elekia's arms wrapped around him, Sashal's body held between them. *What wouldn't she do?*

NO! Geram's voice slammed into him, severing his mind from his hands. But music, the art of his hands, his voice, that was all he had left. Surrounded by lies, decades of deceit, it was the only truth he *knew*. Like a swimmer against the current, he pushed back against Geram's shield, wanting, needing to feel the bones, the sinews, the calluses, even if they were all burnt away. He reached for the seared skin, the crisped muscles, swimming after the pain. As he dove for it, the barrier melted, pulling him into a funnel, a whirlpool of his thoughts spinning down into blackness, spinning faster and faster until he knew nothing but the blackness, then nothing at all.

†††

The prince's wails and pleas abruptly ceased, and the Lathan lieutenant gagged and went rigid, his eyes rolling up into his head as he fell over, foam on his lips. The guards and Vendrael blinked at each other, the sizzle of flesh the only sound. Pulse thrumming, Earnk pressed his back to the wall and stared at his father. *Your voice might have graced my courtyard . . .*

"Get them off him," Lornk roared, and guards sprang forward with mitted hands.

"What happened?" his father demanded. "Lieutenant, what happened?"

"He's not there," Vendrael gasped. A healer held a candle up to Ashel's eyes while another slathered slotaen on his hands. The stink of burned flesh mingled with the sunny citrus of the ointment, and Earnk's stomach roiled with bile.

"What do you mean he's not there?"

"I get nothing from him," she replied. "His body's just a shell."

The Lathan lieutenant groaned and pushed himself to his knees. Lornk strode over and kicked him. "What did you do?"

Swaying woozily, Geram shook his head.

Lornk glared at him, then the guards. "Take them back to their cell." Grabbing Earnk's arm, he pulled him into the hallway, eyes shooting daggers. Earnk stumbled after him, stunned. In the office, Lornk shoved him into a chair and paced behind the desk. "What do you know about this Geram of Alna? Did you know he was a Listener?"

"Yes."

"Why didn't you tell me?"

"It's in my report. I didn't think it worth noting except it would raise his value on the market." His own questions simmered for answers; soon they'd be boiling. *He doesn't love you, he doesn't want me.*

"Talent like that is priceless."

"I had no idea he had that kind of strength."

"You should have recognized it," Lornk said.

"I've done my best." *Do you know you have an aunt? My sister is a queen.* Mother's screams the day she died itched in his ears, the squeak and thud that cut off her final wail like a spigot.

"Find out exactly what he did, then break him. I want him doing that for me." His father stopped pacing, caught and held Earnk's eyes. "Don't you see the potential for something like this?"

"I don't think I can break him." *He doesn't love you, he doesn't want me.* Who did he want, this Citizen of Traine who never took a wife because he loved his mistress, but who defied custom and never married the mother of his child? *She would have been First Councilor, but she set her sights higher.*

The cruelty in Lornk's eyes faded. Sitting behind the desk, he leafed through Earnk's papers. "I know bending a will to yours isn't a thing you enjoy, but you must learn to do it if you want to succeed as Relmlord. I'm confident you can. You've mastered every other task I've given you."

"What about the prince?" *Your voice might have graced my courtyard, my solarium, my dining hall.*

"Well, whatever's happened to him, we have to restore him, of course." Lips curling, his father chortled. "I can't return an imbecile to his mother. It might prompt more nasty notes."

"You said he was my cousin."

"He is your cousin. Whether he is more than that? He resembles his mother more than anyone else."

Breath short, Earnk stared at his father, trying to make sense of that response.

Lornk's hand swept the air between them. "The prince is secondary. I want that Listener ready for Kara when she gets here."

Earnk leaned forward, his heart thudding. He wanted to understand about Ashel, but he *needed* to understand this. "What do you mean, ready for Kara?"

With another chuckle, Lornk leaned back and put his feet on Earnk's desk. "I might get that holiday sooner than we thought. I must admit Kara has acquired some dangerous habits. But with that Listener's help they might be turned to our advantage. I'll show Elekia a Dagger of her revenge!"

Slowly, Earnk stood. Wait, he told himself. Vic wasn't here yet. Vic probably wouldn't make it through the desert at all. He should find out what Geram did, find out the truth tying together Ashel, his father, and Latha's queen. But perhaps his mother's legacy of madness had just been bequeathed. Perhaps years loving a woman he shouldn't tipped him off the knife blade into the black pool waiting beneath it. He didn't listen to his own urgent cries to stop as he drew his knife out of its sheath.

"*Our hearts belong to others,*" his mother used to tell him as they sat in the library reading together, "*but our heads—our minds—are ours alone.*" Is that why she threw herself down the tower stairwell? Did Lornk take away her mind as well as her heart? "I can't let you do that to her." Earnk lunged across the desk, sweeping the knife toward his father. Lornk sprang backward, hit the chair, and toppled backward to the floor. As his father regained his feet, calling for his bodyguards, Earnk vaulted the desk and thrust again. The knife sliced smoothly through wool and flannel, bit skin. Lornk's hand wrapped around Earnk's wrist, and with a twist, the stoneknife clattered to the floor. The guards burst into the room as Lornk wrestled Earnk's arm behind him and pinned him on the desk.

"Treachery!" a guard gasped as the other dragged Earnk away from Lornk.

His father stared at him from the uprighted chair, his face pallid. "He reopened the wound. Call Trellerend."

"You can't do that to her," Earnk cried.

Lornk shook his head, jaw bunching. "Put him in the filthiest hole you can find."

CHAPTER 20

SAND CAST

The breeze blowing off the Kragnashian headland stoked the sun's blaze and fired the sand. Land and sky were a vise, squeezing sweat from every pore as the hot air dried the throat. Vic counted the barrels being loaded onto a sledge, hoping they'd brought enough water. "Captain," she called to Carl, her command third. "Ask the ship captain for two more barrels."

The hint of a sneer twisted his lips before he pressed them together and answered. "I wouldn't add more weight, Marshall. The horses will already be pulling their limit in this heat."

She nodded, swallowing a curse. The ship lay at anchor in a turbulent bay, their supplies ferried ashore in a pair of rowboats. The last of the horses kicked and struggled in a winch as sailors lowered it to the water. Its squeals resounded off the yellow sand, and its herdmates shied and whinnied in their traces. A pair of cavalry troopers bobbed in the surge below the animal, dodged its hooves and teeth as it thrashed. Draylune soothed with soft words and stroking while her partner Nedden unfastened the winch harness. When the horse was free and swimming for shore, the troopers lay back and floated in the sea, relieved all the animals had survived the voyage and debarkation.

As Vic paid the ship captain, he peered at the yellow sand and shook his head, but he kept his thoughts to himself. Before the company had all the provisions sorted, his ship had become a speck, running before the wind off the headland.

When everything was loaded, the horses trudged up the dunes on splayed hooves, harnesses creaking as the sledges rutted the sand. The humans gouged the dune after them, backs bent under packs. Reaching the top of the first rise, Vic shaded her eyes and gazed at the yellow landscape undulating to the horizon. Already grit rubbed against her heels and sweat rolled down her back. She resisted the urge to cast off her djellaba, knowing it would be her only defense against the sun. Wineyll and Bethniel clambored up the dune and stopped beside her.

"How long before we meet the Kragnashians?" Vic asked.

"I'm sure they sent out a greeting party as soon as Mother's message arrived in Direiellene. They'll find us soon," Beth replied.

"Shouldn't we wait here for them?" Wineyll asked, staring at the endless dunes.

"We don't have time for that," Vic said. Bethniel nodded, then slipped down the slope after the others. "Keep up the dagger practice with Carl, Drak, or Valion," Vic told the minstrel. "Relmans and"—she waved at the desert—"Kragnashians may not be charmed by your flute."

Grinning, Wineyll glanced at the case at her hip. "I am pretty good."

"Nobody's that good. Not even Ashel."

The girl's smile faded and she followed the company down the dune. Vic watched her go, blinking at tears that dried before they reached her cheeks. Ashel—she prayed to Elesendar or fate or pure damn luck he was well. He's the son of a sovereign, not a powerless slave, she reassured herself, but her spine clenched at the memory of Lornk's glacial gaze. The land ahead taunted her, promising failure. Clearing her throat, she fell in after the company.

† † †

The first afternoon, the heat killed a horse and nearly killed three troopers. After that, they marched at night, when the air was cooler. Although they followed the course prescribed in Elekia's agreement with the Kragnashian Center, no guides appeared. Only sand surrounded them, as featureless as the ocean, the sky endless, empty blue by day, heavy with glitter by night. Progress slow, in a month they'd walked the distance they'd expected to cover in two. In two they'd covered only half the route to Relm, when they thought they'd be crossing the Plu—though without the Kragnashians' help, Elesendar knew how they'd manage that. The Umbrachlorn Plu looked like a river on maps but was a gash in the earth's crust, bubbling with sulfurous mud and lava, and only the Kragnashians knew how to cross it. Dune after dune sucked strength from calves; grit blistered heels and ravaged throats. Time and distance blended together, marked only by the emptying of another water barrel and the butchering of another horse, killed for its flesh and to spare the water as the sledge grew lighter. As the supplies shrank and the Desert People failed to meet them, discontent grew.

"Cut again?" Valion, one of the junior officers, asked one morning, hefting his canteen after Marenye, the quartermaster, doled out the day's ration.

"Could be worse." Marenye angled her head at thin strips of slaughtered horseflesh drying in the sun.

"This little water won't leave me far from that," Valion complained.

"But there'll be blood stew for supper," Bethniel cut in with a laugh. "And as a bonus, I'm not making it."

Valion raised his canteen. "Hear that, boys and girls? Her Highness is letting someone else cook tonight! Three cheers for Latha's Heir!" A ragged hurrah and round of guffaws echoed off the sand. Vic exchanged a smile and wink with Bethniel, but the levity evaporated as quickly as spit on the hot sand.

The sun paced across the sky, dragging a cape of green-gray clouds. People talked of rain over their blood stew and fresh jerky that evening, yet only sand showered them. And on the horizon, one smudge stayed stubbornly brown while the setting sun painted other clouds pink and orange.

Skin prickling, Vic called over the captains and jutted her chin at the smudge. "Another sandstorm." Each had stalled them for hours, and one had halted progress for two days when they had to dig the sledges out from under a dune.

Drak shrugged. "The wind's blowing it away from us."

"Hope it stays that way." At Vic's wave, the company plodded up the next slope. No one spoke, in mindspeech or aloud. Throat aching, Vic forgot everything but pulling each foot out of the sand and pushing it forward. No one had ever been this deep into Kragnash. They might find themselves on flat ground at any moment. Vic smiled, imagining her legs free of sucking sand, running for the joy of running across a hard-packed plain.

Without warning, the storm slammed into them, thrashing skin and clogging nostrils. Horses whinnied and charged toward the lights at the head of the column, sledges rattling behind them while their drivers shouted and sawed the reins. Orders flew from the captains: "Get the tents up!" "Cover the provisions!"

"Horses' tent first," Vic shouted. Canvas tore out of hands, whipped and cracked above heads as sand pelted them. Troopers fought the animals, hanging onto their lines as they bucked and kicked and tried to bolt away. At last the horses were inside their shelter with troopers to tend them. Stinging sand blizzarding around them, a second tent went up and everyone else dove inside.

Prayers for sturdy seams murmured as the wind shook the canvas like an angry mother punishing her child. The air reeked of fear, cloying against the skin, and the lamps cast fitful shadows of elbows and chins and noses—all sharp angles. Its fury indefatigable, the storm raged for hours. Vic dozed on a camp stool, jerking awake each time the gale spun and hurled sand from a new direction. Others bedded down, but few slept as a wall bulged inward, the willowwood struts bending toward their limit.

With a low rumble, sand began to slide out from under them. Shouts echoed as canvas stretched and seams popped. The ceiling caved inward. "Hold those struts!" Drak yelled as troopers scrambled in the landslide. Lamps fell and went out. A bedroll caught fire. Pouring sand snuffed the flames, pitching them into darkness. People tumbled into one another amid screams, crashes, and clatters. When the motion stopped, the tent was a crawlspace, the air thick with dust. Coughing, Vic ordered a roll call; eight names went unanswered.

"Listen, the wind's stopped," Wineyll said hopefully. "Do you think it's over?"

"I think we're buried," growled Carl.

"Find some lanterns and get us some light," Vic snapped. "Carl, get a team and start digging. Drak, find those missing troopers."

Lamps flared alight, and Bethniel crawled through the crowd to Vic's side. "Maybe we should stay here until the storm's over."

The princess was shaking, her eyes big as saucers. Vic

swallowed a curse at Elekia for sending her daughter on this mission. "As bad as it is outside, it's also where the air is. We don't know how long we have in here."

The princess pointed at a broken strut, jutting out of its sleeve. "They're hollow."

Vic blinked, a grin blooming despite their dire straits. The willowwood struts *were* hollow, each segment a little smaller than the next, down to the width of a man's thumb, so they could be pushed together or pulled apart to alter their length as needed. They were also strong enough to hold the tent up in the storm, until a mountain fell on them, and even then they had saved the company from being crushed altogether. "Carl," she said, "disregard my last order. Use the willowwood to get us some air until the storm blows itself out."

An hour later, troopers lay in the sand, exhausted from the effort of pushing the struts through to the surface and digging for their missing comrades. They found them all, seven still alive, though one of those was coughing blood. Air moaned through the willowwood, and the stream of sand piling beneath each duct told them the storm still raged, but at least they could breathe. Vic slept a few hours, then moved among the troopers, speaking to them as one speaks the night before a hopeless battle, of faith and bravery and luck. Bethniel spoke as well, reminding them that Elesendar still made His rounds above the storm, that He still watched. Some nodded and shared comfort and courage with their comrades, but others turned their heads away when the princess mentioned their god. Vic settled next to Orlon and put a hand on his shoulder, urging resolve. Fists curled into balls, the healer chewed on his lip. "I'm sorry they took him," he muttered. "I'm sorry."

The apology bit like an accusation. It was madness to try to cross Kragnash—the desert had proved a barrier stronger than a thousand-foot wall. Despair sinking into her bowels, Vic retreated to a corner of their tomb to listen to the wind, as the others did, in silence.

Chapter 21

Under the Knife

The deepest cell in the dungeon stank with mildew and raw sewage. Earnk lost track of time, fell into a fitful sleep disturbed by visions of Vic as his father's mindless slave. When he woke, sweat soaked his clothes and pasted hair to his forehead. His chest and limbs ached, and a hammer banged the inside of his skull, measuring the minutes and the hours. After an eternity, Trudin opened the door.

"You're on hard labor until your trial," she said.

He snorted. "He's letting me out of the filthy hole, then?"

She scowled. "If it were up to me, I'd kill you and be done. But your father has a generous heart."

They stopped at a storage room and she gave him a rough blanket, threadbare and crawling with blanket bugs. Knotting it around his shoulders, Earnk followed her up the maze of stairs and tunnels to meet the other Relman prisoners. The stairs robbed him of breath, and his chest heaved a coughing fit as they neared the others. Trudin waited for him to finish, tapping an impatient boot.

"Took you long enough," Fran grumbled at them.

"It's a long way up here. I'll be glad when he's tried."

"Worn out from your walk up the stairs, Marshall?" Fran

asked, shoving Earnk into line with the others. "Well, you'll join these scum soon enough, or your head will be on the block."

Outside, the sky sagged, dropping slowflakes like an overstuffed pillow. Earnk hugged the blanket around his shoulders and watched his feet stumble along the road. With the clarity of delirium, he thought of the sweet heat of Elsa's winter teas, the comfort of quilted down and a glowing hearth while snow gathered on window panes. A year and more ago, Elsa had warned Lornk that the Commissar had his eye on their house and mines. She'd urged him to let Earnk remain in Traine and steward the properties so Parnden couldn't claim them as abandoned. Father had agreed, but Earnk had refused. He preferred the straight-talking, hardworking people of Relm to the sophisticated schemers of Traine. Now Trudin, one of those straight talkers he'd admired, tagged his calves with her baton, her face etched deeply with hatred.

Several miles into the woods they reached the firecutters' camp. A woodsman's song and the cadence of axes drifted over a stack of cut logs to the prisoners. Beside the woodpiles, empty carts waited on the track to Lordhome. Fran and Trudin directed them to fill the carts, and that morning the prisoners stacked them full of wood and dragged them to Lordhome and back.

When they stopped to eat, even Trudin and Fran looked tired. The prisoners washed down their bread with bites of snow. Earnk sat apart, sweat steaming off his face and neck, freezing on the collar of his tunic and the fringes of his hair. He rubbed snow on his burning forehead but had no strength to eat his own loaf.

A pair of antimilitia—Relman rebels who'd been caught with poisoned knives inside the palace—whispered to each other. The woman took a sharp breath and flicked her thumb at one of the woodpiles. Her partner, a tiny man with huge hands, shook his head and rubbed his chin. Earnk's gaze followed theirs to an axe haft jutting out of the jumble of small kindling logs. No blade could be seen, but the woman looked determined to use the haft. Her partner shook his head again as Fran ordered everyone back to work. Earnk stumbled toward the pile with the axe handle, snowflakes melting the moment they touched his skin.

The tiny antimilitiaman glared at Earnk as he joined him at the pile. Earnk tried to remember his name—Mallosh, Malber, something. The man was small, but his arms bulged with muscle and he easily freed the axe and passed it to the woman. Wiping a hand across his eyes, Earnk reached for one of the smaller pieces of wood. He did not warn the guards. He tried to remember the man's name.

The woman hefted the axe, hiding its graystone blade with her body as she ran her thumb along the edge. Earnk shuffled toward the cart, arms full of kindling. A violent trembling seized him and his knees gave out. Sticks spilled across the bark-strewn ground. Cursing, Trudin pulled him to his feet. With a shriek, the antimilitiawoman turned and swung the axe at Trudin's neck. The guard toppled over Earnk, knocking him flat as the rebel sprinted into the woods. Mallach—that was it—Mallach darted to Fran and shoved him as the crossbow fired. The bolt thunked into a log.

Shouting and the pounding of feet filled the air, while Earnk lay pinned under Trudin's dead weight. His sweat misted around them, fogging his view, darkening it into black.

† † †

Geram hunkered on his cot, shivering. Across the cell, Ashel's body sat rigid, his eyes blinking at regular intervals, bandaged hands resting on his lap. Blood pulsed beneath ravaged skin and muscle. But he did not live. Geram tried again to reach him, drawing on all his experience to thrust his mind into Ashel's and Listen for something more than a heartbeat. But if Ashel hadn't been sitting in front of him, he wouldn't have known he was there.

In a corner sat the little jar of slotaen Earnk had given them. Geram had seen miracles from the ointment—skin green with infection turned brown and healthy in days, a blistering, bleeding burn healed in weeks. But Ashel's hands would need months of treatment, and the supply Earnk had brought them would run out in a day. Elesendar, to lose something so valuable—his heart ached in sympathy.

And fear stifled his lungs. Each day brought him closer to the auction block in Traine. What would it be? The mines? A bilge slave? Either promised a short, miserable sojourn toward death. Or would they break him and turn him into some Citizen's personal Listener? Having seen the Relmlord's methods, Geram prayed for the bilges.

Water dripped down the walls; torches guttered and hissed. In the quiet, he Heard his name: *Geram.* Not a spoken voice. *Geram, where are you?* A panicked voice. *I can't see you—see anything.*

Ashel?

Where am I? Geram, what did they do to me? I can't see, or hear, or feel anything.

Ashel's body sat beside him, unmoved, unalive. The voice was like his own thoughts, lightning fast ideas rather than words or images. Elesendar. "Ashel," he whispered aloud, then clamped his mouth shut. *You're inside me.*

What happened?

I don't know. I tried to take your pain.

Put me back! Panic like a klaxon in his head. *Where is my body?*

Right here. Ashel, calm down. It was hard to sound soothing to your own thoughts. *Collect yourself—literally. I don't want to put you back until you're sure all of you will go and all of me will stay.*

As if in prophecy, sour harp notes echoed through his head.

How is my body? Ashel asked, sounding calmer. *Is it alive?*

Yes. It's breathing. It even looks pained by your hands.

My hands. What about them?

Some healers put slotaen on them, and we have some more. I think you may be able to flex your fingers again. I hope. The trouble with having somebody in your head was that you couldn't lie to him, even when a lie was what he needed to hear.

Flex my fingers? But play? Geram, I tried to hold out. Elesendar, it was more than I could bear.

You held out. Are you calm now?

Yes.

Do you feel whole? A few bars of orchestra music fluttered by.

No.

Elesendar's Shrine, Ashel. Collect yourself. I need you.

A bitter chuckle not his own slipped past Geram's teeth. *Well,* Ashel said, *looks like you've got me.*

Ashel floated through the depths of Geram's memory, searching for himself. Catching stray harp notes, harsh words spat by his mother, his sister's giggling, he drew them toward the core of thought and feeling he believed was himself. But with each memory he retrieved, another frayed off and drifted into a swirl of furled sails, leaping fish, and rough sailors laughing and drinking. He'd hear a deep voice singing a dirge and grasp at it, certain it was one of his old masters, only to find it was Geram's Uncle Arnan, singing the fish into his nets. Geram's memories ran through and around his own like the confluence of one river meeting another. Ashel struggled not to drown in those thoughts. But sometimes the whirl stilled around him.

A hand reaches for a naked arm. Tears darken honey-colored eyes, but Ideigin smiles like the sun when he touches her. Her cheek pressed to his shoulder, she weeps, grieving a brother executed for piracy. The crime doesn't matter to either of them. Blinking tears and starlight out of her eyes, she reaches up to draw his mouth down to hers.

Waves crash over the prow. Uncle Arnan yells at him to slacken the halyard. Salt stinging in his eyes, his hands fumble with a wet line and stiff knot. Arnan shouts again, and a wave smashes the deck, sweeping him overboard.

A lump choking his throat, he watches Father step down from his throne and offer it to Bethniel. Lips pressed tight, he wills the blood to drain from his face as his sister bows to the Senators and Prime Minister and dances up the dais steps. Father stands beside it, smiling as Bethniel hops into the chair. Her feet dangling, she declares her first proclamation as Heir: "My brother, Prince Ashel of Narath, apprentice to the Music himself, should sing for me." He bites the inside of his cheek and sings with iron on his tongue.

Shaken, Ashel sifted through the jumble faster, collecting every bar of music or roll of dice, hoping he wasn't gathering Geram's memories as well. But he shrugged off worry and moved on through any stillness that didn't seem familiar. As the gathered thoughts grew heavy and dragged against the opposing currents, he began to search not only for himself, but for a way out. Echoes of sleep sloshed past. Exhausted, he surrendered to the whirlpool, dropping into its center. There, a door stood ajar, opening on his bedroom at the manor. Clothes draped the chairs and sheets of music lay scattered on the floor. On his bed, his harp sat with tangled, broken strings. Rumpled blankets urged him to curl up and rest. He hugged the net of memories closer and stepped across the threshold.

The latch clicked, and seawater poured into the room, stinking of fish and rotting seaweed. A whirlpool swept sheet music and clothing and furniture down a funnel while Ashel clung to the doorknob, fighting to open it while slimy tendrils snagged his ankles, tugging him toward the vortex. Mustering all his strength he pulled on the door, and it burst open on the warmth of a paneled library.

† † †

Pain tore through Geram's head. Blinking, eyes tearing, he focused on the winged serpent coiling across the greater part of the mantle, on the crackling fire beneath.

"That was quite a feat yesterday," the Relmlord said, shrewd eyes scanning Geram's fists and face.

"What feat?" The wave of hurt subsided, leaving him breathless.

The Relmlord scowled. "Don't bother with the pointless evasions, Lieutenant. Vendrael figured out what you did." He made a shallow bow. "Your Highness."

Geram gazed at the fire, jaw bunching.

"How did you do it? I'm fascinated."

"It's a trade secret."

Lornk chuckled. "Vendrael concluded it was an accident. Do you know how to put him back?"

He considered lying, but saw nothing to be gained by defiance. "No."

"Not good, my friend." He must learn to control it, Lornk added to himself.

Fists clenched, Geram shook his head vigorously—too vigorously. *He won't, he can't,* Ashel said. *Don't let him use you.*

Ashel, stay quiet.

Lornk tapped his fingers on the mantle while Geram regained control. The Relmlord's ashen face belied his amused smirk, and his tunic bulged unnaturally around the middle. "Geram of Alna. Alna is not so different from Traine, which makes it very different indeed from the rest of Latha. What draws an Alnan to fight in Elekia's war?"

"Patriotism."

"How noble! What do you think of my home?" the Relmlord asked.

Geram had never seen finer furnishings, not even in the Courtesans Guildhouse. "I've heard the Ruler's manor in Narath has more windows."

Lornk's smile widened. "Indeed it does. But so drafty. Stone's the thing, Lieutenant. Latha will know its value sooner or later. Probably sooner, given the news I've had. A rescue party took ship in Cabanarl. The Blade and Latha's Heir were aboard."

Geram hung on to the arm of the divan to keep Ashel from flinging him at Lornk's throat. "What?" he croaked.

Laughing, one hand pressed into his side, Lornk wagged a finger at Geram. "I see control is definitely a problem, Lieutenant. But to answer your question, the queen has foolishly sent a company to attack me from the west, and my agents tell me Princess Bethniel is with them. My mistress"—his voice whetted on the word—"leads them. So I shall not only retrieve my property, I'll end this ridiculous conflict. Now you can guess what I want you to do for me. Take a few days to think about how you could help me, without, of course, another accident.

I want my property compliant, but not vacant. Oh, and restore the prince. I wouldn't want his dear sister to be distressed over his condition."

† † †

During the walk between Lordhome and the lower tunnel, Geram managed to keep Ashel's thoughts and feelings at bay by focusing on each step and nothing else. But in their cell, a slow dull pounding assaulted his temples, and the air came stiffly into his chest.

Elesendar, Bethniel.

Geram sighed. *Ashel, keep quiet, or I can't sort out which thoughts are yours and which are mine.*

If he did this to me, what will he do to my sister? You must put me back.

You aren't whole. I keep hearing music, Ashel.

We may not have time to wait. I'm tired. I have to sleep, but I can't here. I was going to, and then there was a flood, as if your thoughts were trying to drown me.

Geram's chest tight, he took a shallow breath, and another, trying to give what comfort he could to the prince. But Ashel's anguish infected him, and every muscle, his very blood, ached. Elesendar, help us, he prayed. All the times he had thrust himself into another's mind, he'd always kept himself separate. He'd done it by instinct, but now he needed to puzzle out the how or he'd never push Ashel from his head. In his earliest training as a counselor, the other Listeners had spoken of a focal point. *I need something to focus on. Something not you and not me, but apart from us.* His gaze fell on the tiny candle flickering near Ashel's breathing body.

Squashing his own doubts, Geram sat on the floor and put the candle between him and Ashel's feet. *Ashel, gather yourself.*

His throat was itchy and raw, and he fought a dizziness borne by torch smoke. Focusing on the flame, he centered himself on the wick at the base of the flame. As Ashel ransacked their memories, looking for his own, Geram remembered the bully who'd bloodied his nose until Geram learned how to make his fists mean something. He heard the sneers of the Caleisbahnin, with their silks and steel, as he helped his uncle deliver the day's catch to the fishmonger. He recalled the fear and suspicion in the Loremasters at his school, who didn't trust him not to cheat on his exams and who were certain that he would learn their secrets and use them for ill. All these memories now lay strewn about like old clothes, soiled by Ashel's agonies. It was time to restore order. But first and foremost, he needed to put Ideigin away.

As children, he and Ideigin had swum with her brothers for mullas dropped beneath the wharves, harried fishing skiffs in their tiny sloop, rolled marbles beneath the feet of dockworkers, stole feathers from pirates' sheaths. Ideigin used to stand on the corner across from the Weavers Guildhouse and moon the Guildmaster when he came out, then go sit beneath a window of the Minstrels Guildhouse and cry over the ballads practiced above. Geram still could feel the weight of her heavy locks, thick and frothy like his aunt's best ale. The sun on the bay washed her in honey brown from her hair to her feet, but Elesendar painted her smokier.

The summer before he joined the army, he would meet her as the last customers left the brothel where she journeyed, and they would walk across town, spread a blanket on a westside beach, and watch dawn break over the water. They rarely talked. They frequently made love, and afterward she would snuggle in his arms, reaching up occasionally with her finger to poke his nose, giggling at the honk he made when she touched it.

She'd had a baby on her hip when he saw her last winter, late in the afternoon in the main market square. They'd both said hello, asked the usual polite questions, and moved on. That was love in Alna—ardent but not always permanent. He'd stowed his memories of their youth away, a silk scarf better admired inside the box than held in the hand where the light of day might show the flaws. At the end, her lips had tasted bitter.

Geram placed his hands on his knees, palms up as Ashel's were placed. While the prince wound up his thoughts, Geram's chest reflected the movement of Ashel's rib cage. His buttocks began to groan against the stone floor. Slotaen wept from the prince's bandaged hands, staining his trousers. The candle flared as the texture of the wick changed. Drawing in a single deep breath, holding it, Geram closed his eyes to the flame, to Ashel's body. In the darkness, Ashel had spun his thoughts and memories into a cocoon of crystal threads that whistled the harmony of a top. *Now*, he said to the top, spinning it toward the tiny flickering warmth and the emptiness beyond.

The crystal jolted out into the darkness, hopping toward the heat, toward the void. Its whistling was the cry of flutes, the whine of fiddles, the beat of drums. Adoring applause, teasing giggles, scornful words echoed from it. A choir of cerrenil leaves, the ring of crystal and the lull of bells. As the sounds faded, they left only the drumming of Geram's heart. Sighing, he reached for Ideigin to put her away, first of all his painful memories.

He caught a snag of her sparkling laughter on the beach, but the thread jerked in his hands, tugging him toward the void. *No,* he whispered, his voice grim, and braced himself against the pull. Her laughter hardened into a scream as she stretched between him and the darkness. "No," he said aloud. Something banged like a hatch open in the wind. Ideigin's shriek scaled upward, her line slackening and snapping taut, burning the palms of his hands. "No!" he shouted, pulling on the shred of her with all the might he'd muster against a halyard in a storm. Then, as if the wind changed, the line snapped back at him, the boom swung, and the black sea sucked him down.

† † †

Vic kneels in front of a fire, combing tangles out of long wet hair. Water drips from the ends, steaming on warm flagstones. She smiles. "You look cold."

Earnk holds his hands to the flames. "I've been in Lordhome."

"I know." Wind howls down the chimney, snuffing out the fire. "Your father told me."

She stands and walks to Lornk's side. Grabbing her hair in a fist, he kisses her. Earnk tries to stand, to protest, but cold chains bind him to the ground. "You should have stayed in Traine," his father says. "Now look what you've done."

"Come on, get up." A hand shook Earnk's shoulder. He opened his eyes, blinked at a guard. He didn't remember the journey back to his cell. "You're due for questioning." The guard hauled him to his feet, shoved him out the door and down the hall. Sweat ran into his eyes as they walked into the forge room. He shivered, remembering Ashel's hands.

His father waited there, garbed in silk pantaloons and a quilted robe, and his hair smelling of Elsa's bath oil. Earnk brushed at stains on the doublet she'd embroidered for him.

"You look ill."

His eyes darting at the guards, Earnk touched his temple, scabbed and swollen. "Filthy holes will do that to a man."

Lornk crossed his arms and looked at the ground between them. "Why you tried to kill me was a mystery until I heard about yesterday's fiasco. How did they get to you? What did they promise you?"

"Who?"

"How long have you been antimilitia?"

"Did she escape?" Earnk asked, knowing his father wouldn't accept any of his real reasons for wanting to kill him. He didn't understand half of them himself.

"Who was she?"

He shook his head, his stomach lurching. "I can't remember her name. It's in the report I filed when they were arrested."

"But yesterday you helped her."

"I'm sick. I stumbled."

"The other one admitted you helped them. He said she couldn't have escaped without you."

"They got lucky, I guess." At Lornk's signal, the guards came forward and strapped Earnk to the chair. Vendrael stirred the coals, began to heat up her tools. "I want you to tell me everything you know about the antimilitia," Lornk said. "Who they are, where they are, and who is their leader?"

Earnk coughed, but felt like laughing. "I doubt you'll enjoy tormenting me as much as you did the prince. You *care* about him."

His father gazed at him, lips serene, eyes burning. "Maudlin self-pity is never a surprise from you, but always a disappointment," he said in Relman, but added silently, "I thought you understood there is purpose to everything I do. I am not a gratuitous man."

"And *I'm* the leader of the antimilitia," Earnk sneered aloud, startling the guards.

Lornk shook his head sadly and nodded for Vendrael to start. "Get the truth out of him."

CHAPTER 22

THE REWARDS OF GREED

Sand spilled through the willowwood tubes, measuring long hours. When the strident whistles finally faded, and the last grains of sand rattled into the crawlspace, eyes studied the sagging canvas and lips exchanged murmurs of the damned.

"We survived the night," Vic said, pulling the eyes to her and silencing the whispers. "We're not done until we're dead."

Carl ordered two troopers to dig under the canvas and head for the surface. Before their boots had disappeared, both came scuttling back into the shelter, sputtering sand. "It's like swimming through rocks," Selmar said, coughing. "We can't make any headway."

"We'll have to hope the horse teams can dig us out," Drak said.

"How long will that be?" someone asked.

The big captain shrugged and shook his head. Vic studied the sagging canvas and willowwood struts. "Drak," she said, crawling over troopers to her command second and waving Carl over. Even seated, neither man could raise his head; their shoulders pressed against the canvas ceiling. "We didn't use more than fifteen feet of willowwood to reach the surface. It's not that far—we could all push through together, dragging the

308

tent with us to keep the sand from falling into what we've dug."

"We'll have to dig laterally," Drak said, "and there's no telling how wide this dune is."

"We go at an angle. We can't wait for the horse teams—they may not be able to see sign of us."

The captains agreed and issued orders for gear to be gathered and stowed in packs. Drak broke down one of the camp stools and fashioned a plow that he pressed into the canvas, while troopers clambored over each other to line up in wedges, the largest taking point in each row to support the tent as the company crawled forward. Bethniel and Orlon wrapped the injured trooper's arms over their shoulders. Wineyll gathered the dead trooper's boots and said a prayer for him. When all were ready, Drak, Carl, and Valion—the largest and strongest—threw their weight against the plow, and the canvas inched into the sand. Thighs straining, they pushed again; one of the remaining struts snapped, and canvas pressed down on them.

"We expected that," Vic called over squawks. "It's going to happen. Just keep the canvas between you and the sand above, and stay together."

The three men at the head pressed forward, and the wedges condensed into a tangle of arms and knees, faces pressed into rumps, shoulders straining under the weight of the sand. The ducts twisted and broke away, and the air grew dense. Vic's eyes stung with sweat. Yet they slid slowly ahead like a great worm. "It's working," Marenye cried. The captains and Valion pushed again and again, and inches turned into feet. Spirits rose with each press forward, until suddenly a yelp came from the front and the plow and Drak slipped out of sight. Carl and Valion dove after him, and fresh air wafted beneath a flap of canvas. The first rank rose to their knees, the captains clamboring back up the dune, and soon everyone crawled out of the sand tomb and tumbled down the slope, coughing and laughing.

On the other side of the ridge, whoops and tight hugs wove through the reunited company. The horseteams had survived the night unharmed, and the sledges lay only *half* buried. In celebration, Vic ordered an extra half ration for all, then presided over a memorial for the lost trooper. Carl oversaw the repair of the damaged tent, and Bethniel led a prayer of thanks to Elesendar before they retired inside for the rest of the day. Listening to contented snores, Vic closed her eyes and felt the sand flay her cheeks and grind into her eyes, stripping her away like fire denuding a piece of ore.

Lornk's eyes shine, his teeth gleam. Fingers creep slowly down her belly, wedge into the space between her thighs. Her breath draws in with each press, out with each release, heat surging. Craving sifts through every nerve. "I have something for you," he whispers. "Come look." Trembling with need, she slides off a bare black mattress and follows him to a pile of clockwork gears. At the top sits a figure made of brass, the limbs and torso a cage round a network of gears. Drawing her with him, Lornk climbs to the figure. "My finest creation. Isn't he beautiful?"

The head turns, revealing a bronze facsimile of Ashel's face. Gears whir, and the figure's lips open over bright ivory teeth. "Hello, Kara."

Vic jolted awake. Afternoon sunlight stoked the tent's heat and cast diffuse shadows across snoozing figures. Tears ran into her hair, and she rolled over and pressed her face into her blanket. Each time she woke from a dream of Lornk, she expected to see white stone walls and jagged glass in a window. In Kragnash as in Traine, the days passed like too many versions of the same nightmare. Fetching a comb, she unplaited her hair, brushed it free of sand, and folded it back into her braid. We're still alive, she reminded herself, as fiercely as she'd reminded the company during the storm. We're still alive.

Shouts from the watch echoed down into the bowl where they camped, followed by screams from the horses. Vic scrambled toward the tent flap, Carl and Drak on her heels. Enormous beasts lined a dune crest, three on their way down the slope.

"Shrinejump," she breathed, her eyes rising to huge triangular heads and bulbous eyes. She'd walked upon the woolen Kragnashians woven into the carpet of her room; she'd seen pictures of them in books, read about their stature and strangeness, but the actual sight of them shivered down her spine like a forgotten memory. The creatures sweeping toward them stood at least three times as tall as Drak, sported elaborate tattoos on segmented thoraxes and abdomens, and bore powerful mandibles large enough to grasp a trooper and snap her in half. "Holy Shrinejumping fuck," she said aloud. The carpet in her room showed people *fighting* these creatures.

"Marshall," Bethniel scolded as she emerged from the tent, "mind your language!"

Antennae jerked and waved, mouthparts clicked. Bethniel clapped at the creatures, speaking in mindspeech for the company's benefit. "I am Bethniel of Narath," she spoke her name aloud, "Lathan Emissary and Heir."

One creature dipped its head and rippled toward her on a shining gray curtain composed of thousands of legs. As wingcovers snapped and mouthparts clacked, Bethniel translated: "You have trespassed into our lands. Why have you come?"

Vic exchanged a puzzled look with the princess, then stepped forward. Bethniel clapped and snapped her fingers, translating Vic's response: "I am Marshall Victoria of Ourtown, in command of this mission to rescue Prince Ashel of Narath from captivity and end Latha's war with Relm. Per the agreement between Queen Elekia and the Center, we seek your help crossing the Umbrachlorn Plu."

"What will you give us in return?" Bethniel said while the Kragnashian spoke, then clapped her reply: "We will honor the contract sealed by my mother, Ruler of Latha, when she informed the Center of our arrival."

"Have you iron? Copper?"

"We have diamonds in agreement with the bargain already struck," Bethniel clapped irritably.

The Kragnashians conferred, and the largest said, "We will share water with you tonight. The horses smell like good meat. A messenger will come at sunset to bring the Dealmaker's Offspring to our camp."

"Who?" Vic asked as they watched the creatures flow smoothly up and over the crest of a dune.

The princess's shoulders twitched. "The Dealmaker is what they call Mother—I'm the Offspring. That was odd, though. They act like they weren't expecting us."

Vic frowned. "Maybe it's not the escort party—maybe something happened to them, but it's a group of Kragnashians, and we need their help, whatever it takes. Lieutenant Marenye, time to break out those diamonds. Drak, you'll come with us tonight. I'm sure the princess could use an extra pair of hands to talk to our guides." She grinned up at the captain. "Plus I may need to climb on your shoulders so I can speak to them eye to eye."

† † †

That evening, Bethniel ducked out of the tent with a large crystal bound to her forehead, shoulders back and proud as the Ruler she'd be one day. A breeze dusted sand from the crests, but not a cloud marred the purpling sky as they met a small

Kragnashian—this one only as tall as Drak—at the top of a dune. Laughter and hope echoed from camp as they followed it down the other side.

A sharp whistle welcomed them when they sloshed into the Kragnashians' camp. A single silken dome stood in the center of four large sleds, all packed and arranged in a circle. Bethniel cocked her head as she scanned the hollow. "More oddities. They should be ready to camp—they usually sleep at night."

Drak scowled. "I don't like this, Marshall."

Vic nodded. "Agreed. Marenye," she said, turning to the quartermaster. "Take the diamonds back to camp and tell Carl I want two spear squads watching this place while we meet with them."

Marenye saluted and dashed over the crest, loping through the sand as fast as she could go. The small Kragnashian guiding them spun after her, clicking wildly, but Bethniel clapped at it, telling it Marenye had only left to tell the others the meeting had begun.

"What if it comes to a fight, Marshall?"

"It won't," Bethniel replied firmly, frowning at Drak.

"Spears," Vic said. "We should have brought our own."

He nodded. "I'll bring some back."

"You will not!" Bethniel said, drawing herself up. "This is diplomacy, not warfare, and right now, I'm in charge. You are both here to assist me in negotiations, understood?"

"We're here to protect you," Vic retorted.

"No, you are not. Your mission is to rescue my brother and end the war. My mission is to make sure you get to Relm so you can do it. Don't interfere with my job, and I won't interfere with yours." Bethniel strode down the duneface toward the waiting Kragnashians, and Vic and Drak hurried to flank her. The largest Kragnashian chittered a welcome, signaling for them to go inside the dome, where white light glowed from orbs set in floorstands, the air clear of smoke or scent of oil. The Kragnashians invited them to sit on a large cushion woven from white fibers. Bethniel lowered herself gracefully into the nest. When Vic sat beside her, the material molded itself around her thighs and back, and she felt like she'd sat upon a cloud. Drak remained standing. Three Desert People sat on a floor spun from the same fabric, while a fourth served the party, passing round a transluscent bowl containing a blue gel. Beth drank first, handing the bowl to Vic, then clapping her thanks.

Vic sniffed at the gel, found it odorless, then tipped it into her mouth. Her sinuses draining and eyes tearing, she flexed her jaw. "What was that?"

"You don't want to know," Drak said with a wink as he took a sip and passed it back to the creatures. The leader sucked at the gel, then faced them, thousands of tiny facets on its eyes sparkling in the white glow. Each segment of its underbelly bore stylized paintings of horses and hammers—the trades it had profited from, Vic guessed. How had the Wizard Meylnara enslaved these creatures? They made Vic sorry for every bug she'd ever stepped on.

The leader clacked mandibles and snapped wing covers as Drak translated: "I welcome you to my nest. Please tell us your desire, and we shall try to make an agreement."

"I thank you for your hospitality," Bethniel replied, clapping and snapping fingers, "and formally convey greetings from my mother, Elekia of Reinoll Parish, Ruler of Latha. As stated by Marshall Victoria of Ourtown, we are headed to Relm and have been promised your aid reaching it."

The Kragnashians chittered among themselves, and then the leader spoke again. Bethniel's eyebrows furrowed, she touched the curls spilling out the top of the headwrap bearing the diamond. "It claims to know nothing of Mother's agreement, but it wants to buy my hair."

Vic suppressed a shiver as her scalp recalled the pull and saw of Lornk's scissors. "Why?"

Beth shrugged and shook her head, eyes going to the Kragnashian as it spoke again. "It'll give us five barrels of water."

"For hair?"

The princess's mouth tilted in consternation, then shook into a smile. "For my hair. Hair of the Heir." She quickly unwound the headwrap, combing her fingers through the black mane to shake it loose. Vic marveled at how months of sweat and sand had hardly dampened the luxurious spirals. The leader squealed, and one of the others approached, a bundle of its legs twisted around a shining steel dagger.

"Your Highness, no!" Drak exclaimed, putting himself in front of her.

"I said I'd sell it, Captain. Stand aside," Bethniel commanded.

"Beth, how do you know they won't cut your throat?"

The princess cast Vic a scathing glance. "If they wanted to kill us, they'd have snapped our heads off the moment they saw us. Captain, stand aside!"

Drak reluctantly dropped back, and the Kragnashian set to work, pulling small bundles of hair taut and slicing it inches from Beth's scalp. The princess grimaced and winced, but otherwise held still and silent until only black fuzz covered her head. The Kragnashians put some of the hair in another white bowl, chittering excitedly as they poured a viscous liquid over the hair and stirred it around.

Bethniel tied the diamond back round her forehead. "How do I look?"

Vic exchanged wry glances with Drak. "Still gorgeous." Then a lump formed in her throat. "You look even more like Ashel."

The Kragnashian leader clacked another question, and Bethniel looked at Vic quizzically. "It wants yours now."

Vic shook her head emphatically. "No. I'm not going to let it shear me like an erin."

Bethniel huffed indignantly. "I did!"

"*You* enjoyed the attention."

"If you weren't my sister . . ." Bethniel grumbled, then spoke to the Kragnashian, her lips curving petulantly at its response. "It must really like red, because it said it'll provision the company all the way to Relm, for a single lock!"

Vic glanced at Drak, who stared suspiciously at the Kragnashians. "I should have gone back for the spears," he growled.

Scowling, Vic wished she had enough saliva to spit. "Tell them they can have some hair for the provisions *and* if they take us across the Plu. But I'll cut it myself."

Beth nodded approvingly and passed on the demand. The Kragnashians conferred, then handed over the dagger. "We will give all aid required to cross the Plu." Admiring the balance and gleam of the steel, Vic pulled the thong off the end of her braid and shook it loose, slicing off a lock from behind her ear. Looping the hair round her hand, she offered it to the leader and reluctantly returned the dagger. They put her hair in another bowl, poured the same liquid over it, and squealed as they stirred it.

"I see a whole new opportunity for Lathan merchants," Bethniel said thoughtfully as the creatures pressed their heads together, antennae beating wildly and mouthparts clicking. The leader's tail curled upward, and filigreed wings fanned from another creature's back.

"What are they saying?" Vic asked.

"Not sure—they're talking very fast. Captain?"

Drak shook his head. "It's hard to make out. Something about a fulcrum?"

Bethniel nodded. "I heard that too, but it's so odd that can't be right. But, yes, they're saying, 'The one and fulcrum are confirmed. We must take them—'" The princess blanched.

Two of the creatures moved to block the pavilion's opening, while the leader loomed over them.

"Spears!" Drak swore, launching himself at the smallest, hitting it hard enough to clear a path. Bethniel darted out as Vic dodged a pair of snapping mandibles and dove after her. Outside, they zigzagged through the loaded sleds as Desert People flowed up the dune, cutting off escape. Vic ran wide, hoping to outflank them as the creatures converged. Shouts echoed as troopers charged into the bowl, spears raised. Vic ducked the sweep of a mandible, rolled out of reach, and scrambled on all fours toward a gap. A Kragnashian struck Valion, sending him flying. Drak was caught in a pair of mandibles, roaring and pounding the chitin with his fists. The creatures swept easily after the humans, batting weapons away, mowing them down. Troopers lay prone all over the bowl. Vic howled and drove her dagger at the nearest abdomen. The crystal blade glanced off the chitin, and the creature snagged Vic's hood and yanked her off the ground. Another restrained her legs and arms with a sticky silken cord. They flipped her upside down as a third Kragnashian appeared with a large sack full of orange goo. Slotaen. Her face plunged into sunshine. Serenity seeped into her pores. Elesendar, she thought as her eyes drooped closed, not again.

White walls. White ceiling. White floor. Finding herself surrounded in white, Vic bit her tongue, dread gripping her throat. But the walls weren't stone and her waist and wrists were free of a mistress's jewels. Her eyes closed in relief, but in her gut, fury still raged.

She lay atop one of the cushions; as she sat up, the material puffed out to fill depressions left by elbows and shoulders. Her clothes, clean and neatly folded, lay beside her. Shivering, she pulled on tunic and trousers and socks, swallowing bitter memories. The slotaen had cleaned out all the vileness left by months of sand with too little water, but she shuddered at the memory of a Betheljin slave trader's hands around her waist.

On the floor lay her boots, the leather buffed to a soft glow, and they seemed to fit better than they had before. The floor gave a little under her weight, like a tarp stretched over the hull of a dry-docked boat. Around the oval room, the wall material thinned to transparency high overhead. At one end, a seam marked what had to be a door. A brown foot and hand hung over the side of another cushion. Shrinejump, Vic thought, her knees weak. The hand jerked. With a squeak, Bethniel snatched her tunic to her front and sat up. "Well, that was a diplomatic success," Vic said bitterly.

The princess glared as she slipped the shirt over her head, then rubbed her shorn hair. "Damn, that feels weird." Standing atop her cushion, she tried to peer out a window. "We must be in Direiellene."

"Why would they kidnap us?"

The princess shook her head, mouth grim. "I'm guessing the Waters of the Dead."

"What are those?"

Bethniel cast her a scathing look. "Some history buff. They called it the Elixir in the time of wizards? You've never heard of it?"

"Beth, I studied *real* history, not the fancies of poets and hucksters." She grimaced, thinking of Ashel's admissions about Elekia. "Frankly, I only accepted that your mother's powers might be real last winter, and I've been too busy fighting a war to study up on how she might have gained them."

Bethniel's glare softened. "Well, the Waters are how. The Kragnashians make anyone who comes to Direiellene drink it."

"So they make you a wizard?" Vic's mind leapt at the advantages Elekia's power, weak as it was, could give.

"It's not a boon." Bethniel's shoulders hunched around her ears. "The Waters are the price of entry into Direiellene, and the price my mother paid for my father's throne. The merchants who trade with the Kragnashians, they never leave the beach because the Waters kill most people, and it's a horrible death. Of those who don't die, most go insane."

"Your mother didn't."

Bethniel shrugged. "I guess she was one of the lucky few."

Warm air drafted into the room, followed by a Kragnashian. It bowed its head to Bethniel. "I welcome Latha's Heir," the princess translated, "and apologize for the manner of your transport here. But it was necessary that the One should come here and speak with the Center, and that the journey should be made quickly and in secret."

"Where are our people?" Vic demanded. Bethniel translated the question, adding, "Are they safe?"

"We intended no harm and respectfully remind the Heir that your clan attacked us. We killed none of your clanmates and have tended the wounds of those hurt. The others remain well and have been told where you are. As we promised in exchange for the follicles of the One, your clan will be provisioned until you reach Relm."

"Why must I speak to your Center?" Vic asked. "The Lathan Ruler gained permission for us to cross your lands before we even left Narath."

Bethniel continued, "The Ruler was told we would meet guides within days of our arrival, not months, and it was never our intent to come to your sacred city. The Ruler will not be pleased with this breach of contract and will demand recompense."

The creature's antennae whipped to and fro. "We found you on our lands by chance."

"By chance?" Bethniel snapped. "What happened to the party sent to guide us?"

The Kragnashian quivered. "You must ask the Center. Come."

Scowling, Vic clenched her fists, wished for a spear, but she and the princess followed the creature down a spiraling hallway. Bethniel swallowed repeatedly, eyes wide. Shrine, she's out of her depth, Vic thought. Relaxing her fists, she clasped the other woman's hand, pasted on an encouraging smile that she feared looked more like a grimace. Their guide touched a spot on a wall, and light and heat spilled into the hall as a panel slid aside. Vic's jaw dropped as they came outside. Thousands of cocoon-shaped buildings obscured the desert in a haze of white, broken by scattered brown-green copses. Orange, the sky could signal dawn or dusk, but she didn't trust her sense of direction to guess which. The oven-like air made her think dusk.

Cables stretched from hexagonal doorways, connecting the cocoons around them. They stood on the landing of a wide bridge leading to a mountainous trio of domes. Thousands of Kragnashians, most smaller than their guide, crawled along the bridge and cables above them. Those headed away walked on top; those coming toward them walked upside down below. Bethniel grabbed Vic's arm and pointed toward the top of a nearby building. Hanging by half its feet from a cable anchored to the roof, a Kragnashian held a grub in its jaws and was using its excretions to caulk a rent in the building.

"That must be a larva," Beth said, then turned to their guide as it spoke. "It says we should ride. Our boots won't stick to the bridge, and we won't be able to keep up with the traffic."

Vic nodded and they scrambled up the creature's abdomen. Faster than a galloping horse, their guide sped past others on the bridge, clicking at them to make way. More Kragnashians carried larvae to repair holes or spin out new cables. "They don't gain their intelligence until after the first metamorphosis," Bethniel observed grimly.

"What do they feed all these people?"

"They must have crops and herds somewhere. And they're cannibals."

"Kragnashian leather is Kragnashian leather."

"Best leather money can buy."

Vic shifted in her seat, hair rising on the back of her neck as she watched thousands of Desert People swarm all around them.

Hexagonal cells fit together to form the domes of the Center's complex; whorling stonework adorned the arching doorways. Anchored to the path at odd intervals stood stone statues of horses and trees and humans. The bridge divided in three as they approached; the widest lane led straight to the middle dome, but the traffic split off to the other two.

Two guards with grotesquely large mandibles stood before the central dome's entrance, an opening so large a merchanter might sail through. Within, birds soared in cool air to the ceiling, dove back toward a park of trees and grass. Vines climbed over trellises and arbors, and the scent of flowers teased Vic's nose. Vic fought against tranquility as their guide shuffled across a cable to a huge dais in the dome's center—a stone foundation, then a band of copper glowing like sunrise in all this white. A gleaming parquet floor capped the stone and copper, together forming a small mesa. Dismounting, they approached a nest draped with blue erinsheen and gold silk where sat a Kragnashian twice as large as any they'd seen. Following Bethniel's lead, Vic bowed to it, both arms extending straight from her sides.

"I bring greetings from my mother, Ruler of Latha," Beth clapped and snapped.

The Kragnashian in the nest gazed between them, its eyes twinkling as the facets caught the light. Vic stared back at it, unwilling to buckle under its gaze. Finally it spoke. "The Dealmaker has twice done what few humans dare once. The first bargain remains only half paid." It stared hard at Bethniel, then turned to Vic so abruptly she took a step back. Squaring her shoulders, she spread her feet, determined to hold her ground. "You have a solid face."

Bethniel clarified: "It means you look honest, for a human. That isn't a compliment, it's an observation."

The Kragnashian continued, "I am the Center. All aims are to me. How can I profit you?"

Vic kept her eyes fixed on the Center's. "We wish to know why no guides met us as promised."

"We found no sign of you and assumed your party had been lost at sea. You may keep the diamonds."

Bethniel pushed her shoulders back. "No sign? We were to meet you en route!"

"The route was searched; no sign was found. You may keep the diamonds, but you must pay for entry to Direiellene." The Center slid off the nest and came to stand directly in front of Vic, forcing her to arch her neck to keep eye contact. "You are the One. You must take the Waters of the Dead. Three leagues south of this city lie the ruins of the Oppressor's fortress. A pool is there. You must drink."

Bethniel stepped between them. "We did not come to Direiellene of our own will. The People brought us here. The price shall not be paid under duress."

"You are the One," the Center said, ignoring Bethniel. "From century to century since the death of magic, we have allowed humans to take the waters because magic grows from belief as a tree grows from soil. Belief washes away unless it is replenished. We have allowed the humans to come because we have waited for you to come. You are the One who will destroy the Oppressor."

"You, Captain, have a famous wizard for a namesake . . . It's a mystery how an Oreseeker ended up on the Council. But it's a historical fact a woman with your name fought in that war."

"And had a lover and a husband. She was busy."

"This is absurd!" Vic broke eyelock with the Center. She looked down at the Center's garden, choked, then doubled over, her voice caught between a sob and a laugh. She heard the Kragnashian move away and felt Bethniel's hand on her neck as she tried to catch her breath, only to lose it again as her shoulders shook and her lungs heaved.

"I'll fix this," Bethniel promised.

Scraping the tears on her face, Vic straightened. Another chuckling sob bubbled out of her. She didn't know herself if she was laughing or crying. "It's the two of us alone here," she said. "How can you?"

Bethniel pressed her lips together and clapped and hummed at the Center. "You forced us to come to this city. No contract is valid when made under duress."

"All land beyond the beach is Direiellene, and when you did not meet your designated guides, you became trespassers. We are at peace with Relm. You entered this country to end your war, but in doing so you disrupted our peace. We must be compensated."

"You may have the diamonds as originally agreed. We came as agreed and traveled the designated route in good faith. It is not our breach if the designated guides failed to find us." Bethniel added silently, "I doubt they looked very hard."

"Your entire company are trespassers, but we are satisfied

to have only the One take the Waters of the Dead. That is the price of entry to this land, and the price of your return to your companions."

"I'll take them," Bethniel blurted.

The Kragnashian's eyefacets turned to an oily black. "The Heir will die if the power comes to her."

"Shrinejump." Vic paced, her heart pounding blood into her face, heat traveling to the roots of her hair. Her fingers curled into fists and punched the air in front of her. She knew she shouldn't show her anger like this but couldn't help it—didn't care to. Curtly signaling Bethniel to follow her forward, she strode up to the Center. "She will not take your Waters, and I cannot. I am not who you think I am. I cannot be. I do not believe it."

"Your face is among those of the dead waiting by the Waters. Sometimes the magic takes time to grow. If no magic manifests by the Plu, we will help you cross in exchange for your herd."

Bethniel said, "We have already paid for help crossing the Plu."

The Center stared, stock still, then moved back to its seat. "The One must drink. There is no negotiation on this point."

Vic looked at her boots. With Elekia's power, she might squash Lornk with a wall of air as he'd stifled her with blankets. Yet she gaped at the idea she had killed someone a thousand years ago. The entire world was full of mad religions: talking trees birthing humans, giant insects with time-travel prophesies. Curious to see this face at the pool, she was enraged that once again someone wanted her as a tool. Logkeeper. Mistress. Blade. How much of choice and how much of circumstance put her here? How much of either would save Ashel and push Lornk from her heart once and for all? Nausea bubbling up her throat, Vic turned on her heel and strode to the edge of the dais where their guide waited. Pointing at it and then at the door, she signaled she wished to leave.

Bethniel clapped something at the Center, then ran down to join them. Hanging itself upside down on the bridge, the Kragnashian hooked the tip of its abdomen over the edge of the dais near their feet. Vic slid carefully down to rest cross-legged between the creature's legs. The Kragnashian's body swung slightly as Bethniel joined her, then it started off, its legs whisking along the bridge. The entire ride back, Vic held her hand over her mouth as bitterness welled from her stomach.

In their room, they found a basket of plump blue fruit and a jar of water. Vic took a long draft from the jar. She wasn't used to talking out loud for so long, and the sun was just as hot here as in the rest of the desert. Ignoring the fruit, she climbed up onto her cushion and tried to peer out the windows, but she could see nothing but the yellowing sky. It had been dawn after all.

"How far are we from camp?"

Bethniel swallowed a bite of fruit before answering. "The city's in the southwest. The old maps showed Meylnara's keep about three hundred leagues south of the coast, probably twice that from camp."

Vic swore. "How long has the company—"

"I'd wager we came here by Device. I'd be surprised if we've been gone more than a few days to a week."

"A single day is a day too long. Shrine-fucking-jump, Beth. Some of those people are pretty rattled by the journey so far—I don't know if Drak can hold them together." And how many more days had Ashel been at Lornk's mercy? She thought of the clockwork facsimile in her dream and felt sick again.

"Vic," Bethniel said quietly. "Do you remember you dreamed of Kragnashians when you went into Fembrosh?"

"Yes," Vic said grimly.

"Fembrosh remembers the past. A wizard named Victoria was with the Council when they defeated Meylnara and freed the Kragnashians."

"Don't be ridiculous!" Vic snapped, anger foaming to a head. "With all their technology, our ancestors could never travel in time. How could I be 'the One' to do anything a thousand years ago? I don't know what they're up to, but I'm not going to save anybody from the Oppressor. At least not that one!"

"Of course you're not *the* One. But the Kragnashians believe you are, or might be, so why not use that to our advantage?"

"If you think so, what were you doing volunteering?"

Bethniel's cheeks darkened. "It just popped out."

"You had to clap it, Beth!"

She shrugged sheepishly. "I don't know what was in my head. It just seemed . . . the right thing to say." Eyes fixed on intertwined fingers, Bethniel grated, "I couldn't take the throne if I were a wizard." She looked up, mouth flat. "My mother flouts the laws she's supposed to uphold, but I won't."

A pang of sympathy squeezed Vic's lungs. "She does what she believes is best for Latha."

Bethniel snorted. "The Vic I know would never defend my mother. You haven't even drunk the Waters and you've already gone mad."

"Death or madness. Some choice, Beth."

"Or wizardry, if you're lucky."

A low growl bubbled from Vic's throat. The day Caleisbahn pirates had taken her from her homeland and sold her to Lornk, they'd put her on the road here. Every fork she'd chosen since—escaping from Traine, joining the Lathan army, refusing Ashel's marriage proposal—had led her here, and it was a dead end.

CHAPTER 23

VOICES

Coughing, Earnk rolled onto his back and stared at the ceiling. Voiccs itched in his mind—not his ears. He Heard the guards' musings on dinner and dice games, the healers' worries over bandages and medicines. Had the fever catalyzed an ability to Listen, or had he always had the talent? Surely if he had been able to Listen all his life, he'd have been better able to predict his father's actions.

Like letting him live. Phlegm clogging his throat, he hacked into a handkerchief and swallowed honeyed water from the jug beside his bed. Whitewashed walls, clean sheets, and smoke-free lamps belied the fact he was still a prisoner, condemned to fifteen years' hard labor for collaborating with the antimilitia. After the trial, Lornk had ordered Earnk admitted to the infirmary so he could begin his sentence in good health. Earnk knew better than to think mercy motivated that decision. *There is purpose to everything I do.* Tugging aside the blanket, Earnk picked at the angry weals snaking around his calves, laced over the soles of his feet and between his toes. Slotaen had almost healed the burns; only a brown lint of dead skin dusted the sheets. Grimacing, he pulled the covers back up. He'd made up names, numbers, places, information about the antimilitia to make them stop, all while Vendrael reported every word as a lie. Then he'd wept and begged his father's forgiveness, which had fueled his anger. Lornk Korng wanted a son stronger than the one he had. Perhaps one strong enough to deny him, even as skin and muscle burned. Stomach lurching, Earnk slid under the covers, hiding from that possibility.

Trellerend came in and put one of his large red hands on Earnk's forehead, then pulled back the blankets to look at his legs. "Time to walk," he said after examining the skin between Earnk's toes.

Hobbling through the hallways, Earnk kept his eyes on the ground. None of the healers would meet his gaze, least of all Trellerend. He and his father had dined at the healer's house; Earnk had crawled on the floor with his daughter, hunting for lost jacks. Around a corner, they came to a guarded door, and Earnk winced at the onslaught of silent raving emanating from that room. Trellerend's jaw tightened and untightened as they passed.

"What does my father think of that?" Earnk asked. Within the room, Geram bellowed silently about a flag. Rubbing his temples, the Relman guard asked Trellerend for headache medicine.

Trellerend promised to bring relief, then answered Earnk. "He's concerned the prince will die when the Listener does."

"I'm surprised he's not more worried about the Listener. Such a useful tool for him."

"Or weapon against him," Trellerend murmured, his eyes as flat as his mouth.

"No matter what I said during"—Earnk waved at his feet— "I'm not antimilitia."

Trellerend's eyes narrowed. "I know."

† † †

Half dozing in flickering lamplight, Earnk imagined different ways he might die. Another prison-wrought illness, scourged at the whipping post, shanked by a prisoner whom Earnk himself had sentenced. He tried to reach for old dreams, of sitting before a fire, Vic nestled warm in his arms while snowflakes dusted a window. But each time he conjured it, that vision melted into Kara taking his father's hand, so he returned to morbid daydreams of vengeful thieves and merciless guards.

A scream ripped the silence, resonating through the stone. Flexing his jaw, he rubbed his ears, beginning to discern words. *Eyes, my eyes. No music. Stop. Get out. Stop seeing. Stop.* His temples ached with each word, as if they were blows Geram aimed at him. *No music. Songs. Sea. Sight. Stop!* Rubbing his own eyes, Earnk realized with the clarity of a seer what the Lathan Listener meant.

He fell out of bed, legs tangled in the sheets. Shouting for Trellerend, for the guards, he struggled to the door and banged for someone to come. A key turned in the lock, and Earnk yanked it open and flung himself into the corridor. As he rounded the first corner toward the Lathans' room, a guard hauled him up short. Footsteps pounded toward them; Earnk struggled, still shouting for Trellerend. The healer appeared, red-faced, and told the guard to release him.

"Get to their room," Earnk said, panting too hard to speak aloud.

"Why?"

"His eyes—"

A scream split the air. The other guard shouted for a healer. Rushing around the corner, Trellerend led them into the Listener's room. Geram clawed the air, straining against the grip of a guard. Blood covered his fingers, ran down his cheeks onto the pillowcase, one eye bulging out of its socket. Half sobbing, half screaming, the Listener writhed in the sheets.

Trellerend ordered one guard to run for help and Earnk and the other guard to hold the Lathan. Sitting upright in a bed on the opposite wall, Prince Ashel's body blinked at them.

Mouth contorted, Geram kicked while the guard pinned his arms and Earnk held his head still. Trellerend carefully slipped the eye back into its socket. "He's scratched his corneas," muttered the healer while he tore strips from the sheet and wrapped them across Geram's face. "It'll be a miracle if he keeps his sight." While Trellerend worked, a silent barrage of madness pounded Earnk's temples as Geram raged. Yet his legs gradually stopped thrashing, his arms slowly relaxing, as the bandages thickened. As another healer came in, pushing a cart of ointments and bandages, Trellerend stood back, running blood-slicked hands through sandy hair.

"Don't know why we care if he scratches his eyes out or not," the guard grumbled as she escorted Earnk to his room. "Lousy Lathan's going to die in a day or two anyway." She looked at him suspiciously. "How'd you know something was going to happen?"

Earnk shrugged. "Maybe I'm a Listener too."

"Hmph!" she said, then slapped her hand over her mouth.

After the guard locked him in, Earnk pressed throbbing temples against cool flintrock. Geram's cries had dimmed, but Earnk could still Hear his agony.

He dreamed of running down an endless hallway with seawater churning behind him, a riptide tugging at his ankles. Doorways lining the hall emitted smells and sounds—brine and the slap of waves, rich ale and the tumble of dice, perfume and laughter, stale wine and blame. Angry surf chased him, licking his heels if he slowed, never giving him time to escape. A bass drumbeat rolled after his footsteps until, realizing the drum was the ache above his eyes, he woke.

Quiet rasped in his ears. The lantern wick turned low, shadows haunted the room. At the door, Earnk Listened for the guard and Heard nothing, but the latch gave under the weight of his hand. Very slowly, he opened it. The guard sat propped against the far wall, chin resting on his chest. A flask bearing the healer's Guildmark toppled out of the man's fingers. Earnk slipped down the hallway. What am I doing? he wondered. He wouldn't get out of the Tunnel, and if he did, how far would he get in the highland snows without boots or cloak? Peering round a corner, he saw the guard in front of Prince Ashel's room slumped against the wall, another healer's flask beside him. Trellerend. The healer wanted him in that room. Pressed against the wall, Earnk shut his eyes and weighed his options. What business had he with the Lathans—if Geram and the prince died, it would spare Vic. Does she love Ashel? he wondered. And if she does, would she blame me as much as Father for his death? Gingerly, he stepped over the guard's legs to enter the room.

The room smelled of slotaen, stale urine, blood. The bandage around Geram's head bulged over some kind of poultice, his wrists loosely bound to the bed frame. Ashel's body lay on its side. Its eyes stared at Earnk but did not see him.

He placed a chair next to Geram's bed and leaned over the other man. A febrile heat warmed his face. If he'd run a fever this high for weeks, it was a wonder he lived. Gingerly, Earnk touched the Listener's hand.

Geram's head jerked and he clutched Earnk's hand, his grasp like iron. "Get him out of me."

"How?"

"He drowns my memories. Get me out." That was Ashel's voice.

Geram growled, biceps bunched, and his bonds broke. "He fills my mind with bitter songs played by instruments I never heard." The Listener hauled himself upward, dragging Earnk with him.

"I don't care if I'm whole," Ashel said. "Make him put me back."

"No!" Geram shouted aloud. "Nothing of you!"

Earnk's heart pumped blood toward the sinews of the hand clasped in Geram's. He studied the bandaged face, the mouth on the verge of a snarl. What did he know of this man? Even if he could help him, why should he? Behind him, Ashel's body breathed hoarsely. If he could help Geram, he'd release a man who claimed not only Vic's affections, but his father's. *That voice in my courtyard.* Let them die, he urged himself. What did he know of them? Geram's hand clenched tighter, his need, his suffering urgent. How long had Earnk inured himself to others' pain? The last person he'd given aid and comfort to was Vic. Seeing the emerald accusation in her eyes if these men died, he returned Geram's grip. "Focus on your hate," he whispered, following instinct.

Geram's arm relaxed for a moment, then he threw his weight forward. Grunting, Earnk held his arm upright. As Geram pushed, Earnk squeezed his eyes shut and pushed back. They struggled. The sheets rasped as Geram rocked into a better position. Earnk leaned forward and blinked sweat out of his eyes. Sweaty palms began to slip against each other.

"Why are you still alive?" Earnk gasped. "What are you trying to live for?"

Leaking a groan, Geram's lips shrank back over his teeth. The sound billowed into a battle cry as he bent Earnk's wrist backward and shoved his arm down. Spent, he flopped back onto his pillow, and Earnk collapsed across his own arm. The headache was gone. Geram's hand, still clasped in his, became cool. Whatever had happened, it was done.

"Why did you help us?"

Earnk peered at the prince. Ashel pushed himself up, flexed bandaged fingers. *Your voice in my courtyard.* Roguish Betheljin minstrels still sang of the night the Lathan prince stole the hearts of Trainer Citizens right out of the Relmlord's pockets. Swallowing bile, Earnk said, "You're lucky."

The skin around his eyes and mouth tightening, Ashel shook his head. "How so?"

"The Blade leads a company here to rescue you."

"I know. You know. And that makes it a lost cause."

Earnk pulled his hand free from Geram. "I should get back."

Ashel cleared his throat. "Why did you help us?"

Another question lurked beneath that one: are we brothers? Earnk shook his head. "My father lied," he said, cracking open the door. The guard's snores trundled through. *Your voice in my courtyard.* "He lied," Earnk insisted aloud, then slipped into the hall.

Ashel stared at the door. Stared at the shadow Earnk left lingering in the room, over Geram, in Ashel's heart. But now when he blinked, his vision darkened. When he turned his head, his perspective of the room changed. Instead of looking out of Geram's eyes and seeing his own body lying across from him, he saw Geram's body out of his own eyes. And his thoughts sounded amid blessed silence. He felt like he did the first day he could sing again after a cold. So many days spent wishing to feel normal and normalcy left him so giddy he could no longer remember how illness felt.

Slowly, he got out of bed and tottered to the chair next to Geram. He watched the other man's chest rise and fall, his lips and cheeks soft in repose. Twice Ashel owed Geram his life. No, three times, he thought, flexing fingers sore but healing. He would play again—not as well, but that was better than not at all. "Thank you," he whispered. Whatever happened now, he was alone.

And he had to act. Not like a madman, but act. Vic, his sister—they'd be at Korng's mercy if they made it through the desert. His jaw clenched, Ashel assumed the stance of a royal, opened the door, and kicked at the guard sprawled in the hall.

The guard mumbled, his eyes winking open one at a time. Seeing Ashel, he cursed and jolted up.

"I want to talk to the Relmlord," Ashel said before the man rose past his knees.

The guard cursed again, peered into Ashel's room, and swore another oath.

"Now," Ashel told him.

Halfway down the hall, the man paused. "How did you get out? The door was locked."

Ashel crossed his arms and lifted an eyebrow. The guard's face slackened and he looked around again. Finally, he bellowed the name of another guard.

"What's going on here?" a healer scolded as she rounded the corner. "Oh, my," she gasped, seeing Ashel.

"I want to talk to the Relmlord," Ashel demanded again.

"Arlek, you idiot," she hissed. "Get to Olmlablaire."

"But—"

"You drunken oaf! See if you can deliver messages better than you can guard prisoners!"

Arlek scrambled down the hall, taking the healer's flask with him.

Ashel waved at his nightshirt. "Where are my clothes?"

She shook her head. "Not worth the soap to wash them. Go back into your room, and I'll find you some trousers."

"And boots."

Nodding, she shut the door after him. As the lock turned, he collapsed onto his bed, trembling head to foot. Standing those few moments left him as tired as a man who'd won the annual race around Narath's walls. Before long, the door opened on the tall, sandy-haired healer. He went to Geram first, laid a hand on his forehead and held his wrist in the other. Frowning, he asked Ashel how he felt.

"Well enough."

The healer moved the chair back against the wall. "How did this happen?"

Ashel shrugged. "I don't know. All of a sudden, I was just here, in my own body again."

"Hmph. Uman is bringing clothing, and then the guards will take you up to Olmlablaire."

Ashel nodded and wondered where the Device was.

† † †

Outside the Tunnel, patches of dirty snow melted under the late-autumn sun. Mud sucked at their boots, a dull slurping with every step. Ashel took deep breaths of the crisp air and refused Vendrael's arm. He imagined he looked as weak and sick as he felt. Yet he clung to a minstrel's stamina for the performance of a lifetime. And I'd always thought I'd meet that cliché on the stage, he thought.

His first sight of Olmlablaire grabbed his attention. Cut-stone walls surrounded a courtyard checkered with alternating patches of grass and stone, adorned with fountains. In the center stood a statue of the Architect, facing her masterpiece. Stonework vines sprouted out of the earth, wound around the pillars and lintel of Olmlablaire's grand entrance, and from there ascended the towering façade of the mountain home.

The Architect had taken the network of caves within this cliff and turned them into a palace. From the ground, the many windows and balconies adorning the cliff could not be seen; the rock appeared unbroken all the way to the top.

Inside the main entrance, a passage wider than Narath's broadest avenues opened onto a great hall. Ribbons of smooth stone cut through unaltered rock, sparkling with mica and pyrite. The different faces of stone spiraled together to an apex adorned with a massive, glittering chandelier. A mosaic of Relm, each county a different shade of gold, spread across the floor. Ashel missed a step at the green tiles marking the Kiareinoll, putting the Relman border well north of its legal boundary.

"I expect we'll have to relay the floor to show all of Latha," Vendrael gloated.

He held his neutral expression, hid hope behind despair. He had to put himself in a position where he could be of some use, and a dungeon was certainly not that place. Whether she Heard that last thought or not, Vendrael pursed her lips and led him up a wide staircase past a host of servitors and clerks, warleaders and ministers. Conversations faded into stares, and murmurs followed in their wake. Finally the Listener approached two doors carved from single cerrenil trunks, each with a brass doorknob.

He'd glimpsed the library through Geram's eyes, but seeing it for himself was staggering. Few collections in the world could have held more volumes. Books shelved a dozen feet up, tapestries hanging between cases, lamps profuse on the desks and tables—Vic would love this room. Vic. Grimacing, he thought of her struggling through the desert, thirsty, burned by the sun and wind. And Bethniel. An image crept into his heart, of his sister lying in the sand, one hand clutched around a shriveled water skin, Vic sprawled a few feet away, her hair streaming in the wind.

Stop. Firmly turning himself back to the moment, he sat on the divan before the fire. He had to act, do something, and now he waited for the Relmlord, ready to admit his name and . . . Ashel put his head in his hands, aware of Vendrael's eyes on his back. What would he do? If he could find the Device and escape, how would that help?

"So," Lornk said effusively from the doorway, "how are you?"

Ashel stood and bowed. "My lord." Protocol served a purpose, allowing him an extra moment to gather his wits. Under the bandages, his fingers itched.

"Your Highness," the Relmlord purred, smiling like a cat. He sat in a large armchair next to the fire and told Vendrael to shut the door on her way out. "Well?" Lornk asked. "You wished to speak with me." The fire crackled for the space of a dozen heartbeats. "I'm a busy man."

"Did you kill my father?"

"What? No more denials of being royal?"

"Did you?"

Lornk's fingers drummed on the arm of his chair. "No." He looked squarely at Ashel. "I have wished him dead, but never ordered it done. I wanted to pull him from that ill-got throne first."

Ashel's blood pounded in his ears. "Did she?"

"Did she? You'll have to ask her."

His eyes fell on his bandaged hands. *What wouldn't she do?* Elesendar, surely not that. He returned his gaze to the Relmlord, raised a hand, and asked his last question, aloud, voice shaking. "If what you said is true, why would you do this?"

Lornk sat forward, his eyes deep, cold blue, his face chiseled stone. "Because you look like her."

"What does that mean?"

A vicious smile played at the corners of the Relmlord's mouth. "I would speak plainly, but I fear offending your sensibilities, Highness."

"Your innuendos offend me more, my lord."

The older man snorted softly. "Did you love Sashal?"

Ashel trembled with growing rage. "He was my father."

"Yes, well, I loved him as a brother, until he and your mother betrayed me. Elekia and I were—are—wed by Lathan custom. The horse breeder's daughter had hooked the biggest fish in Knownearth, short of the Commissar of Betheljin. I wanted your mother as my First Councilor more than anything in the world. But she declined. She said she wanted to wait until she could bring more than herself to the marriage. Then next I knew, she and Sashal announced their betrothal, and shortly after, they declared themselves wed."

Ashel stared at the fire, his belly aching as Sashal's midnight shout rang in his mind: *"Why didn't you declare with him, if you loved him so much?"*

Lornk chuckled ruefully. "No man likes to admit being a cuckold, and so I let their sham of a marriage stand, yet I always wondered if I might see myself in the infant Elekia bore the following spring, should I ever meet him. Then one day I noticed a young man standing in front of a mural of the Lathalorns."

"And did you?"

"I suppose I saw some reflection—your jaw, the shape of your eyes, perhaps, and especially the way you carry yourself. But I would be surprised if Sashal didn't see as much of himself as I do, because you look like *her*."

Suppressing a shudder, Ashel met Lornk's gaze. "I won't sign that declaration."

A corner of Lornk's mouth turned upward. "Well, perhaps I was mad to think you would."

† † †

Ashel slept that afternoon in a room on an upper floor of the palace. It had no window, but fresh air came in through ducts chiseled out of the stone. A fireplace, two overstuffed chairs, and a feather bed rubbed against each other in the small space. A rug woven by Semena herders protected bare feet from cold stone. A comfortable room by Lathan standards, a luxurious prison by any.

His stomach woke him to find the healer, Trellerend, in one of the arm chairs. He sensed Vendrael, outside the door, Listening.

"It's good that you slept," Trellerend said. "Your body hasn't in nearly a month."

"Neither had I."

Raising an eyebrow, Trellerend picked up a roll of bandages from the small table between the chairs. "I need to change the dressing."

"How is Geram?"

"He sleeps. I don't know if he'll wake."

Ashel's stomach growled audibly while Trellerend worked. He stopped and went to tell Vendrael to have some food sent up, leaving Ashel to stare at his left hand. Raw and crimped, it looked as if he'd never use it again, except it stung, it itched, and he could feel the tips of his fingers when they touched his thumb. Patches of healthy brown and healing pink skin had replaced the blackened crisps. Holding his wrist, Trellerend slathered the hand with slotaen, and the fierce sting faded.

"Isn't this too expensive to waste on prisoners?" Ashel asked.

"No one ever intended you should lose your hands."

Ashel snorted. "And this is a man beloved by his people."

"Yes." Trellerend stopped wrapping bandages and went to the door again. He peered through a crack, came back and tucked a note from his pocket under the blanket next to Ashel's leg. "Midnight," he hissed before Ashel could ask anything, then shook his head to prevent any questions.

Soon afterward, Vendrael came in with a servant carrying a tray loaded with meat and fruit. Trellerend directed them to set the tray by the fire and helped Ashel get out of bed without revealing the note. After they'd all gone, Ashel retrieved the slip of paper and pulled up all the baffling he possessed against Listeners.

War room. SE corner.

At midnight. The note also contained a series of directions—it had to be about the Device. This could be some cruel game the Relmlord was playing with him, but he had to take the chance that Trellerend, for whatever reason, wanted to help him.

His skin itching with a million pinpricks, Ashel stood and looked around the stone chamber. A damp chill slid off walls, tripped along his arms, raising goose bumps and heightening the tingling left over from travel by the Device. The room held nothing but the knob and the sconce, its gems now fading to blue. Thin, yellow light filtered from a passage leading up. Shutting his eyes, Ashel saw—in a memory belonging to Geram but drawn from Vic—her flight to this chamber, heard Lornk coming down the passage behind her, felt her desperate hope to die because she could not live and be his. The gray walls and floor resonated with despair; Vic, hundreds of Lathan prisoners, Elesendar knew who else had passed through here because of the Relmlord's cruelty. And now me, Ashel thought, moving toward the hall. Now me.

At the top, he slipped carefully into a library redolent with must. Rain thrashed the outside walls, and a courtyard lamp cast speckled silhouettes of the windows on the carpet and bookcases. Glass cases lined the wall behind a heavy table. Peering at the spines, Ashel felt a momentary longing. The library surpassed Lornk's assemblage in Olmlablaire—only the Archives in Narath, the Guildschool Collection in Mora, perhaps the Library in Caleisbahnin might contain so many precious volumes. Scattered throughout the bookshelves, spines embossed with silver rumored wealth, power. He flexed his fingers, gritting his teeth at the cracking skin around his knuckles. Only Trainer wealth could have paid for such extravagant vengeance. *Because you look like her.* Peeking out a window at the granite pavement, the garden golden and ready for harvest, Ashel saw a courtyard filled with sunlight and gaiety, himself bowing from a small pedestal in the corner, people clapping, Lornk nodding his head with pride, an arm around Mother's shoulders. Elesendar, no. Sashal—*my father*— wouldn't be the cad who trysts with a married woman. *If you loved him so much . . .*

The heels of his hands pressed into his eyes, he bent over to hold back a sob. That he had found his way to the Device might still be part of the Relmlord's vengeance—or worse, his mercy. With Bethniel on her way to Lordhome, Lornk could afford to let Ashel go. The image of his sweet, lighthearted sister in that dungeon, Lornk's hands around her neck, kicked Ashel's breath away. Hugging himself, he thought of the times he had held her while their parents fought, trying to insulate her from their fury with his songs. Who would protect her from the Relmlord—Vic? By Geram's memories, her strength would shatter like an eggshell when she saw him. Neither could guess some spy had already betrayed their mission; surely nothing but defeat awaited them if they reached Olmlablaire.

Taking a slow breath, Ashel looked out at the courtyard again. A single guard, shoulders hunched under a cloak, paced between the shadows. The wall to his right lacked windows, but a small wooden door suggested an easier exit than the main gate. The rain had gutted half the lamps in the courtyard—the perfect night to escape. And the perfect night to return.

PART 4. TEMPER

CHAPTER 24

AWAKENING FIRE

Briny would have been a compliment to the taste scalding Vic's throat. Her spine cringed, her eyes teared with each swallow. When the flask was empty, she threw it aside, one hand over her mouth, the other pressed to her stomach. Heaving bile, she swallowed and gagged as the shadows crept across the rock.

Around her, twelve statues guarded a single shrunken geilmor hunched over the grotto. Rough-hewn and angular, the faces looked only vaguely human, but the Center had pointed to the one beside the pool, the thirteenth face, and said that it was Vic's own image. The only resemblance she could see were two jade ovals for eyes and a rusty streaking that might be taken for hair.

Coughing, she crawled beneath the gnarled trunk. Shriveled thorns cast a meager shade over the cistern. White crusted rings told the tale of deeper water and a tastier drink in years past. Gagging, Vic watched sweat drip off the end of her nose and splatter in the dust between her fingers. Elesendar, this stuff *is* killing me.

When they'd arrived, the symbolism of the place stirred the Logkeeper in her. A tree living where none should live. Waters that transferred their powers to those who drank them.

345

Twelve stones facing inward toward a thirteenth, a chosen one, one foretold by legend, by myth. As a girl she'd scoffed at the Ancients' myths, as a young woman at Lathan legends of wizards. The last thing she ever expected was to become one.

She tumbled onto her back, sucking in the hot, dry air. A gust shivered the geilmor. Dry leaves sifted into the well, fell on her face, pricking her forehead and cheeks. Vic groaned. If she died here, would she return as a gekko or a tree?

"Vic?" Bethniel's hand reached through the noxious haze to touch her shoulder. "Are you all right?"

She managed to shake her head. "No."

"You probably shouldn't have drunk the whole flask. The Center said most people manage only a few swallows."

Now they tell me. "Why didn't—" Vic gulped down another assault from her stomach. "Why didn't it tell me that before?"

"It didn't expect you to drink the whole thing. It's also time to go."

Breathing deeply, Vic sat up. Squinting in the heat, Bethniel felt her forehead and cheeks. The statues glared at each other, their shadows stretching across the sand as the sun ballooned into red. The central statue's shadow pointed directly at Vic, an accusing finger. "What happens now?"

Bethniel shrugged. "Do you feel different?"

Carefully, Vic stood. With her first step, she had to grab the princess's arm. "I feel awful. Tell the Center that I drank its waters, and if I die, I want them to take you across the Plu for free."

Bethniel grinned. "I don't know about wizardry, but I could almost believe you'd drunk from the waters of diplomacy with a demand like that."

† † †

Half a day from Umbrachlorn Plu, the earth began to rumble, sifting the sand into soft mounds that bore witness to the war between wind and earth. The earth had more stamina and more patience. The company's shadows lengthened into an army of two- and three-headed silhouettes as the dunes frayed away to a plain, black with the furrows and lumps of old lava flows. A sulfurous fog obscured the sun, and obsidian sliced out of the ground. The Kragnashians who bore the company stepped gingerly here. A shudder rattled the thorax under Vic's thighs. The creature paused, then moved on, holding a bundle of its legs off the ground. A trail of green ooze shrank in the heat behind them.

The Plu loomed out of the fog, hissing and sputtering, globs of mud burping rotten eggs into yellow air. Umbrachlorn Plu oozed from the feet of the Lathalorns in the north to well beyond any maps the humans had or the Desert People would share. Many an explorer had been lost, led to her death by rumors of silver and copper at the end of this river of earth.

Vic signaled for the company to dismount, closed her eyes, and tried once more to lift herself off the Kragnashian's thorax. She imagined herself rising smoothly into the air, her brow furrowed with effort. At last, her lungs aching for breath, she opened her eyes and sighed.

"No luck?" Bethniel asked, standing below.

Vic shook her head and slid down the abdomen. No luck for weeks. Two days choking on the bile churned up by that poison, and every day since trying to make it work. She pictured herself swooping through clouds, causing earthquakes, healing wounds—everything the wizards of old could do, but she could not muster enough force to sweep a hair off a sleeve.

"Drak!" Her captains stood together, surveying the border. Drak winced as she approached but quickly smoothed his features into good-natured discipline. Bethniel had advised keeping the bargain with the Kragnashians secret; Vic wished she'd listened as she watched the others dismount, wary eyes darting between her and the Plu. "Have everyone collect their gear from the sleds and line up by the ford. I want two days' rations in every pack, and don't let anybody forget to fill their canteens."

As Drak stepped away shouting orders, Carl scowled. "Two canteens apiece won't go far, Marshall."

"No, they won't," she murmured, eyeing the yellow clouds. "But there must be water over there, or the nomads wouldn't be able to live."

"We could die before we find any."

Her gaze snapped to his. Uncertainty and mistrust had grown like weeds while she and Bethniel were gone. Bethniel had been right—there had been a Device that shortened their travel time between the Kragnashian capital and their campsite, but the company had still been left alone in Kragnashian custody for three weeks. "We haven't died yet, Captain. Tell Drak to tell them we need the water and sledges taken across as well."

Carl stomped away, and Bethniel took Vic's arm. "It's rocky on that side, Vic. Without horses, we can't pull the sledges. And even the Kragnashians can't carry the horses across *that*."

A gleaming white cable slung between a pair of ramps spanned the river of boiling mud, joining Kragnash with Relm. A trembling began; the cable bounced and swayed. Hands jerked to sides as a jet of mud and boiling, sulfurous water shot out of the river and splattered the bridge. Steam hissing off the cable, Vic doubted the Desert People, much less anyone else, would have survived that dousing. She hoped the Kragnashians knew the timing of the geyser. "We brought wheels, Beth," she reminded the princess. "We can pull the wagon ourselves."

"Are you sure you've been trying?"

Pressing her lips together, Vic glared at the princess. "Of course I'm sure. Wizardry was never part of this plan."

"You survived, you haven't gone mad. It's going to work, kick in somehow."

"Will it? What if it simply doesn't? I don't feel any different, except I've had a bloody headache since I drank that stuff."

"Well, *they* seem to think you can do it."

"*They* can't seem to tell me how!"

"Let's ask them again."

With a growl, Vic followed Bethniel to the lead Kragnashian. "Tell me again what your water did for me," she asked while Bethniel translated. "How does this work?"

"The water releases your mind to what you already know," Bethniel said as the leader clicked and rustled. "Use what you know of the air around you, of the sand, of the sky, of the sea. Use—Shrine, it's all nonsense."

"*You* wanted to ask it again. Tell me what it's saying."

"Use, uh, sky, air, sea." She sighed and started again. They had gone through this almost every day since leaving Direiellene. "Sand grains—no. Particles, building, complexes." Bethniel stopped translating and clapped at the creature. It snapped its wing covers, and she shook her head and waved her hands. It chittered, she stomped. Its antennae went rigid and pheromone billowed from it, gagging them and panicking the horses. A nervous, silent murmur swept through the company. Wineyll slipped to the front of the crowd.

"Marshall, it's talking about atoms."

Vic's eyes snapped to the minstrel. "What?"

"Like the Logs. Atoms, particles, molecules—of air, water, sand. I can Hear it through Bethniel."

Vic shushed Bethniel's furious clapping, asking her to translate again. "What does science have to do with wizardry?"

Hands slammed over ears at the high-pitched trill echoing off distant dunes. The horses strained against their leads, screaming. Gossamer wings stretched all the way out of wing covers, lifted the creature in a slow hovering hop. "Everything," Bethniel shouted over the din. "Science has everything to do with wizardry. The atoms . . ." She looked at Wineyll and shrugged.

"The atoms," Wineyll continued slowly, "come together and move apart. They are in motion, are everywhere, are . . ." The minstrel shrugged as well. "I'm sorry—the rest of what it's saying is too—we, Lathans, humans I guess, don't have words to translate it into." Bethniel nodded.

Oreseekers would know, Vic muttered. The Oreseekers waited for generation after generation for someone to come who understood the Logs fully, who knew not only the formula for the acceleration of a warp wave, but knew what a warp wave was and what to do with it. They waited and waited for men and women to come and take them home. And the only people left in the world who could even glimpse the meaning of these things were eighteen-foot insects, who were already home.

"Marshall," Drak said, "they're ready to start ferrying people over. They say we have only a short window between geysers, so we should hurry."

Nodding, Vic signaled they should proceed. The clouds broke over the eastern horizon, the setting sun mocking her between mountain peaks. Wizard—paugh! She could hear Lornk laughing in a valley guarded by those mountains. "I'm still coming," she muttered. "Maybe slower than I hoped, but I'll still be there before winter solstice." Unless they all died of thirst in the badlands or became snowbound in the passes.

She picked her way to the rim of molten mud, stepping carefully between jagged obsidian. Dusted with sulfur, the shards gleamed sharper than the velvet-wrapped dagger in her pack. The dagger she couldn't look at, the one she'd kill him with. Kill him. Could she? Since she'd left the Center's city, he had stalked her dreams more often, and more often she had awakened, heart thudding, from nightmares where she submitted wholly to him, handing him the devotion he so desired.

A bubble popped on the surface of the river, hot mud splattering her face. Blinking, Vic wiped stinging droplets off her cheeks. The Kragnashians said to use molecules. Molecules of air gathered even under her boots. Molecules of air tore meteors apart and made them shine like stars. Wind could blow a house down, whip the sea into waves big enough to drown a merchanter. It could whip up dunes and carve pinnacles of stone. She understood the air's power, but how was she supposed to use it?

Elekia used it. She would thicken it around you to push you, lift your head to face her, slap your cheeks. Vic wanted to believe she could sweep into Lordhome and single-handedly save Geram and Ashel, defeat the Relman army, and exact her revenge on Lornk because she had a wizard's power. But wanting wasn't having. Logkeeper, mistress, Blade. Wizard just didn't fit; Ashel would say the poetry of the three would be spoilt by the fourth. Ashel—the clockwork version of him had haunted her dreams along with Lornk. She hoped he still *could* say something, anything, about poetry.

Another tremor waved the mud into slow ripples. The rumbling grew louder, and Vic edged backward. Like a cat about to pounce, a bubble gathered itself, growing larger, mounting quickly while smaller boilings plopped and slurped around its base. Her pulse quickened as she backed another step and a deep sucking noise echoed from the surface of the river. Someone screamed her name, and the bubble burst. Boiling mud showered the shore; she flung herself away, covering her face with her hands. A thump loud in her ears, she landed on her side, pain biting through shoulder and leg. People shouted near her, around her, and hands gathered beneath her shoulders to pull her to her feet.

"Am I burned?" she cried, her leg aflame.

"No," Orlon said, lifting the robe over her head, "but you've got some nasty cuts. I need water."

Vic blinked at the faces around her. Orlon tore her trousers away from the wound. Drak was smiling, looking much younger in his uncertainty. Carl scowled; Marenye, the quartermaster, clutched his arm and looked up at his face, not Vic's. Laughing softly, Bethniel shook her head, looking so much like her brother Vic's throat swelled. "What?" she asked them.

Valion shouldered his way into the circle, casting her a wink and a grin. "Let her see." The group parted. They stood a hundred yards from shore, behind even the sleds and horses, a distance only a bird could have flown. "What shall we call you?" Valion asked. "Victoria, the Muddy?"

She looked at the Plu, at him, at the mud splashed all across the robe Orlon had tossed at her feet.

"Looks like it just kicked in," Bethniel said, grinning smugly. "May I present, Madam Victoria of Ourtown. A wizard."

With a cough, Vic began to chuckle, then to laugh. Bethniel giggled. Valion, whooshing, arced his hand from the river to their feet. Drak slapped Valion on the shoulder and bellowed. Marenye grinned. Carl relaxed his shoulders and nodded, the lines around his eyes fading. Orlon admonished Vic to hold still, so she grabbed him around the neck and mussed his hair, laughing harder. Outside the circle, the Kragnashian leader edged toward them. Vic shook her head at it, thought of the air under her boots, and suddenly a great wind rushed at them from all sides. Her cuts stung like mad; her hair pulled out of its braid, rippling wildly above her head. The wind swelled within her lungs as if they were balloons, and she drifted up, still laughing.

So this was joy. She looked down at the company gathering below her feet, their hair and robes whipping in the wind. Taking a deep breath, she raised her head toward the clouds, pulling them all off the ground. Elation and fear echoed as she rose with them. They moved slowly over the rocks, crossed the yellow line marking the river's exhalations. Wind roaring, the hot vapors rising from the Plu buoyed them higher. Vic laughed again. It was so easy. Just like learning a new Log, or mastering a new parry, using the power was impossible until the "how" clicked into place. Then, like Bethniel said, it just happened.

The company bobbed over Relman soil, plain hard-packed earth free of obsidian and lava. Regretting the loss of something precious, Vic released the wind. Her scream ripped the air as she and the others plunged to the ground, landing in a jumble of elbows and knees.

Coughing, Vic rolled off the pile and apologized. "Anyone hurt?"

Wrenched shoulders, bruised hips, and several sore heads, but nothing broken. Bethniel brushed dust from her trousers and nodded at the Kragnashian's leader, scuttling over the cable past its fellows bearing packs and barrels. It swept up to them and bowed. "We agreed to provide all aid that was required to cross the Plu. No aid is required." Gravel tumbled in its wake as it spun round and sped back to Kragnashian soil, drawing its fellows with it. The earth rumbled again. Trailing Desert People whistled and pressed into those ahead of them. The geyser blew; the last few Kragnashians still on the bridge shuddered and keened in the spray.

Bethniel and Drak exchanged shocked looks. "I've never heard of a Kragnashian reneging on a deal."

Vic swallowed sour bile. "They didn't. They promised all aid we *required*."

Curses rippled through the company as the Kragnashians dumped their provisions, leaving packs and barrels scattered over the jagged black rocks, then headed out, driving the herd of squealing horses ahead of them.

"I guess they were in a hurry," Valion whistled.

"You can do this," Bethniel whispered encouragingly.

Vic took a breath. "I guess I have to." The gashes in her leg and arm gnashed as she brought up the wind again, directing it beneath the packs on the other side. They bounced into the air like popping grain, one shooting beyond sight, whistling back down to bounce up again before it touched the ground. Holding her breath, Vic tugged the jumble closer. Strays slipped toward the Plu, but she snagged them, sending others too high again. When she took a quick breath, the packs dropped toward the mud. She flinched and bobbed, her hands instinctively grabbing air as if she were juggling the lot. This was harder than moving herself and the company beneath her. The wind tore at her hair as the packs edged closer. Djellabas flapping loudly, the company backed away as the jumble swooped toward them and finally landed. The wind died. Vic's knees buckled.

A cacophony of hands wrapped around her. The grips were solid, but her ears rang in the silence of Lathan voices crying her name.

"Let me just sit," she mumbled. Orlon pushed something between her lips, wrapped her leg and shoulder with bandages. The hard, sour thing in her mouth stilled the swirling and she found herself leaning against Bethniel's shins. Around them, the company sorted through the packs, some unrolling blankets.

"No. Drak, Carl," she called. The two captains came over. "The sun's as hot on this side as the other," she told them. "Take the company east, find cover, and wait for me."

Carl shouted for people to get ready to move. Drak knelt beside her. "Are you sure?"

She nodded. "We need the water in those barrels. I can fly now—I'll catch up."

He shook his head, keeping his voice low. "You can't fly far, and can't lead a company, if this . . . power . . . takes this much out of you. It isn't natural, Marshall."

"Lornk Korng isn't *natural*. I'm new at this—ten minutes new. Go ahead. I'll catch up."

His face pensive, he scratched the dirt, retrieved his pack. Vic leaned away from Bethniel, waving her and Orlon on with the others. The princess grasped her shoulder and turned away to find her gear. Orlon looked more reluctant to leave her.

"I'll be fine."

"We're in Relm now," he reminded her. "Nomads could be anywhere, everywhere."

"They're more likely to notice all of you than me here by myself. Drak, leave me a trail, but one only I'll know."

Inclining his head, the big man offered a small smile. The company left, and Vic slept.

Heated by the morning sun, her hood stifled her. Coughing, head throbbing, she sat up. A few feet away her pack lay unopened, the bedroll tied beneath it.

Her bandages brown, they needed changing and she needed the water. A few swallows from her canteen shrank her swollen tongue, but as wet sips turned to dry gulps, she chided herself for not following her own orders. Across the Plu, the gear waited like the remnants of a battle. Temples pounding, Vic stood and brought up the wind.

Whipping her hair across her face, it swept over the mud,

dusted the sulfur from the obsidian, ruffled the canvas sacks scattered on the shore. She lifted the sledges and tents and brought them tumbling over. The bags of food, the quivers, the bows, the spare daggers, and finally the sack of sulfa came swooping across. A quiver dropped into the Plu, burst into flame and sank with astonishing speed. Vic swallowed—if that had been the sulfa, or worse, one of the troopers . . .

Gear collected, she collapsed onto one of the tent sacks and waited for the world to swing back into focus. A dried fenelfruit cleaned the film off her teeth and tongue, and the weight of something in her stomach steadied her head.

This is all wrong, she thought. She couldn't carry all the gear by herself, not without a tornado. Such a storm would exhaust her, maybe kill her, and every nomad for miles would see it.

Elekia pushed things with her mind without so much as a breeze. Think, Vic told herself. It isn't the wind that burns up meteors. It's the air itself somehow. It's the pressure of the air.

On shaky legs, she walked up the ramp to the bridge. Hardened with a waxy, seamless coating, the ramp spun into the cable, its fibers a long, twisting bundle, the surface slick as ice. The earth snored, and the cable swung slowly. Cursing, Vic thought of those hundreds of Kragnashian feet sticking to this as if it were covered in glue. Why did they pick her? Was it simply the extraordinary coincidence that she bore the same name as a wizard who had lived a millennium ago?

Not that it mattered. She looked at the Lorn oc Re, swallowing a breath at the peaks. Snow crowned the mountains, pink in the dawn sun, a promise of clean, of cool, of victory. With closed eyes, she tasted the kiss of it on her lips, the ice melting in her mouth and the chill sliding down her throat. Shivering with pleasure, she remembered the shock of it against her neck when she was a child. Her face and arms tingled with the memory of a frigid breeze, and her nostrils filled with the smell of the ocean, her ears with the creak of fishing boats and the call of sea birds. Ourtown. Her eyes fluttered open, and for a moment she thought she saw the boats tilted on the sand, nets laid across their frames, smoke rising out of the chimney holes in every lodge. The sun, low on the horizon, but not gone yet for the winter, bathed the town in a warm amber glow. But she shook her head at the vision, heard a black rushing in her ears, and then the stink of sulfur spoilt the smell of the sea.

Concentrate, she ordered herself. Wishing she were home now didn't do anybody any good. *"Don't think you'll be a Logkeeper by dreaming about it,"* Martha used to say. *"You must work for your dreams. Metal doesn't fall from the sky, you know."* Four barrels sat on the other side, unmoved by Vic's wind storms. Couldn't the wizards of old make water? They would have had to pull the hydrogen and oxygen atoms out of the air and stick them together somehow. How could they isolate them? Damn, questions like these kept her thoughts on tangents. Focus. How could she move the casks without wind?

The queen again. Elekia didn't so much move the air as thicken it. Vic reached up and grabbed a handful, but her fingers closed around nothing. She tried again, seeking to grasp enough molecules to hold. A breeze whisked the hair off her shoulders. No. No wind. Telepathy and telekinesis. Mindspeech and wizardry. Both powers of the mind, both subject to the *state* of mind. Martha and Olivet had taught her to keep her head clear, her thoughts cool as she recited a Log or assessed an enemy's camp. But Lornk had taught her how to release her mind and live in the physical moment. With him, she'd known absolute clarity, not of reason, but of time and place and being.

Her fingers bent, wrapped around something solid. *"Let your mind go, my treasure,"* his voice whispered in her ear. *"Let it go and come to me. To me. Come, Kara."* Skin at the back of her neck cold, she reached with her left hand, felt substance beneath those fingers as well. Her right hand reached higher. Standing, she tried a foot. The rungs of a ladder formed beneath her weight. She let go and hung in midair, supporting herself with the energy of the matter surrounding her. Telekinesis, wizardry. "Who cares what you call it!" she shouted, as loudly as her lungs could manage. Victoria, Kara. Just names, without meaning. With a rush of fey laughter, she flung herself across the Plu, picked up the barrels, stacked them. Then she jumped to the top and danced an angry jig, facing the Lorn. "I'll come to you, Lornk Korng!" she shouted. "I'll come as Kara and I'll spit in your face!" The earth rumbled, and she lifted the casks, lined them up, and marched them across the lava. Her throat ached for the water sloshing inside. Her loins ached for Lornk's caress. "I am not yours!" she screamed, with each word shooting a cask into the sky. Each shrank to a speck against the azure, then hurtled back, growing to the size of a fingernail, of a thumbprint, of a palm, of a head. They'll smash, dundlehead, she chided herself, and thickened the air beneath each to land it gently. Casks safely aground, she rocketed into the air, closing her eyes to the sting of rushing wind. Her chest tightened as she pulled away from the earth's hold, and when she remembered to breathe, she couldn't pull the icy air into her lungs. At last she stopped and saw the Plu winding out of sight in the south and the blue smudge of the ocean to the north. From here, the earth bent away from her, but directly below, the Lorn oc Re beckoned with its white peaks, a mother welcoming a hungry child. Up here, you forget everything but beauty, she thought. Up here, you see forever. She held herself there, shivering and growing woozy in the frigid space but entranced by the gold and blue hues of the land beneath her. Finally, eyes dry and lungs burning, Vic dropped back into life.

As she neared the land, the fire in her chest mellowed and

deepened, became the black heat of Lornk's touch, pressing, releasing, controlling her breath, controlling her. Sinking on weak knees beside the barrels, she fought the white spots blooming and shredding behind her eyelids. *What are you?* I'm a Logkeeper. I'm the Blade. I'm a Wizard.

Mud hissed as the earth began to shake again. Heat bubbling, she staggered up, dizzy, fighting Kara's craving, embracing Victoria's power. Knocking against each other, the casks hopped across the undulating rock. "I am not yours!" she cried again at the mountains. Steam whined, screamed, roared out of the Plu. As the geyser thundered, the pleasure and pain Lornk had given her blew sparks across her mind, down every fiber of bone and muscle, through every drop of blood, making even the tiny hairs on the backs of her fingers stand straight. She wanted to hug her chest to her knees, her neck and shoulders ready for his fingers, her ears for his warm cajoling. But instead she stood with her fists ground into her eyes, waiting for the memory of him to sink back into the folds of the earth. As the last drops of mist cleared, Vic wept, her sobs loud after the eruption.

She found the company in a dry ravine where the sentries stood watch atop an asymmetric rise of scree. She had stacked all the equipment on the sledges and floated them along Drak's trail, impressed that the company had traversed the entire plain in one night. As she drifted up the rise, Orlon and two other troopers emerged from a cleft in the rock, but they would not greet her until she put the sledges down. She ordered the wheels found and attached as Orlon inspected her bandages and felt her forehead. "You've been in the sun too long," he said.

Vic nodded, letting the man's square hands support her. It felt odd to be on her own feet after riding on wishes. "Any Relmans?"

"None. We passed an old campsite."

"I saw it." Dry horse droppings and a rotted water pouch. With a deep breath, she walked into the ravine. The stone walls arched together, the gap a blue crease, bright in the afternoon glare. The company lined the walls, most asleep. Inside, the air cooled Vic's cheeks, and she brushed back her hood, mopped the sweat from the back of her neck. Soft snores echoed off the rock.

Stirring as she passed, Carl sat up. "Drak and I climbed up the ravine this morning. You should take a look."

"Let me sleep a few hours, then senior command will meet up there."

At the rear of the ravine, she bedded down near a jagged stone forming a rough natural ladder out of the cleft. She slept soundly, too exhausted for dreams, but woke to a hammer pounding in her skull. As she pushed herself up, fingers rubbing a temple, Orlon came over and handed her a canteen. Choking on the bitter flavor, she spluttered and shoved it away. "What is that?"

"You're dried out from heat and sun. It'll help with your head too."

"I don't think I can hold it down."

"Drink it." He pushed some dry flatcakes into her hand. "Then eat."

Bethniel and the captains appeared, the princess taking the canteen as the captains climbed up the ravine. "I'll make sure she drinks it."

Vic watched the princess ascend halfway, then grabbed her pack and slowly followed. "Does your mother get headaches?"

"I don't think so, but then with her you never know. She's so severe."

"Aren't I?"

"No. You're . . . determined." Grunting, Bethniel hoisted herself out of sight. Vic swallowed at the pain, tried to squeeze it out of her eyes. When she opened them, Bethniel's head shadowed the exit. "Are you all right?"

Nodding with pressed lips, Vic started climbing again, her knees scraping against the stone. The rock was cool, smooth, almost clammy, but the handholds offered a solid grip. The darkness of the cleft soothed her eyes, but she forgot the throb in her temples when her head emerged into the light.

"Beautiful, isn't it?" Bethniel sat cross-legged beside the opening; the captains lounged beyond.

The sinking sun blazed over a cacophony of arches and pinnacles towering above flat-topped mesas, ragged fissures, fluted ridges. Blue and gold, orange, purple, red, even pale green striped and swirled in intricate patterns toward distant blue peaks capped with white.

Vic climbed the rest of the way out. "It looks like another twenty-five, thirty leagues to the mountains."

"About what I figure." Drak tossed a stone over the edge.

"How long then?" Bethniel asked. "Three days, a week?"

"That's thirty leagues as a bird flies." Vic pulled a roll of maps from her pack and weighed the corners down with rocks. Their only map of western Relm showed a road heading out of the Lorn oc Re and ending at a shaded area marked "badlands." The map offered no details, and they couldn't tell whether they camped north or south of the road. "The badlands are a bloody maze, and it's nobody's Nine Day. We don't have time for trial and error." Vic rubbed her temples. More delays! They were finally within Relm's borders, but no nearer Lornk's mountain stronghold. Yet each passing day brought them closer to winter. If the Center's party had met them as planned, they'd have had time to nose their way through these lands. Instead, the white-capped peaks ahead promised only snowbound passes and failure. "I can scout ahead, find our way from the air."

"Marshall," Drak said, "you look like you might puke, on your own boots," he added with the shadow of a smile. "You're in command; you can't go flitting around like a bird and making yourself a target for nomad crossbows."

"We cannot lose any more time."

"We steal horses to haul the water," Carl said, "and we capture a guide too."

Vic sipped from Orlon's canteen. The bitterness sent a shiver down her spine, but the throb in her head had diminished. Her eyes scanned the fissures and spires separating them from the Lorn. Raids were common in the badlands, and nomad sentries were likely as sharp and wary as the Dagger on its best day. "If we send a team to steal horses and they're caught, then what?"

"We go in and get them," Carl said fiercely.

"And we'd have to find and kill any messengers headed to Lordhome," Drak grumbled. "It's too risky. We shouldn't go near any nomads. We send scouts ahead to find the way through. It's the only way."

"Trial and error, Drak. The only way is for me to scout from the air."

"Marshall, no. Shrine, you've been sick as a cat since they . . ." Carl rolled to his feet, his eyes on the mountains. "When I signed onto this mission, I didn't know you. I believed what troopers said round the tap, that the Dagger was a sham and you were only a captain because you sucked the right cocks and licked the right cunts."

"Captain!" Drak angled his head at Bethniel, whose cheeks flamed red.

"Apologies, Highness, but that's what they say."

Hot ire pumped up Vic's neck. She knew very well what people said, though few had ever dared state it so bluntly to her face. "Your point, Captain?"

Carl knelt in front of her. The sun, sinking behind him, haloed his head and shoulders. He spoke aloud, voice thick and urgent. "I was an ass. I joined this mission thinking I deserved your glory. I thought I'd earn acclaim by saving the day when you led us into disaster. But Shrine's bitch, under that sand, I didn't see a way out. I would have let us die. But you—you kept us alive, and you led us out. If there's another disaster, Marshall, I trust you to lead us out again. And I'll follow you. I'll do whatever you ask." He took a breath. "But I can't do my job if you're too sick to do yours."

Vic stared at the captain, the outrage of a moment ago draining down her throat. She knew her loyalists—Orlon, Drak, Marenye, a few others—and she would never have counted Carl among them. Drak and Bethniel looked just as surprised. But she wasn't going to turn him away. Shrugging, she angled her chin at the view. "Thanks, Captain, but I can't lead us out of this disaster if I don't know where the Shine I'm going."

"We capture a guide." Carl hit fist to palm with each word.

"They are civilians," Drak said just as forcefully. "Stealing horses, fine—but taking people? That's what the bloody Relmlord does."

"We capture a guide," Bethniel interjected. "And we make sure no one can follow us or send word to Lordhome." Vic and the men exchanged wide-eyed glances. Bethniel's face was hard, her eyes glass, and Vic felt as if she looked at Elekia stern on her throne rather than Beth cross-legged on a rock. Elbows on knees, the princess leaned forward, resting a glare on each of them. "My brother has been at Lornk Korng's mercy for months. Winter is shutting down those passes. If we don't get through the badlands now, we'll never make it to Olmlablaire. And we cannot risk the Relmlord having warning that we're coming. There is too much at stake."

"Highness, the nomads travel as families." Horror stretched Drak's features, and his voice trembled. Everyone spoke aloud now. "There are children, old people. You want to murder them?"

"I want to save my brother and end this war. We've come too far, been through too much, to fail within sight of the Lorn oc Re!"

Tension yawed between them like a bowstring. Drak went to the cliff edge and gazed across the badlands, while Carl nodded his alliegance to Vic. Her eyes fixed on the distant snow, she heard herself shout at Lornk while the Umbrachlorn Plu bubbled behind her. Would she kill innocents to keep those promises? Searching her gut, she knew she had to reach Olmlablaire. It was the only way she'd finally break Lornk's hold on her. Standing beside the older captain, she put a hand on his arm. "This mission is to save Geram, too."

The big man glowered. "He'd be the first to tell you killing Relman children is wrong. I didn't volunteer for *this*, Marshall."

Vic studied the spires and arches, wondering how long it would take to nose through with scouts on foot. How many of the countless channels below led to a dead end?

"Marshall?" Wineyll poked her head out of the ravine, climbed the rest of the way up. "I can help."

"Get back down the ravine, girl," Carl growled.

"Captain, wait." Bethniel said, then turned to the minstrel. "Did you Hear us?"

She shrugged. "I couldn't help it. I think I can hide whoever goes to steal the horses. And if you can kidnap someone, I can find out what he or she knows."

Vic's eyes darted to Bethniel before returning to Wineyll. "How many people can you deceive at the same time?"

The minstrel disappeared. Carl cursed and leapt to his feet as Drak stumbled backward off the edge of the cliff, arms pinwheeling. Vic caught him in a net of air and set him down on the rock. Breathing heavily, he nodded his thanks.

"Do you see her?" Bethniel asked Vic. When she shook her head, the princess said, "That's at least four."

The minstrel reappeared and Vic gave her a hard look. "How many illusions can you do at the same time? How long can you maintain them, and in how many people?"

"I'm not sure, Marshall, but this is why you brought me, isn't it?"

Vic nodded, seeing a way out of murder. "Carl, send scouts to find a nomad camp. Wineyll, while they look, I want you to find your limits. Start with fifty people and work your way up or down from there."

After the younger captain and minstrel climbed down, Drak shook his head. "Vic, no. She's too green."

"Every one of us was too green the day of our first battle."

"Wineyll can do it," Bethniel assured them.

"And if she can't?"

Vic grimaced, but her heart beat steadily within the ice that formed round it the night she carved a message in a rapist's skin. "Then I'm leading you all to hell."

CHAPTER 25

NOMAD

The tents crouched together in a small box canyon. For three days, scouts surveilled the encampment, noting when the guards changed and when the absolute quiet of deep sleep descended. In that hour, the company crept down a slope toward the sentries, a pair of men leaning casually against a boulder. Vic knew that stance, like a coiled spring, ready for release. The guards' gazes passed over the slope, across the Lathans, and on to the spires of rock that might hide an enemy. Vic's lungs released a long breath, and she glanced over her shoulder at Wineyll, perched on Valion's back, the girl's lips pressed together in concentration.

Loose gravel scattered across the hardpan incline, pulling Vic's focus back to her toes and heels and the imperative for silence. A scratch and tumble behind her snapped her head back around. Down on one knee, Valion struggled to stay upright as Wineyll clung to his back, one arm flung out for balance. Below, the sentries raised gnarled bows, but a pair of Lathan arrows whispered first. One pierced a guard's throat, another sank into the second man's chest. Gravel spraying, the company sped toward them, archers firing again to make sure of the kill. At the canyon's entrance, Vic left Bethniel and a pair of troopers to hide the bodies and stand guard. Then she led the others inside.

A hundred yards down the trail, they found a boy whittling, intent over his knife and a stick of knobby wood. At Vic's nod, Valion pounced on the boy, delivering a sharp blow to the back of the head. Orlon shouldered their guide's body and trudged out of the canyon, his cheeks bloodless in the starlight.

The company stole forward, faces baring fierce snarls and wary eyes. White framed Wineyll's blue irises. A second boy, perhaps looking for the first, came down the boulder-strewn path and stumbled into Drak. The captain's knife plunged into his neck, slicing off the boy's shout. Wineyll, a hand clapped over her mouth, froze.

"We had no choice," Vic whispered. "He would have alerted his camp."

The minstrel nodded, swallowing hard as Drak shook his head over the body. "He'll be the last we have to kill."

A tense lump formed in Vic's stomach, twisting her awareness, sharpening her sight and hearing as they reached the camp. Crouching behind boulders and scrub, the company surrounded squat, circular tents. A clothesline hung thick with tasseled robes—good camouflage for a large party moving through the badlands. Vic signaled for two troopers to gather the garments while two others approached the horses tethered near the canyon wall. A bray echoed, and Vic's heart leapt to her throat. Clucking softly, Draylune and Nedden padded forward and palmed muzzles, unhooked bridles. When four horses walked complacently out of the canyon behind the cavalry troopers, Vic took her hand off her dagger. Then a whicker from a tethered animal prompted a new chorus of stamping and braying.

"Someone's awake," Wineyll hissed.

Throat closing, Vic squeezed the minstrel's arm. "Do what you can."

Wineyll's eyes glowed in the darkness. "I'll try," she whispered shakily.

A head of brown hair ducked out out of the largest tent, followed by the bare chest of a man Drak's size. He carried a crossbow in one hand; a stoneknife jutted from his belt. A man who knew how to defend his people against raiders. Expelling a slow breath of air, Vic bounced softly on her heels. It was a bloody shame.

"Everything all right, Hemen?"

Vic started, hearing the Oreseeker's tongue, the words out of a dream. At her side, Wineyll closed her eyes, and Vic Heard the voice of a boy telling the man that yes, everything was fine.

"The code, Hemen." Stretching, the man walked around his tent toward the herd. Vic flashed hand signals at her people to get ready. Nodding, troopers licked fletchings and signaled the troopers beyond them. The nomad stopped and blinked at the horses, his shoulders tensing.

Eyes still closed, Wineyll's lips formed the word sixteen, sixteen, but in the boy's voice she said, "Elesendar set without flame tonight. The clouds broke His light. Everything's OK."

Shrugging, the man turned from the animals and peered toward the boulders. "Come out where I can see you, boy. Where's Mane?"

"More are waking," Wineyll told Vic, her voice on the edge of a whine.

Vic gripped her arm. "Just answer him."

Rubbing her palms on her thighs, Wineyll drew in a breath and held it. "Mane went to relieve himself. I'm right here." A figure—the ghost of the boy Drak killed—stepped from behind a tent. "I'm right here," Wineyll repeated. "You can go back to sleep."

The man nodded, looked around the camp again. "That's all right, I'm up now. Here"—he squatted next to a glowing firepit and picked up a kettle—"you want some tea?"

A Lathan arrow flew, striking the man in the shoulder. The pot clattered, the man fell back, roaring. He rolled to his feet and dodged behind the shelter of a tent, crying alarm. Yelling, the company leapt out from the rocks. Half-dressed men stumbled to meet them, shrugging off sleep like rain on a hot day. A bloody shame, Vic thought again, charging into the camp and plunging her dagger into the stomach of a trilling Relman. Another man leapt at her, but then hesitated, perhaps startled to find the killer a woman. Before he recovered, Vic ducked inside his reach and rammed her dagger through his ribs.

Valion struck a nomad's head with his foot, slashed another's belly open, and picked up a brand from the fire and tossed it through a tent flap. Children screamed, women rushed out of the tent, carrying babies into the bedlam. The nomad leader stood at the center of the fray, shouting orders. Another tent caught fire; wailing children tumbled out. A little girl crashed into Vic, another skidded around her, and Vic spun and fell. Cursing, she rolled to her feet but dropped to the ground again as a stoneknife whistled behind her. Twisting around, she kicked her attacker's knee and heard the muffled crunch of bone. With a vicious howl, he collapsed, and Vic raked her dagger across his neck. A screaming woman rushed forward, fingernails aimed at Vic's eyes. Sidestepping the woman's charge, Vic caught her from behind and plunged her dagger into her heart.

Angry trills vibrated as bodies sprawled across the camp. Blood mucking her brown braids, a little girl lay facedown in the yellow embers, her clothes already smoking. Wiping slippery fingers on her trousers, Vic caught sight of Carl fighting the nomad leader. Blood wept down the man's chest, but Carl staggered back, clutching his ear. The man roared and advanced, stoneknife raised. Vic reached for her bow, but then pitched forward, landing facedown, pinned beneath a heavy weight.

"Filthy bitch," a voice growled. "To dress like a man, fight like a man." His hand reached underneath her and yanked at the laces of her trousers. "Let me remind you what you are."

"No!" Vic cried, pushing off her assailant and tossing him into the fire. Flames roared up, quenching his scream. Heat scorching her face, she looked across the camp. Nomad women herded the children into a large tent sheltering beneath the cliff. One woman paused at the flap, her hands over a boy's ears, her eyes a mirror of the terror that had birthed a girl named Kara in a silent white tower in Traine. As Vic and the woman stared at each other, the cries of battle, the slither of stone against crystal, the thud of boots and fists faded, and Vic heard only her own breathing, felt a thumb on her windpipe and a palm on the nape of her neck, smelled perfume, and the sweet must of an animal skin on the floor. Her face lined and harsh, the nomad woman had known the hardship of sun, thirst, starvation. She may even have been kidnapped from some neighboring tribe and forced to marry into this group. Come with us, Vic wanted to tell her, wanted to offer her the rescue she'd never had. The woman's eyes flicked from Vic's face to the fire, white hot around the nomad corpse, and she drew the child inside the tent. The hand around Vic's throat tightened, choking her. *What are you?*

A firebrand flew at the tent, struck the fabric, and exploded, burning faster and hotter than the Dagger's poison ever had. As heat roared upward, enveloped in screams, the scent of Trainer perfume drowned in the stench of burning hair. Shaking herself, Vic scooped up her dagger, but the Relman men stood transfixed by the conflagration. "Finish them!" Valion cried, plunging his dagger into a man's heart.

Soon, only Lathans stood in the angry light. Vic counted heads—no one, no Lathans, dead. Wineyll sobbed behind the scrub. In a gruff voice that carried over the fires, Drak ordered all the horses cut loose, all the remaining tents taken down. The troopers moved slowly, none speaking. As they worked, Vic squatted beside Wineyll and grasped her arm. "Pull yourself together. We need you still."

Wiping her nose on her sleeve, Wineyll shook her head. "How can you stand it?"

Vic tasted a Relman rapist's blood on her tongue. "I can, because I have to."

"And what if I can't?"

Vic's grip tightened. "You will, because we need you to." Ashel's beatific smile, as Wineyll had painted it the night they met, loomed in memory. "You will, because *he* needs you to."

When they walked out of the canyon, the nomad boy broke from Orlon's grip and threw himself at Drak's throat. The big captain fell back a step and for a moment looked as if he'd allow the boy to throttle him. Then, lips flat, he broke the boy's hold and wrestled him to the ground. Howls echoed off the surrounding spires, and Vic ordered the boy bound and gagged.

"Wait," Wineyll cried. She placed her hands on the nomad's cheeks, and his rage scaled down to grief.

Nomad and minstrel were of an age, both too young, too green, for the night's horror. Vic had been no older when she first supped on hatred and vengeance. "I can stand it because I have no choice," she muttered to herself.

† † †

The nomad never spoke a word after Wineyll quieted his screams, but the minstrel learned his name—Mane Thrushwind—and found their passage through the crags in his thoughts. When he first realized Wineyll plundered his knowledge, Mane began sending them to impassable cliffs or other nomad encampments, but Vic anticipated lies and sent scouts roving ahead. Soon Wineyll learned how to dig deep enough into the boy's memories to tell false from true, and the company moved quickly through secret trails along tight ravines. When they camped, Mane sat, chin on knees, refusing to eat, drinking only when a pair of troopers held his mouth open while Orlon forced water into it.

Vic watched his suffering, the anguish of a Caleisbahn ship hold and terror of a white room in Traine digging at her conscience. Bile churned each time Wineyll ravished the boy's mind, and Vic knew each rape damaged the minstrel as much as the nomad. But the Lorn oc Re moved swiftly closer. A day out, Vic ordered most of the horses released. Water would be easier to find in the mountains, and the large herd would only slow them down. Mane watched the freed animals trot away, tears blazing trails down his cheeks. "You should have killed them too," he spat, speaking for the first time. "You know my thoughts, but you know nothing about me. Those animals were as much my family as the mother and father, sisters and brothers you burned alive."

The next morning, the badlands melted into a narrow plain. The road to Olmlablaire cut across it, then wound through steep hills fronting the mountains. Coughing hoarse sobs, Mane fell to his knees. Wineyll, cheeks hollow, took his head in her hands, and after a minute, the tears stopped and he grabbed her wrist.

"Say my name," he told her.

"Mane Thrush"—she choked, then cleared her throat, speaking loudly and clearly—"Mane Thrushwind."

"Now, you kill me."

"I'll do it," Carl said.

Vic held up her hand, holding Wineyll's gaze and thinking of the velvet-wrapped dagger in her pack. "It's your choice."

White as a sheet, the girl swallowed hard and pulled her dagger from its sheath.

"You've taken my name," Mane snarled, "now take my life with it."

Sucking in a breath, Wineyll grabbed his hair and pulled back his head. His adams apple bobbed. Her hand shook. Squeezing her eyes shut, she sliced, and the boy fell backward. "That was for Ashel."

CHAPTER 26

OLMLABLAIRE

Winter had seized the mountains, but the sun still rose early, painting a warm image of dawn on the farmer's bedroom wall. Vic watched the light creep through the treetops to stretch shadows of a corral, a barn, and a well across the snow. Her own silhouette broke the pattern of panes on the wall until the candle she held blossomed without match or flint. Swallowing with a dry throat, she snuffed the candle with her palm, but not so quickly it didn't burn. She heard the nomads' screams when the candle flamed. The cries were still in her ears when the fire went out.

The road into the Lorn oc Re had jerked through the lower slopes, taking them past dry rocks and brown trees that waited for the snows above to melt and moisten the earth. As they passed the first quiverfills and manarks, true mountain trees, as Valion laughed and lobbed a snowball packed from the first patch of snow, and even as Vic laughed with him, brushing the snow from her hair, she'd sworn that Lornk would pay for what had happened to the nomads.

She'd promised to hear his screams instead of theirs.

Below, Draylune came out of the barn with a pair of milk tureens yoked around her neck. Her braids bounced as she walked, even with the weight swinging at her sides. The farm nestled in a secluded outgrowth of Olm valley, connected to the main vale by narrow, overgrown wagon ruts. The company had watched the house all day until the family went inside for dinner. Then they had simply walked through front and rear doors with bows drawn. No one had even been scratched, and the family, a gray-bearded man, a grandmother, two grown daughters, and a son Wineyll's age, moved into the cellar. From there they complained about their food, the cold, the straw brought them from the barn. Vic might have laughed at these grievances if she didn't still hear those children screaming.

With a grunt, she left the window and glimpsed her face in the mirror. A gaunt woman with frozen eyes stared back. Head shaking, she went downstairs. In the great room, she stopped and traced the curves of a rocking chair. Coals pulsed dimly red in the hearth. Dried flowers came to life as sun brightened the petals. Drak's laughter boomed from the kitchen, followed by Bethniel's giggling. Something caught in Vic's throat as she stood in the light of a waning fire and a waxing sun. Geram could laugh like that too, fearlessly, without acknowledging how close danger might be. She tightened her mouth and went into the kitchen.

"Morning," the princess said, pouring Vic a cup of tea. "I made some cereal."

"Don't eat it, if you value your stomach," Drak warned.

Vic sat, thanking Bethniel for cup and bowl while the princess stuck her tongue out at Drak. Carl leaned back in his chair, a foot hitched over a knee, eyes on the ceiling. A raked mound filled his bowl. Drak's bowl was empty. Vic sipped her tea and took a spoonful—not bad for one of Bethniel's efforts. "We need reconnaissance," she said.

Carl unlocked his legs and arms. "I'll go."

"No. I'm going."

Drak's face sobered. "You can't."

"I will. If Ashel and Geram are still alive, I may be able to get them out before we attack."

"Marshall"—Carl's chair slapped back onto the floor— "we've been through this. We're not the Dagger; you cannot be the Blade here."

"And I'm not the Blade any longer. That woman was lost in the desert." In a nomad camp. "I have to go, and I'm taking Wineyll with me. One: I can escape if we get caught. Two: Wineyll speaks Relman."

"So does Orlon."

"I'll need her skills to find Ashel and Geram."

Drak laid a big hand across Vic's fist. "She's only a girl, Vic. You've seen what she's been like after that nomad boy. Send Orlon. He speaks Relman too."

"He's the only healer we have."

"All right, send Harma or Frearth to scout the perimeter."

She shook her head. "No, not Orlon, not Frearth, me." The velvet-wrapped dagger waited upstairs. "I have business to finish."

Door creaking, Draylune carried in one of the tureens. As she stamped snow from her boots, Drak took his hand from Vic and studied the dried ribbons left in his bowl. Carl heaped his cereal into a lump. Vic glared between them and ate. Angling her head upstairs, Bethniel took the milk from Draylune. When the trooper was gone, she walked to the head of the table. "Vic's right." Her voice carried the same hard edge as it had when she'd ordered the massacre. "We need reconnaissance. We need to know where Ashel is, because the Relmlord will surely want to kill him when we attack. Plus"— Bethniel looked straight at Vic—"if the Marshall can assassinate the Relmlord, the confusion might aid our assault. Remember where we are, gentlemen. One company isn't much against squadrons." She paused, taking a breath to voice her words. "If Vic gets caught, she can escape. If Wineyll gets caught, she'll do better than most of us at hiding her thoughts. And Wineyll speaks Relman; she'll pass for Relman."

"You don't speak Relman, do you?" Carl asked, his eyes begging a denial.

Vic met his gaze, sorry to disappoint him. "Anyone who asks will be told I'm mute. I write and read Relman, so I can use notes if I have to. If we're not back by tonight, leave. You'll have to send Harma to scout the perimeter then. Don't send Orlon inside because they'll be expecting someone."

"Vic, your place is to lead, and that doesn't mean being first into the fire."

Smiling ruefully, Vic put her hand over Drak's. "My father used to say something like that. Maybe I'm not doing my duty, but to me there's a lot more at stake than Latha's war. If I have to, I'll resign as marshall, even from the army. You can have me court-martialed when we get home. But there's nothing you can do to stop me from going."

Neither answered. In the silence that followed, Bethniel returned to the stove and started stirring her cereal. "You'd better put on some proper Relman farm-girl clothes."

"I will." Vic tucked into the rest of her cereal. Carl returned his gaze to the ceiling. Drak's head rested in his hands, elbows propped on the table. When she finished, she put her bowl and cup into the tub of water warming on the hearth.

"Good luck," Drak said.

"Tonight," said Carl. "We'll see you tonight."

Vic nodded. "I—we'll be back."

Wineyll was sleeping in the attic with three other women, all curled into the corners of an enormous old bed. Her breath steaming in the cold, Vic crept over rolled rugs and quarry tools, finding the minstrel awake and staring at the rafters. "I'm going with you," she whispered. Selmar sighed and turned over.

"Go get some breakfast."

Wineyll nodded and slipped out of bed, shivering. She looked a lot older than her years as she pawed through the packs on the floor, found her flute case, and looked inside. The girl rolled her lower lip under her teeth. Vic's own grief welled, and she went to find them clothes.

In the daughters' room, Orlon stood at the window, wearing a sweater twice his size. He jumped when she came in.

"Nervous?"

He shook his head. "I didn't think we'd actually make it."

"We're not there yet."

"The war will be over in a week."

"One way or another," she muttered, but brightened for his sake. "I'm sure you're right."

"What are you doing?" he asked as she rummaged through the bureau.

"Wineyll and I are going to Lordhome to find Ashel and Geram and get the layout of the place."

"Is that wise?"

Her hands paused over folded sweaters. So they wouldn't shake, she picked one and held it up to herself. "That doesn't really matter, does it?"

He shook his head. "I guess not. Let me come with you."

"No. The company needs you as a healer, not a spy."

He chuckled. "Who's to argue with the Blade on matters of reconnaissance? Good luck, Marshall."

She smiled, taking the hand he offered. "Thanks. You'd better get some breakfast—maybe you can cure Bethniel's meal of its lumps."

He laughed on his way out, promising he would try.

† † †

The golden face of Mount Olm towered over a lake glittering under the noon sun. Winding through dense forest, the road sloped down into the valley toward a stone bridge, rising on the other side through orchards with shining limbs. Seeing no outlet for the lake, Vic wondered where the water went.

"This is a natural cistern," Wineyll replied. "The water comes out again a few miles from here, and then it's known as the River Re." The minstrel stared over the valley, the sun highlighting the copper in her hair. "My mother is Relman," she said. "I thought you should know."

Vic clasped her elbow. "Can you keep hold of yourself? It's not too late to go back."

Jaw bunching, the girl nodded. "My mother is Relman, but I grew up in a Lathan Guildhouse. Ashel is my brother, Vic. I'm not turning back."

They descended to the lake, crossed the bridge, and entered the orchards. Vic's teeth ground as she imagined Lornk appearing from behind a tree. This valley was his home as much as Traine—he could be anywhere, out for a ride or a hunt or a stroll. A sudden yelp of laughter prompted a quizzical glance from Wineyll. Her first purpose here—to rescue Ashel and end the war—flashed in her mind like lightning illuminating a door lost in a storm. Months of tension in the company, delays in the desert, the Kragnashians, all these things had wiped out any thought of her purpose, or she wouldn't be here now, walking toward the Relmlord's palace with no help but a girl still frazzled by her first kill.

Pursing her lips, probably Hearing everything, Wineyll crossed her arms and walked faster. Vic quickened her own pace, and a bend in the road led them stumbling into a group of people digging in the embankment, watched by a pair of Relman troopers with crossbows perched in crooked elbows. Legs hobbled by leather thongs, the prisoners swung their picks in an uneven, halfhearted rhythm. Vic's breath caught when she saw them, but a search through the haggard faces failed to reveal Ashel or Geram.

Straightening her hat, Wineyll shrugged off her gloom and sauntered up to the male guard. "How much farther to Olmlablaire?"

He pulled himself off a tree, leering. "You going to need a place to stay, honey?"

"Leave her alone," the other guard clipped, not taking her eyes from her fingernails. "It's another league or so up the road. You girls looking for work?"

Vic smiled goofily and rubbed her stomach. Wineyll nodded. "I hope there's work to be found—"

"Vic?" The question, spoken directly in her mind, cut through Wineyll's flirting. One prisoner stood still, his pick on the ground beside him. Recognition hit like a hammer. With a beard catching icicles and hair that caught shadows, Earnk stared with the same eyes that had restored her to herself, long ago. "Vic"—he spoke with more assurance—"he knows you're coming."

"Quit gawking and get back to work." The leering guard jabbed Earnk with his crossbow.

Wineyll tugged Vic's sleeve. "Thanks for the directions. Maybe I'll see you later." She winked at the guard and tossed her hair as they turned to go.

The man flourished his crossbow and bowed. "Now that's a pretty miss," they heard him say.

"Shit, she's as likely to spit on you as sit on you," the other guard replied.

"Who was that?" Wineyll asked after they had rounded the next bend, the prisoners out of sight.

"A ghost," Vic gasped, trying not to howl. She'd expected she might have to face Earnk in battle, harbored wild hopes he'd be in Traine or Re when they arrived. She had not thought to find him a prisoner doing hard labor, and wondered what he'd done to earn his father's wrath. "We're in trouble."

"I Heard. How could he know we were coming?"

"Spies," she ventured. "In the manor or in Cabanarl." Or with the company itself. She riffled through every face. Not Carl or Drak. Marenye, Valion, Nedden, Harma, Garth, Draylune—each name came with a denial. Over the months since they'd left Cabanarl, she'd gotten to know these people, trust their loyalty, especially after the nomad camp. Besides, few knew their destination before they set sail. Truth struck like a lightning bolt: Orlon. He had survived the ambush on the Dagger, brought word of Ashel's capture, and known the plan from the start.

Her feet stopped on the cusp between the orchards and fields. "This is more dangerous than I thought. You should go back."

Wineyll shook her head. "No. You need my help to find Ashel."

"Can you send them a warning?"

The girl's eyes grew wide. "I—I don't know. I've never tried anything like that before. Nobody has."

"Here." Vic pointed to the embankment. "Sit down and try. I'll wait ten minutes, then we have to go on."

†††

Ashel studied the chessboard, gaming out stratagems while Lornk's eyes shifted from piece to piece. The logs snapped in the hearth, but the warmth hardly touched the chill, and each exhalation sent another puff of vapor over the board. The tea in Ashel's mug had already gone cold.

Lornk slid his rook across the board. "I've meant to ask for some time: how did you get back into my house in Traine?"

Ashel smiled an oily courtier's grin. "The dark and rain made it easy to slip past the guards. When you're not there, I expect they're lax in their duties." He placed his bishop quickly, hiding his hands under the table. His fingers looked like diseased twigs—skin mottled pink and brown, fingernails mere nubs. He touched each fingertip with his thumb while he waited for Lornk's next move. At least he had fingertips. At least his hands worked.

Lornk frowned. "I thank you for uncovering a dangerous security breach."

"You're welcome," he replied congenially. He'd run straight to the Guildhouse that night, written a letter to his mother, telling her in oblique language that Lornk knew about Vic's rescue party.

My sister's imminent arrival has prompted this message and has probably enabled me to send it. When you receive this letter, I will be in the south. I don't know what I can do while I'm there, but I know I can do nothing if I'm not.

After entrusting the message to Jovial, he had climbed the hills back to Lornk's house, slipped through the gate and back inside. Lornk himself had caught him materializing in Olmlablaire. *"Isn't this a surprise. I leave the bag open, I don't expect the cat to climb back in. Now that you have, I suppose I'd better keep a closer watch on you."*

And so began the long wait. Ashel had spent the time locked in his room or in this library.

"Your mother has sent a massive force against me on the plains." Lornk took Ashel's remaining knight with his queen. "Seems unwise, with winter coming on."

"Many of my mother's decisions have been unwise." He let

a hint of scorn show as he placed his rook.

"You've exposed your king."

"Have I?"

Lornk guffawed softly, his eyes scanning the board. "Now I see what you've done." After a minute, he reached for his remaining knight, but a knock on the door froze his hand. An officer asked for a private word, and Lornk stood. "Another enjoyable game. I regret duty calls me away."

"We'll finish when you're free."

One corner of Lornk's mouth pulled upward. "None of us are ever free, Your Highness. Escort the prince back to his room," he ordered Ashel's guard.

† † †

Whether the warning had reached Drak, Wineyll couldn't say. Even if he had Heard her, neither she nor Vic knew what he would make of "Orlon—traitor," but Wineyll had said a longer message would be lost to wind and trees. Vic hoped Drak had understood and arrested the healer, but her stomach knotted in dread, reminding her that Orlon had also been dressed in farmer's clothes that morning. If he had beaten them here . . . "I'm going to see what that ghost knows," Vic said.

"He's the Relmlord's son?"

"Yes. Stay hidden here and I'll be back." She circled the orchards, traveling unseen through the surrounding woods, moving slowly through har vines, ramshackle branches, straining limbs of the underbrush. If she didn't know better, she might have thought the forests of the Lorn had the same power as Fembrosh, and they wanted to keep her from meeting him. Nothing would do that.

Coming back into the orchards, she flitted from tree to tree until she found the prisoners' detail. They were still digging, their trenches pointless when the only water that might run through them would freeze before it got here from the river.

"Earnk," she called to his mind alone. He didn't look up, but hesitated a moment before raising his pick for another swing. He hacked at the dirt a few more times, straightened and spoke to the guard, signaling toward the trees. The woman nodded.

"A guard doesn't come with you?" she asked as he circled to her hiding place.

"I'm a model prisoner." He looked at the thongs sewn around his ankles. "I couldn't get far anyway."

Her hands shaking, Vic swallowed the lump in her throat and reached up to touch his face. He grimaced but looked down at her, his cheeks yellowed from old bruises, his temple blue with a new one. Last she heard, Earnk Korng was the chief interrogator of Olmlablaire. "I thought you were dead," she whispered. "In Traine, I thought he'd killed you. Later—"

"Later we both became infamous among our enemies." Taking her hand, he looked at her fingers, touched them briefly with his other hand, released them. Then he rolled his head back and blinked at the single cloud blowing across the valley. Vic had forgotten his eyes, the depth of their blue, the black eyelashes and the golden eyebrows. She swallowed again, her skin tingling from his touch.

"There's a spy with you," he said. "Father knows how many are in your company and he knows the princess is with you. You must be very careful."

She brushed the information aside and spoke from her heart. "What happened to you?"

Looking away, he swore softly. "Your prince is alive." She blinked to dam tears she didn't want him to see. His voice hardened like the ice on the roots beneath their feet. "I've heard he's kept in the palace now, treated as an honored guest."

The tears spilled. "And Geram?"

"I don't know. He was dying last I heard."

Gasping for fresh air, she scrubbed her cheeks. Geram was dying, probably dead. She was too late to save him—told as much by one she'd never tried to save. "And you," she whispered hoarsely, "how did you end up"—she waved at him, at the others—"here?"

He smiled that rueful way that used to make her cry at night. "He forgave me, and I did everything he asked of me."

Ears pricking, she stepped back. "Is this a trick?"

"No." He glanced over at the guard scanning the trees. "I'm sorry, Vic." Wrapping his arms around her, he stroked the back of her head with one hand—the same caress Lornk had used to calm her those first nights in Traine. Her ears and fingertips pulsing with blood, she pulled away. "I'm sorry," he stammered again and stumbled back to the others.

She watched him get his pick and start working again. A little man in the crew angled his eyes toward the woods and asked something, but Earnk shook his head, mouth closed and eyes down. The guard shouted at them, thumping Earnk on the shoulder. Wincing, Vic ducked out of the orchard and back into the forest. Her head reeled from the sight and touch of him. Their brief, painful courtship had fallen through the cracks of memory, but as she stumbled back up the valley, recollections swarmed around her. The books he brought her. His irritation when she scolded him. His enthusiasm over each step she'd made, settling into that household. Breathing hard, she scanned the mountain peaks around her. How much power would it take for her to leave? To fly off somewhere and forget all this had ever happened. To fly home. Would Martha or Father recognize her? Could she take up the sash again and walk from town to village, teaching, guiding, delivering mail? Could she forget she'd left people she cared for in the hands of a man she hated? Strapped to her calf, the answer waited, wrapped in velvet, thirsting for blood. Reaching into her boot, she felt that metal ringing for revenge, and her breathing steadied. She came here for a purpose; Earnk's status as prisoner or prince didn't matter. What Earnk thought of her now didn't matter either. Her shoulders straightened, her feet rose again off the ground, and she bolted for the upper valley.

As she and Wineyll walked the last half mile to Olmlablaire, Vic observed the number of guards at the gate and on the walls. Only four men walked the parapets; three women stood before the thick iron bars of the portcullis—a light roster if Lornk expected an assault. At the gate, a stocky guard asked what they wanted. She shrugged at Wineyll's request for work and passed them through with directions to ask at the kitchens. Inside the courtyard, Vic noted the placement of the arrow slots—invisible from the other side—and the additional twelve troopers manning them. Once through the gates, the company would have twenty yards of open space to cross. Snowdrifts heaped against five dry fountains; shoveled paths a yard wide led from the gate to two doorways. The statues among the fountains might offer some cover, but they'd have to slog through deep snow or run down tight channels to the main entrance—a massive stone port, polished to a mica shine beneath a façade of weaving vines and peeping animal eyes. Four troopers guarded that entrance with crossbows. No one stood before the pair of humble wood doors standing open to the east, near the junction of the mountain's granite and the manmade wall, a half-frozen waterfall cascading beyond that.

The usual noises of a busy kitchen clanged out, and Vic and Wineyll followed the trail leading there. They had hardly crossed the threshold when a slender woman greeted them. "Looking for work are you? Well, you couldn't have come at a better time. There's an officer's banquet today." She pushed a basket covered with warm towels into Wineyll's hands, and another into Vic's. "My name is Vendrael. Follow me." She led them around the preparation table, through the jostling cooks, and out into a hallway. Hollow voices echoed, a wordless sound of a crowd far away. Vic's stomach muscles clenched as she followed the woman. She flexed her fingers around the basket and shook her shoulders out of their hunch. Vendrael passed through a door of polished cerrenil planks. Vic took a breath and held it, then shouldered the door aside, imagining his smugness melting into surprise, imagining him sitting frozen to his chair by her will as she crammed the biscuits down his throat.

The room was empty. A cream-colored linen cloth covered a table long enough for twenty. Lanterns hung from the ceiling and burned in stone sconces, illuminating a fine wool carpet woven with another battle between wizards and Kragnashians. The One indeed. Vic laughed softly, thinking, *if they're right, we know who wins this battle, don't we? I still have to kill a wizard a thousand years ago.*

"Something funny?" Vendrael asked, lips curling.

Vic shook her head like an imbecile, while Wineyll made excuses. "My sister's prone to fits—but nothing serious. Where should we put the bread?"

Vendrael angled her head at a banquet table. "On the end there. You can fetch the rest of the food from the kitchen as the cook prepares it. I'll leave you to your work."

Vic pilfered some bread after the door swung closed behind the woman. "We all right?" she asked, handing Wineyll a roll.

The girl nodded. "So far so good."

"Earnk said Ashel's here in the palace; somebody's delivering his meals."

The minstrel nodded, eyes shining. "I'll find him."

They ferried dishes from the kitchen, Wineyll hunting through minds until she flashed Vic a smile. After they dropped off a pair of covered platters, Wineyll grabbed Vic's hand and they ran down a twisting hallway, the passage walls becoming rough and narrow. A winding stairway landed at a wide hallway, the glassy floor divided by a wool runner. Hearing voices, they dashed up another flight. Here, the ceiling lower, the weight of the mountain forced Vic's neck into her shoulders. Weak light flickered from sconces, illuminating a threadbare runner.

They reached a junction where the hallway teed off, one branch bending sharply, the other heading straight. A door opened in the straight hallway; mandolin chords drifted out, then died as the door clicked shut. Vic and Wineyll ducked around the sharp bend, and a moment later, a tall man, his fingers stained with healers' herbs, walked past. Gathering her skirt, Vic darted across the junction to look down the straight hall.

A single hooded guard leaned against a doorway, humming. From the rhythm of the guard's toneless wheezes, she recognized the song Ashel had written for Elesendar's Landing. Biting her lip, she rolled back against the wall, pressed her hands against the rock to steady them. His song, written for her, he'd said, swelled in her mind into the thousands of voices singing it the night Sashal had died. She'd found Ashel. To stay was foolhardy; they should leave now and go back to the farmhouse. Lornk knew they were in Relm. He might even know she was in his palace. But Vic's heart still lurched with the rhythm set off by Earnk's unexpected touch. "Help me get down this hallway unseen, then go back to the kitchen," she ordered Wineyll.

"But—"

"It'll look suspicious if we're both missing for long. Do it."

The minstrel's lips pouted, but she nodded. "You can go."

Skirt twisted tightly against her thighs, stomach clenched, Vic zipped down the hall while the guard stared at the floor and hummed. Breaking the lock and slipping inside, she shut the door before he could even wonder at the sudden draft behind him.

Ashel stared at her, a mandolin held loosely in one hand. "How?" he stammered, turning with the instrument between the bed and the chairs, finally leaving it on the table as he took a step toward her. "How did you get in?"

She whispered his name, smiling through the tears in her nose. Earnk had reminded her of all the evils in her life; Ashel made her think of Fembrosh and the Wind, skipping stones and chess pieces. She covered her mouth so she wouldn't laugh out loud. "I'm giddy," she said.

"Vic." He sat heavily on the bed, his eyes mournful. "How did you find me?"

"I heard you were held in the palace." Her gaze fell on scraped and bloody fingertips, mottled skin, and her smile melted. "What happened to your hands?"

Grimacing, he curled them into fists behind his back. "I should have left my harp at home. It didn't do me much good, and I lost it."

Stepping closer, she pushed his hair off his forehead. His cheeks hollow, he looked thin and weary. "What did he do to you?"

"You shouldn't have come." He grasped her wrists and pushed them down. "The Relmlord has been waiting for you."

"I know. I think Orlon must have betrayed us."

His head jerked up. "Orlon? Well, I suppose so. A lot has happened. Geram—"

"I heard he was dying?"

"He was very ill, nearly passed into the trees, but Lornk had him submerged in slotaen to . . . keep him on the path."

"Why?" Even with Lornk's wealth, that seemed an unlikely extravagance.

"A lot has happened," he repeated. Shutting his eyes, he took a breath, gazed at her again, his irises wells of darkness.

"I know now how he can . . . infect you. I'm sorry I didn't understand before."

Her arms urging toward him, she hugged herself instead. "What did he do?"

Grimly, he chuckled. "Showed me my limits."

A sob loosened in her chest, and her shoulders began to shake. Rising, he drew her into an embrace, and the wail that had been growing since she saw Earnk bled into the fabric of his tunic.

Apologies whispered against her hair. "I'm sorry. Sorry I had no patience, sorry I blamed you."

She looked up into glimmering dark eyes and felt a tug toward him, toward a thing they shared now. Instinct drove her to touch her lips to his. His arms lifted her, their mouths opened into a full kiss, and the warmth she'd felt in the rosen grove melted over her, enlivening every hair, every particle of blood and muscle and bone. Life itself flowed into her, easing the pain in her head, calming the churn of nausea that had lived in her belly since she took the Waters of the Dead.

He hoisted her higher, asked with a smile, "What are you doing, Captain?"

She giggled and nipped at his lips. "It's Marshall now, Your Highness. And I'm not sure, but it feels *good*."

He laughed softly. Lips and tongues tasted cheeks and necks, each brush of skin on skin a jolt of urgency. *I have unfinished business,* she'd said to Silla and Maynon, but here, now, in Ashel's arms, she wanted life with him far more than she had ever wanted Lornk's death. A protest—you don't love him, you can't love him—flitted through her mind. Love or not, it's close enough, she answered herself, kissing him hungrily.

He inhaled sharply, sank onto the mattress, drawing her with him. "We don't have to declare," he mumbled, his lips exploring below her collarbone.

She palmed his cheeks, made him look at her. "Yes, we do." He beamed, and she pulled that smile into her own.

"This is a familiar scene." Lornk's voice froze the air. Her skin pebbled with cold, Vic rolled off the bed and faced the Relmlord, standing in the doorway. Ashel wrapped his arms across her chest, shielding her. "I'm glad to see my property still beautifully intact."

"You don't own her," Ashel snarled.

Lornk laughed and entered, a guard on his heels. "Come, my dear—let's see this power the Kragnashians sold you. Orlon arrived an hour before you and told me all about the spectacle you showed the nomads."

"If you know about that," she said, "you should be terrified."

"Oh, no." He chuckled. "I'm thrilled to see what you've become. Come"—he stretched fingers out to her—"let me see you now."

"Let me go," she said to Ashel, fumbling at his arms. Her skin was burning, but her vision was clear as crystal. "Let me go," she repeated. Ashel's hold tightened and Lornk's grin spread.

"You heard her, Your Highness. She knows what she is."

She looked up Ashel. "I do know," she said aloud. "Let me go."

His gaze locked on the Relmlord, his muscles bulged once against her shoulders before his hands dropped to his sides.

"Ah," Lornk breathed. "You're not a girl anymore, are you?"

Her fingers trembling, she took Lornk's outstretched hand. Her chest ached, as if her heart had stopped. *His* dagger quivered against her calf. Ashel drew in a breath. Lornk's fingers curled into a fist, locking her hand to his. As she stepped closer and his scent filled her, a shiver rippled from shoulders to knees. "Do you crave me?" he teased.

Dropping her head, she rammed her shoulder into his gut, pulling him into the blow with his own grip, straightening to throw him. Growling, he twisted off her shoulder and used his momentum to wrench her wrist behind her back. Ashel grabbed his arm, wrestling his hand away from her neck, the three of them groaning together for a moment before the guard slammed into them and everyone tumbled over the footboard of the bed. As the men grappled with each other, Vic slipped free. In a flash, she flew out the door.

She sped down the hall and around the corner, tore down the stairwell, froze at the first landing. Ashel. Panting, she looked up the steps winding back toward Lornk. Ashel's raw, red fingers haunted her. *He showed me my limits.* And Lornk knew what she was, wasn't afraid. Her heart thudded, breath came in wheezes. *Do you crave me?* Her fingers tingled where he'd touched them, arm hairs frizzed with electricity. Ashel. *Do you crave me?* She heard the ticking of the floor clock in his palazzo, felt the click and catch of the gears. *I want your devotion.*

"He won't hurt him," she whispered. "Not now. Not now he knows what I can do." She needed time, another day, an army at her back before she faced him again. You'll come back, you'll save him, she promised herself as she raced downstairs.

She met Wineyll running up. "They know!" the girl panted. "That woman, Vendrael, she's a Listener. I'm sorry I didn't Hear it—"

Shouts echoed toward them. "Come on," Vic ordered, grabbing the girl's hand. She dragged her into a sprint when they reached the first floor. Somewhere, a klaxon sounded. As they wheeled into the kitchen, guards were running in from the courtyard, shoving aside cooks and scullions. Vic turned back into the corridor, flying now and dragging Wineyll behind her, turning right at each bend, knocking down anyone who stumbled across their path. Abruptly the hallway widened into a tunnel, and well-dressed people leapt for arched doorways as she and Wineyll flew by. Ahead, a great hall filled with troopers.

"Hang on," Vic warned, then flew down the corridor and up over the heads of the crowd. Weapons clattered on the floor. A woman screamed. Vic circled the ceiling. Her eyes shut, Wineyll chewed on a wail.

"Shoot them down!" Lornk cried from the middle of a broad staircase, then ran for the wide hallway opposite. Vic swooped across the ceiling; the first volley pattered against the stone. Wineyll peeked out, mewling another half-stifled scream. Her grip tightening around the girl's wrist, Vic shot toward the tunnel leading out, guards diving out of her way like grain before the wind. Lornk stood beneath the arching stone, arms spread wide. Vic swerved, but Wineyll's body swung toward him. The minstrel shrieked and Lornk sprang, tackling her in the thighs. The impact jolted through Vic's arm; she lost her grip on Wineyll and tumbled against the wall. Dazed, they all lay still for a moment, Lornk on top of the minstrel, her breath wheezing painfully. As Vic righted herself, her eyes crossed Lornk's. The admiration in his smile unnerved her.

Around the hall, guards leapt to their feet and ran toward her. More footsteps echoed from ahead. She scrambled back into the air. Shouts and curses boomed behind her. Ahead, a solid beam of iron barred the exterior doors. Four men guarded them, bows drawn. Vic stopped midair and held up her hands in surrender. The heat of Lornk's touch raged in her gut, but she held it in, let it build. Troopers dashing from the great hall called for her to hold. Raising a wall of air around herself, she pushed all the power the Kragnashians had given her at the beam. The metal groaned, and the doors exploded outward, door guards sailing with them. Arrows whizzing at her back, Vic shot out the opening and into the sun.

CHAPTER 27

FIRE WATER STONE

Like dawn on a bad dream, she had finally come. The sunrise of her hair, the timbre of her voice, the scent, the taste of her had fired Ashel's blood. He could not let Lornk have that brightness, to dim it into the pale shadow Geram had known in the Kiareinoll. Roaring out from beneath the tumble of bodies on the bed, he ran after her.

To his left, a copper-colored braid whipped around a corner. "Wrong way," he shouted, but then he'd never followed that hallway—the war room and the library lay in another direction. Cursing the touch of her skin still tingling along his arms, he dashed after her. Probably even Geram couldn't guess how deeply he loved this woman and how much he didn't want to. Damn—how could anyone so small run so fast? Turning the corner, he stopped at a convergence of hallways without a hint of her. Behind him, Lornk shouted at the guard in Betheljin and switched to Relman midsentence. Over the blood pounding in his ears, Ashel heard himself chuckle.

He turned left and ran faster when he caught a whiff of snow and dust, like the scents in her hair. *She said yes! And now she's left me.* He ran down deserted halls, the lamps less frequent, the light dimmer, and he wondered if she'd been a vision he conjured to jolt himself out of indolence. But his lips whispered no. The taste of her—that had been real. His feet stumbled, and he stopped amid deep shadows and dust. Something about her had changed. She'd kissed him, and he'd felt a tingle of energy pass between them unlike anything he'd ever known. He dared not hope it was love, but she'd kissed him and agreed to wed him. She'd done that, just now, she'd said yes! Love or not, that was something.

She'd also left him, and he'd lost her. "Go back," he muttered, but his feet ran toward squares of sunlight punctuating the gloom ahead.

A pair of gauze-covered doors framed sections of glass, their light illuminating footprints, some heavily dusted, others fresh. The balcony outside would have to be several levels above the courtyard, but it might give access to a ledge that in turn might offer a route down the mountain face to the valley. Looking hopelessly back down the hallway, he flexed the doorknob and went out.

Smelling of resin and silence, cold flashed through his doublet, crimping muscles already tensed with her touch, but he stood still for a moment and held the ice in his lungs, letting it cool his heart. A waist-high buttress of stone surrounded the balcony, natural jags and fissures blending it into the mountain face. A few leafless potted trees and a small, carved table with delicate filigreed chairs stood alone in the cold. Ashel whistled softly at the chairs, one artist's admiration for another's artistry. A movement in the corner drew his gaze off the table, startling it into focus on the figure facing him.

"You." Ashel slumped back against the door, resignation shaking his knees.

Orlon shut his mouth and narrowed his eyes before speaking. "Your Highness. I'm glad you're well."

Ashel thought of sails and sea salt. A bitter wind ruffled his collar. "Geram isn't."

Shaking his head, Orlon leaned against the wall. "I'm truly sorry."

The wind steals a flag from his grasp. A girl's tears glisten on his thumbs. The music of the waves, and the empty silences where his own memories used to lay. A roar and a rush of wind blurred into more memories not his own, more darkness where his thoughts used to lie. When Ashel's senses returned, he had Orlon pinned against the buttress. The healer's eyes bulged at the dagger Ashel held against his throat. Another of Geram's memories: how to disarm an enemy and kill him with his own weapon.

"I've dreamed another's nightmares," Ashel rasped in a voice like icicles against the eaves. Some things had to be said aloud, or shouldn't be said at all. Orlon began to choke. "I've walked the edge of madness—"

A klaxon sounding, shouts echoed. If they were shouting about her, they hadn't caught her.

The fear drained from Orlon's eyes, but horror froze his mouth in a scowl. "If you still love her," he said aloud, in Relman, "you walk a sharper knife than madness."

The wind gusted ice, and Ashel's spine stiffened. "Was it you?" he grated. "Did you kill my father?"

Teeth clenched, Orlon shook his head. "No."

Rage tightened his grip around the hilt of the dagger. Orlon shut his eyes, and the dagger pinched into his flesh, drawing a line of blood. The shouts from below rose to a strident pitch. A heavy bang summoned a screech and a crash, tearing their gaze downward. The polished granite doors lay in the snow, and a red-gold figure flashed over the courtyard walls toward the valley. Awestruck, Ashel stood, his fingers slack. The dagger dropped into the snow.

"The Kragnashians did that to her," Orlon said, eyeing the hilt jutting out of a drift.

Victoria of Ourtown, legendary heroine of the Wizards' Council. Ashel remembered laughing with Vic over the coincidence of her namesake, then a thought colder than the frigid air seized his heart: she's forsaken me.

Orlon dove for the dagger. Ashel snatched it up, stabbing into the other man's lunge. A hesitation, a plunge through flesh, a choke and a gurgle. Vic sped away, shrinking into the distance until she vanished. Orlon coughed, and a final rattle bled into the snow. Desolation cramping his chest, Ashel looked over the sides of the balcony. Sheer cliff walls offered no escape. He sank into a chair, staring down the valley.

> "You should be terrified."
> "Oh no." He chuckles, his eyes hungry. "I'm thrilled to see what you've become."

She'd left him, but could he blame her? If that hunger had been aimed at him, wouldn't he have fled too? She'd never break free of Lornk without help. He scanned the cliff face once more. Nooks and clefts offered a way down for a daring climber, but should he make it, what help could he give outside the palace? "She'll come back," he promised Orlon's corpse. Leaving the dagger lodged in the healer's chest, he went inside, back to his room.

† † †

Once when Geram was very young, hardly tall enough to see over the tables in his aunt's tavern, he had gone with his uncle to fish and, curious about a silver flash beneath the surface, had toppled over the gunwale into the sea. As he sank, the sun dimpled a school of ellesfish in silvered hues of blue and pink. Water swished through his clothes and the fins of fish who scattered and converged around him, and the cold crept through his hair like the fingers of his mother.

He lived now in that memory, the only one Ashel hadn't smudged. The only place he didn't hear harps or drums, rattling dice or furied politicking. No bassoons, no guitars, no whining fiddles. No teasing, no shouting, no disapproval. The groan of his uncle's boat sounded a bit like a droning pipe, but the water muffled the creaking, and the fish arched toward him, a thousand bodies approaching as one welcoming friend. He reached toward them with small hands, the sleeves of his tunic billowing over his wrists. His aunt's stitches swam around the cuffs, surrounding them with little sea bursts, sunclouds, merrywings. Uncle Arnan would be coming for him, but Geram wished he wouldn't. The fish reminded him of Arnan, the needlework of Aunt Celina. But if his uncle dove after him, his memories of their gentle warmth would be sullied by the cold passions of Ashel's family.

When he felt the tug toward the surface, he sucked water into his lungs, clawed at the hand on his collar, kicked, screamed. Still, he slid over the gunwales onto the deck and lay coughing for air next to a net of fish coughing for water. Each gasp hoarsened into a sob, and darkness swathed the deck, stilling it, softening it, resolving it into a mattress beneath weak elbows. Voices spoke aloud in a language he did not know. Someone, not him, was crying, trying to be quiet about it. It was still dark. He smelled sunny slotaen and stale death. The silence of the sea leaked from his ears, and he finally began to Hear.

"What a rare and precious thing you are." Lornk Korng's voice caressed someone. Geram shivered, blinked. He raised a hand toward his face.

"Don't." A girl, one he could not Hear, wrapped moist

fingers around his wrist. Her voice was thick, slow, toned, even in mindspeech.

"Do you remember where you are, what you've done?" Lornk shouted.

"I'm not deaf." Longing for the peace he'd known under the water, he remembered everything.

The Relmlord chuckled like a man trying not to roar. "No, my friend, you could never be that." Trellerend cleared his throat loudly. "Your warden disapproves of my witticism," Lornk said. Trellerend grunted. The girl's hand still held Geram's, squeezing so tightly it hurt.

He felt the slotaen evaporate off his skin, the rub of linens wrapped around him, and wondered how long he'd been here, bound to this bed by an unwillingness to live with a duality only death could sever. Ashel knew he was awake, was trying to ignore it as guards escorted him down to the palace cellar. Geram's throat tightened. He could see stairwell lamps flickering along Ashel's route, but he couldn't see the people standing next to him. "I don't know what use I am to you now," he said.

"Nonsense. They say the blind have better Hearing than the rest of us. You should treasure this as a gift!"

"Stop it!" The girl's voice cracked like a whip, and the Relmlord grunted in surprise.

Then he chuckled again, low and angrily. "Unwise, my dear, to sting unless you have venom in it."

"There's plenty of that."

"Not enough to keep you from getting squashed," Lornk replied. Geram felt the Relmlord's eyes return to him. "I kept you alive so you might help me with the task ahead."

He straightened his shoulders. "I won't help you."

"You might, when you know my purpose, Lieutenant. I'm going to save the world." The girl squeaked in pain as her weight left the bed. "Trellerend, get him dressed and send him up to the house. If he won't help me, perhaps this girl will."

Marking Vic's flight to the farmhouse, clouds rolled over the valley from the south. Her temples pulsed against skin tight as leather in the sun, and the farmyard crawling with Relman troopers didn't ease the pain. Swallowing deep breaths, she swooped to the roof of the barn, where she listened to the farmer describe his ordeal to a Relman officer. The squadron had been too late—the Lathans had left soon after midday.

Relieved, she flitted back to the woods and circled the yard, looking for Drak's signs. They'd headed away from the road, leaving her a gekko track—made with the first three fingers of the left hand for a few paces between trees. She traversed the trail, sweeping away any stray footprints. Clouds bunched over the valley, but she doubted snow would fall before Relmans found the tracks. She was surprised to find them not already marching up the slope.

After the first mile of sweeping, the snow began, and Vic moved straight along the company's path. Dizzied by the surging behind her eyes, she bumped into one tree and then another before she returned to the power of her feet. Flakes sifted slowly through the leaves and branches, the woods cold and dark. Alert for Relmans, she stumbled upward, switchbacking on the steep surfaces, heading straight when the grade leveled. A scratch in bark, a pile of rocks, arrangements of twigs pointed her way. As she came across these signs, she destroyed them, cursing Drak for leaving a way for the Relmans to find them, blessing him for having the confidence she'd be able to follow.

As the mountain angled higher, she saw more signs of the company. Here someone had fallen. Here they'd stopped to rest. Heavy, wet gems the size of her thumb sifted over the trail, easing the throbbing in her temples. With a deep breath of cold air, she began flying again.

The ache returned almost immediately, but she fought it with blinks and soared past the tree line. Here, the wind swept the rocks clean, but snow whipped around her like sheets blowing in the laundry yard. At last she came to a lump of boulders jutting out of a granite slope, a wooden door hiding among the rocks. Her ears heard nothing but swirling snow, but the mindspeech behind the door battered the bones above her eyes. Gulping the bile in her throat, she knocked.

The door cracked open.

"It's me," she snapped.

A hand snaked out and pulled her inside. Heat and darkness washed over her as the door scraped back into its frame.

"Give her some air," someone said.

"Not likely in this gekko hole," grumbled Carl.

With a groan, Vic fluttered her eyes open and sat up. Faces rushed forward and back, slowly coming into focus. Bethniel knelt beside her; Drak's and Carl's faces peered from above. Marenye passed a damp cloth to the princess, Valion hovering behind her. "What happened?" Vic asked, waving the cloth away.

"This is Caileanne." Drak nodded to a stranger wrapping a scarf around her head. "She came about midmorning. When we heard Wineyll's warning, she led us up here."

Vic shook her head, eyes on the woman. "Who are you?"

"We call ourselves the antimilitia," she replied, throwing her cloak over her shoulders. "You'll have to move tomorrow, but you'll be safe here tonight."

"You can't leave in this storm," Marenye protested.

"I've left my child alone. I'll be all right. Rimma will come tomorrow."

In a whirl of snow and wind, the woman stepped outside. Pollard passed a steaming mug to Drak, who gave it to Vic. Harlolinde flared her nostrils. "Thank you." She raised the cup, then turned to business. "Orlon?"

"Missing since morning," Carl spat.

"Did you find my brother?"

Vic squeezed Bethniel's hand, regret cramping her chest. "He's well." Lornk won't hurt him, she assured herself again. "The Relmlord is holding him in the palace. Wineyll"—she answered their glances at the door—"is alive. The faster we move now, the more likely they will stay that way."

"How many of your people can we count on?" Vic asked.

Shortly after dawn, another antimilitiawoman had turned up at the grotto and led them down the valley to a small system of caves, screened by a thick copse of geilmors but only three leagues from Lordhome. Rimma seemed eager to show a martial discipline Vic found ridiculous, but fierceness refracted from her eyes, warning off those who might scoff at her.

"They're all cowards. They think you should wait until winter deepens and reinforcements can't come up from Re."

"Has he sent for them?" Drak asked.

The woman looked toward her eyebrows. "Not that we know of. He's doubled the guard on the gates, and the officers are all carrying swords now."

Collectively, the company swore. Vic swallowed. "Then he's desperate, if he's incurring that expense."

"But not desperate enough to order reinforcements?" Carl growled. "He's playing with us."

"He can get Caleisbahn mercenaries from Traine any time," Bethniel reminded them.

Rimma cast her eyes across the group, resting them on Vic. "They say you blew the doors off Olmlablaire. If you can do that, you should fear nothing."

"Vic can't fight the whole Lordhome guard herself," Bethniel snapped. "If we go in bashing the place apart, my brother will end up dead."

"You're sure there's no way in besides through the main entrance and kitchen doors?" Drak asked.

"We tried the ventilation shafts last summer, but only Mallach and I were small enough to make it. Ten of us tried, and they found only one of the others, stuck in a shaft." She shuddered. "The only way most of you could get in is through a door."

Vic tapped her fingers on her thigh as the company settled into a stumped quiet. This was her forte—doing what couldn't be done. She was the Blade. She tickled her enemy's noses and was gone before they scratched. But instead of battle plans, her head filled with the stroke of Earnk's hand down her hair, the pressure of Ashel's arms across her collarbone, the ignition of Lornk's fingers wrapping around hers, the darkness that touch left in her.

"If the only way in is through the front door, let's go," Carl said. "Tonight. Before they can gather their courage."

"If the guards are doubled," Drak disagreed, "we should wait a few days, let them get tired out, let them get sloppy. Tonight they're expecting us."

"We're outnumbered three to one! Will sloppy make that much difference?"

"The longer we wait, the more time he has to assemble mercenaries from Traine."

As they argued, another voice echoed, one tight with controlled panic and need. Vic brushed the memory away, trying to focus on the command conference, trying to figure out their best course. But the other voice insisted she listen, insisted he be Heard, nagged until she held up her hand and asked them all to be quiet.

Vic, he said, *if you're coming, come tonight.*

Elesendar, Geram. His voice shrank the fog left by the other three men waiting for her in Lordhome. Was he dead that she could Hear him so well, know him so well?

They're expecting you, but come. It will be your only chance.

Her head jerked as he left it, empty, blank, and then in washed the calculations of the Blade. Carl and Valion exchanged grins as she leapt to her feet. Signaling Rimma to sit, Vic picked up a stick and drew a diagram of the courtyard outside and the great hall inside. "Our first priority is to secure the Device."

CHAPTER 28

WIZARD

Geram had always been able to talk to people over distances, especially those he knew well. A single word had always been enough. He'd never had a conversation before. Not that it would do any good. He felt like he'd just called Vic to her death.

A draft turned his head toward the door. The Relmlord entered, and Geram faced the fire, wrapping his fingers around the grooved arms of the chair.

"My friend." Clothing crinkled. Lornk smelled of mud and exotic spices. "I've arranged a place for you in Traine."

Goose bumps prickled down Geram's arms. Blinking, he wondered what his eyes looked like, with the corneas scratched away.

"Oh, you're worried no one will want you. But what's happened is an asset, I assure you. Naturally I'd prefer you stay on with me."

"I won't help you." He kept his voice low.

"The girl will."

Geram shrugged. "If you're so sure, why do you need me?"

"Because you know *her*," Lornk growled. "And you know she is mine." He leaned closer, his breath on Geram's neck. "She fears me, because she knows what she is. Elekia thinks

405

she forged the Blade, but she forgets that Kara was mine first. She'll be mine again, sooner or later. It will be much less painful for everyone if you made it sooner."

"I won't help you."

"Hmm. Well, perhaps our young minstrel can. You must tell her what you did to the prince, and also how you restored him." His clothing swishing, he stood, padded across the floor. The latch click echoed in the quiet.

Don't let her do it, Geram.

Ashel, you Heard that?

I've nothing to do down here but Listen to you. I Heard you speaking with Vic as well. Tell her not to come. Send her away. I don't think she can win.

Why?

Wineyll's loyalties aren't with Latha, they're with me. If Vic comes, Wineyll will do what Lornk wants.

After she's seen what he did to us?

For a while, he Heard nothing coherent from Ashel, but he felt the other man's fingers rake through his hair. Ashel's small candle flickered against the darkness of his own vision. He felt the stone bench beneath Ashel's thighs as he slumped into the upholstery of his own chair. His fire crackled. Ashel's candle sputtered. *Wineyll may find a way to avoid our problem,* Ashel said finally. *Technically, she's not the best musician in the Guild. But she can make people feel her music.* One of Ashel's memories flashed in Geram's mind, of a room full of troopers and craftspeople weeping as Wineyll played. *I don't think Vic has a chance,* Ashel finished.

He felt the door draft again. Wineyll and a guard entered, the girl rushing to take his hand.

"It's me. How are you?"

"Whatever he asks of you, you cannot do it."

She sniffed. "Of course not."

"Then you haven't seen Ashel."

Her hair rustled against her shoulders. "No. I know they're holding him in a cell in the bowels of this place, not down in the tunnel with the other prisoners. We'll have to get a message to the marshall"—her voice tightened—"that they've moved him."

"Don't blame her, Wineyll."

"What makes you think I do?"

An answer too quick for truth. "What makes you think you'll stand up to the Relmlord?"

She pulled her hand away. "I am a Lathan, even if I'm not a trooper."

"Korng burned Ashel's hands."

She gasped.

"He almost lost the use of his fingers. And that was for something much less important, almost trivial. Do you understand me?"

Silence, then, "Yes."

From Ashel's memories, he imagined what she looked like, sitting across from him. A small, fair-skinned, dark-haired girl with large blue-green eyes. Daughter of one of Latha's most renowned master minstrels. A master herself at stagecraft. Always cheerful, always a quick study. He smelled soap wafting from damp hair and the drerwood fumes from clothes recently unpacked. Then he felt the vibration of her chair as she shuddered.

"When did you"—she paused, and he imagined her eyes shying away from his—"do that to yourself?"

To cover a grimace, he faced away from her. "What happened between Ashel and me was an accident. I didn't mean to do it. It almost drove both of us mad."

"How—"

He reached across the small table and snatched her hand.

"Don't ask. You don't want to know. You don't want to do this—not just for what it will mean for Latha, for the war, for the wars that could follow if Relm conquers us, but you cannot do it for yourself. You've spent as much time with Vic as I have—but you've probably never really been inside her head." He thought of Vic, sitting atop that pile of brass gears, desperately searching for a hidden key. "What's in there, you don't want to know that closely."

"She's ruthless—"

"She's . . ." What was she? Angry, arrogant, cunning—he tried to remember all the adjectives he'd used in his reports to Command.

> *"Hey, Shrink." A nut bounces off his head, and Vic chuckles. "Tell them I'm the most incredible shot you've ever seen."*
>
> *"You're not." Grinning, he pens another sentence into his report.*
>
> *"The best fighter."*
>
> *"Wrong again."*
>
> *"Ha. How'd I get to be captain of the Dagger then?"*
>
> *He laughs. "Because you're the sharpest."*
>
> *"Right. Make sure they know that."*
>
> *"They do."*

But what did that mean, the sharpest? The smartest, the most dangerous? Yes. He held a deep breath before continuing, "I've gotten about as close as anybody to knowing who Vic the Blade is, and what I know frightens me. Don't get wrapped up in her anger. Don't become party to her memories."

She snorted softly. "She can't remember anything worse than what I can."

Elesendar. "Has he hurt you?"

The fire cracked, and one of the logs collapsed, the embers settling into a steady chorus of small snaps and pops. Geram had never been able to Hear people's emotions, but Wineyll's shame bled into him now. "No," she said aloud, her voice choked. "That hasn't hurt."

In the storeroom below, Ashel surged to his feet and slammed his fist against the door, seething. Buffering his own rage, Geram clasped her hand. "In Alna, we believe love is a *choice*. And rape is rape, even when it feels like seduction."

"I know." She pulled her hand out of his, dress rustling as she stood. "But I'm still an inlander. The wisdom of sailors and courtesans won't help me." The volume of her voice fell as she stepped toward the door. "Nothing will."

Elesendar help us, Ashel said when she'd gone. *Warn Vic not to come.*

Geram reached out and Listened to what she planned to do. *It's too late,* he told Ashel. *They're moving.*

† † †

"You up to this?" Drak asked, catching Vic rubbing her temples.

She felt as worn as a bowstring after a battle. But, thrusting her hands into her pockets, she nodded. "Do I have a choice?"

Bethniel pressed her shoulder and offered her hand. "Squeeze as hard as you need to," she said. Thanking her, Vic raised the raft. Rimma had led them to a woodcutters' camp, where Vic had assembled logs into a floating barge that would serve as transport and shield. The breath of a hundred troopers misted around the vessel as it nudged forward over a landscape black with shadows and white with frozen waves. A hooter called. Vic gulped at the cold, then let go of the princess's hand to dig her fingernails into the bark instead.

When they reached the edge of the woods, Vic's heart leapt at the sight of a fortress defended. The interior of the courtyard dark as pitch, light from lanterns along the top of Lordhome's walls spilled across the open field, long ovals broken by the shadows of passing guards. The gate cast hatches across the road, broken by another pair of silhouettes. Glancing back, Vic saw wide eyes and narrow, fear and readiness. None of these people had assaulted a stronghold. Lathan troopers fought among trees and open land. Shutting her eyes and bowing her head, she thought of the star—the ship—hanging above the planet, keeping watch until they could go home. Preserving itself until humanity found again the means to reach it and relearn its secrets. How far the humans of Knownearth had drifted from the Oreseeker's goal, but how much closer to home they had come? For the people behind her, and those ahead, *this* was home. One worth fighting for, worth dying for. "Elesendar," she prayed aloud, "guard our backs and guide our hands. Get your teams ready."

Arrows rattled out of quivers, bowstrings thrummed soft and low. The raft bobbed as the archers lined the edges and set their feet. Behind them, another rank of troopers prepared to light the sulfa. Vic held up her hand.

"We're ready," Bethniel whispered.

The raft hurtled across the field, blowing Relman guards off the parapets. Lathan bowstrings thwanged, cutting short the first Relman warnings. Relman arrows thunked into the wood. A Lathan jerked back, a bolt in her eye. The broken granite doors had been wedged into the main entrance. Vic circled the courtyard, and the next Lathan volley aimed for the shadows running on the battlements. Sulfa grenades bounced into the courtyard, exploding among screams. An alarm began to ring. Shouting, Relman troopers scrambled out of the kitchen. Arrows and bolts flew at the company like sea spray. Their vessel bounced like a skiff as the Lathan archers jostled for firing positions. Vic let them fire once more, then swung toward the blocked entrance. Carl ordered the second volley of sulfa lit, and as the raft sailed past the doors, a dozen grenades struck the stone, exploding in the raft's wake.

"It's no good," Valion cried, pointing back at the doors, still stuck in the doorway.

"Everyone down!" Vic yelled. Outracing Relman arrows, the raft plunged toward the stone. Below, Relmans screamed warnings. The massive logs slammed against the doors, the impact throwing everyone backward. Relman troopers leapt aboard; the raft rolled and bucked.

"Marshall," Drak yelled. "Get us in or set us down!"

In the raft, arms grappled, teeth and knives rent the air. Carl kicked a Relman off the raft. Valion chopped at the hand of another. Across the snow, more Relmans swarmed at them. "Hang on!" Vic shouted, bracing herself as she swung them away from doors. The raft rammed the statue in the middle of the yard, knocking it from its base, and a pair of struggling troopers sailed off the edge into the fountain below. Vic held her breath, aimed the logs back to the doors, and poured all the strength she had into the wood. The impact flung people off their feet. Elbows jabbed into guts, heads cracked against bark. Stone screeching, they burst inside.

The raft skidded through the tunnel into the great hall, finally stopping beneath the massive chandelier. Calling his squad together, Carl scrambled over the wood and ran toward the stairs. Drak rolled out with a score of troopers and headed for the kitchens. Vic led the rest back down the tunnel to the entrance. Relmans thronged inside to meet them. Breaking the first wave, she threw their bodies onto the following ranks. The Lathan troopers followed with arrows and blades, killing those on the ground. Arrows whistling toward them, Valion tackled

Vic, landing on top of her, and a wet heat melted into her tunic. Relman crossbows winched for a second volley; daggers and stoneknives rained in both directions. Vic pushed out from beneath Valion, picked up the doors, and jammed them back into the doorway.

The sudden quiet stilled their panting for a moment. Gently, Vic rolled Valion onto his back and brushed black hair off his forehead. His gaze already glassy, blood spilled from a corner of his mouth. Closing his eyes, Vic asked how many were left.

"Carl had two dozen, Drak twenty. We're two score," Rimma replied.

Over thirty dead in the first assault. She stood. If her head hurt, she couldn't feel it. "Come on," she said. "Let's find the Relmlord."

Only the flickering of the candle had measured time while Ashel sat alone in a storeroom. Geram had Listened to Vic all day, and through him, Ashel Heard her faintly. When the door finally opened for a trio of guards, he knew the company waited at the edge of the clearing, and he wondered if the ache behind his temples belonged to Vic or himself. *Leave her alone, Geram*, he said. *It's out of our hands now.*

Lornk waited in a room smelling of grain and spices, but holding only a rough-hewn table and a few chairs. Beside the Relmlord lay a broad cleaver. Ashel stopped, his throat knotted, his right hand balling into a fist.

"We have little time," Lornk said. "The others are on their way down."

Ashel swallowed a breath. "Why—"

"I want you to know . . ." The Relmlord walked toward them. Ashel's foot inched backward, but the guards blocked the door. He locked his knees straight. "I wish things could have been different."

Ashel eyed the cleaver, then the man. A day's worth of beard stubbled Lornk's cheeks; faint lines of wisdom creased the corners round his eyes. The insanity of it all tickled the back of Ashel's throat, tugging up one corner of his mouth. "So do I," he agreed. "This is senseless." Hands itching suddenly, he shook his head. "What in the Shrine can you gain by this?" Held prisoner in his belly, laughter roared with ire.

Lornk grinned. "I haven't done anything yet. Perhaps I won't have to."

Ashel moved toward the wide-armed chair waiting at the end of the room, guards shadowing him. He felt stunned, euphoric with certainty. Geram, occupied with negotiating stairs, didn't feel it yet. A fey chuckle slipped past his teeth as Ashel lowered himself into the chair and fixed his eyes on the cleaver. The blade sucked in the torchlight, waiting for blood. "Tell me I truly am your son," he said, "if you really want to hurt me."

"I don't want to hurt *you*," Lornk asserted, grasping Ashel's shoulders and blocking the cleaver from his sight. "Believe that—it was never you, it never will be you. But the stakes are very high here. Victoria of Ourtown has a destiny. You know what it is. The *world* needs her, and my purpose has always been to ensure she does what the world needs, when the time comes."

Ashel gripped the chair arms with pale knuckles, astounded at the lunacy Lornk Korng hid so well beneath his urbane charisma. The night Lornk let him escape, he had come back to do what he could to protect those he loved, and yesterday he'd seen how badly Vic needed that protection. So he would do what he could: he would accept the inevitability of that cleaver. The chair arm was ill-sanded, and a splinter jabbed a finger— perhaps the last feeling he'd have there, he cherished the sting. "You won't stop her," he said. "She's not here for me."

Lornk's eyes caught fire. "Good."

"Ah, good," he repeated, as a guard led Geram and another brought Wineyll through the door. "We're all here now."

† † †

Geram used his guard's vision to see his way to a chair at an unfinished wood table. Wineyll settled next to him. At the end of the room, Ashel sat surrounded by guards. Geram's guard blinked, and his view of the room went black, then resolved itself from Ashel's perspective.

Get ready, Geram, Ashel said. *This is going to hurt.*

"I've decided to give you one last chance to make this painless," the Relmlord announced, turning to Wineyll. "Either of you."

"You can't," Wineyll whispered, her face turning the color of pale granite, her eyes locked on the table. His biceps quivering as Ashel's muscles tensed, Geram caught the sight of a guard and saw the stone cleaver on the table.

Blind again, Geram jolted out of his seat and reached for the weapon, but his hand struck only the table. The guards slammed Ashel tight to the chair, fought to uncurl his fingers. Ashel roared as Lornk pressed the cleaver down. Geram dropped back, grinding his teeth, his index finger spasming as Ashel's blood throbbed out. Wineyll's shrieks pierced their ears. Numbness welled up Geram's shoulder, and his heart rippled with Ashel's pain.

Lornk shouted, "That was so you know I'm serious." Then he bent down and whispered in Ashel's ear, "That is my gift to your mother." Breath stuck in his chest, Geram stared down at hands holding his right hand—no, Ashel's hand—tight to the wide arm of the chair. Blood bubbled from the knuckle where the index finger had met the palm.

Wineyll's screams scaled back to sobs. "I don't know what to do."

A klaxon echoed through the palace as Vic attacked the walls. "Don't," Geram and Ashel groaned with one voice.

"Arlek," Lornk ordered, handing him the cleaver, "take another finger."

† † †

"Where is the Relmlord?" Bethniel demanded.

"I don't know," whimpered the warleader, sweat streaming down his bald head. The stoneknife emblems on his collar rattled when Vic shook him and tossed him up toward the chandelier.

"Might he be found within his chambers?" Bethniel asked politely, her mindvoice cutting through the man's cries. "Or has the coward fled to Traine? What kind of Lord leaves his people to face a wizard's wrath?"

A boom reverberated, followed by two more—Relmans trying to break through the doors. As the battering settled into a rhythm, Vic dropped the warleader. His scream echoed off the domed ceiling and did not end when she caught him a dozen feet from the floor.

"Tell us," Bethniel gritted over his squealing, "where we will find him."

"I'll show you," he pleaded. "Just put me down."

As Vic lowered him, her grasp on the air supporting him weakened, then fell away. The warleader thunked onto the floor, and Vic staggered, a soft shush filling her ears. She felt fingers press between her thighs, lips graze her neck, and a hand wrap around her throat. *Do you crave me, Kara?* Lornk whispered. Her breath stilled in her lungs, and she waited for him to release it.

"Vic, what's wrong?" Bethniel shook her arm. "What happened?"

Lornk's grip vanished. She shook herself, blinking at the princess and the warleader groaning on the floor. Shrinejump, stay focused, she swore at herself. Using her power, she yanked the warleader to his feet. "Take us to him."

Down in the tunnel, a crash followed a final boom as Relmans hammered through the wedged doors, and a flood of enemies roared toward them.

† † †

"I had her," Wineyll screamed.

"Try again."

"Don't do this." Geram shook from the effort it had taken to rip through the link Wineyll had formed with Vic. The girl had appalling strength and skill at illusion.

"They're overwhelmed up there," she said to him alone. "I won't let Ashel die."

"Arlek, be ready," Lornk threatened.

"Please, wait! I'll stop her this time," Wineyll cried.

Ashel's agony moved through Geram's blood to his heart, from whence a paralyzing ache spread to his fingers and toes. Laboring for each breath, Geram pushed his awareness into Wineyll's, glimpsed Relmans swarming down the tunnel toward the Lathans. *Don't let her do it*, Ashel groaned, and Geram dove after the other Listener, grappling for the outcome of the war.

† † †

Air seared exposed muscle and bone, and agony ripped up Ashel's nerves into his spine, sending spasms along his vertebrae and out into his limbs. Two fingers gone, eight left, then his tongue. All I am: my hands, my voice. Months ago, when Lornk had burnt and restored Ashel's flesh, he had stolen and returned Ashel's deepest ambitions. Now this madman, who might be his true father, chopped them off and cast them away. Blood welled with each lurch of Ashel's heart, and his life's purpose drained onto the floor.

Sweat soaking his hair, he panted, trying to slow his heartbeat. Two fingers gone, eight to go, then his tongue. His mind shied from the pitiful freak Lornk would make him, but through Geram he could Hear Wineyll rooting through Vic's memories, using them to turn her into another kind of monster. "Wineyll, please, stop."

"This is her fault!" she spat silently, maintaining her illusions in the chamber far above. "She left us here." Her fingers tugged and twisted her hair into knots, but her face was flat in concentration.

Butchered hand quivering, Ashel clenched his other fist, straining against the guards holding him. "Think beyond this moment. Think what will happen to Latha if Lornk controls Vic, with the power she has now. Think!"

"I don't care about Latha. I only care about you."

"Then stop, for me."

"You still love her, after this?" Wineyll gripped the table, her shoulders hunched up to her ears, but her face remained preternaturally calm.

Geram sat still as a statue, but Ashel felt him wrestling with the specter Wineyll had sent against Vic. Through the other man he glimpsed the dull simulacrum Vic would become if Wineyll succeeded. The sight of raw meat and bone at the end of his hand kicked him in the stomach, but when he closed his eyes and saw the Blade—bright, fierce, and flawed—he felt her hidden wounds as severely as his own. Ashel's heart steadied, the agony ebbed, and he answered, "I do."

"This is taking too long," Lornk complained. "Arlek, take two more."

Vic thickened the air across the tunnel opening. Relman troops banged pikes and daggers and swords against the invisible wall, some climbing on their fellows' shoulders, trying to go over it. "Take us to him," she demanded, throttling the warleader as she raised the barrier to the ceiling. Her head pounded with the dual effort.

"Shouldn't we retreat?" Bethniel asked. "Regroup at the top of the stairs?"

"We have to find him," Vic replied, tightening the vise around the warleader's throat. "Above or below us?" The warleader clutched his neck, his face purpling.

I'm below, Kara, Lornk murmured, his hands snaking back into position—the one at her throat demanding obedience, the one between her legs enticing devotion. *Come to me.*

"Vic!" Bethniel screamed as the warleader stumbled free and the mob of Relmans charged across the mosaic floor, screaming.

Clockwork gears ticking softly, Vic blinked at the princess. Heat stirred deep in her belly, and blood pumped toward her loins with an urgent need to finally give her devotion to Lornk. "He's below. I need to go down."

"Shrine, what's wrong with you?" Bethniel grabbed Vic's arm and tugged her toward the broad staircase. The squad formed a cordon, but Relmans swarmed, blocking retreat.

"I need to go down," Vic repeated, shoving Bethniel away. The Lathans froze, mouths agape, and Relmans attacked. Pikes struck, daggers slashed. Blood and cries splattered as the ring of enemies thickened around them.

"We surrender!" Bethniel cried, ordering weapons down. "This is not the time to go mad," she hissed at Vic, using her mother's commanding voice. "Pull yourself together and get us out of this!"

Let them bring you to me, Lornk whispered.

Lathan daggers and bows clattered on the floor, and a Relman housemarshall pushed into the circle. Caught in Lornk's ghost embrace, Vic stared dumbly as he yanked out her dagger and ripped away her bow and quiver. "The Blade's gone dull, it seems," he smirked, backhanding her across the face. She fell, hair spilling out of its braid. "My Lord will be very pleased to meet you, Your Highness," he said to Bethniel.

What are you? Lornk teased.

Not his, Geram said, his mindvoice as clear as her own thoughts. *Not his,* she Heard Ashel say, a far-off echo. Lornk's grip loosened. *You know who you are,* they said together.

Who I am. Logkeeper, mistress, Blade, she recited as Geram grappled with the spectral hands holding her. The ghost of Ashel's last touch pressed against her shoulders, while his agony bled through Geram's thoughts. *Ashel,* she asked, *what's happening to you?*

Never mind about that, Geram groaned. Lornk's grasp began to tighten again. *Focus on who you are, at this moment only. Be that. Be that now or you'll be his for the rest of your life.*

Lornk slipped past Geram's defense and pressed fingers into her flesh once more. She fought the grip this time, twisting, rending with her nails. Who I am, she repeated. *Mine,* Lornk purred. *Not his,* Geram urged. *Your own,* Ashel promised. She felt a twinge in her right ring finger and pinkie, and Geram and Ashel disappeared. But in their wake, she heard the faint wail of a flute, smelled the acrid stench of burned flesh, and felt the simmering fury of lost innocence. *Come to me,* Lornk's voice had called to her in the desert, and she remembered the answer she had shouted in response. "I'll come to you," she muttered. Her hand dug into her boot, took hold of a hilt wrapped in velvet. "I'll come to you," she said aloud, drawing the dagger out of its enfolding cloth. A chuckle hard as iron shook her shoulders. "I'll come to you!" she shouted and dug the bronze blade into the floor, raking stone into handfuls of dust. "I'll come as Kara and spit in your face!"

Howling, she ripped herself free of the spectral hold and rocketed upward, smashing through the domed ceiling. She tore through floor after floor of the mountain palace, boulders tumbling in her wake, and burst into the bitter night, where fury steamed off her skin. Lornk had stripped her to her core, tried to shape her into a clockwork doll that moved and breathed at his command. But she'd broken that mold and forged herself anew: an alloy cast in blood and sand, tempered with a wizard's power. Everything she had done—from the mutilated rapist to the inferno in the nomad village—she had done to prepare for this moment. Her fist aching to crush his throat, she plunged back into Lordhome and punched through the floor. Stone and screaming rained after her; the mountain rumbled, but her rage boomed over it all.

Down, his specter had said, go down. The ground quaked around her. She swept through corridors, boring down to the next level when she couldn't find stairs. When her blasts tore out chunks of rock but did not penetrate the granite, she knew she had reached bottom. She ripped door after door off its hinges. A succession of storage cells held wine, canned fruit, grain. At last she heard their voices over the stress of the stone. At last she found them.

She blew the door to splinters, crushed the skulls of the Relman guards. Her hair crackled around her. Dust fogged the room; she swept it aside and found Wineyll hunched over crossed arms, sobbing hoarsely while Geram bent over her, an arm round her shoulders. Skin mottled, trembling, Ashel sat with his right hand wedged beneath the opposite arm.

Lornk scowled, fingers tapping elbows.

"What have you done?" Vic asked.

"Tried to win you back, my dear."

His dear. She bit her tongue to keep from screaming, and iron washed her gums. The dagger's hilt felt cool on her palm. She held it up. "Remember this?"

"Ah," he stepped forward. "That must have cost Elekia a fortune."

Vic walked toward him around the table, stepping over the bodies of the guards, slapping the blade against her thigh. Pushing back his chair, Geram felt his way toward the door and stationed himself there.

"I received your note," Lornk said. "The one you sent to claim your independence. The messenger died soon after from a dreadful injury."

She grinned. "I hoped you'd finish what I started with him."

He raised an eyebrow. "You were correct to assume his actions would matter to me. But your actions matter more—who you are, what you are, you could have become without so much bloodshed."

The cajoling flattery pulled at the strings he'd tied round her long ago, in a white tower. Her knees quivered with Kara's desire to beg his forgiveness. But the rage that had brought down a mountain held her up. "Every drop of blood I've kept in here." She pointed to her heart, then grabbed his ankle with the power and yanked him upside down. He grunted in surprise, crossed his arms, and frowned. The lack of fear on his face vexed her. Bringing the dagger to his throat, she hissed, "Before I drown you in your blood, I have one question: what are you?"

"Vic," Ashel croaked, "leave him to my mother."

The stink of iron wedged into her awareness. Dark red soaked Ashel's trousers, migrated through the fabric of his tunic. "Elesendar," she gasped. Four fingers lay in the muck, mocking the cruelties she'd sworn to avenge. She dropped Lornk; the dagger slipped from her hand and landed with a dull ring in a pool of muddied blood.

Battlefield instincts kicked in. "Wineyll, come here," she barked, sharp as the cleaver clutched in a dead guard's hand, then she snatched Lornk and slammed him against the wall. "Why would you do this?" she demanded, cinching her power round the Relmlord's throat while Wineyll tore a strip from her skirt and wrapped Ashel's butchered hand.

"To be sure of you," he choked out.

"Take him back to Latha," Ashel panted. "Let him face justice from all our people. Killing him now won't free you, because you freed yourself long ago. All you have to do is accept it." With his intact hand, he reached for her hair. It stretched to his fingers, hissing softly as it met his skin.

"I can't." Her eyes welled with fury, and she increased the pressure on Lornk's windpipe.

Fighting for breath, he said in mindspeech, "You will hold the world in your hands. The fate of all of us—of humanity—will depend on how you follow your destiny. I need to show you the path—"

"You're insane!" Tightening the noose, she turned back to Ashel. His dreams lay on the floor, defiled and broken. Shrine, she could have saved him if she'd only thought beyond herself yesterday. Wineyll held the bandaged hand between both her own, her eyes deeply shadowed. In a flash of insight, Vic understood what had happened here—Wineyll had tried to save him by turning Vic back into Kara, while Geram and Ashel had fought against her. The weight of Ashel's sacrifice bore down like the stone creaking overhead, and her knees slapped into the blood beneath his chair.

"You're not his," Ashel said aloud over Lornk's fading gasps, "and you're not my mother's creation either. You are your own." He stroked her head, his touch draining her hair's energy. "You're not a weapon, not a tool, not a pawn. You're a scholar and a soldier and a wizard, and you made yourself." As her hair came to rest on her shoulders, the ice coating her heart melted. She let Lornk's body slump to the floor.

"Is the Relmlord dead?" Wineyll asked.

Her eyes on the bloody mess she'd made, she shook her head. Ashel touched her cheek with his good hand, his fingers pressing gently, urging her to look at him. Her throat constricted, holding down the grief surging from her belly. She longed to step into his arms, drink again from that well of life that had slaked her thirst and eased her heart, but the dreadful sting of her failure pushed her away. Standing, she looked at her blood-soaked knees. "I owe you . . ." Her voice cracked. She took a breath and finally met his gaze. "I owe Latha more than just a corpse." Ashel nodded, his face tight with pain.

The ground shook with the noise of a rockfall, and dust billowed into the room. "Marshall," Geram said, "we need you to lead us out of here."

Lornk's body rose and hovered. Wineyll wedged herself under Ashel's shoulder, eyes daring Vic to touch him. She took Geram's arm instead. The bronze dagger lay where she'd dropped it, its blade the color of dawn and stained with blood.

† † †

The Woern Saga will continue in **A Wizard's Sacrifice.**

ACKNOWLEDGMENTS

This novel would not exist without the advice and encouragement of friend and fellow author C. C. Aune, whose constructive and instructive critiques formed the sand cast for this story. Comments from my editor, Amanda Rutter, guided the hammer blows that fashioned the finished product. Both provided invaluable insights and helped me realize my vision. I couldn't have done it without you, ladies.

I also thank Patrick Maloney, Amy Quale, and the rest of the crack team at Wise Ink Creative Publishing for their help bringing this book into being. Steven Meyer-Rassow's outstanding cover design succeeded beyond my wildest dreams in capturing Vic's struggle, and the map and interior design are beautiful.

My husband and daughter deserve utmost thanks for their patience and encouragement, especially when I was working behind a locked bedroom door. Enthusiastic thanks also go to book blogger Rebecca Tyndall (aka the Literary Connoisseur) for being an early supporter and cheerleader for my work. Many friends and associates in writing groups provided crucial feedback on portions of this book, but special thanks go to the Refugees—a group of extraordinary people who have helped me grow as a writer and as a person.

BOOK CLUB QUESTIONS

The following questions may inspire some lively conversations with friends. Best enjoyed with snacks and beverages.

1. Queen Elekia treats Vic with alternating contempt and kindness. In your opinion, what are the queen's real feelings and motivations?

2. What do you think Vic is searching for in Geram's vision of her atop the pile of brass gears?

3. Lornk shares something about his past to Ashel. What are the implications of this confession?

4. Were the deaths of the nomads justified? What ramifications do you expect from this action?

5. Vic and Ashel swap traditional roles of hero and heroine in this story. What do you think about the juxtaposition? Did the change in role make either of them more or less appealing?

6. *A Wizard's Forge* is a loose retelling of "Rapunzel," as told by the Brothers Grimm. What elements of *AWF* do you think might have been inspired by that fairy tale?

BIOGRAPHY

A.M. Justice has danced tango beneath the wings of angels, played hide-and-seek with harbor seals, and sought distant galaxies from dusk to dawn. Hiking to a remote swimming hole, exploring an ancient cathedral, and sharing a good meal with friends are among her favorite things, but she likes nothing better than sitting with a cat on her lap while watching a beloved movie on TV.

For insights and updates, join the Citizens of Knownearth mailing list at amjusticeauthor.com or follow @amjusticewrites on Twitter.